Red Hot Blues

Red Hot Blues

Reggie Nadelson

St. Martin's Press ⋈ New York

A THOMAS DUNNE BOOK.
An imprint of St. Martin's Press.

RED HOT BLUES. Copyright © 1995 by Reggie Nadelson.

Library of Congress Cataloging-in-Publication Data

Nadelson, Reggie.
    [Red Mercury blues]
    Red hot blues / by Reggie Nadelson.—1st U.S. ed.
        p.   cm.
    "A Thomas Dunne book."
    "First published in Great Britain by Faber and
Faber Limited under the title Red Mercury blues"—
T.p. verso.
    ISBN 0-312-18166-3
    I. Title.
PS3564.A287R43   1998
813'.54—dc21   97-46498
                                                      CIP

First published in Great Britain by Faber and Faber Limited under the title *Red Mercury Blues*.

First U.S. Edition: March 1998

10 9 8 7 6 5 4 3 2 1

For Anne Graham Bell

Part One

NEW YORK

Chapter One

"THERE WERE BODY PARTS HANGING FROM THE TREES."

I was in my car coming back from Brooklyn when the radio started playing news of an airplane crash in the Midwest, and a nurse who got to the scene first was saying, "There were body parts hanging from the trees." While I listened, a weird white fog seemed to boil up fast and low off the river.

It had rained hard all morning, rain like steel needles driving into the East River, the river spilling over its banks in places and now the fog chasing me back from Brooklyn. I raced it halfway up the Brooklyn Bridge. Then traffic stopped dead.

I lit a cigarette as the fog crawled up my windshield. In the gloom, cars' warning lights flashed yellow. A couple of kids got out of the car in front of me, tried to climb the struts of the bridge, disembodied heads sticking out of the mist, hands clinging to the railing.

On the other side, the tops of buildings, eerie monsters, poked up out of the rolling white fog, the mist on them in sheets like ghosts on bayou trees I'd seen once. Then they disappeared. Manhattan was a lost island state. Remote. Isolated. Invisible. Part of a mysterious archipelago, borders cut off by fog. On the bridge I sat, smoking, waiting. The fog cut Manhattan off: I couldn't see my way home.

I had gone to Brooklyn early to get caviar for Dawn's wedding—you can get good stuff cheap for cash at Fish Town in Brighton Beach. It gives me the creeps, Brighton Beach, it pulls me back, the signs in Russian, the sound of Russian, the talk always about money along the boulevard where the elevated train makes dark shadows even at noon. Babushkas reach out and push prescription meds, hoods in gold chains and thick leathers swagger, old men flap their hands at you if you take a picture. Mind your own business. Keep to yourself. Shut your mouth. As I came out of the store that morning, a woman stumbled and dropped her bag so apples bounced on the cobblestones; she scrambled to get them;

no one helped her. Ten, twelve miles from Manhattan and you were in Russia.

I'm not crazy about doing business with the Russians, but Dawn's mom asked me and I'd do anything for Dorothy Tae, deal with Russians, fish for sturgeon. So I went, then I beat it and now there was a couple pounds of the best Osetra in a blue can in a cold-pack on the backseat of the Mustang and I was sitting on the bridge in the fog. I switched off the news, put some music on. Tony Bennett was doing "Steppin' Out." I sang along, then caught myself singing in the rearview mirror and laughed outloud.

It was over.

The fog rolled out. The rain quit. Suddenly. The way tropical rain quits. The city was locked back in a suspension of humidity heavy as chicken fat or depression. The sun came out again, bloated and yellow, leaking smudgy color into the sky. It was very hot, a stinker for September, as I drove off the bridge near City Hall, up Lafayette, and thought of the first time I'd crossed the bridge, when I was nineteen, coming in from the airport. I'd ordered the taxi driver—it was a rattletrap gypsy cab—to take the Brooklyn Bridge. A big shot. I was aching to show I knew the way. I didn't. I didn't know shit. I wanted to be cool, but I was scared. And then I saw the skyline: impossible, arrogant, beautiful. It made me want to cry. It made me feel I could dump the past. Twenty years later, it was home.

"Dickfist. Asshole. Sonofabitch piece of dogshit, move it!" The guy in the next car leaned on his horn. He was white and he wore a Knicks cap backward. The light had turned green, I was gazing absently out the window. He had a point.

"Lighten up," I yelled back pleasantly and headed for Broadway to deliver the caviar, get a shower and change into my tux.

"You got some secret?" a pretty girl at Dawn Tae's wedding asked me that night. I was laughing outloud for no reason except that I was drunk. And happy. Later on, when things were lousy, I would remember having a completely wonderful time at the wedding. Dawn could have had it someplace fancy, but she wanted it here; this was home. For me, too. The Taes, who run the best restaurant in Chinatown, are also my landlords, having refurbished the space in the building upstairs for lofts. They put in a separate entrance so you don't have to go through the restaurant. It works great.

"I'm a happy man," I said to the girl in blue satin. Under her thin jacket, as we spun onto the dance floor, I could feel her pliant flesh. Over her head, mirrored balls the size of melons spun and sprayed reflections of hundreds of people into silvery shards of light. The smell of lilies, chilies, and girls' perfume bloomed in the heat and everywhere, vases blazed with red roses. Red for luck.

I knew I was drunk. But it was the kind of Champagne drunk that made everything sharper. Later, the scene would come back as if out of a Christmas window on Fifth Avenue: the room very bright, the dancers spinning, the bride parading, old men in armchairs snoring, children spilling over their feet, waiters hefting loaded trays, the guests all moving in set patterns, as if driven by invisible motors. Sleek as a seal, Mr. Tae beamed; Peter Leung came from a good Hong Kong clan; Dawn had married well.

The band played "Cheek to Cheek." I'd trade any classical stuff you could name, even Horowitz playing Chopin, for Astaire, not to mention Dreck Doggy Dog or whoever the dead rap fool was, and I danced with kids who stood on my feet and old ladies who pushed me around in intricate two-steps. I danced with girls in sleek silks, perched like exotic birds on four-inch heels.

"I'm in heaven."

The girl in blue satin looked up at me like I was a little cracked and I realized I was singing outloud. Born happy, my mother said once: a freak of nature.

"How you doing, detective?" Ricky Tae, Dawn's brother and my best friend, drifted by.

"Great," I said. "Great."

As we danced, I realized the girl in blue, who had a high forehead, a great smile, and terrific tits, had nothing on under the satin jacket.

"What's your name?" she said.

"Artie," I said, pulling her closer. She smelled good.

"You're Ricky's policeman, aren't you? I thought cops were brooding. You know, brooding. Disaffected. Sick of life. Saddened by experience."

5

"You've seen too many Al Pacino movies. I am the cheerful cop," I said. "You want to come upstairs and try me? I live upstairs," I said. I didn't bother her with all the facts, didn't mention I was on leave and thinking of quitting the department, or that the more misery I see, the more I'm convinced there is only one message, which is to live it up. She wanted brooding, I could try; I gave her the young Brando. She giggled, then drifted away from me. Dawn passed and I put my arm out and caught her.

"She didn't like you?" Dawn looked spectacular in a red suit.

"She was hoping for Al Pacino," I said. "You look wonderful. Maybe you married the wrong guy."

"I wish it could have been you," Dawn whispered, only half joking. We'd been kidding around for years, ever since I moved into the building; sometimes we used to make out on the stairs.

But it would break her father's heart if Dawn married a round-eyed cop, and we both knew it.

"Let's just dance," I said and we moved out onto the floor and everyone made room for us because we were good. From the bandstand Ricky sang "I Love You Just the Way You Are." Everyone laughed and danced, the lights spun and I held Dawn and smelled the roses.

She said, "You're drunk. I've never seen you drunk."

"You never got married before."

An hour later, I ran up the stairs to change because my shirt was soaked. Earlier, Dawn and her girlfriends had commandeered my place for a dressing room and it was drenched with delicious smells: powder; hairspray; the smell of girls, and perfume. Dawn wore Joy. A red silk slip was tossed over my bed. I put my face in it, then snapped on the CD; Ella Fitzgerald sang "Give It Back to the Indians."

Glancing in the mirror, I grabbed a fresh shirt. I was thirty-nine, six one, in pretty good shape. I sucked in my gut. God, I was slaughtered. I lit a cigarette, did up my shirt with fingers thick as egg rolls, inhaled the smoke, and the perfume mixed with it and gave me a rush, like pure oxygen, or pure pleasure. I would find a nice girl, get married. Be a real American. Have fun. Listen to Ella Fitzgerald. Tony Bennett. It was okay. I was safe.

I was halfway down the stairs when my phone rang. The answering machine picked it up. Something made me go back. Something was wrong. The pulse in my neck pounding, I played the message.

Gennadi Ustinov had been shot.

My head exploded. Shot. Shot where? I stood, rigid, frozen, watching myself listening to the voice on the machine. Gennadi Ustinov shot in the face on *The Teddy Flowers Show*. Shot?

As I ran out into the street, I was uncomprehending, the city hot as hell, me running, trying to outrun the nightmare I could feel pulling me back, sweat dropping like rainwater from my hair into my eyes. The soft hot tar dragged at my feet.

I ran three or four blocks up Broadway and saw a cab. I ran for it, blocking it, hitting my fist on the hood to get the driver's attention so hard, the skin on my knuckles broke. I threw myself into it. The driver's name was posted on his license: Petrov, Fyodr. I started barking orders and the angry driver became meek, tugging a tuft of hair. "Okay, mister" he said, "Yessir," he mumbled, subservient, scared of me. I realized I was shouting in Russian.

He drove like a crazy man, and all I could think was, Please don't die. Don't die. Then I realized my knuckles were bleeding.

Chapter Two

DON'T DIE!

Even before I got to his room in the intensive care unit, I could hear the machines breathing. In. Out. In out. In out. It was after midnight, the hospital was quiet. From halfway down the corridor, I heard the sounds of a man in outer space.

In the room, on a bed, under greenish lights, Gennadi Mikhailovich Ustinov lay motionless, attached like a spaceman by corrugated plastic tubes to the machine that breathed for him.

Banks of machines winked. Jagged green lines on the black monitor showed his heart was still beating, and he was wired to a tangle of IVs, anchored by these fragile connections to life. His face, half covered by the plastic cone he breathed through, was drawn; he was old, he was older than I remembered.

There had been pictures. With his book coming out, there had been photographs in the papers, but his age never showed because he was a vain bastard, and you could fool with pictures. I pushed the hair out of my eyes and leaned over him and a nurse motioned me away, but an FBI agent whose name I couldn't remember said to her, "Let him be."

The agent had been there when I arrived at St. Vincent's, had shaken my hand with a brief, dry gesture of sympathy.

"Don't die, please," I whispered to Gennadi Mikhailovich Ustinov now, this time in Russian. "Don't goddamn die on me."

I said, "What did you do? Who wants you dead?" But there was no answer.

Except for the nurse, a single intern, and the agent, the room had emptied out and I was alone with him. I stood by the bed looking down. How many times in recent years had I picked up his phone messages off my machine? He always spoke English, as if to show he knew I was now an American. I never called back.

"Shall we meet, Artyom?" he wrote. I never answered the letters. I saved the tape from the answering machine, though, and put it in a drawer.

"Shall we meet?"

Don't die.

People used to joke around, used to tell my mother I looked exactly like Gennadi Mikhailovich. Uncle Gennadi, I called him, the way you called your parents' best friends, for respect and love, and they'd tease Gennadi: So maybe he's yours, they'd joke, so maybe he'll grow up and join the KGB. Maybe I'm Gennadi's kid, I once said to my mother when I got to be a teenage smartass and she slapped me. The only time. That was for grown-ups, that kind of talk, but otherwise, she giggled about it; it was only a joke.

"Please," my Aunt Birdie wrote me from Moscow. "Please see him. Please, Artie, for your father's sake."

On the narrow white bed, breathing through tubes, oblivious, was the man who had been my dead father's best friend: Uncle Gennadi. I had not seen him in twenty-five years. Then Birdie wrote me again. I had agreed. We were to have met the next day at my place. In his last letter, he had asked me to show him where I lived. "I am so happy we shall finally meet," he wrote; now we never would.

The FBI agent materialized behind me and put his hand on my shoulder as I watched the green lines on the black screen go flat. Doctors hurried in, rubber soles of their shoes making busy noises on the linoleum. In a furious phalanx that cut me out, they surrounded the bed and went to work on the body that lay on it.

"I'm sorry," a doctor said. "You'll have to go."

"Is he dead?" I said. "Is he dead?" No one answered.

"Who would want to kill an ex-KGB general these days?" some news knucklehead with big hair chuckled knowingly as I wandered into the street outside the hospital. I needed a smoke.

"Everybody," I said to her. Go away, I thought. "Everybody."

On the street, a camera crew lolled against a network truck, waiting hopefully; their lights were already up. Half a dozen blue and whites were parked along Twelfth Street, and up near Seventh Avenue a couple of barricades cut off the through traffic. Men in suits disembarked from limousines and cabs, were whisked into the hospital, the newsguys running alongside them, arms flailing, equipment aloft.

Trying not to yawn, young cops patroled the perimeter, the boys scratching their brutal haircuts, the girls struggling to keep their hair up under their caps, weighed down with handcuffs, guns, nightsticks, and fatigue. I felt for them, but I couldn't reclaim the young Artie Cohen from this footsore street life.

Then, out of one of the big cars, Sonny Lippert bounded energetically, racing toward the hospital. He saw me; Sonny never misses a trick.

"Artie, I'm sorry, man." He was solemn. He pumped my hand like a man at a funeral.

"Yeah, well, thanks for letting me know, Sonny." It had been Sonny Lippert's voice on my answering machine telling me Ustinov was shot. A few weeks back, during some bonding built out of too many beers, I had confided to Sonny I was going to see Ustinov. It was a mistake.

"I'm a sweet guy," he said.

Like me, Sonny was still wearing a tux; his was unwrinkled. He shook hands with half a dozen cops on the street. Sonny Lippert is plenty ambitious; he has a huge network of buddies and he keeps it well oiled.

"I got to go in. I'm on the job, man. On this case, no one sleeps," he said. Sonny works out of the Federal Prosecutor's office now, and he takes an interest in anything Russian, but he never lets you forget that he was a detective once. He wears attitude that says "I'm a real cop."

"What office you running for, Sonny?" I once heard someone ask him and Lippert imploded with rage.

"Hey, Sonny, where's the shooter?" I called out.

Sonny pushed me away from the cluster of cops, against the hospital wall.

I taunted. "Where is he?"

"We lost him."

"You lost him? You lost a Russian who shot a KGB general on a live television show in the middle of New York City?"

"How do you know the shooter's a Russian?"

"My penetrating intellect." I looked down at Sonny. "What happened?"

Sonny tugged at an imaginary crease in his jacket, as saliva formed around his mouth. This could be a big case.

"We don't know. Security sucks. There was like this chaotic thing, you dig? Audience screaming. People on the floor. He walks out. He walks out of the studio. Disappeared. But what else do you know, Art? Huh?"

"Nothing at all, Sonny."

Sonny went in, I crossed the street and found a piece of wall I could lean on outside an apartment building. I fumbled for cigarettes, hands numb.

A few yards away, leaning against the wall of a brownstone, was a woman, a leather bag dangling off her shoulder, a cigarette in her mouth. She had red hair. A female detective in uniform stood at the curb, watching her. The woman pushed the heavy red hair off her neck and looked in my direction.

"Can I borrow a light?" she said.

"Sure."

I dug some matches out of my pants pocket, lit the cigarettes. She was almost as tall as me.

We stood for a minute smoking, silent conspirators. It was a stinking summer night. The relentless low rumble of thunder was never more than an impotent whimper, you could feel fights brew up all over the city, spiraling to the surface. Across Seventh Avenue, a few junkies dealt China White, a college kid pushed Prozac at a buck a pop. "Business is looking up," said a guy I used to work with at the Fifth Precinct. A lot of people saw the shooting as a turning point: the palmy days of New York as a low-crime town were ending, the illusion was over, the mayor slipped in the ratings, West Coast gangs got a foothold, cops were mad as hell and pulled random strikes, and heroin in a pill you could smoke flooded the market. All around us, walkie talkies, police radios, cellular phones, and self-importance crackled and buzzed in the city night air like crickets in the country. Somewhere a bottle shattered on the pavement.

"You're a cop," she said, pushing the red hair off her neck again, twisting it nervously into a knot.

"Does it show?"

"Can you call off your guard dogs?" She nodded at the cop on the curb.

I shrugged. The waiting, the tension, the growing hangover from all the booze I'd drunk at the wedding made me glad for some distraction. "I don't have much clout these days."

"I'm Lily Hanes," she said. "It was my show. You understand? He died on my show."

"He's not dead yet," I said, but she didn't answer.

Lily Hanes had been sitting in for Teddy Flowers that night and I think she talked because she was scared and I was there and I'm good at listening. The pulse in her forehead made a blue vein stand out in the white skin and she licked her dry lips and talked and I waited for confirmation that Gennadi Mikhailovich Ustinov was dead.

"I really liked him a lot. I liked Ustinov. It was hot and I was nervous as hell, and he was nice."

I didn't say anything.

11

"Look, I'm a reporter, not a talk-show host. I was just Teddy's backup. It was the end of the summer season. The ratings dry up like my Aunt Martha's skin in Boca Raton, you know? But it was a good gig for me. I was nervous. We were trying out this new studio space over by the meat market and I didn't know my way around. 'Think of the show as a dinner party.' Teddy always says that. 'Try to be a good hostess, Lily,' Teddy says to me on the phone. He's out in Bridgehampton screwing around and telling me to make like Martha Stewart. I'm always surprised someone doesn't punch his face in."

"What about the audience?"

"They were restless. They come to see Teddy needle the guests. That's what makes it a hot ticket. It's like some Japanese game show. They like him cruel. They were disappointed he wasn't there."

"He sounds like a prick."

"Teddy is a prick."

She sucked her cigarette. I wanted to put my arm around her. She smelled of almonds; maybe it was her shampoo.

I said, "You think someone set Flowers up?"

"I set it up," she said. "I did it."

"What?"

"Ustinov writes a book. A tell-all about the KGB. I was interested. I invited him. What I remember is he spoke this wonderful English. We were in the make-up room and Babe—that's the make-up woman—is working him over and I ask him where he learned it. 'At Harvard University, of course,' he says. Of course. On an exchange program. 'I was not the only KGB agent there, naturally.' That's what he says. 'I was not the only KGB agent there.' "

"I know," I said.

"What?"

"Nothing. Go on," I said, but she was silent.

Outside St. Vincent's at one in the morning, I was listening to this pretty woman with red hair, waiting for confirmation Gennadi Ustinov was dead and I was numb and excited at the same time. She pushed her hair back again and finally tied it in a ponytail with a rubber band.

"He was so charming." Lily Hanes put her hands over her face for a minute. "We kidded around. I asked if he had a KGB uniform under the bed. He said he preferred Brooks Brothers, but he did have an Aston Martin with an ejector seat and an exploding fountain pen. A Mont Blanc. Naturally. We all laughed. Then he fucking drops dead on me."

She was trembling and I thought she was coming unglued. I got her inside the hospital where it was cool and we found a waiting room and sat on orange plastic chairs. A cleaning woman pushed her bucket in our direction and we held up our feet like obedient children so she could clean around us. The disinfectant stank of rotting apples and made me gag; it was the smell of mornings in Moscow, the smell of whatever they used to wash away the drunks' vomit.

"Please. Please try to remember. Who else was there?"

"There was this real angry Russian woman in the front row who wanted to stick it to the general. In sort of a peasant blouse thing. She had these tendons in her neck that stuck out, she was so mad. Like a chicken. I remember that."

"But on the panel?"

Lily rubbed her face. "What?"

"The other guests?"

"A Russian DJ or a record producer, something like that. Sverdloff. Big guy. He seemed okay. Smart. Also a stripper from one of those nightclubs in Brighton Beach. Olga was her name. She called herself Anna K." Lily laughed emptily. "I think Teddy dug her up. Or maybe I did. I can't remember. She whined a lot. Wanted her own dressing room. Tomas Saroyan. Made his money selling private health care. Other stuff, maybe diamonds. And Leonid Zalenko."

"The fascist?"

"I used to think New York City cops were fascists. Or Richard Nixon. I was a fool."

She got up restlessly, leaning her hip against a table that held only an empty coffee carton. Her skirt rode up over her thighs and they were silky and tan. She swallowed drily. "You think there's any soda around?"

In the background I was conscious of people milling, waiting, hushed. Ustinov would rate. A big player in the old days, a parliamentary deputy under Yeltsin, he'd get dignitary status. In the waiting room, officials muttered in Russian and English and the orderlies washed the floor. I found a soda machine and got some Cokes.

"Zalenko stank," Lily said. "Literally. He chewed garlic."

"Why's that?"

"Maybe to keep away the werewolves in Gorky Park," she said and rolled the cold Coke can on her neck, then swallowed the soda in two gulps. Scrambling in her bag, Lily found some fossilized Juicy Fruit. Like a schoolgirl, she tore the stick of gum in half and offered it to me.

"Zalenko had an agenda. Ranting about Mother Russia. The West. Ustinov just backed off. He didn't like Crowe much, either."

"Crowe?"

"Gavin Crowe. British writer who lives in Moscow. The kind of guy who always knows everyone. Short. Bad teeth."

She was breathing hard, sweating badly. "He just fell on me."

"Are you okay?" I asked and she turned away girlishly.

"God, I'm so tired." She leaned back and closed her eyes.

"Who fell on you?"

"The show started, someone got up and pointed a gun."

"One shooter?"

"I think so. I can't be sure. I felt paralyzed. Like those dreams where you can't stop someone from falling? Something heavy fell on me. It was covered in blood. It was Ustinov."

"What else?"

"Stuff people tell you about wars. People screaming." She fingered the pink jacket she carried; it was smeared with blood. She had come to the hospital without changing. "All I could think of was Jackie Kennedy's suit in Dallas." Finally, Lily put her head in her hands and cried. "You know what he said?"

"Go on."

"Ustinov knew I was nervous. During the opening commercial, we're still off camera, he looks at me and he has these wonderful blue eyes and he puts his hand on my arm. He says: 'They are warming up, I think. I think this is going to be quite a lot of fun,' he says. It was going to be fun."

* * *

14

Around five in the morning, maybe later, the FBI agent came into the waiting room and told me Ustinov had been declared dead officially.

I went back out to the street with Lily Hanes. A stale half light came up. Even at dawn it was stinking hot. The reporter was still waiting, chirpy and hard-eyed. "Who would want to kill a KGB general?" she kept asking.

Afraid to let go, I held Lily's arm tight and she leaned into me wearily. I wanted her to hold me. I put my arm around her shoulders.

Suddenly she pulled away, like I was some guy she'd slept with and didn't recognize in the morning.

"I just worked it out. You knew him, didn't you? I mean you really knew Ustinov. Before. Didn't you?"

"Yeah, I knew him."

Sweat ran down her neck as she wrapped her arms around her bag, clutching it as if to protect herself from me. She edged toward the curb and I felt like a criminal. I followed her.

"Let me take you home. You shouldn't be alone," I said idiotically.

"You knew him," she said again. "What's your game?"

"Come on."

"I can manage." She was scared. "Leave me be, okay?"

I reached for her arm, but she turned and ran down Twelfth Street. Before she went I saw in her eyes something I'd avoided for a long time: it was my own past.

Her voice cold as ice, she called out, "What the hell are you?"

When I dragged myself home around six in the morning, I was someone I barely knew. I was angry. Scared. I switched on the answering machine and there was a voice I didn't recognize. It spoke a literate, purring Russian that made me feel my soul was being fingered. I switched it off; I didn't want to hear from any Ivans.

On the morning news, commentators did a lot of self-aggrandizing analysis; on ABC, Vladimir Pozner appeared and spoke some sense. All I took in was that Ustinov was dead. I hadn't dreamed it. He was dead.

The smell of girls was still in my apartment, but not of Joy. Automatically, I put Lily Hanes' name and the address of the TV studio in my computer. It was morning. Through the building, there was the clatter of kids shouting, dogs barking, TVs playing, plumbing, sex; it was early September, still summer, and the windows were all open. Normally, I love the noise of the building coming to life. I ignored it all.

Inert, hungover, sitting in front of the TV, I barely heard Ricky come in. He had a cigarette hanging out of his mouth and a tray with a coffee pot on it. He had changed out of his wedding suit into gray sweats and he put the tray down on a table, poured some coffee, handed me a mug, and sat in the sling chair, one leg hooked over the arm.

"You okay, man?" Rick said quietly.

"I'm tired."

"Have you eaten? You want some food?"

"No thanks. You heard?"

Ricky gestured at the set. "I saw the early news. I'm sorry, kiddo, I'm really sorry." He tossed me a pack of smokes. "You want to talk?"

"You think it could have been an accident?"

Ricky looked at me. "When birds fly outta my butt."

"Sonofabitch survives the entire Cold War and gets knocked off on talk TV." I needed some sleep. "Give me a couple hours," I said and Ricky nodded. He's a kid, but he has real emotional tact.

"I'm going," he said. "Get some sleep. I'm here. We're all here, okay?"

I got a beer from the fridge, trying to put things together in my head. I climbed out the window onto my fire escape and snapped a few withered leaves off the geraniums I had set out in pots; they were dying in the heat and the stench was bitter.

The phone rang, I scrambled back in and grabbed it. A man's voice spoke in Russian. The same voice, oozing concern, imploring attention, demanding tribute. It drenched me like napalm.

"Wrong number." I slammed the phone down.

It rang again. I let it ring. Sonny Lippert's voice played into the answering machine: "I want to see you."

I grabbed the receiver, "Not now, Sonny."

"Today, detective. Today. Before five. My office. You hear me? You listening?"

I would have dragged myself over to the TV studio where he was shot, but it would be ass deep in people; it would take all day for the cops on the job just to interview the audience from *The Teddy Flowers Show*.

Although I was officially on leave that month, I called my own station house and got the boss and told him I might want to offer my assistance to the Sixth where the investigation was being run. He said it was fine as far as he was concerned, but Sonny Lippert had already got to him and asked for my help personally, and Sonny was an old buddy of the boss.

I took off my clothes, put some shorts on and crawled back out and up the fire escape to the roof where I keep my bike in a shed. My back against the rough boards, I could see the river. The city made itself up out of the sludgy morning torpor, skyline sharpening up for business in spite of the murderous heat. I finished my beer and dozed.

Half asleep, I remembered that during the siege of Leningrad, when there was nothing else to eat, Gennadi Ustinov's grandmother gave him wallpaper paste. "It wasn't bad, you know," he told me once when I was a kid. "It didn't taste that bad."

He survived all of it, the war, the Cold War, Stalin's wrath, Brezhnev's corruptions, Yeltsin's drunks, and ended up murdered on a TV talk show one hot night at the end of the summer, wearing his Brooks Brothers suit. For a million reasons, or, this being New York, none at all. But I didn't believe that.

Ustinov had written a book revealing how the KGB did business, but so had half the assholes in the former Soviet Union. There had to be something else. Already I could feel the answers were in Moscow. Already the knowledge made my flesh crawl. But I'd think about that later.

I went back inside and sat at my desk in front of the open window. Dawn had put roses the color of apricots there the night before and they caught the light. On my desk was the transistor radio in the shape of a baseball Ustinov had given me when I was a kid and I picked it up and turned it in my hands. "What is Mets, Uncle Gennadi? What is Mets?"

17

If you grew up in Moscow, even when you're long gone, you got messed up remembering. When the KGB kicked my father out of his job, no one talked to me about it. No one said anything: It was a topic for grown-ups only. But, nights, I'd see my father's crumpled face through the kitchen door as he bent over the table, working out sums on tiny scraps of paper: how much was left, what we could afford; if they would take him away. Gennadi Ustinov disappeared from our lives, but no one mentioned it.

When my father died, I found the scraps of paper piled in his dresser drawer with his socks, the diminishing returns of a ruined life in those little sums neatly written in his impeccable hand.

The years went by, the thing in the pit of my belly evaporated. It was over, I told myself. I had unloaded the past. I was never going back to Moscow. Not even close. Going back was like death.

Chapter Three

"I'M NOT GOING TO DO IT," I TOLD SONNY LIPPERT LATER THAT DAY AS soon as I saw him. "I'm not."

"Artie, good to see you, man," Sonny exclaimed as if he didn't hear me, shaking my hand in the waiting room of the temporary federal building in Brooklyn where he works, greeting me personally like I'm some VIP.

Sonny Lippert is a small man, but tight as a bullet; the dark curly hair holds his head like a hood. He's maybe fifty-five but looks ten, fifteen years younger. Sonny Lippert has hard eyes like pebbles, a cunning mouth, skin like a girl.

"You didn't hear me, Sonny. I'm not going to do it."

"I don't think you have much choice, Art." When Sonny calls me Art it always sounds like a threat.

"In Brighton Beach, they kill cops. They kill cops' families."

Allowing himself a faint smile, he said, "You don't have a family."

Sonny's ardor shriveled faster than a cold dick when I said I wouldn't be an ear for him in Brighton Beach. He was convinced Ustinov's killer was an Ivan. I was too, but I wasn't going to do his dirty work. He said he had to take some calls and left me in the waiting room. I could wait. Sonny made me wait almost an hour.

I looked around the waiting room of the building. There were half a dozen unmarked doors leading from it. Raw blue industrial carpet covered the floor. The chairs were gray plastic. The smell was plastic pine. From behind a bulletproof glass wall, the couple of retired cops who worked as security guards kept watch and drank coffee from Yankees mugs.

"How ya doing, detective?" called one of the guards after Sonny beat it.

"Hiya, Eddie. Joe. Grandkids good?" They beamed and nodded, and went back to comparing family snaps and chortling over gossip in the *Post*.

I know Eddies and Joes all over town. I know their birthdays. I send cards. I'm everybody's favorite guy.

"It's not what you know in this town, but who," Dan Guilfoyle told me when I first joined his squad. Danny had showed me how it worked, how the NYPD graded its precincts, who got a bone, which specialists would help you, who the wireheads were, even who you could call down at Quantico and Langley, where they have experts who analyze weapons, blood, DNA, fibers, foodstuffs, radiologicals, even feathers. There are guys who only examine frigging feathers. When Danny retired from the West Side of Manhattan out to Sag Harbor, I missed him a lot.

Waiting, I watched cops come and go, watched agents pass silently through the unmarked doors. The FBI shared some offices here along with Organized Crime, Eastern District, and other Feds, part of the interlocking, impenetrable, competitive justice system in New York that would by now be in gridlock due to Ustinov's death.

Most of the time, the NYPD only talks to the FBI when someone orders them to. The federal prosecutors compete for collars with the attorney general. On this one, there would be State Department, CIA, who the hell knew?

In the city alone, there are entire divisions of specialists—

Intelligence, Bomb Squad, Hazardous Materials, special squads, PR people. Down at Police Plaza, there are so many of them it's hard to figure out who is where, which is why some wise-ass dubbed it the Puzzle Palace. Then there are the private security guys, tough as hired assassins because they don't have to follow the rules, and contract security firms like Kroll, big as governments. A guy I know in that line had been sniffing around me. It's good money, but I'd had it with institutional life and I'd already applied for my PI license.

"Agent or attorney?" Joe or Eddie would call every time the elevator opened.

"Counselor" is how the lawyers addressed one another, like courtiers, and they were slick as high-bred dogs only dressed in rich men's clothing. The agents wore bad suits, muscular hips straining against the cheap fabric.

I waited for Sonny.

"It's not what you know but who," Dan would say. "The rest is academic, boy. It's like fixing your toilet. You don't have to know how it works, do you? All that matters is knowing what plumber to call, what's his number, and if he owes you."

I owed Sonny.

"You can go in now, detective," Joe finally called out and I went through the door, past Rhonda, Sonny's long-suffering secretary, into his office.

Sonny Lippert was all smiles. "Sorry for the delay, Artie. How about some coffee?"

Sonny's so cheap he can make a nickel cry and I figured he'd ask me a buck for the brew, but what the hell; I could play his game better than he knew.

I smiled back. "Love some."

Rhonda appeared bearing a coffee pot big and shiny as an imperial samovar. Sonny waved her away. "I'll make it. Yergacheffe," he said, sticking his nose in the coffee bag. "Ethiopian. Starbucks. Costs a bundle, babe. So. You think there's a connection between Ustinov's death and the Russian mob?" Sonny fussed with the coffee while he talked.

"How would I know, Sonny?"

I knew the point for Lippert was always the Russian mafia in

Brooklyn. It was his obsession. The Ustinov killing was probably outside his jurisdiction, but he wanted a piece of it for himself anyway. The Russian mob was the prize that would get him elected District Attorney , he believed, and he wanted the job bad.

Sonny has all the accoutrements in his office, the leather chair, the view from the window, the pictures of the wife and kids, a baseball in a lucite box on his desk signed by Jackie Robinson himself, or so he says. Maybe this buys him street cred in Brooklyn, or maybe it actually matters to Sonny; I never ask.

"What's wrong with the Feds? With the cops, for that matter? Also, I hear they got a special squad going."

Sonny made coffee. Then he made the speech.

"Come off it, you know what's wrong. For years, the department graded the Brighton Beach precinct 'residential'. Hardly any of the cops speak Russian. We've got zero penetration in the community. We're no further along than we were ten years ago and you know it, man. The FBI picks up Ivankov, they brag they don't even know Russian like it's some goddamn badge of honor. We don't know who's running things. We don't know how tribute is paid. You go in a deli on Brighton Beach, the cash drawer is empty, there are eight bullet holes in the wall, someone's bleeding, you ask the goddamn Russian behind the deli counter what happened. 'Nothing,' he says. 'Nothing.' "

"Things are changing." I knew it was bullshit.

"Please! No one testifies. They'd rather go to jail than rat on one of their own. Also, they kill for fun."

"What do you want?"

"I want to see a structure, capos, underbosses. How am I gonna do this with a few cops who speak lousy Russian, some dumber than a lox. I try to get some federal attention, I get Jews screaming at the Justice Department. They don't want publicity. They're afraid bad PR will hurt immigration. Brighton Beach is Jewish. The mob there is Jewish. I'm Jewish. I can't help it."

"I can't help you."

"You have to. I need you," Sonny said.

Outside thunder grumbled over the river. The heat had to break soon.

"I like my work. I like being a regular cop."

"Cut the crap, Artie. You've been on leave for a month, you're thinking of quitting. You think I don't know? Anyhow, you were never a regular cop. You were my cop. My cop. Dig?"

A long time ago, when I first got to New York, before I even went to the academy, I met Sonny Lippert and he cut some corners for me. He helped get me my citizenship. He helped me get a job I wanted. New York could always accommodate oddballs like me, he said. More than once, he helped me and I owed him and he didn't let me forget. I did stuff for him, still do from time to time. I speak Russian; I know Hebrew from the years we left Moscow and went to Israel. I have nice suits. I can check diplomatic abuses without anyone making a fuss. I can soothe ruffled diplomats and I don't hold my knife and fork like they're weapons.

"I do your errands, Sonny. I run interference for you. I keep Jewish groups sweet. The FBI likes me. The CIA likes me. Even goddamn Mossad likes me. But I am not, repeat not, going to live in Brooklyn with the frigging Russkis. Why me?"

"I told you. I need an ear. Eyes. On the street. Ustinov is murdered on the TV. Who by? A regular Ivan, a hit man who wants to make a few bucks? A cleaner, some kind of hired assassin with a political agenda? These days, the putzes at immigration let anyone in. I don't give a rat's ass about one dead Russian more or less, but finally, finally I got a legitimate reason to squeeze those bastards in Brighton Beach till they bleed. I'm going to make people so scared of the Russian mob, I could nuke the place and people would send money."

I stood at his window; lightning sliced the sky.

"You've got your head up your ass, Cohen. This is not a nice city. This is not George Gershwin's wonderful town, whatever. It's a sewer and the Brighton Beach mob want to bend over and crap on it some more and all I'm asking is a little help."

"Leonard Bernstein."

"What?"

Wonderful Town. Leonard Bernstein wrote it."

Sonny came and stood beside me; I think he would have put his arm on my shoulder, if he could have reached it.

"Look, babe, I know you're upset. This Ustinov was your

friend. I'm your friend, too, know what I mean, it's important, man, I need you. I do." Lippert was turning it on like a Hollywood producer. "Maybe something about this business scares you," he added, real solicitous.

I remained silent. It was none of his affair.

Sonny Lippert turned away, leaned back in his chair and put his feet on the desk. Sonny's shoes were polished black calf with little tassels; the socks were cashmere. When I got to New York, I was crazy to have shoes like that. I bought some, but for years, afraid I'd ruin them, I left them home in the closet.

Outside, it started raining. I wanted to know why Ustinov died, but I didn't want to do Sonny's errands anymore, and I wasn't going to Brighton Beach for him.

"Maybe Moscow can help you," I said.

Sonny grunted. "Maybe I could ask Jane Fonda to give Jesse Helms a hand job. Jesus Christ."

"You're sure it's the mob."

"I saw an advance copy of Ustinov's book. Suddenly this ex-KGB guy comes over all moralistic about the mafia. Maybe they didn't like it. Maybe they want to warn a few others. Maybe they didn't like his neckties. I don't know. Help me."

"I'm sorry."

Sonny sipped his coffee for a while and let me wade ass deep in his silence. After a lot of time, he gave me a tight self-satisfied little smile.

"Okay," he said.

"Just okay?"

"Yup. I was only trying to throw you a bone. You don't want it, you're out. No sweat." He got up. The meeting was done. I couldn't read his meaning; Sonny has canals in his brain so polluted you could drown in the crap.

"I didn't say I wanted off the case completely. I offered to make myself available to the Sixth."

"If you don't feel able to help me, I don't think you ought to do zip on it. Maybe you're overloaded emotionally. Schlepping baggage from the past."

I wondered if he would produce any more travel metaphors. I said, "What about the gun?"

"We'll find it. We usually do."

"What about the shooter?"

"A thug. A cowboy. In from Moscow, a couple grand. Beats hanging in Moscow sniffing nail polish remover. I don't really care. I told you I don't really care about Ustinov. I want the people who hire the killers, the extortionists, drug dealers, pimps, the Russians who screw up my city."

"Can I see the tape?"

"What tape?"

"He was killed on a TV show. There's videotape."

Lippert shrugged. Suddenly he was busy. "Take some vacation, Artie. Go visit Danny Guilfoyle."

"My leave is almost up. I'm going back to work."

"What I am saying is I think you ought to finish out your leave time. Take more. I think you are stressed. I already talked to your lieutenant. So long, Art." He turned his back and picked up the phone. I went out and slammed the door so hard it rattled.

On Rhonda's desk, as I was going, I saw an open filebox with Ustinov's name on it, but Rhonda was watching and I left and waited by the elevator.

"Detective Cohen?"

The light laconic voice startled me with its formality. It was the agent I'd seen at the hospital the night before whose name I couldn't remember.

"Agent Roy Pettus," he said, holding out his hand.

I had the feeling the meeting wasn't accidental. Pettus was a big balding self-contained man, maybe forty-five, with the face of a middle-aged infant. The skin was thin and pink, the eyes round and light blue and he had no eyelashes. What hair he had was yellow, like straw, and even on a stinking hot day he wore a heavy tan suit; the jacket was wrinkled.

"If there's anything I can do," he said quietly and handed me a card.

"Thanks."

"Keep in touch, detective. Maybe I can get you something you want," he added, and walked briskly away through an unmarked door.

Chapter Four

WHAT I WANTED WAS TO GO HOME. I WANTED TO GO BACK TO WORK. I
wanted the heat to lift and I wanted Lily Hanes to answer my
calls. Downstairs from Sonny's office were courtrooms and on the
wall pictures of presidents, dead and alive. It smelled airless. It
reminded me of Moscow.

I called Lily Hanes' office from the car phone. All I got was her
husky voice on a machine. Leave a message. It wasn't my message she wanted; I was the enemy. There wasn't any point going
to work. I'd been by earlier. Everyone said, "Hi, nice to see you,
man." In this miserable heat they were up to their asses in murder, and I wasn't one of them anymore.

I conned a girl at *The Teddy Flowers Show* into promising me the
name of the security firm that did its work, and also into giving
me Lily's home number. It was too easy. Then, in spite of myself,
I turned the car around.

Along the river here were the old Brooklyn Navy Yards where
an invasion force was once launched and now, on legs like pick-
up sticks, herons pecked the garbage. But the herons were on their
way out. All along the river the Jehovah's Witnesses are buying
up old brownstones, schools, putting up their publishing houses,
gyms, hotels. WATCHTOWER, their big sign read, as the glassy-eyed
zealots devoured the neighborhood for God. I knew a girl, a
painter, who lived around there in the neighborhood they call
Dumbo for Down Under the Manhattan Bridge Overpass. She
had a great view. Those righteous bastards forced her out.

I love the river.

If you grew up in a landlocked city like Moscow, five hundred
miles from water, stranded in the interior and inescapably provincial, the New York archipelago, the coastal city of bridges and
rivers, islands and wetlands, has dazzling glamour. I like to imagine it as a great port, waterways crammed with ships, and when
I feel lousy I still go over to the river and bike, or sit around, maybe
fish a little. I bought a sailboat intending to see the city from water
level, but it's in pieces now, rotting in the shed on my roof.

Down along Shore Parkway, I saw a kid and his father fishing. They shared an umbrella and I was jealous. I wanted to put my head down and sleep. Instead, I kept driving. Maybe I owed it to Ustinov. Maybe what you knew wasn't as bad as what you dreaded. I turned onto Coney Island Avenue and drove to Brighton Beach.

Little Odessa, they call it. Parallel to the ocean, Brighton Beach Avenue runs east from Coney Island, under the El, so the trains roar overhead and the tracks filter the light and make the street mysterious. The place is completely Russian; everything is Russian: the Black Sea Deli, the Kiev Bakery, the Shostakovich Music School, a shabby car parts operation named Cosmos Auto Supply. The Anchor Bank welcomes customers in Russian, the signs are all Russian. On New Year's Eve, people shoot one another up at the Café Arbat.

Ten miles from Wall Street and you're in a time warp; provincial Russia meets turn-of-the-century Brooklyn at the end of the line, the first step up the ladder, the last coming down. When the wind blows in, you can smell the ocean, the salt, sometimes the garbage.

Except for when I bought the caviar for Dawn's wedding, it had been way over a year, maybe more, since I'd really been in Brighton Beach. I went to see my mother's cousin. Genia called me when she got to America and I went to see her in a shoddy two-story house made of masonry and raw brick and cheap gray siding. Out front was a rusted tricycle. Genia lived there—I guessed she still did but I never called—with her daughter and her father; to make ends meet, they rented a room to transients.

In the parlor where the brown drapes were drawn tight over the windows, I was seated on the good chair, its silver brocade covered in plastic to save the fabric. I drank tea while the daughter played the flute. She was a skinny pale kid who refused to learn English. The old man didn't speak English either, and he interrupted the music with angry stories about his heroic days in the Red Army, half in Russian, half in Yiddish, which I didn't understand.

The melancholy in that brown room in Brooklyn had them suspended in a cloud of inaction, halfway between Russia and America, and it infected everything, except for the kid's flute-playing. Lost in Brooklyn, I thought. For a minute, I panicked. I felt I had gone back to Moscow. So I drank their tea and ate the apple cake. I looked at family pictures of people I didn't recognize. I gave the kid some money and fled. I never went back to see them after that. It was late winter and old men wandered the boardwalk, clutching piroshki to warm their hands, staring at the ocean.

On Brighton Sixth Street, not far from my cousin's, I found a parking place. It was getting dark. I didn't know what I was looking for and I had no weapon. I should have had a gun but I was on leave and when I left Sonny I didn't really plan on coming.

I hate guns. I can do it okay. The Israeli Army did that for me, I frigging won prizes for shooting things. And I was used to a weapon, it had become like a body part I couldn't do without; I think maybe that's why I was quitting the department. But around here without a gun, I would feel worse than naked.

I found a screwdriver in the trunk of my car and stuffed it in my pocket. It would make some kind of weapon, it was better than nothing.

The rain stopped. People came out of the houses carrying stools and boxes and they sat on them, fanning themselves with Russian newspapers, gabbing in Russian. As I walked, I snatched pieces of the talk and it was always about money. Whichever way I turned, I heard footsteps in back of me, but they belonged to my own demons. Demons that until Gennadi Ustinov died I had figured were long gone. I was wrong.

"Artemy Maximovich?"

The soft male voice crept up behind me at the Arena Café where I had stopped for some supper. On my table were pelmeni in a tin tray, flabby dumplings like the balls of sick old men. What was in them? Horse meat? Dog? Who the hell knew. I stabbed one with my fork and looked up.

He was a clean-shaven, ascetic man and he wore eyeglasses with steel rims like Trotsky's. He resembled a bookkeeper and, as he sat down next to me, he placed a small notepad on my table.

When I had arrived, maybe half an hour earlier, he had been at a table of men, Russian men, all smoking. The biggest of them had shoulders like a weightlifter and he shoveled kasha and fried eggs into his mouth without removing the cigarette. No one looked at me. Outsiders were unwelcome. That's where Sonny Lippert was wrong. I could speak Russian, but I was an outsider; this circle was closed.

"Cohen's the name," I replied.

"Whatever. Artemy Ostalsky, Artie Cohen. We know who you are. How do you do?" the man said.

"So?"

"We think you should stop chasing phantoms." The man switched to English as if it was code. "We know who killed Gennadi Mikhailovich Ustinov. Soon the killer will also be dead. There is no mystery."

"When pigs fly."

"Excuse me?"

"You heard." I put money on the table and crushed my cigarette in the dumplings.

"I tell you this only because you also cared for Gennadi Mikhailovich."

The man used Uncle Gennadi's patronymic with real respect. All conversation had stopped. It was so quiet in the restaurant you could hear the man eating kasha swallow.

"We understand how you feel because your Uncle Gennadi as you called him was our friend also."

I sat where I was. The man took his glasses off and rubbed the bridge of his nose and I saw he was blind in one eye.

He put the glasses back and stared at me. "I think it would be better if you go home."

But I didn't go. I didn't reply. The man returned to his table and waited for my next move.

I waited. But for what? For Ustinov's killer to walk in and ask for borscht? Looking for evidence of the mafia in Brighton Beach was like looking for Elvis in Memphis: It was everywhere and nowhere. In Brighton Beach, people would tell you there is no mafia. Mainly mafia is Chechens in Moscow, they say. They spat when they said it: Caucasians were dog turds, although after Grozny there was more respect.

The waitress ignored me. She had big tits, a big ass, stone-washed jeans, plenty of gold around her leathery neck. She had tried flirting at first, but I didn't play and she figured I was a snob. I tuned in to a pair of women at the next table. They were eating chocolates from a large box on their table, gossiping.

"He gave me diamond earrings."

"Mine gave me a big diamond Rolex. Fake, like him."

"Stupid prick."

Next to the bar where a babushka smeared circles on the counter with a dirty rag, a beaded curtain jiggled in the breeze from the air conditioner. Through it, I could see a rack with leathers, furs, stuff someone had hijacked at the airport.

I had fought Sonny about coming here, and here I was. Is that how he wanted it? Planned it? Did he know in his gut even before I did I would go after Ustinov's killer?

The women picked through the chocolates, inspecting each piece, biting one, discarding candies they didn't like, dreaming of gold and diamonds. They whined, they shouted. Gimme candy. Gimme Rolex. Gimme gimme. I felt lousy. What I hated most was it was always what I expected: the crude comic book of Russian life, half remembered. What did all this have to do with Uncle Gennadi?

"Can I get a cup of coffee please?" I called to the sullen waitress.

"No more coffee," the waitress said in Russian.

"Okay. Tea."

She brought tea in a thick mug.

"I'd like a glass." Tea in a glass reminds me of my mother. Also, I wanted to annoy the waitress.

"No glass."

The men watched. I finished my tea. I counted my money again. I wiped my mouth. I took a toothpick and inserted it in my teeth and smiled at the women. The place was electric with anxiety. No one spoke.

I was not going to leave because some self-important little hood told me to, whoever he was, however the hell he knew my name, but I was scared. Memorizing the faces around me as best I could, I counted up to a hundred, then I lit a cigarette and smoked it to the butt, crushed it out, got up, put on my jacket, pocketed my cigarettes and moseyed to the door. I turned to the bookkeeper. "I'll be back," I said.

He smiled, a tight, mirthless Russian smile.

"Life, as your beloved mother always told you, Artyom, is not a movie," he said and, as I got through the door, I knew that someone had been waiting outside the restaurant all the time, watching me, waiting for me. I turned my collar up against the warm drizzle that had started again, that carried with it the stink of some heavy cologne, the kind for men who swagger and wear jewelry and leather coats.

It hung on me, the smell. Sometimes it *is* like a movie, that's the trouble, I thought, walking slowly away from the Arena, trying not to show I was scared rigid, sensing men on my back. I could feel them watching from the café window.

Light from Fish Town where I got the caviar for Dawn's wedding—another life, it already felt like—spilled on the wet pavement. In the windows there were dead slabs of smoked fish crammed together: pink salmons, white chubs with mottled gold skins, translucent sturgeon slices expensive as fur coats. Bright green pickles in barrels of brine stood next to black breads that weighed like warheads.

A silver Jaguar pulled up, a man in leather got out, went in, picked up a blue can of caviar, tossed it from hand to hand. He paid with a wad of cash, then got back in his car.

"Everything is cash around here," a cop I knew once told me. "Safety deposit boxes are what you could call the financial tool of choice."

Next door, a trio of teenage creeps loitered in the doorway of a shabby newspaper store, and one of them cursed an old woman when she emerged. They stood in her way and laughed at her, but when I went over to help, she grabbed her bundles and pushed through the barricade of fleshy hoods, then hurried out of sight. You didn't mess in people's business here. As a left, I could still smell him.

I could smell the cologne, and I hurried away and up on the boardwalk that runs parallel to Brighton Beach Avenue. I wanted to lure him into action, get it over with. I walked. Someone followed. On my right was a crumbling housing project Russians call the Great Wall of China. It kept the "schwarzes" on the other side, they crowed.

The boardwalk was deserted, the only lights from ships a million miles out on the horizon. Behind me, footsteps drummed faster on the wet boards, someone following me carelessly, brazenly. I walked faster.

Sweat oozed off my head. He came after me, so close now the stink of cologne made me gag. I took another breath and grasped the screwdriver in my pocket. I could feel his breath on my neck. I spun around hard to surprise him, to face whatever monster was waiting for me.

Chapter Five

"Hi."

A huge man in a black leather coat hailed me cheerfully. He wore a Dodgers baseball cap backward on a square head big as an Easter Island statue. He had black hair in a ponytail, pock-marked skin, and light gray eyes. When he smiled, which he was busy doing, an incongruous dimple appeared in his chin. I figured he was about my age. I'm pretty big, but he must have been six five and he weighed maybe three hundred pounds, but he was solid.

"I said how are you?" he said to me in Russian.

"Fuck off," I said. I was beginning to sound like them.

"Sverdloff, actually. Sverdloff, Anatoly. Tolya usually for friends," the man said, switching to English. He made a mock bow. "I am not going to fuck off, unless you are going with me. I have been trying to call you every hour." The voice was educated, familiar.

"Who the hell are you?" I asked, but I knew. I remembered his name. Lily Hanes had told me. Sverdloff was the DJ on *The Teddy Flowers Show*. He was also the Russian on my answering machine, I realized, and I started walking fast again, toward Coney Island where the big wheel loomed in the wet shadows. Sverdloff kept pace with me.

"You've been following me."

"Yes. You don't take my telephone calls," he said. "I have things to talk about." He looked like a hood. He could have been a weightlifter. But except for occasional lapses, he spoke the elegant English you learned at the Moscow language schools. Puffing a joint, he blew sweet-smelling marijuana into the damp night air.

"Shall we go for a ride?" He pointed at the ferris wheel. "Up there?"

"What do you think this is, *The Third Man*? I'm busy. Say what you have to say and go. And get rid of the dope. It's illegal," I said, feeling irritable, sounding pompous.

Sverdloff flicked the joint toward the sand, making it spin like a pebble on a pond, looked over his shoulder and kept walking.

"So?"

"I was on *The Teddy Flowers Show* last night."

"I got that."

"I am quite a famous Russian," he said.

"Sure you are."

He shrugged, his expression neutral. This one did not threaten or tug his forelock like the cab driver; there was no fear. "You want to talk, Okay. You don't want to talk, also okay. But there are things you should know," he said and pulled a piece of paper with a number out of his pocket. "You feel like talking, call me, please," he added, waved and walked away, lighting up another joint.

I smelled the disease and the presence of death even before I felt the ice-cold steel disturb the molecules near my cheek. It was deadly quiet on Brighton Sixth Street where I had parked the car. No one would come.

As I opened the car door, someone rammed me so hard I was trapped. I couldn't stop the huge force and I fell onto the seat. He punched me, then reached over and yanked out the car phone and hooked the webbed seat belt under my neck and held it. I could taste blood in my mouth where he'd knocked a tooth out. Blood filled my mouth. I gagged on the blood. With the other hand he used the knife, turning the flat, cold blade against my skin until I felt liquid run down my cheek. Then he seemed to fondle my neck, my cheek, my forehead with spindly, brittle fingers. He grasped my hair by the roots, grunting with effort. I could just see dark glasses, a blue watch cap, on the edges of vision. I got the sense of a pale Slavic face for an instant, but he put the knife in my eye and I couldn't see at all. I could feel the point of the knife in my eye as it grazed the surface.

I began gasping. I heard footsteps. They receded. Out here, no one would help. On Brighton Beach, you could commit murder in broad daylight in view of a dozen people drinking tea and later everyone would claim all they had seen was their glass.

The creep held my head and twisted it so the pulse in my neck pounded. His breath was putrid, and I gagged as he moved the knife back and forth across my face, then my eyelids. He mumbled something in Russian, but I was losing oxygen and couldn't hear. A picture floated in front of my eyes of a wounded soldier on Omaha Beach, his eyeball sliding down his cheek. I was half unconscious; the creep had my windpipe. Then I heard him.

"I can arrange so you never see your children again," he said. The voice was high pitched. He spoke in Russian.

The creep's accent was crude, but I knew what he meant: It was a standard mafia threat. They didn't kill you the first time, they threw acid in your eyes so you never saw your children or anyone else because you had become a blind man. Or they cut off your lids so you could never blink, never sleep, never weep.

Somehow I got air in my lungs.

"I don't have any children," I said.

Warm blood dripped on my face. It was humid, viscous, sticky, mixed with saliva. I heard something metallic clatter on the side of the car then fall onto the sidewalk.

"Don't be a smartass," someone else said in Russian, this time in a cultured accent.

The seat belt snapped back in place. The creep's arm flopped like a rag doll's for a second, then whatever held him up let go, and he bounced away into the gutter and lay there, breathing hard.

"Sverdloff, Anatoly." The voice boomed cheerfully, switching to English: "Remember me?"

It was the goddamn Russian. I needed another Russian like I need a third tit.

"Shall I kill him, please?"

"Don't bother," I said. "I'll get help." But the phone was out.

"You're okay?"

In the split second Sverdloff took to make sure I was alive, the creep summoned some kind of animal will, got out of the gutter, and ran down the alley into the dark.

Sverdloff went after him. It was no contest. He came back, panting.

"Okay. Thank you. Now I owe you. What do you want?" My face hurt like hell.

"I believe this is yours," he said and bowed and presented me with my tooth on his ham-sized hand, like a waiter with a platter. The guy was a joker. He smoothed his coat. "You want me to drive you home? You look lousy."

A couple came toward us, laughing, arms linked. When they saw us, they saw trouble and turned abruptly and went in the other direction.

"No." I didn't want anyone around. I didn't want a Russian around. Any Russian. Okay, so he helped me. But I knew I owed him now. "Thank you."

He said, "What do you need?"

"I want to find the creep who killed Ustinov. Also the piece of shit who just attacked me."

"Same guy?"

"How would I know?" I said. But I knew.

"I think this too. We can talk?" he said.

"Sure. Talk."

"Not now. Go home. Clean up. I'll call you soon. You know the Batumi?"

"The nightclub? Why there?"

"Perhaps I can introduce you to someone interesting. Also, I like noisy places. When you talk, it's safest to sit where you can see the enemy."

I grinned. "I haven't heard that kind of paranoid crap for years."

Whipping a pristine handkerchief out of his pocket, Sverdloff picked up the knife and delivered it to me.

"You've been away from home too long," he said and set off back toward Brighton Beach, the leather coat billowing cheerfully, like a Halloween costume.

Chapter Six

WHAT WAS LEFT OF THAT NIGHT, LIKE SOME HOMELESS BUM, MY OLD raincoat over me, I slept in the car. Lay in the backseat, pieces of Kleenex stuck on my bloody face, listening to rain hit the roof. Heroic I wasn't; I had been too shaky to drive home. But I didn't want the big Russian around with his talk of going home to Moscow.

I felt instinctively that the creep who cut me probably killed Ustinov or had been set up by the same people. It meant he probably knew my connection to Gennadi; either that or he had been following me. When did he start following me? At the café? At the hospital even?

The creep's bony fingers when they caressed my face had been bare; there would be prints on the knife.

I lay in the backseat of the car thinking how Brighton Beach could suck you up and leave you for dead.

In the night, the rain stopped.

As soon as it was light I went down to the ocean, took off my shirt, washed my face in the saltwater. It made my face sting and I was running a fever. There were some Band-Aids in the glove compartment and I stuck them on my face, then I found a pay phone next to Nathan's up on Coney Island. I got coffee, but I still felt like I slept in a toilet and I needed help. Maxine Crabbe was at home and said okay, she'd look at the knife. But Maxie, who's in forensics and a friend, sounded reluctant. Maybe she thought I was going to come on to her.

Instead of the highway, I drove back through Brooklyn's interior. A few Hasidic joggers were out early on, running for God. When I got to the deserted federal building all I saw were some destitute old guys snuggled up to the statuary.

"You all right, fella?" The guard recognized me and he was solicitous. I told him I had fallen off my bike and feigned embarrassment. He let me go up.

Eddie was on duty and I said I'd left my briefcase and he waved me into Sonny's office. He didn't believe me but he didn't like Sonny and I had a couple of spare Knicks tickets for the coming season; his grandkids were fans.

From the end of the hall near Sonny's office I could hear the click and buzz of a printer; someone was at work early. But Rhonda kept her office impeccably and I found the filebox with Ustinov's name on it easily in a credenza next to her desk. The video was inside. I took it. There was the sound of footsteps outside the office and I closed the filebox and put it away as the door opened softly.

"Hello, detective." It was Roy Pettus.

I moved into the hallway where he stood and closed the door behind me. I had the video in my hand. Pettus didn't mention it.

"You need a doctor?" He looked closely at me.

"Scratches is all," I said.

"I hear maybe you fell off your bike." He cracked a small smile. "What about some coffee?"

Agent Pettus did not appear a voluble man or a sociable one, so the offer of coffee surprised me.

"Not here," he said.

We left the building silently.

We went to a coffee shop near the Promenade. Some gulls were doing advanced t'ai chi over the river.

"You're up early," I said inanely.

Pettus was silent.

"You fellows situate yourself where you want and I'll be right with you," said the waitress. She had a face as used as her hair.

The place was almost empty, except for a taxi driver in a turban eating pancakes and an elderly couple making eyes at each other over the ninety-nine-cent breakfast; maybe they couldn't sleep much either.

Roy Pettus folded his jacket once, laid it carefully on the booth and slid in next to it. I sat down opposite.

When the coffee came, he leaned forward slightly. Without any melodrama he said, "What I been considering telling you is we think someone is after you."

"Who is it?" I asked, pulling a cigarette from the pack in my pocket.

"You mind not smoking?" Pettus said.

"Sorry," I said.

"I been trying to quit. It's a bitch."

As we exchanged civilities, my heart raced. Cut to the chase, I thought, but I knew Pettus would take his time. He ordered a toasted English muffin. I drank some coffee. My teeth hurt like hell.

"Could I please have marmalade instead of that grape jelly?" he asked the waitress.

Come on!

"You got a name?"

"No," he said. "No name."

I tried not to panic. I needed a smoke. "You're telling me you heard this stuff even before Ustinov was murdered?"

"Could be. People been sniffing around. Someone accesses your file. Wants your file under the Freedom of Information Act. You believe in synchronicity?"

"Sure."

Pettus grinned. "Course, we don't just send the file. Normally, we drag our butts. Then we send it with the good stuff blacked out. This time, we got orders for a rush job, orders from somewhere we couldn't refuse."

"When?"

"Two, three weeks ago. That mean anything?"

"Around the time I got the letter Ustinov was coming."

"He wrote you?"

"Through his book editor. A guy name of Frye," I said.

"Phillip Frye?"

"Yeah." I left my Aunt Birdie out of things. "You think it's connected with Ustinov?"

"Someone who didn't like Ustinov. Someone thought he knew

too much. Someone who thinks if he told anyone here what he knows he might have told you."

"And how would he know I knew Ustinov?"

"This is New York City. Rumors slip around like greased pigs. Lippert knows. I know."

"Any leads on the cleaner or his gun?"

"The NYPD doesn't exactly share their stuff with us 'less someone orders them to." He was mildly sarcastic.

"The videotape any help?"

"Not much. We got tape of the show by the mile. But videotape is deceptive."

"We're talking an Ivan? A cleaner? A hired gun?"

"Seems like."

"But why kill him now? Why on TV?"

Pettus shrugged. "It only makes sense as a warning. Revenge. You want to tell me about the cuts on your face, detective?"

I was silent.

"Did you know I once handled your case?" Pettus said.

"Yeah?"

"I did some work for immigration in those days. I was interested in you. You spoke languages. You were smart. We figured you for a KGB plant."

"You're kidding."

"I don't kid," Pettus said. "After you were cleared, a lot of people wanted you, but Sonny Lippert was first in line. He got you what you wanted, I guess."

I looked at him. "What do you think I wanted?"

"A regular life. No past. A little adventure, but not too much. I'm guessing." Pettus stirred half-and-half into his coffee, watching the swirl, like a man dreaming of Wyoming where he came from and there was time.

"I know you're officially on leave, maybe quitting the department. It's none of my business. I also know you have a personal stake in this. I'd be grateful if you'd keep me posted. I'll give you my home number."

"Sure," I said.

Pettus was straight, I figured, and I knew I'd need help. But he'd want something in exchange, so I told him about the creep in Brighton Beach.

"Where's the knife?"

"In my car. I'm taking it to Maxie Crabbe. You know her?"

"I know Maxine. You want me to send it over for you?" He was asking me to trust him. I nodded.

"I'm gonna level with you, detective. Ustinov's murder is not my turf exactly. A case like this goes straight to top brass out of DC. But I been following the Brighton Beach mob locally for years. We used to go easy. You remember how the CIA advertised in Russian-language papers? It was an invite to every creep to make a few bucks. But back then we had some control. Now we give out visas like peanuts on the airplane. You know we opened an office in Moscow?"

"I heard." I was restless. He was holding back.

"My opinion, it's worthless. Go home. Take care. These Russians are scary. I interviewed one guy, they made him cut off his own ear and eat it while they watched."

"Thanks."

"I got you something."

Pettus hoisted a scuffed brown leather briefcase onto the table. He snapped open the old-fashioned brass locks and took out a package in a plastic bag and handed it to me. It was from the duty free at Sheremetyovo Airport.

He said, "This was with General Ustinov's things. It was addressed to you."

"What's in it?"

Pettus smiled slowly, picked up the check, extracted a five dollar bill from his back pocket. I saw that from time to time he allowed himself a part: he was Gary Cooper in *High Noon*.

"Fudge," he said.

"Fudge?"

"Yes. Fudge. Some photographs. You have an aunt name of Mrs. Birdie Golden?"

"Yes."

"She the type of lady asks a KGB general to carry fudge to New York City?"

I grinned. "Yes."

"You'll be in touch?"

"Sure. Does Sonny know you gave me this stuff?"

"No."

"Why are you doing this?"

"You should have been a New York smartass with all that education and the clothes. But you never were," Roy Pettus said.

Pettus was hard to resist; I have always been too easily flattered by powerful men, maybe because of my father, or Ustinov, or the system I grew up in.

"Anything, what?" I said to Pettus. "What kind of *anything* do you want?"

"Who the cleaner is. Why he shot Ustinov. If someone else is involved. The meaning of sex, death and rock and roll."

I looked up, surprised.

"Hell," he said. "I went to Woodstock."

"Why does Lippert want me off this thing?"

"Maybe he wants this franchise for himself."

"You hate the guy."

"No," Pettus said mildly. "I just don't like the ambition. It's like cataracts. Blurs the vision. He once screwed over a couple of my men. And detective—"

"Yeah?"

"Let me know what you think of that video you swiped from Lippert's office."

Roy Pettus scared me. This was no conspiracy theorist looking for a high. This was not a guy who got his hair in a braid lightly. Gennadi Ustinov was dead on a TV show. Someone was after me.

It was still early, downtown Brooklyn still pretty empty. It was hot, but I was shivering and I trotted out to my car and put the bag Pettus gave me on the front seat, gingerly, like it was a bomb. Pettus followed me and I gave him the knife. He waved and I got in and turned on the ignition; the car stalled. Goddamn antique piece of Mustang crap. I was going to buy a new car next time instead of this thing that plagued my life. I didn't know what was wrong, but I didn't wait to find out. An empty cab cruised down from the Heights and I grabbed the bag and ran for it.

The driver was Russian. Halfway over the bridge, he slowed to a crawl. There wasn't any traffic. It was terribly quiet.

"What's happening?" I said.

"Car overheats," he said blandly, and I recalled this was the exact spot where someone shot at Zilber, the Brighton Beach hood, from a passing car; the bullet got him smack in the eye.

Chapter Seven

GENNADI USTINOV SMILES OUT AT ME, EYES BLUE, CHIN ON HIS HANDS, elbows on the table. Even coming at me through this crap video I stole out of Sonny's office, he is still a handsome man. I remember the face and it makes me ache. Dapper, alluring, he has a face you want to talk to, confess to. He leans forward, he appears completely candid and looks only at you, inviting secrets. It was his trade.

Ustinov always wore American clothes, his vanity invested in the effect, the Brooks Brothers summer suit, a blue button-down shirt, a red silk tie. He loved America.

He was made for television: The cameras loved the cheekbones, the pale blue eyes were cool for a cool medium, the Slavic mouth, the voluptuary's smile warmed up the face. He leans forward energetically as if he has something to tell me.

Beside him on *The Teddy Flowers Show* is Lily Hanes. He speaks to her but I can't hear. The camera pans down the table to the other guests, then to the audience. A man is on his feet, his arms outstretched. There's a gun in his hand, but he turns and puts his free hand in front of his face like he knows the camera will steal it.

In the audience, people screaming, running, flopping onto the floor. Ustinov tries to get up from the table, then falls over and slides off his chair. Over and over, I hit the remote and rewind, then push forward and watch him fall. He falls on Lily Hanes in her pink jacket. They slide off their chairs onto the floor.

I switched the tape off. My face hurt. I was running a fever, from the cuts, or an infected gum, or from fear. I had stopped off at the dentist's when I got back from Brooklyn and he fixed me up temporarily and shot me up with antibiotics, but I couldn't sleep.

I sat at my desk smoking, and cigarette ash fluttered on the pile of papers, Xeroxes and faxes, rap sheets and immigration forms and green card dossiers and all the background reports I'd been able to call in from friends around town so far. The fax chattered constantly. A friend who works at the *New York Times* tapped into a database and it spewed stuff about the Russian mafia onto my fax. Nothing much I didn't know. It's never about information, anyhow; it's about figuring out what the facts mean and getting proof.

Maxie had the knife, but she would have to look at it in her own time, on the sly; it wasn't her case; it wasn't mine either.

I froze the video on Gennadi Ustinov.

They were golden boys together, him and my father, as kids, as young men, Khrushchev's best and brightest; they were going to get socialism right. Best friend, surrogate uncle, the glamorous Uncle Gennadi who came back from America with jazz records and beautiful shoes and radios in the shape of baseballs.

Little by little my father got pushed, the KGB not liking its top guns married to noisy, contentious Yids who questioned the system, which is what my mother became, in their eyes. Quiet Jews were okay, noisy Jews not so good. Did Gennadi stick by him or betray him? We never knew. No one ever said. When I was fifteen, we left for Israel. That was that.

I pushed play and watched the characters jiggle into life. Lily Hanes had them lined up like the cast of those British mystery novels Russians used to love—my mother adored them—suspects at a dinner party: Sverdloff; the stripper; the yuppie, Saroyan; Zalenko, the fascist; Crowe, the Brit. A Russian game of Clue; Comrade Red in the parlor.

I focused on Zalenko. He was a bald man with a beard that made him look like his head was on upside down. Zalenko spoke good English and his eyes glittered with the sheen of the zealous. He was rumored to be Zhirinovsky's successor, the new nationalist sweetheart with good connections to the American Right and the Christian Coalition.

My mind wandered. I watched Gennadi Ustinov die again. The more I watched, the more I was convinced the creep on Brighton Beach the night before was the man with the gun in the video. I would get a blowup made off the video, but from what I could see here, he was a real Ivan: angular face, high cheekbones, thin mouth. Ukrainian, maybe. He had been handsome, but he looked sick, greasy strands of pale hair falling on his forehead.

"Talk to me, you piece of shit," I whispered at the screen in Russian. "Talk to me. Tell me why you did it."

I flipped on the news. Shootings were up. Some right-wing terrorists had trucked a van into the city crammed with fertilizer from upstate. With Ustinov's murder, already, the pundits were pontificating about the meaning of an on-air shooting, live, on television.

It was the kind of thing Ustinov might have once invented himself for a propaganda lecture: a man shot to death on television is the result of rampant abuse of promiscuous freedoms in the United States, he would have said. Sitting at the kitchen table in Moscow, my mother would have snorted with laughter and made fun of him for saying it.

It was all a long time ago. The bad stuff had faded; it seemed to belong to another guy in an old photograph from a different life, the kind where you look at yourself and think, Who's that?

After all, what was the big bloody deal? People had really suffered in that miserable sonofabitch country. I didn't go to the Gulag. I didn't starve. It was the dread of never knowing, and, later, the unspoken things.

By the time I was fifteen, I was out of it. At nineteen, I was in New York. Methodically, like a million other immigrants who wanted to unload the past, I put it behind me. I didn't see Russians or read it or talk it except for work when I had to. Ironically, it was useful for work. Even as a kid, I had a knack for languages like everyone in my family, but only a knack, like karaoke.

No one in New York cared where I came from. New York was the air I breathed; it was all I ever wanted anyway.

I switched back to the tape. On Lily's other side was the Englishman, Gavin Crowe. Lily Hanes looked wonderful. She had a sexy, friendly face. She had great legs. She was smart.

You're a pervert, I told myself. Your father's best friend is getting blown away in front of you and you've got the hots for a woman with red hair and long legs.

I got a cold Corona out of the fridge. I called a guy who owed me one and got my car towed from Brooklyn and fixed. For a while, without meaning to, I dozed in my chair. I was feeling so lousy, I didn't wake up until around 2 A.M., so I went to bed. In the morning, I got on the phone and schmoozed some more people at *The Teddy Flowers Show* and discovered that Gavin Crowe was supposed to be staying at the Chelsea Hotel.

In my opinion, the Chelsea Hotel, which is next door to a dump that sells lobsters and Spanish grub on Twenty-third Street, is a shithole. A bunch of artists and writers who couldn't afford better made it a shrine and Sid Vicious croaked there, also Dylan Thomas, I think.

When I got there, Crowe was in his room smoking Russian cigarettes.

"Hi."

"Hi. Been living it up some?" He gestured at my face.

Crowe was smaller than he appeared on the video. Five two, maybe less in his socks. He wore high-heeled cowboy boots with lifts in them and bell-bottom pants. Briefly, in the sixties, according to the dossier I had, he'd played in some British band no one ever heard of. He was some kind of writer, he said. Crowe, who had the lousy teeth and pitted skin you get from bad food and too much booze, was English and he leaned on it.

"You want to talk a while?" I put myself into low gear. He was repellent, but I was cool. Cool it, I said to myself. I inherited some kind of bad gene where the Brits are concerned. In private, my pop called them "Tea-bags." Perfidious Albion, he said. That was why they made good spies to start with and lousy ones in the end. But they wrote great books.

Also they make great whiskey. They talk in whole paragraphs— I went out with a string of English girls for a while so I could listen to the way they talked—but I don't trust them much.

"What shall we talk about?" Crowe said.

"This and that. Gennadi Ustinov. The show. The murder. Russia. You. Me."

"I've got a plane later," Crowe said. "You can buy me a meal, though."

"You're going back already?"

"Well, some policemen did ask me quite a lot of very dull questions. They decided I didn't do it. Bit boring that."

"Who did it?"

"The butler?"

I don't have much of a temper, but I really hate cute. Crowe was almost a foot shorter than me. I dragged him to the window and opened it.

"You see the street? You want to make contact? You want to end up street pizza?" I said. This was not cool but the guy got to me.

"Street pizza." He beamed. "I must write that down. Street pizza, I love it. So, you're from Moscow."

I was silent.

"Oh, relax, darling. I used to do linguistics once upon a time. I'm the Henry Higgins of my generation. I can tell where anyone is from, especially émigré Russians like yourself. Except to me, you sound like a born New Yorker." Modest he was not.

"But I am hungry and I'd like to eat something before I go back to Ma Russia and the upcoming revolution, so if you want me, you'll have to feed me."

"What revolution?"

"Whichever." Crowe was already out of the room.

In the street, he flagged a cab and ordered it to Little Italy. We went into some dump. It was early and the place was empty. Crowe ordered Chianti and linguine with red clam sauce.

"This stuff was on the wall when they shot Joey Gallo over at Umberto's Clam House," he said twirling the pasta around his fork. "Did you know that? I knew a cousin of Gallo's, interesting family. Obeyed the code," he said.

I couldn't believe anyone talked like this except on *Masterpiece Theatre*, which I used to watch with Dorothy Tae, who was addicted to *Brideshead Revisited*.

"Who set up the killing?"

45

"That's easy."

Crowe took a slab of bread off the table, spread it with butter, dipped it in olive oil, ordered veal parmigiana, and ate. He talked with his mouth full.

I got some antipasto and picked at the salami.

"Tell me."

"Zalenko. Had to be. He hired your Ivan. You see why? Ustinov was old guard. Old guard KGB. Didn't like dirty tricks. Believed in the system. Was perfectly decent, after his fashion. Too decent to care about my old man, of course, but that's the point. He wanted to tell all. He wanted to tell more than was good for him."

"Your old man?"

"Spy." Crowe drooled slightly. "Old man was a spy. Minor spy. Finished up in Moscow. Not in the Philby league, of course. No one made my old man a KGB general. Felt he ought to be grateful they took him in at all."

Crowe liked the idea of himself at the center of his own movie.

I said, "Let's get back to Zalenko."

"Yes, well, as Ustinov saw it, it's the nationalists like Zalenko who are destroying the country."

"How do you know all this?"

"Ask my friend Phillip Frye. He got me on the show. He knows where the bodies are buried. There's a paper trail."

"And?"

"Information costs." He stuffed his mouth with more food. "Have you got funds?"

"I'll think about it. Why kill him here?"

"Zalenko is in bed with the mafia. They use each other. When the fascists take over, the mafia will be in place officially. The new Cossacks."

I ate a piece of hot sausage and drank a beer.

Crowe said, "You think Zhirinovsky's bad? Wait till you see the next generation. Very respectable. Young. Clothes from the Gap. Good English. Cozy with the new American right. Practicing Christians, as it were. They hate Clinton. He wants to take away their nukes."

"What?"

"The Russians love their nukes. Russians think America wants them to dump their plutonium, which would make them a third-world country; no nukes, no power. Me, I'll have to get out," Crowe said. "They'll be after me."

I laughed. "You?"

"I'm a democrat, small d to you, of course," he said. "I was there, in my way, in the coup."

"Yeah? Which side?" I asked, but he was impervious. "So how did Zalenko arrange to have Ustinov killed?"

"Easy enough. Bring in a contract killer. Pick one up in Brighton Beach. Doing it on the show made it a public assassination. That's how they operate. I can introduce you. I live in Moscow, but this is my subject. I know my way around Brighton Beach, I know the gangs all over town, Gum Sing in Crown Heights, Koreans in Queens. Russians have ties to all of them."

Gavin Crowe was a mafia groupie; crime turned him on.

"Tell me something I don't know," I said to him.

He helped himself to my smokes and lit up.

"Everyone on that TV show had a beef against Ustinov. Zalenko thought he sold out Mother Russia. Saroyan reckoned he wanted to stifle capitalism, for which read extortion. Officialdom hated little Olga's kind, poor bitch," he said.

"Ustinov was ex-KGB. They were all Russians with a beef. So what else is new?"

"Myself, I wouldn't trust Anatoly Sverdloff."

"Why not?" I was suddenly more interested.

"Ustinov once locked him up. Got him to talk. Ustinov had charm. He could make anyone talk."

"What else?"

"Lily Hanes had the hots for Ustinov, I noticed." Crowe leered and helped himself to more wine.

"Lily Hanes your friend too?"

"Everyone's my friend, darling," he said.

"Maybe it was you," I said. "After all, you had a beef, didn't you? Ustinov treated your old man like the garbage he was, didn't he?" I tossed it out.

Crowe's eyes went dead with hate. "Fuck you," he said.

I said, "Stick around a couple days," and threw some money on the table.

'hat official?"

icial enough for you."

ᴗne other thing," he called as I started to leave.

"I'm in a hurry."

"Ask Phil Frye about Ustinov's book. Ask him where the missing pages are."

Chapter Eight

I FIGURED I WAS MAYBE ON TO SOMETHING, AND WHEN I BEGAN TRYING to get at Phillip Frye I was convinced. After I left Crowe, I spent the rest of the day trying to track Frye down; Frye was coy. At his office his secretary said he was out, at a meeting, gone home, whatever.

Still zonked from the cuts on my face and the growing reality of Ustinov's death, I went home, but the Frye thing bugged me. It bugged me when I called the Chelsea later and heard Crowe left town, so did the fact Ustinov had locked up Sverdloff once. The man in glasses at the café in Brighton Beach bothered the shit out of me. He knew my name. I figured he had to be connected to the creep who cut me, who maybe also shot Ustinov. Sonny Lippert was unavailable and it was my fault. I didn't know how to get help. I was out of the loop.

The vacuum cleaner was propped against the wall and I climbed off the sofa, uncoiled the cord and plugged it in; it roared into life like a fighter plane. The place was a mess.

The Taes had done the bare bones renovation on the loft, but I had painted it myself and scraped the old hardwood floors and waxed them until they were like mirrors. Back when I moved in, more than ten years ago, when Benny Ong was still running Chinatown, it seemed crazy, a cop living in a loft below Canal Street.

Chet Baker was on the CD playing "It Never Entered My Mind." I never could figure how a white man could play such gorgeous stuff. "There's this little white cat on the coast gonna eat you boys alive," Charlie Parker said after he first heard Chet. I even made a pilgrimage to the Lighthouse, the club in Hermosa Beach Chet used to play at. Shortie Rogers, too.

Vacuuming my place made me feel better, and I got up on a ladder and dusted the window sills, then I dumped all the dirty laundry into a bag, scrubbed out the bathtub, and did the dishes. I like cleaning. I like the order.

Until Ustinov was shot, I was a pretty happy guy. I had a life. I got to travel. I liked the job, sometimes a lot.

New York is home. The Taes are family. There are friends. Music. Softball with the guys. Girls. Once a week I eat ribs at Tennessee Mountain with Lois and Louise from across the hall, and I would marry either of them, or both, if they weren't already in love with each other. I even have a little money in the bank because Dawn Tae, who has an MBA and can make money do tricks you never dreamed of, showed me how. I made a little dough, I blew most of it on fixing my place. I bought a few pictures I liked and the Mustang, took a trip to New Orleans and listened to music there and saw the bayou trees. The few bucks I had left I put away.

The day I realized I didn't owe anyone any money was a liberation. I even have a broker named Stephanie who doesn't let me touch it. You can inhabit New York very nicely if you're not sick or poor. I don't have to mortgage myself to corruption the way a lot of the guys are tempted to, and who can blame them?

From time to time a letter comes from Aunt Birdie, and I worry about my mother. After my father was killed by a bomb on a tourist bus in Galilee, she retreated into a kind of *Yiddishkeit* of her own making, looking to inhabit the world of her own grandparents. I get over to see her in Haifa once a year, if I can, and the Alzheimer's leaves her periods of lucidity, but they're getting shorter.

I was making a mozzarella sandwich when the front door suddenly burst open; I scrambled for my gun.

"What is this, the OK Corral? Jesus Christ," bellowed Rick. "This is New York, Artie. Civilization, you know?"

He was carrying an armful of beer. "Look what I got. A fabulous micro-brewery in New Haven."

"You're turning into a beer bore, Ricky. I hate beer bores. I like Bud Lite. What's up?"

"Tastes like cat piss." He sat cross-legged on the kitchen counter and drank with zest. "I read something in the paper maybe means something. Who owns *The Teddy Flowers Show*?"

"What do you mean, who owns it?"

"Is it network? Cable? A syndicate?"

Next door, the kid was playing a Portishead album. "Shut it up." I pounded the wall.

"Jesus, you're wired," Ricky said mildly. "So who owns him?"

"Surprise me."

"CBM owns it. That's who."

"Okay."

Ricky loves this stuff. He likes revealing information with what he considers legerdemain and for a while, he planned on being a professional magician. His mother got fed up with the dead rabbits around the place and cooked one.

"CBM is a media conglomerate that's suddenly buying up all kinds of stuff. Talk shows. Tabloids in small markets. Putting together a mini-network, like Fox."

"And?"

"Today I read that CBM also owns Madison House. So I think how come the same go-getter media outfit that's in bed with tabs wants a staid book-publishing outfit?"

I got onions out from the icebox and began chopping them to go with some eggs I planned on making.

"You want me to do that?"

"No thanks. Tell me what you're getting at."

"Madison House published a memoir by a certain ex-KGB general. Interesting? Do we care both General Ustinov and Teddy Flowers are owned by the same people?"

"I guess. You saw the tape of the show I left you?"

Ricky nodded. "The fat guy?"

"Sverdloff. He's a DJ. A rock-and-roll type."

"He seems familiar. I think I'm going to make some calls," he said. "I got cousins with good connections in old commie rock circles."

Like most Chinese, Ricky Tae has cousins all over the place. I'm ten years older and six inches taller, but he's tougher and smarter, some kind of actual class-A genius when he bothers. He graduated Bronx Science, then MIT, but he went into the family business in the end. "Gimme a plate of perfect dumplings for a religious experience," he always says.

Ricky has a loft in the building too and, early on, when I first moved in, we became friends. Sometimes, when his parents go home to Riverdale, we sit up late in the restaurant talking politics, smoking, playing some chess. It was Rick got his folks to change the name of the place from China Host to the Tiananmen Café; he's the only son and they indulged him and changed the sign.

"Artie? You in there babe?" a voice yelled through the door. It was the casting director who lives two floors down. Her name's Irma but she calls herself Oxygen.

"Later," I yelled back.

"Jesus Christ," Ricky said irritably. Oxygen never pays her rent on time. It drives the Taes crazy. "What do you see in her? She bolshoi ugly, man."

Ricky makes me laugh and I love him. Years ago, I figured out he's sexually ambivalent, and he knows I know, but it doesn't matter to anyone except his father. I can say pretty much anything to Ricky. Once I crossed a line. We were talking about women and why I could never fix on one and settle down and I said to him, "You think I'm a faggot?" and he shot me a look. I knew it was a mistake.

"She's not that bad."

"Reality check, Artie." Ricky looked out the window. "I think you got more company. This place is turning into Grand Central Station. I gotta go."

I leaned out the window and threw the keys to Maxine Crabbe who climbed out of a taxi. She waved and came up.

"Hi, Artie." Max kissed me, but she was nervous.

A string bean of a girl, too tall for her torso, she has a punk haircut, an angelic face, a disposition to match and long loose limbs.

She wanted to be a jazz singer, but ended up in forensics. We went out for a while, but eventually she gave up on me and married a handsome fire chief named Mark and moved to a house on Staten Island where you can practically fish the Arthur Kill from the backyard. They have twin girls.

She had called earlier. She was coming over, she said; she didn't want to talk on the phone. Maxie accepted a cold beer and zipped her purse uneasily. With those two kids, she's always strapped for cash.

"Let me give you the money for the taxi, Max, Okay? It's my nickel."

"It's not that. We're friends, right, Artie?"

"You know that. Hey, I'm not going to come on to you. I like Mark."

She sucked on the bottle. "It isn't that. I'm not supposed to be here. Where did you get that knife Roy Pettus sent over? What's with you and Agent Pettus?"

I told her some of it.

"Look, doll, this Ustinov thing has moved up the ladder. It's mostly all Feds now. Roy Pettus told me I could talk to you about the knife because he thinks you're in trouble and he likes you, but from now on it's going tight as the cracks in some assholes I know. Everyone is frantic. And I'm not even really in Pettus' jurisdiction exactly." She hesitated.

"What? What? Come on, Max. This is me."

"My boss gets this call from Sonny Lippert. He lets on you're on leave, you know? Tells him stay clear of Artie Cohen. Like you have a disease. Why, Artie?" She looked at the wooden counter that separates the kitchen from the rest of the place. "You got anything to eat? I'm starving."

I made her a sandwich out of some sweet Italian sausage and a slab of mozzarella on focaccia.

"Thanks." Chewing, she sat on a stool at the kitchen counter and leaned on her elbows. "Okay. This is really preliminary, but I got some prints. And blood. I love blood," she said with relish, her mouth full. Maxine is nuts for blood. Since O.J. and the DNA thing, blood has become the fingerprints of the nineties.

"Spell it out for me, Max."

"The knife is what they call a boning knife. Only three or four places sell this kind. Fancy chef stuff. Very expensive, over a hundred bucks." She took a list out of her purse. "These are the stores."

"That's not all, is it?"

She shook her head.

"What?"

"Gimme a cigarette."

I lit one for her.

She said, "People talk wild stuff. You know."

"Yes."

"Turn on the stereo, okay. Just in case."

"Sure. But no one's listening." I put on Peggy Lee and George Shearing.

Maxie lowered her voice.

"The weird thing, and it's not my territory, but there have been forensics guys from Washington I've never seen before. Something is going on and it's way out of my league. I don't know, but you should be careful, Artie. Be careful."

"What? What is it?"

"Nothing." She was holding back. She was scared.

"Tell me."

"I gotta go now, Artie. I gotta go."

It goes without saying there was a lot of crap being talked about this whole case, and Maxie had probably stepped in some of it. She was holding back and I was pissed off, but she has the kids to worry about. I called her a few times but there was no answer. I left messages for her boss. Nothing. The shops where you could buy a knife for a hundred bucks weren't much help, either; I got in touch with most of them and came up blank.

For the third time since Roy Pettus gave it to me, I opened the plastic bag. I knew the contents by heart: Birdie's fudge; a book written by a kid I went to school with; a few photographs, including one of my parents and Gennadi Ustinov near a river; a funny note in Birdie's beautiful hand. Jesus, I felt guilty about Birdie, but the guilt never quite outweighed the fear of going back to Moscow. Also in the bag was an item Roy Pettus had added, the flimsy Xerox of a double-page spread out of Ustinov's diary, his last full day alive and the day he died. It was Roy Pettus' real gift to me.

Everything checked out. The hotel where Gennadi Ustinov stayed, the restaurants he ate at, the people he saw. All of it was inscribed in his elegant writing, including me. Breakfast, he had written. Breakfast with Artyom. We were going to meet the morning after *The Teddy Flowers Show.*

In one corner Gennadi had also written CB in tiny letters. Who was CB, or what?

The phone rang. It was Sverdloff. He reminded me I promised to meet him. He wanted to meet tomorrow night. I owed him so I agreed. I took off my shorts and got under the shower. I ran it hot and hard, then I switched it off and grabbed blind for a towel. There was blood from my face streaming down my chest.

"Artie, babe? Sweetheart? You in there?" It was Oxygen screaming through the door. "Hey, I'm bored. Open up." Once in a while she offers me a part. I love it. I would have been an actor if I had any talent.

"You wanna night job?" she screams, clattering past on her five-inch platforms. "I got defectors, I got dissidents, I got KGB, nice uniforms." "Why can't I play an American?" I always ask. "Americans I already got. You want it, you don't want it? I got the director on the phone. I got Mike Newell on the phone."

It was early evening. It was hot. "Don't trust Sverdloff," Crowe had said, but I owed Sverdloff and I didn't trust Crowe. The guy who towed my car from Brooklyn said I owed him. I owed everybody. What the hell, I thought, life is short.

I wrapped a towel around my waist and shouted through the door, "I'm coming."

Hours later, in the middle of the night, Oxygen sat up, rigid as a board, and her hat, which she wore to bed, fell onto the floor.

"What?"

"Outside. There's someone there."

"Go back to sleep," I said.

"No, listen. Listen."

The building was silent. No dogs barked. The babies in 4B

slept. No noise came from the street; it must have been around 4 A.M., the only time New York is silent.

In the black stillness, holding the hand of the woman in my bed, I listened again, hearing now the faint creak of the old building: the walls in these cast-iron buildings are a foot thick, but the hardwood floors resonate, and I could hear them moan, as if in a storm. But it was humid and still out and there was nothing else except the chug of the refrigerator.

Then I heard it.

"Stay still." I swung my feet over the edge of the bed, feeling for my sneakers and a pair of sweat pants, fumbling in the closet for my .38. I turned the deadbolt quiet as I could. Outside, in the narrow hall that led to the elevator and the other two lofts, the light had gone out. There was a faint scuffling, like rats, I thought. But there were no rats here; Mrs. Tae is a fanatic.

Creeping along, gun in my hand, I went down the stairs chasing the noise. In the dark, there was a palpable stink; it was the smell of rotten flesh I had smelled in Brighton Beach.

A shadow moved down the hallway. My mouth went dry. I heard a door slam. Probably Oxygen running home from my place. Then something slimy draped itself around my ankle, something wet, oily. Maybe there was a rat. I reached down and grabbed it and felt blood. It was the bandage from my face. It had fallen off.

I tried to chase the shadow. It danced in the dark. Then it reached up.

A light snapped on. I was ready.

"Ricky? What the fuck."

Ricky had stripped off his T-shirt and was wrapping it coolly around his head and it was already soaked with blood. He was a skinny kid but he had real balls.

"Give me a cigarette."

I gave him one.

"I heard something. I figured you might need some help."

"Thanks, man." I didn't know what to say. Ricky had taken the blow for me. "You want me to get a doctor?"

"Nah," he said. "I hit my head on a door is all."

"Well, thanks."

"For what? I figured if you were screwing the broad, you wouldn't hear a nuclear bomb drop." He pushed his hair back from his lean face. "I gotta get cleaned up."

"I'm coming with you," I said.

"It's okay, I can manage." Ricky was secretive about his apartment—I'd been in it, of course, but only by invitation. It was a sleek place with a few good leather chairs and some wonderful Chinese rugs. Maybe he had a visitor. Maybe he didn't want to tell me about it.

"What would I do without you?"

"Beats me, pal. Get some sleep," Ricky said and went home.

Somewhere I heard a door bang again, and then the eerie quiet returned to the building and by the time I got back to my place, the creep had been inside. I could smell him. My laptop was gone, nothing else. The creep left no other trace at all, except dread.

Chapter Nine

DREAD WAS WHAT I FELT THE NEXT NIGHT WHEN I PULLED UP NEAR THE Batumi Nightclub in Brighton Beach. I spent the day checking what I could around town—but the Feds were a pain in the ass and I didn't get much satisfaction—and by the time I got to Brooklyn that night I was dog-tired. There was a greasy gunmetal sky and a sticky drizzle that smelled of seaweed. Standing in the doorway, light falling on his huge face from the Odessa Deli next door, was Tolya Sverdloff, surrounded by a phalanx of Russian men attending him as if he were some kind of priest.

At night Brighton Beach turns in on itself. The Batumi, like most of the clubs, had no windows. Out front, radio cabs and limos jammed the street. It was Saturday night. It was four days since Ustinov was killed; it seemed like a year.

Standing a few yards from Tolya were a couple of cops I recognized. They were wearing fancy outfits, and when they saw me they looked away uneasily; they were moonlighting as muscle.

"Don't trust Sverdloff," Crowe had said. "Ustinov locked him up."

Local goons in leather—they had leather for brains, some of them—swaggered along the avenue under the El. All wore weapons, some carried streetsweepers. They like knives best in Brighton Beach, though; slice and dice is their stock in trade; connoisseurs use a blowtorch. The Russians leave their signature and I'd seen some of their work.

They have no pretensions about family or honor. They run their business in clans and gangs that splinter and reform according to geography or specialty: Chechens, Ukrainians, Georgians, gas scams, drugs, prostitution. Money's what matters, but they like the killing.

More men climbed out of limousines and greeted Sverdloff, who, chattering like a tour guide in a rich patter of English and Russian, unstoppable, fluent, made his way into the club, some of the men in his wake. Up close, in the light, he was a giant. Like I said, I'm big, but Sverdloff towered over me.

"Tolya!" people greeted him. "Tol!" they cried, slapping his back, punching his shoulder, kissing him three times on both cheeks.

The Batumi was one of the newer joints. The lobby floor was green marble. A pair of gold plaster nudes stood beside the boutique that sold lobsters, crab, and caviar. Sverdloff moved on, wallowing in the attention. A little man in a tux stood on tiptoe to hug him and Sverdloff actually swept the guy off his feet.

"Look on the wall," Tolya Sverdloff breathed in my ear. With me, he spoke English. He liked showing off his English, except as he got drunker, it got worse. He had already been drinking plenty.

A man in a silk jacket stood in a corner, shouting into a portable phone, one hand stroking a photograph on the wall. Mesmerized, he moved his hand over the naked woman. ARTISTIC DANCING, it said in Russian. THE INIMITABLE ANNA K.

"The stripper on *The Teddy Flowers Show*?"

Tolya nodded. "We'll see her perform, then pay her a visit. Okay?"

"You know this girl?"

Tolya grinned. "I'm from Moscow. This is New York City. Everybody knows everybody. You will meet her. It will be interesting for you."

I followed him up the stairs. He turned.

"Did you know Ustinov locked me up once?" he asked cheerfully as we got to the club.

"How come? You talked too much?"

"I tried to screw my guitar onstage at a rock concert in Tallinn. I was quite a big star. Big as Gribenshikov. For fifteen minutes." Sverdloff laughed. "After your time."

Sverdloff's laughter was sucked up by the noise in the main room. He moved in quickly, gracefully, working his way into the heaving crowd.

The walls of the Batumi were made of mirrors. At one side was a bar, at the other a bandstand where a group in silver tuxes played cover versions of Beatles tunes.

On the dance floor men in silk suits, guns under their jackets, moved lightly with babes in tight leather skirts. The men's shirts were silk too, the collars spread over their lapels. They were meticulous dressers and they flicked those collars into place incessantly; their fingers were thick with rings and the nails manicured. And they could dance.

The crowd made room for the best dancers, and they were light on their feet and loose in the hip. They knew all the steps. These were not Moscow intellectuals or Manhattan Jews. They were voluptuaries from the wrong side of the Urals and they really could dance.

"You want to drink something?" Tolya asked formally and we went to the bar.

Around the dance floor people sat at long tables and ate. The tables were jammed with food: smoked fish, chopped liver, pickled walnuts, pickled mushrooms, ham, salami, head cheese, herring, red caviar, black caviar, black bread, and Russian salad, the carrots and peas suspended in bright yellow mayonnaise. There were forests of vodka bottles and Coke cans. People leaned on the table, shouting in Russian, Ukrainian, Georgian, Yiddish. An elderly woman made sandwiches out of bread and fish, wrapped them in Kleenex, then inserted them methodically into her large plastic handbag.

"Mama's got a great big bag," Tolya shouted and leaned on me, laughing.

In the darker corners, men moved restlessly, shadows reflected in the mirrors. It reminded me of the time, on a case in Crown Heights, I went into a Hasidic synagogue. There, too, the men wandered, gossiped, prayed, even selling stuff they had hidden in those mysterious deep black pockets. It was as alien to me as a mosque and so was this. Russians I had known, in my Moscow, people like my parents, intellectuals, ate home at the kitchen table. Here, I could speak the language, but I couldn't read the meaning.

Sverdloff stopped in front of the bar and hailed the bartender. He stared at me for a minute.

"What?" I said.

"How's your face?"

"Lousy."

"Be careful. This guy will come after you again."

Sverdloff ordered brandy. I asked for beer.

"What do you know about Gavin Crowe?"

Sverdloff shuddered. "Nasty piece of goods. Also, the father. I met the father. He did some small business for the KGB. Dirty business. You met him, you wanted bath afterwards."

"Where is he?"

"He is dead. Do you know what one hit costs these days?" Sverdloff asked me. He was really knocking back the brandy.

"Is this a riddle?"

"Someone reliable, two hundred. First-class hitman, two grand. Plus one return ticket to Moscow. Plus maybe one night to lay low in Miami. Two thousand American smackers," he added and I noted that his slang was out of date and felt superior. I said something in Russian.

"In English, Artyom. It's safer around here. I will tell you, Artyom, however, this doesn't feel like simple mafia hit, Ustinov. No, I don't believe this. It feels wrong." He spoke softly.

"What feels wrong?"

"You have information you want to share? Maybe I can help?"
I didn't answer.

"Let's drink," he said.

Under my feet I could feel the floor vibrate with the moving
crowd. At a table in front of us was a sedate party of well-dressed
men and women. Sverdloff followed my gaze.

"Slumming," he said. "From across bridge to view goods. Armani Jews. To see how they spend their many dollars."

"What?"

"Where you been hiding? Look, I am no anti-Semite. My wife
is Jew. My kids, therefore, are Jew. But Russki arrives in this country, he is Jewish, he got friends. First time in Russian history people want to be Jew. Sure, why not? New Jews arrive in America
they get cash, medical treatment, help with houses. They are very
smart cookies."

"That doesn't make them gangsters." I could tell Sverdloff was
plenty drunk because he was dropping articles now like a comic-
book Russian.

"Sure. Sure. But Russian hood with "Jew" on passport gets
same deal as every other Jew. Say I am Jewish engineer. I cannot
find work. I say I am fearful of mood in my country—Commu-
nists' return, Yeltsin leaving, fascists coming, nationalists, army
junta, anti-Semites. I wish to come to America. I omit fact I am also
running extortion ring in Kiev. I arrive. Work hard. Learn English.
Few years later, I am set up again. Anyone make fuss, Jewish or-
ganizations start screaming. In Brighton Beach, no one talks. Who
will talk? Everyone is afraid of reprisals back home. Just like before. Nothing changes."

"Tell me something I don't already know." I felt depressed.
The band launched into a Stevie Wonder medley.

The mirrored bar ran the whole length of the room. Dozens of
men leaned on it. Tolya Sverdloff looked completely at home; he
drank French brandy, calling loudly for VSOP brands by name.
With one hand, he sampled snacks of fish and caviar from a platter on the bar, the other he planted on my shoulder with jovial
bonhomie. I wanted to shake loose, but this was ritual for him.

"It took Italians three, four generations to penetrate legitimate
society. These guys, it's already happening. Smart guys. Ph.D.s.

We Russians are good at paperwork. Paper money." He shook with laughter.

"Who does the dirty work?"

"Look around. They got Olympic weightlifters retired from the Soviet team. They got Israeli commandos not retired. The KGB is also helpful. Scary combo," Sverdloff said, admiring himself in a mirror.

"I read that in *Vanity Fair*," I said.

The lights went out. There was a drumroll. I drank my beer. Acrobats in tights flipped out of the darkness into the colored lights. The show had begun.

The Tom Jones clone followed, then gilded birdcages descended from the ceiling and three girls emerged, dressed in feathers. They were jugglers, but I couldn't see what it was they were tossing around.

Sverdloff looked up. "Stuffed birds," he said.

I asked for Scotch.

"So you were godson to the general," Tolya said. "Listen to me, and watch the table in the corner." He gulped his brandy noisily.

At a round table on a raised platform were eight men all dressed in dark suits and white shirts. They spoke quietly among themselves.

"Petrol," Tolya said. "Gas scams, you say. Medical insurance fraud. You know how much they skim this way? Millions. Billions. They prefer to rip off little people. You know this saying, 'Better steal one dollar from a million people than a million dollars from one person.' "

The men in the dark suits barely touched their vodka. There was only one woman at the table. A tall blonde in a plain silk shirt, hair netted low on her neck in an old-fashioned chignon, she had the exquisite affected posture of a flamenco dancer. Men who stopped to pay court to the suits first kissed her hand. I couldn't stop looking.

"Don't even think about it," he said. "This is Marina, cousin of Elem Zeitsev's wife. You know Zeitsev?"

The smell of bodies and spilled booze, perfume and corruption was oppressive and so were the crude Russian voices. I knew who Zeitsev was, of course, but I let Sverdloff go on, insisting over and over this was the safest place to talk. He liked the risk. He got off on intrigue.

Sweating, I pulled off my jacket, and got a Coke. Sverdloff couldn't shut up. As the show went on and on, the jugglers followed by the fire-eaters and the tap-dancing midgets, he delivered his spiel on Brighton Beach: how the Brooklyn resort named in the 1870s for the English seaside town became a poor Jew neighborhood, as Sverdloff put it; how in the 1970s when Nixon and Brezhnev invented détente, forty thousand new ones arrived, including all the criminals in the jails. The big KGB joke: You want them? Take them, the KGB said and opened the jails and sent the garbage into the American bloodstream like a plague.

Sure, there were real immigrants, real dissidents, but also thieves, rapists, murderers, as there had been during the Mariel boat lift when Fidel did the same thing in Cuba.

The band played "Born in the U.S.A." Sverdloff talked about the rackets, the trade in currency, raw materials, diapers, newsprint. He claimed he once knew Agron, the first Godfather, the old thug who parked his gun at the baths on the Lower East Side then got journalists to write it up. Agron was gunned down across the street from the Batumi. Sverdloff claimed he also knew Balagula. I yawned.

"You don't like it here?" Tolya said. "You prefer somewhere else better?" he asked, and I told him I liked a bar on Broome Street a whole lot better but it was only conversation.

Losing Sverdloff in the noise, I thought about the cleaner, the Ivan, the man who killed Gennadi Ustinov. Who was he? Was he here hidden in the crowd?

"Come on," Tolya said, reaching into a bowl on the bar for a handful of hard-boiled eggs. "I want to eat some dinner while we watch the grand finale." He made for a small table that was empty, signaled a waiter who brought shashlik on a skewer and the band broke into a version of "I Just Called to Say I Love You."

A male chorus line in Czarist military outfits, all holding telephones, pirouetted onto the floor, their tights stuffed with socks to make their cocks bigger. A chorus line of Vronskys, I figured, as the noise of a train came over the loudspeaker and a girl in a hooded cape swept in, and was announced as the inimitable Anna K.

"You think Tolstoy would have approved?" I whispered but Sverdloff didn't hear. I was crying from laughing.

Anna K, whose real name was Olga Gross, began her routine. She was good. Real good. Most topless clubs these days, even fancy ones like Stringfellow's place, the girls take their clothes off so unceremoniously they could be going to the toilet—dress off, tits in your face, ass up, twenty bucks. Smile. Time is money. But Olga took her time. I was impressed.

She removed the cape first, then the long white gloves, one at a time, the hat, the veil. She peeled real slow—a scarf, a tight-waisted jacket that had a million buttons. She undid each one. Then the skirt. Underneath was a petticoat, a corset. She released one breast at a time. She stroked herself slowly. The men in the audience were panting. I was panting. Olga had a dull face and a sulky manner, but she had a sensational body. When she was naked except for a G-string, the silk stockings, and high heels, she pulled the cloak around her and headed in our direction. Tolya was sweating. He had stopped eating.

The girl leaned into him, whipping his face with her long hair, flicking her large breasts, the nipples rigid, over his jacket front, then, lightly, over his face. The music got louder. She tossed away the G-string. Strobe lights came on. In a frenzy, the girl threw herself on the floor in front of him, legs wide, and seemed to pull him down on top of her.

The lights came up. Olga had disappeared. Tolya wiped his face and finished his food. Then he said, "Let's go."

At the back of the club were the dressing rooms and when Sverdloff barged into one of them, we found a naked woman cross-legged on the ground, eating a hamburger and shielding her breasts from the grease with paper towels. Ten or twelve women were in the locker room, some naked, some half dressed. The girl with the burger looked up impassively, then went back to her dinner.

The corridor was lit by a couple of bare bulbs and it stank of booze. A few men loitered.

From the fourth door down came the sound of shrill voices. A man in a gray silk suit emerged and disappeared. The door remained open. We went in.

Inside, her costume on the floor, was Olga Gross. She wore a dirty pink bra and faded Jordache jeans.

Looking up from the cot where she sat, she saw Sverdloff and ran to him. She wound her arms around his neck in a hammerlock and clung to him like iron on a magnet.

"Oh, Tolya, you will help me?" She spoke in Russian.

"Of course. Sure. But first you will help us."

She put a sweater on, then groped for her glasses on a table littered with makeup and cigarette butts. Without the costume, Olga Gross was a plain woman.

"Tell my friend what happened on the TV show."

"I can speak Russian?"

I nodded.

She hesitated.

Tolya said, "Olga, remember what I promised."

She nodded and scratched her face; there were bad herpes and the sores around her mouth showed dried blood. "I have seen the murderer who shot the general. I have seen him before."

"Where?" I wondered why she would talk.

"I tell you this because, like Ustinov, my father was also a general," she said, tossing her limp hair from her face.

Sure, I thought. Him and George Patton and Colin Powell, but I kept my mouth shut.

"A few weeks ago, here in the Batumi Club. He was bothering me all night, but he looked poor, you know? He wore stonewashed jeans," she sneered. "Two nights before the TV show, he was again here, in a silk suit, Versace style. Versace."

"You're very observant," I said.

"Thank you," she said.

"What color was it? The suit?"

"Blue. Green. I'm not sure."

"Where would he get a suit like that around here?"

She looked nervously at the door. "Two or three tailors. I could get you the names, but tomorrow."

"Why should I believe you?"

She looked imploringly at Tolya. "You said."

"How did you get on the TV show, Olga? Who invited you?"

She shrugged. "The woman with red hair. Miss Hanes. And her friend. She was not nice to me. She would not give me a dressing room for the show."

"What friend?"

"The Englishman." Crowe, I thought. Lily and Crowe.

Sverdloff took my arm. "Give me five minutes with her."

I talked to Tolya direct, but loud, so she could hear. I ignored Olga like she was nothing. I behaved like a Russian man. My mouth tasted of bile.

"I want the tailor's name. Tonight. You tell her. Tell her. I want the name. I want to know everyone she saw. Whatever you promised her to get her to talk, it can wait until she gives me something." I was angry at Lily and I took it out on this miserable girl. "Also, I want an agreement she testifies if we need her. In court." I watched as the girl crouched in front of her mirror.

An expression, half terror, half cunning, crossed her thin sallow face. Her lips were encrusted with traces of dried blood. A purplish lesion on her forehead was covered with the wrong color makeup. Olga picked up the vodka bottle, put her head back, and swilled it like medicine. Her eyes watered.

"You ask a lot."

"Her visa runs out next week," I lied. "I checked. She wants to stay, she talks. She testifies. You hear me?"

"You have the picture?" Tolya asked me.

I gave him a picture I'd had made off the video of *The Teddy Flowers Show*. The man with the gun was in it, but the picture was blurry. Sverdloff put his arm around Olga's shoulder and sat with her on the cot.

"Come on, Olga," Tolya cooed and showed her the picture. "Come on honey, come on. I'll help you. We'll help you." He whispered in her ear in the purring Russian he had left on my answering machine. "Tell us. You knew him, didn't you, this guy? Who is he?"

Tolya was gentle and efficient; he behaved tenderly to her. He was the best kind of interrogator, convincing as a priest, crouched beside her, massive arms around her shoulders as if to protect her.

"I promise," he kept saying over and over. "I will help you. Tell Tolya. Tell me everything."

She pulled away from him and disappeared into a toilet next to the room. I could hear her puke.

When she came back, she took the picture from Tolya. "I knew him," she said.

She knew him. Suddenly I understood.

"You knew him in Moscow," I said.

She nodded.

"What's his name?"

"He used different names."

"What's his goddamn name? You tell me his name, you understand?"

"Give me some time." Tolya's hand was on her breast.

I turned away. "I want the name. And she testifies," I said.

Without waiting for an answer, I turned and left them. The girl was hanging on Tolya's neck as if for her life.

Chapter Ten

SUNDAY MORNING I WAS BACK IN BRIGHTON BEACH WHEN THEY FOUND Olga's fingertips in a sealed plastic jar under the boardwalk. I actually went to see Genia, my cousin, but first I made a stop on Church Avenue.

In a Laundromat, I found him asleep on a chair tipped back against the wall opposite a row of dryers. Eyes closed, hat pushed forward over his face, he barely stirred. His name was Brunel Dieudonné. A sleepy spaniel lay over his feet.

"Anyone home? Hello?"

"You don't have to shout, man," he said, a man waking up from an untroubled sleep. He was Haitian and big, with a sweet face and the ingenuous manner of a charming con man. "What's up?"

"We need to talk." I leaned against a washing machine.

"Talk," he said. He got up, dragged some wash out of the machine beside mine and hauled it into a dryer. "You got some quarters, man?"

I dug some silver out of my pocket and gave it to him.

"Talk," he said again, inserting the money into the dryer. He pulled over a rickety bench and we sat side by side and watched the wash go around. The place was full of women doing their laundry and the sour-sweet smell of damp linen mixed with the smell of candied violet breath mints Dieudonné kept feeding into his mouth. Somewhere a radio played and a man read the news in French.

"You work for the security people who do *The Teddy Flowers Show*?"

"Yeah. You a cop?"

"Yes," I said. I didn't see the need to inform anyone that I was off the job, not yet.

"You want a candy?"

"No thanks."

"What you want when I seen ten different cops already?"

"You worked the *Teddy Flowers Show* the other night. You usually work that show?"

"What night is that?" He delivered a disingenuous smile and ate another candied violet.

"Please. You want to do this nicely or you want to let someone else take over. I'm a very nice guy."

He shrugged. Cops were a way of life for a lot of Haitians. "Nobody ever told us you got to look at people going out of the studio, you know? What's the point after they go in? Going in, we say hi, take the tickets. After that, me, I regarding the TV with my dog. We keep a portable in the lobby. Passes the time."

"You watch *The Teddy Flowers Show*?"

"Most nights now we watch Letterman instead. Better show." He laughed uproariously. He was a comic. His jowls shook like chocolate pudding.

"What about metal detectors?"

"We don't use them. Too expensive, they tell us."

"If I show you some pictures, could you try a little harder?"

He shrugged again. It was hot in the Laundromat and I felt smothered by the smell of wash.

67

I got out pictures of Ustinov and one of the Ivan. I already knew but I wanted more proof.

He held them up to the light, then turned them around.

He pointed to Ustinov. "This one is the guy got killed. This one's not so hot. You make it off a videotape?"

"Everybody's a director."

"What you want me to tell you? I see a lot of people. Maybe I see this guy. I don't know."

"Okay. You hear anything. Anything. Give me a call, okay?" I gave him a card with my home number. "Okay?"

"Okay, okay. Maybe I hear something. I got a friend works over on Brighton Beach. He likes the cooking."

On the other side of Beverly Road, I left the urban sprawl for the big houses on green lawns where people drank iced tea in the shade, then I doubled back to Ocean Parkway. It was enveloped in Indian summer heat and women in long skirts and wigs, most of them pregnant, stood under the trees and gossiped and men in black hurried to storefront synagogues. It was a scene from another century. For a moment I wanted to drift into it, park my car, sit on the stoop watching the women and kids, smoke a cigarette with the men, crack a joke, read in the numbers and codes of the cabbala the meaning of life, lose myself in a coherent world.

Instead, I went to see Genia. My cousin was unsurprised by the visit, although I hadn't called her in a year, maybe more. When she opened the door, I saw she was a woman who had given up on surprises a long time ago.

"Hello, Artyom. I will come out."

Behind her, in the house, I could see the old man, her father.

"Is something wrong?"

"We'll walk a little," she said.

"He doesn't like me because I'm a cop?"

She nodded. Around here no one liked cops.

We walked and I let Genia know I was looking for a new job. I took her into a toy store and let her choose something for the kid, a Barbie, I think, a Barbie bride. The old man didn't like me. But Genia would tell him what I said and he would sit on the boardwalk with the other old men. The community was tight; the message would be retailed that I was an ex-cop looking for work that paid nice.

"Stay in touch." I put some money in her pocket. "Be in touch."

I left her outside the toy shop and went up toward the beach. Up at the Coney Island end, not far from the Cyclone, a small crowd had formed. In the distance I could see cop cars and some blue police barricades. Slowly I made my way, startled by a pack of gulls that burst into the sky suddenly, wings snapping like gunfire. Drawn by the stink of burning flesh, one of the gulls swooped down again onto a grill a woman had going on the beach and snatched a hamburger off it.

Roy Pettus was at the back of the crowd. "Detective."

"What is it?"

"Bastards." He was angry. "They cut off her fingertips and put them in a jar. Got rid of the prints."

"Who was she?" I asked, but I knew. Instinctively, I already knew.

"We found the body under the boardwalk. In a garbage bag. They wanted us to find her. It's a message."

"I want to see."

Pettus looked around. "Come on," he said.

A couple of hundred yards farther along, they were loading a body bag onto a truck. My shoes were full of sand.

"Let him take a look," Pettus said to the detective in charge.

"Sure, Roy. Whatever you say."

Pettus unzipped the bag. "You know her?"

"I met her last night."

Pettus shook his head.

Someone figured out she was going to talk to Tolya Sverdloff and killed her. Olga with the sensational tits and dirty bra got scared because I leaned on her. And she told somebody and, because of it, they took off her fingertips and slaughtered her. I told Roy Pettus about Sverdloff because I wanted something from him in return.

"Do something for me, will you?" I said to Pettus. "Before Sonny Lippert gets wind of this."

He waited.

"Maxine Crabbe. Let her take a look at the jar. The one with the girl's fingertips."

"That's way out of line." He looked at the sand. "Okay," he said. "I want to know as bad as you. I hope the bastards who did this fry in hell. I just hope to God they took the girl's prints off after they killed her."

For about forty-eight hours after I got a good view of Olga's body parts, I was out of action. I went down with a flu that made my bones ache so bad I could hardly move. I dragged myself to a few appointments I made at the Russian consulate, hoping I'd get something on Ustinov, but I wasn't in any shape.

By Tuesday, though, I was better. First thing I did was go to see the dentist again so he could finally stick his fingers in my mouth and fix my tooth for good. I lay in the chair while Dr. Pelton Crane regaled me with tales of his last ski trip to Taos and I thought how life doesn't exactly come to a grinding halt because people are dropping dead in Brighton Beach or anywhere else. You get the flu. The dentist overcharges. Women get mad if you're a jerk. Friends get pissed off if you forget their kids' birthdays. You get hungry, horny, tired.

In New York, people are always dying, and I think my lieutenant finally wrote me off that Tuesday because there had been six murders inside twenty-four hours and I was still dicking around on leave, as he put it. The lousy heat went on and on and it made people murderous. Over near the river, a gang of kids had gone up to the third floor of a tenement and killed the old woman who kept yelling at them to shut up because they played Tupak on her stoop all night and she was trying to watch Mary Tyler Moore reruns. One kid was ten. Two blocks away, a crack-crazed man threw his three-week-old baby out the window into a Dumpster.

The lieutenant called me and said he needed help, but I said I had other business. I could virtually hear him shrug. Too many excuses. He knew I was considering leaving the department for good. I was almost forty. There was another life I wanted. But even thinking about it was like considering amputation.

Olga was dead; Crowe was gone, so was Zalenko; Saroyan had slipped between the cracks; which left Sverdloff, assuming the other guests on *The Teddy Flowers Show* even mattered, but it was all I had. I had a make on a knife and a photograph made off a video. All I knew for sure even a week after he died was whoever killed Ustinov would be happier if I was also dead. I was moving real slow. It scared me that with the passage of time, the case would go cold. I couldn't break down doors the way I could when I was official, either. If I didn't watch it, Sonny would come down on me like a ton of bricks. Just my luck, that night I ran into Sonny Lippert at the Garden.

I had promised Ricky's uncles I'd go to a Knicks game. They gave up on Rick in terms of sports years ago, so they nab me once in a while. The Garden always stinks of hot dogs and the excitement of these old guys; it's pretty infectious. "My Uncle Liu dropped dead of a heart attack at the Garden he got so excited during an NBA play-off," Ricky once told me. "At least he had the dignity to wait till he was near the hot dog stand instead of doing it in his seat."

Sonny Lippert saw me at the end of his row before I saw him and he made one of the uncles change places. The whole half, he badgered me, keeping his eye on celebrity row, waving at Woody and Spike and all the other suck-ups who were dying for some seven-foot black guy with gold neck chains to favor them with a smile. I hated this part. The slick coaches making moves for the TV, arms raised in salute, bouncing around the sidelines in their Armanis. It was gladiator stuff: Everyone wanted blood.

"What the fuck you doing here, Art?" Sonny put his arm along the back of my chair.

"Taking in a game, Sonny. Same as you." After the Novocain that morning, my mouth was still stiff as a corpse in full rigor. I drank some beer and tried not to drool in front of Sonny.

"I want you to get your nose out of the Ustinov case. Do you understand? We're closing in. We got prints. We got the gun. I offered you the gig and you didn't wanna dance, now I want you off the streets. You mess with this any more, I'm gonna have you disciplined, dig? I'm not having you mess with my case, not you, not Roy Pettus. Oh yeah, I know all that, babe, check it out." He gave me a sour smile and went off to greet Spike or Woody or some other celeb the starfucking bastard wanted to fawn over.

"I heard it's not your case anymore, Sonny. I hear it's moved up the ladder," I said, but he didn't hear me. I was pissed off, so maybe to spite him, the next morning, I tracked Ustinov's ghost all over town one more time; there was only one surprise.

Chapter Eleven

FOR TWENTY YEARS, GENERAL GENNADI MIKHAILOVICH USTINOV HAD kept a charge account at Brooks Brothers. Everywhere his diary said he would be the day he died, Ustinov had been: the Union Square Café with his publisher where a waiter remembered he ate the smoked steak sandwich, the UN mission to see an old friend, public radio, a couple of other interviews, Brooks Brothers. He had made a note to go to Brooks Brothers; he had gone.

"I took care of Mr. Ustinov for years. We often shipped shirts to Moscow for him via the consulate. He preferred our Oxford button-downs. The blue was very nice with his eyes," said a salesman sadly. "He kindly sent me an autographed copy of his book." He had been in recently, yes, the man remembered. He had come to buy a gift.

"What kind of gift?"

"For a young man. His nephew, I think he said."

I asked what it was, but the phone rang and the salesman was distracted. After a few minutes, I beat it.

It blew me away that Gennadi had bought me a present. I left without even knowing what it was, robbed of even that. I didn't care now what Sonny wanted or what creeps I came up against; I had to know why Gennadi died.

I went to Phillip Frye's office. They said he was out of town, so I went over to the TV studio near the meat market—you could smell the raw meat—and lied my way into Teddy Flowers' office.

Teddy was on the phone trying to wangle an invite to the White

House. He was cool as a cucumber. Most people I like; Flowers I couldn't stand from the beginning.

You know the kind of person you want to use for a barf bag on a plane? Teddy put my teeth on edge. He was so slick, I felt I could rub up against him and slip right off. Teddy Flowers was the go-silk of broadcasting. He had a reputation as hardheaded; I guessed Teddy had invented it himself.

Uninvited, I sat on an office chair with a split green leather seat; *The Teddy Flowers Show* went in for the hard news look, you practically expected people to show up in eyeshades. I pulled out a pack of cigarettes.

"Do you mind?" Flowers said. "Secondary smoke." He hectored me for a while about it. Stupidos are commonplace in his business, but a Teddy is rare.

"I can't give you much time, but I'd like to help, of course." Teddy Flowers flexed his pecs. He had on a tight white T-shirt, he wore Topsiders, no socks, and a towel hung around his neck like a boxer after a fight. Before I could open my mouth, he swilled Evian, emptied his mouth in the wastepaper basket and started lecturing me again, I can't remember what about, health care or Newt Gingrich or China. He saw himself as a hawk for truth. I leaned back, lit up, and blew smoke in his direction, an eye on the door in case Lily Hanes might pass.

"I never met the general. I was in the Hamptons. We put him on the show because I felt Russia was heating up again. Also a favor to a friend."

I said, "What friend?"

"A friend in publishing."

"Phillip Frye, maybe? You two tight? You do each other favors?"

"It's no secret Phil spent a lot on Ustinov's book and it was a dud. He needed publicity, I wanted to help."

"What kind of dud?"

"Phil paid a lot for the book, then he had to kill the juicy stuff, I heard. What I hear is usually right."

"Why had to kill it?"

Flowers shrugged.

"Teddy." A skittish voice came from the corridor.

"My trainer," Teddy said. "I have to go."

"Too bad you missed the big night. Great ratings, I heard," I said.

"I didn't miss anything. I never do. Now I told you, I'm busy. I know all about you. Sonny Lippert told me. I'm trying to help, but you're not listening."

"I've been listening for half an hour," I said. "I want to know how come you use shitty freelance security guards?"

"That's not my decision. It's the station. The station takes care of the support staff."

"What about your own staff?"

"I take care of them. I give everyone a chance. I gave Lily Hanes a chance to do a big show. She blew it."

"She blew it because a guy got shot?"

"Sure. It was her show. This is the real world. I'm busy. You need me, make an appointment. Call my agent." He got up and pulled the door open.

"Hurry up, Teddy," the voice called again.

Lily Hanes looked up. "Hi," she said without much warmth. She sat in a cubicle, glasses on her nose, cigarette in her mouth, legs tucked under her on an office chair, looking at a TV on a shelf above her, the volume off. CNN ran soundlessly like wallpaper. Lily Hanes' image came up on the screen.

"I need some help."

"I'm sorry I freaked out on you the other night. Okay? But I've got stuff to do." She glanced up at the set and snapped it off. "Suddenly I'm flavor of the month. Everybody wants me. *New York* magazine wants to do a cover story. You know what some stylist asks me? Did I take the outfit to the cleaners or was the original blood still on? He said blood would be better for the picture. A guy falls dead in my lap and suddenly I'm big time," she said, more bemused than angry.

"You didn't answer my calls."

"I don't know anything. I told you what I know. Also I've been getting some creepy calls. I don't pick up the phone much."

"What kind of calls?"

"Heavy breathing. Middle of the night. Usual stuff. It's nothing," she said.

I didn't tell her my computer was gone and that her name was in it. Maybe I should have. But I mentioned the studio gave me her home number.

"Shit. The security here sucks." She shrugged but she looked worried. Then she said, "I liked Ustinov. I put him next to me. Someone killed him. I feel guilty, Okay? I feel really fucking shitty. It also happened to be on my birthday."

"I'm sorry."

"Yeah, well, what more could a woman want for her forty-fifth fucking birthday than a dead Russian general in her lap?"

Even after all these years, I never get used to how these clear-eyed, intelligent New York women swear like coal miners or peasants. Not that I don't have a mouth like a toilet.

"We already did this. Didn't we? We went through all this that night." She took off her glasses, rubbed the bridge of her nose, and, for a minute, her face settled into middle age.

"What about Teddy?"

"Teddy? Teddy's good at what he does. He got into this game before a lot of the others. He's connected. We're not talking naked astrologers on public access channels, you understand. Teddy's a cult for people who buy Salman Rushdie novels and maybe don't read them. People watch the show 'cause it makes them feel smart. TV talk is cheap, Teddy talks good, and he's got low cunning. He knows where people live."

"He was out of town that night."

"Look, I was glad to get the gig. It was good exposure. Now Teddy's mad because he missed it."

"You think Teddy Flowers could have anything to do with the murder?"

"Honestly?"

"Honestly," I said.

"I wish I did. I don't. He would if he could, but he's not that dumb."

"Tell me about Gavin Crowe?"

"I met him once, detective, or whatever you're called."

"Artie is what I'm called," I said, and added, "You weren't in a nightclub in Brighton Beach with Gavin Crowe?"

She gave me a weird look. "No, of course not."

The phone rang.

She picked it up, listened. "I told you, Phil, I'm busy." She covered the mouthpiece with her hand and looked at me. "I'll see you, okay? Maybe after the show tomorrow?"

"How about tonight?"

"Sure. Come by for a drink tonight. Okay? Artie?"

Teddy Flowers was in the hall when I left Lily's office and he grabbed my arm. "You still here?" he said.

"On my way. But tell me one thing."

"What?"

"Who's Phil?"

"Phil?" He looked toward Lily's door. "Phil Frye, like I told you, is Ustinov's publisher. He is also"—he gave a nasty chuckle—"he's also Lily Hanes' main fuck."

Killing time until I could go back and see Lily Hanes, I hung around with the Taes and ate a plate of scallops in black bean sauce Dorothy Tae put in front of me. Staring out the window of the restaurant, I watched a black woman in corn rows and kente cloth selling aromatherapy utensils, potions, and oils off a push-cart in the street. Circling her was the girl on Rollerblades who danced there every day. Across the street in the coffee shop, I could see the owner, Mike Rizzi, eating a piece of lemon meringue pie.

The dusk was colorless. The humidity gathered, fall was overdue, the sky heavy. Lily Hanes hadn't told me she was connected to Frye, who published Ustinov's book. She hosted *The Teddy Flowers Show* where Ustinov got murdered. The TV show and the publishing company were both owned by the same people. I played some backgammon with Mr. Tae and he let me win. Ricky kibitzed. It didn't help much.

When the phone rang, Mr. Tae answered it. He handed it to me. "He says he figured you might be with us." It was Sonny Lippert.

"To what do I owe this pleasure, Sonny?"

"Cut the sarcasm, man. You better get over to Brooklyn pronto."

"I'm busy."

"Someone punched out your cousin. Her face is a Russian sunrise. Her wrist's broke. The old man is up in arms, he's gonna sue the police department because 911 didn't show fast enough, he wants to kill someone. The girl is catatonic. A guy they rented a room to has disappeared."

I went to Brooklyn, but by the time I arrived, the old man, Genia's father, had posted himself and his cronies outside her room at Coney Island Hospital. "Stay away," he screamed in Russian. "Stay away from us. We don't do business with the police."

I felt like a punching bag. At a pay phone, I called Lily. A woman at the studio said she had gone home. She had said to come by later and now she was gone and I was pissed off. I planned to say so. I called her house, expecting an answering machine.

"Can you come over here?" Lily's voice was very quiet. "Please, I could use some help," she added and there was more than a whisper of fear as she gave me her address. She said come over and I drove like crazy.

At Lily's building on Tenth Street, there was some heavy-duty security downstairs—a guy from a private firm, a regular cop. I wondered why. I showed my badge. I went up.

She answered her door wearing an old bathrobe and sneakers. The red hair was in braids. She looked young, scared, and glad to see me. I was surprised.

"I'm sorry to drag you down here at this hour. I'm having kind of a rough time." She sat down hard on a chair and stared at the wall.

"What's going on? I know things have been rough. They've been rough for me, too. I can go. I can come back. Tell me what you want me to do. Please."

Lily's living room was painted yellow and there were big sofas and good drawings and the walls were full of books. A coffee table was a jumble of tapes, Kleenex, wine bottles. On an old-fashioned upright piano were photographs of Lily with Gorbachev and a tall thin couple posing with Pete Seeger; they were a stringy pair, but Lily had their good New England bones.

"I'm sorry about the mess, I'm sorry about everything. Do you want a drink? Wine?"

"Sure."

Lily left and came back in jeans and a T-shirt, a bottle of red wine under her arm. She poured it into a couple of glasses and sat down. She smiled some. "Okay. I'm better now. I'm glad you're here."

"Talk to me, Lily."

"A guy came through my door with a knife," she said, drinking some wine as she started her story. "He knew who I was. He knew where I live. He knew how to find me."

Chapter Twelve

LILY HAD COME HOME EARLY FROM WORK, AROUND SEVEN, EVEN BEFORE the show went on air; she felt lousy. Her heart was pounding. Her head ached. She had to get away from the show, from Teddy, from all of it. Her friend, Babe, called and said she'd come over with food, but Lily said no, she wanted to sleep.

"You should eat," Babe said over the phone.

"I'm not hungry."

"You'll feel better. Promise me, okay?" So Lily promised and called the Chinese take-out. Then she buzzed José the doorman, like she always did when she was waiting for the regular take-out people and told him to send the kid on up; that was her big mistake. José did pretty much what Lily asked because José was hoping for a TV career and figured Lily was a better bet than Richard Gere who lived across the street. José was a practical man.

Lily put some music on and dozed. The doorbell woke her. She went to the door and slid open the peephole. The man's face was obscured by a large bag of food.

"Who is it?"

There was no reply.

"Who's there?" she said sharply, then felt sorry about her tone.

A lot of these Chinese kids were just off the boat and didn't speak any English.

He shouted something. His English was barely intelligible. Lily felt bad, she was sick of the paranoia; it could turn her into some kind of vile rightwinger if she wasn't careful, and so she reached for the chain on the door.

Then he moved back and, through the peephole, she saw his shoes. Why did a Chinese take-out kid have on fancy leather shoes? How come? The man outside her door knocked softly again, patiently. Through the peephole she could only see the shoes and legs and the paper bag full of food. She couldn't see his face. Her flesh felt like spiders had crawled under her shirt.

"Leave the food outside." She knew he wouldn't leave it. He would wait, patiently, for the money. She only had a credit card. The card machine wouldn't fit under the door. If she didn't pay him, he would lose his job. Worse, they might take it out of his miserable pay. Lily's mind raced. She buzzed José; there was no answer. José took his dinner break at eight; you could set your watch by José's breaks.

"Stop this!" she said and realized she was talking outloud to herself, and she reached for the door, but she left the chain on. The man outside was ready.

Dropping the bag, he put his hand through her door and grabbed for the inside knob. Like her worst nightmare, she watched the hand come around her door. The man mumbled at her in a language she couldn't make out at first; he wore a dark blue cap and sunglasses.

"Get out," Lily screamed.

He swore at her, voice muffled, and she braced herself and shoved the door, but he was stronger. He pushed back. The door-knob turned. She felt herself reel, his weight on her like the dead general. Her ears rang, she was dizzy.

The hand appeared again, fingers groping for the doorknob. Lily was losing ground.

Somehow, she leaned back and got some momentum then crashed into the door with her shoulder as hard as she could, so hard she smashed the man's hand. She heard the sound of tiny bones breaking, like a Cornish game hen when you chopped it in half with a big knife. There was the sound of pain on the other side, something clattered on the floor, the man pulled his crushed hand back and Lily saw a blade glint. She got the door shut, snapped the locks, and was on 911 to the cops in seconds. But he was gone, through the basement, out into the night streets.

Later, José the doorman told the cops he didn't pay much attention to the man. Sure he was hanging around a while, but he looked respectable, the kind of guy who could be visiting in the building. So he was there when the delivery boy asked for Lily Hanes. José went on his break. The creep saw his chance, his luck was good or maybe he made his luck. He followed the boy into the elevator, punched him, dragged him out on the second floor, punched him again, grabbed the food and went up to Lily's. Later, they found the Chinese take-out kid in the stairwell nursing a black eye. Lily thought about moving, leaving. He knows where I live, she thought.

Chapter Thirteen

"He swore at me in Russian." we were at a local bar later that night. Lily wanted to get out of the house and we went around the corner for something to eat. I got a beer; she had red wine.

"You speak Russian?" I looked at her.

"School stuff," she said. "I'm hungry."

"Weird how all this doesn't stop you from being hungry," I said. "I thought that."

The place was dark, cool, and nearly empty, only a few late-night drinkers at the bar.

"I'm scared, you know. Someone knows where I live. Where I order take-out. A vindictive thing is out there and it's after me. Did he know? Was he hanging around waiting for a chance? Did he plan it? I've lived around here most of my life. I grew up here. I went away, when my parents died I came back. Stayed on. I know every crack in the streets. I used to tempt fate stepping on them."

"When was that?"

"When I was six."

"Where's the knife?"

"I guess he took it." Lily finished the wine in her glass. "Look, thanks for coming."

"Thanks for asking."

"Is that a come-on?"

"I better say this now so it doesn't get in the way later. I need your help finding out who killed Gennadi Ustinov and why, but there's something else and you should know it now." I was sweating like a fourteen-year-old.

"Spit it out."

"I'm a cop. I'm on leave right now, but I am a cop. A cop, not a brain surgeon. If I could have been a brain surgeon I probably wouldn't have been a cop. Okay? But that doesn't make me a Neanderthal fascist pig either."

"So?"

"I want to have dinner with you."

"Is that a euphemism?"

"You could call it that. But I won't mention it again. We could just meet up and talk about the assassination and stuff. We could meet in public places. And if you decide sometime you want to have dinner with me or any of the things it's a euphemism for, you could tell me."

Lilly smiled. "That's a pretty good line."

"Thank you. You want to eat now?"

"Is that an invite?"

"No, you can pay."

Lily ordered a bacon cheeseburger rare with fries; so did I.

The burgers came. She ate a huge bite; juice dribbled down her chin onto her T-shirt. She laughed. I laughed.

"You know Ustinov's publisher?" I said.

"I know Phillip Frye."

"But you didn't tell me that."

"It's personal."

Suddenly I thought of something. "Is he a Brit?"

"Yes," she said, and I knew I was right. It had been this Phillip Frye she had been with at the Batumi when Olga met her, not Gavin Crowe. But I was going to put my foot in it if I didn't shut up. "I'm sorry. It's none of my business."

"The show was my idea," she said. "My subject."

"You spent time in Russia?"

"Some. I wanted to see for myself."

"See?"

"What my parents cared about so much," she said a little bitterly. "My parents were true believers, you know? They didn't believe in Stalin, exactly. They believed in Trotsky and Pete Seeger. I finally went to Moscow like everyone else when Gorby came in. It was the hot story."

She had a slow, easy way of talking. She was a friendly woman. There was no agenda. She didn't sulk. There were no smuggled messages. She rubbed her eyes with her fist like a kid and a trio I hadn't heard before played "Desafinado."

"Stan Getz does that better."

"Yeah," I said. "You like Stan Getz?"

"He's the best," she said, and I fell for her completely.

"My parents were the kind of old lefties who saved their passion for the cause. Righteous New Englanders, you know? Took in everyone. Fellow travelers. Hippies. Black Panthers. God, how I longed for one dinner alone with my parents. They put all their emotion in it, what they had. I think having a kid scared the shit out of my mom."

"How do you know?"

"After she died, I found a letter in her stuff. From my grandma. Her mother. I think you should take Baby Lily home, it said. I must have been almost a year old. I guess she dumped me when I was born."

"You've done okay."

"Yeah, I even outgrew being a good little girl to get their attention." She was pink from the wine. She leaned forward on her arms. "It was okay. It makes you tougher, you know? There's not that much I'm scared of."

"Except how you feel?"

"Nice guess." She shifted her weight. "I don't know why I'm telling you all this. Maybe I like you."

"I hope so."

"There's something else I should tell you." She leaned closer. I hoped she was feeling as weak-kneed as me. I could feel her breath.

"I really like Tony Bennett. Maybe more than Sinatra. It's your turn." She waved at the waiter for more wine. "Your turn."

"What do you want to know?"

"How much is there?"

I told her most of what I knew so far. It wasn't much.

"You think it's a mafia hit?"

"That's the obvious answer, but why? What did Ustinov know that every other KGB apparatchik didn't know?"

She looked at me. "This matters to you."

"Yes."

"Big case."

"It's personal."

"Tell me." She drank red wine and wiped her mouth with the side of her hand. She reached over and put a hand on my arm. She made it tingle.

I drank, took a deep breath, and looked into the light gray-blue eyes. I knew there was part of her I could never get at, but if I could surprise her, maybe I could seduce her. I never talked about Gennadi to anyone, except a little bit to Ricky Tae.

"Tell me," she said again.

I told her. About Gennadi Ustinov and my father.

Lily listened, head on her hand, as if what I said was the most interesting thing in the world. It was a real talent.

I leaned back and looked at her.

"I called him Uncle Gennadi. All I cared about was Uncle Gennadi. Gennadi would come back from America like a movie star, with magic presents and stories and records and news of another planet, like he'd been to the moon." I drank. "God, how I wanted to be an American. Not an intellectual. A real American." I felt I could tell her anything. "My mother said I was born to be an American. I was always cheerful, she said. The family joke."

Lily poured more wine in my glass.

"After a while Gennadi Ustinov disappeared. Maybe he betrayed us, who knows. My father lost his job. We lived lousy for a while. I spent a lot of time hating. You know? Even after I got here. Everything Russian. The whining. The ideology. Superstitions. I hate the moods, the inertia. Also, I hate borscht."

"So you cast yourself as a New York cop."

"Yeah, well, that's the point, isn't it, in New York everyone gets to choose a part, and I can't play the tenor sax. I gulped my drink.

"Gennadi tried to see me. I always refused. Then I thought, what the hell. I said yes. I was over being mad. Over being Russian. I had become someone else. I wanted to see him. I got to the hospital and all I saw was a dead man hooked up to a lot of tubes."

"I'm really sorry."

"Me too."

"What's your real name?"

"Artemy Ostalsky. Everyone always called me Artie. I took my mother's last name."

"So Artemy Ostalsky became Artie Cohen." She wiped her mouth with a napkin. She smiled shyly for such a big noisy woman. "Do something for me?"

"Sure."

"Anything you find out about the case, will you tell me? It's a great story. I'd like to be in there first."

She sure knew how to ring a guy's chimes, I thought wryly, but I said, "Sure. So how about you try to get the unpublished pages of Ustinov's book?"

"You know about that?"

"I know."

"Touché," she said. "It's a deal." Lily held out her hand. I shook it and kept it. It was warm.

"There's something else, isn't there?" she said.

I was a little drunk by now. "Yeah. This case? I know in my gut it will end back in Moscow. I know it. I just feel it. And I'm not going back, ever. Ever."

Lily leaned over and put her arms around me. "You don't have to go back," she said. "Okay?"

"I'm supposed to be taking care of you."

"What's the difference?"

The piano player looked at us, grinned, and launched into "Someone to Watch Over Me."

Lily laughed. "They like us."

"Me too."

"I thought I was too old for this stuff," she said.

"Nah," I said.

"Will you walk me home?" She put a warm hand on the back of my neck. She leaned over and kissed me for a while.

"Is that a euphemism?"

"Yes," she said and kissed me again.

By the time I left Lily's the next morning I felt better than I had since this thing started more than a week before. It was a great day, a cool marine breeze had blown the humidity away and I left the car and strolled a while, smoking, whistling. On my way down Broadway, I stopped off at Dean & DeLuca. It was on Maxine's list and I had been in before, but I figured I'd drop by again.

Asking around, I finally found a salesman who remembered the man who bought a fancy boning knife. The knife that cost more than a hundred bucks. I hadn't talked to this guy; he had been on vacation all week.

"A Slav of some kind, I believe," he said politely. He was small and neat and had a cook's thick competent hands and a real eye for detail. It's always the detail, the routine, that blows a creep's cover.

"I remember because it was the day I was going on my little vacation. And it was early. I came in to do inventory on the cookbooks, so I know. He came in just after we opened. The shop was empty. I noticed him right away. He walked like he was in pain. I thought to myself, this was once a very pretty boy."

"Go on."

"I watched him. You see them sometimes, foreigners. He was mesmerized. He inspected everything, cheeses, breads, then he stopped here and pointed to the glass case. He only had a few words of English. He carried a little pocket dictionary. I asked if I could help him.

"He said, 'My mother is, you say, cook? In Russia.'

85

"I said we say cook too and he gestured around at the knives and I said all cooks like good knives, and he asked which and I opened the case to show him what we had.

"We did this in sign language, mostly, but I made out he wanted something for boning, chickens, I suppose. I showed him something cheaper, but he liked this one." The salesman removed the fine steel knife from the case and held it out. It was identical to the knife the creep used to attack me on Brighton Beach.

"I really felt sorry for him." He put the knife back and locked the glass cabinet.

"Why's that?"

"He wasn't rich, clearly, but he obviously cared very much it should be the right thing for his mother. You could see the way he looked the knife over. I thought he must be a cook himself. I felt sorry for him."

"Sorry because he was poor?"

"No. He was sick. Poor bastard. He was sweating, he took off his cap—this is why I remembered him so well—and his forehead was covered with some very nasty lesions. Worst I've seen. I knew the poor bastard had AIDS."

Chapter Fourteen

THE STREET WAS FLOODED WITH SUNLIGHT. I BARELY NOTICED. I FOUND a phone and called Roy Pettus.

"Tomorrow," Pettus said.

"Now," I said.

"Not here." Pettus had something on his mind; it wasn't me.

"Where?" I was desperate.

"I'll try. I can't promise. I got stuff on. Later. I'll let you know where."

Around five I was sitting on a bench downtown by the river, behind the World Financial Center. I watched the boats in the marina and waited for Pettus.

A while later, Roy Pettus arrived, took off his jacket, put it neatly on the bench, pulled two cartons of coffee out of a brown paper bag and handed me one of them. He had on a white shirt and a striped tie.

"What is it?" he said. I told him about the man who bought the knife. I told him about the lesions.

"I see."

"What else do you see, if you don't mind telling me? What else is there?"

Shading his eyes from the sun, he glanced out at the river, then put the coffee down and leaned forward, making a temple of his hands. "We got some prints off the knife now. We got the video. Now you got the description from the man who sold him the knife. Blood. The jar with Olga's fingerprints. Everything matches up. I think we have some kind of ID."

"Russian?"

"Russian, maybe Polish. We found a guy at JFK who probably remembers him. You know why?"

"I don't know."

"The man's name was Lev. The customs man's father's name was Lev. Both Polacks, he said, with the same name, so he let him through easy. Because he was named Lev."

"Olga?"

"The fingertips in the jar belonged to Olga Gross." He looked up again. Out of the blue, he said, "Tell me something, detective, you ever give nukes any thought?"

"What?"

"Nuclear weapons."

What was he talking about? I had been cut by a man with AIDS, I probably got his blood on me, Pettus was on some other planet. "I don't know. We made them. Russia made them. Whatever."

"I'm talking about the stuff you put in them, the radioactive stuff."

"My father used to say strontium 90 would get in the grass from fallout from American bombs. The cows would make poison milk, he always said."

Pettus did not laugh. "In Wyoming we said that about the Russkis. We prayed for the souls of the poor Commie children after every mass. I worried about their conversion. I'm not saying the nuke stuff is happening here, I'm just saying I'm scared. For years, there's been smuggling out of Russia into Europe. Into the Middle East. Big spills. Enough uranium to make bombs. Plutonium. More and more of it."

I waited.

"An ex-KGB general gets shot on TV in New York City. There are rumors. I get interested."

"What rumors?"

Pettus was distracted. "This is what I do, detective. I worry about this kind of stuff coming into the country."

I waited.

"I was thinking about the World Trade Center bombing. About Oklahoma City. What if someone uses a nuclear device next time? But it's rumors that's the worst part. I think about every copycat, every wannabe terrorist. Think about it: someone calls the mayor and says, hey, Rudi, I got a radioactive device I'm setting in the Midtown Tunnel. Rush hour."

"This isn't just hypothetical, is it? Is it?"

Pettus remained silent.

Pettus threw his coffee in the garbage. It sloshed over the side of the paper cup as it fell.

"Let's just say I worry a whole lot," said Pettus. "You ever hear of a substance named Red Mercury? Remind me to tell you about it sometime." His normally bland baby's face glowed with messianic fever; he was obsessed. "It's not the grand scenario, the melodrama, the movie version of stolen nukes, it's the squalid leaks, the two-bit atomic smugglers that scares the bejesus out of me. The notion of nuke-shit, of radiologicals coming into the U.S.A., into New York City, maybe next door to you and me, detective. Stuff can kill you just as dead as a big bastard warhead."

Finally, I grabbed his shoulder. "Listen. Please. What does this have to do with me?"

"I don't know. I'm telling you this by way of background because you're involved with the Ustinov thing and now you're in some trouble and I'm real sorry you are because I like you."

Quietly, this Jesuitical cowpoke was driving me nuts with talk. Maybe he was crazy. I was shaking so badly I slopped hot coffee on my arms. Again I told him about getting cut, about the creep on Brighton Beach who had AIDS.

"I'm sorry, detective. I've been preoccupied. I hear you. I don't have the answers. Like I said, we got an ID on him, we'll try to get to him. Meanwhile, I guess you ought to get yourself checked out. You're right. The creep cut you with his knife. He got his blood on you."

Part Two

NEW YORK

Chapter One

"His name is lev. the creep who cut you is named lev. he's an Atomic Mule."

Sverdloff hoisted his bulk up onto a stool at the bar next to me, grabbed my wrist with a hand the size of my head and said, "Listen to me. Listen to me, okay? You must hunt him down and kill him."

It was the night after I met Roy Pettus by the river. My arms were black and blue from the goddamn needles some dismal medic stuck me with to take blood. At the bar on Broome Street where I usually go, I was in a lousy mood, nursing beer, eating fried potato skins. I thought of going over to the Soho Steak for dinner, but I couldn't face it. I put a great track Tony Bennett did with Bill Evans on the juke box; nothing helped.

I was tired. I could feel my lids fall like they had weights. I was hating this freelance life. I missed the station house, the squad, the bang of metal lockers, even the rancid smells of sweet-and-sour pork that died in take-out cartons, the fossilized pizza. I missed my work and the people. Someone put Harry Connick on the jukebox. "For Chrissake, turn it down," I mumbled.

Ten days since Ustinov was murdered and already the case was drifting to the back pages of the papers. There had been another murder on TV—some diet show—and reporters were hungry for something new. The Feds loved it; they didn't have to let on they knew diddly squat about Ustinov or about Brighton Beach. I knew. Brighton Beach sucked me in and chewed me up. The old bitterness about Russians sloshed over me. I rubbed my bruised arm. The doc who tested me for AIDS said he'd try to have results Monday, maybe sooner, but he was overloaded. He made encouraging noises about research and I said, sure, thanks, and started drinking real early.

"You look lousy," said Bob, the bartender, and pushed a Bud across the bar.

"Thanks, I try," I said, drank it, and asked for Scotch.

Which is around when Sverdloff appeared and started talking

about this Lev. Same name as Pettus got off immigration, but I wasn't going to let on to Sverdloff.

"How did you find me here?" I was not gracious.

"You told me you like this place." He gestured to the bar.

What a jerk I'd been to mention where I like drinking to him. I swallowed some Scotch and tried to ignore him.

He grabbed my shoulder. "Listen to me, please. Do you know the story by Borges about the race of the prisoners?"

It was how Russian intellectuals proved they were good guys; they talked you to death.

"The prisoners are permitted to race each other, but first they have to cut their own throats. Whoever dies last wins. They all join the race. It is the story of the atomic mules."

I polished off the Scotch. "One more," I said to Bob. "Go on," I nodded at Sverdloff, who was speaking Russian.

"He is dangerous and he is sick. He attacked you. He visited your apartment. He needs money. He wants to sell me his shit."

"What shit? What are you talking about?"

"I'm telling you, this Lev is an atomic mule."

"An Atomic Mule."

"Yes. He is a mule, what they also call a sample man. He transports radioactive samples. He says he has plutonium. Uranium. Cesium. He has top quality certificates of validation from Russian research institutes. He says he has Red Mercury."

"Where?"

"In his suitcase."

"Probably under his bed."

"Yes. Under his bed."

I looked up at Tolya Sverdloff, who was a kidder; he wasn't kidding.

"You saw the stuff?"

"I saw enough." Sverdloff was edgy, angry. He bent over the bar so his huge bulk made an impenetrable shell. Then he hauled himself up off the stool, signaled for more booze, and pushed me toward the back room where we sat in the window under a couple of hanging plants.

"You want to pay attention now?"

94

A plant hit me in the head. Out the window I saw the white girl on Rollerblades I sometimes saw near my building. She was doing figure eights under a street light in the middle of the road. "How come he trusts you?"

"After Olga, I felt bad. I let her down. I wanted the guy who killed her. I looked for him."

"Did he do Olga?"

"Yes. I felt bad about it. So I talk to people on Brighton Beach. Hoods. Cops. On the boardwalk I gossip with the old men, guys who always got food in their beards. I saw him there. From no place. We make Russian guy talk."

"How come he trusted you?"

"I made him my friend." Sverdloff laughed bitterly. "Like the KGB used to say, I let him find a niche in my heart. I made him trust me."

Chapter Two

"Going through immigration didn't make Lev nervous," Tolya said. "He told me it was easy."

"Easy?"

"Just listen," Tolya said and then I shut up and he told me everything he had learned from this man who called himself Lev Ivanov.

Lev Ivanov was the name on his papers, nicely forged documents—he had done the alterations on the photograph himself, he bragged to Tolya. He had a real letter from a cousin in Buffalo inviting him for a visit, which was still necessary for Russians, but easy to fix, a few bucks here and there. Americans were pushovers for a well-dressed foreigner who was white, a Polack like him with a respectable pair of gray leather shoes and a plaid sports jacket.

As Lev retrieved his suitcases from the luggage carousel, he knew he resembled a newly minted capitalistic business-class guy. He got in line behind a woman wearing a large fur coat. The customs officer kept her twenty minutes. Lev's turn.

"He told you all this?"

"He told me. He told me he carried a copy of Agatha Christie. He told me he has two Samsonite-style suitcases, good imitations. Polish-Russian joint venture. He acts out for me how he puts them on the counter at customs. There's a fat inspector, big belly, nice manners. 'Nice cases,' the inspector tells him. 'I like them Sammies.' "

Sverdloff was into it, playing all the parts, an actor. Something made me keep my mouth shut; I ate pretzels and listened.

"The customs officer glances in the big case, gives Lev's underwear a casual poke. He points at the small suitcase and shoulder bag, but doesn't open them. He looks at Lev's documents. 'Samples?' he says. Lev nods. His visa says he is a suitcase salesman from Moscow selling these joint-venture goods; he is also hoping to make contact with American manufacturers. The suitcases are the samples.

"The inspector waves him through, smiling. 'You are really Lev? My pop's name too,' he says, then adds in Polish with a Brooklyn accent: 'Welcome to America, Lev.' "

My mouth was dry. "This nukeshit is in the suitcases?"

Tolya nodded. "Our second meeting, Lev tells me. We eat dumplings together, then he spills the beans. He says he decides to trust me because I am a true Russian, not some Jew, excuse me, like everyone else around Brighton Beach."

"Cut to the chase."

"He leaves the airport and gets to Brighton Beach."

"When? When was this?"

"A few weeks ago, maybe more. He lies low. He makes contact with a man he says looks like Trotsky—eyeglasses like Trotsky—who gives him some money for expenses. More money is coming, the man says. Arrangements will be made. Lev orders a new suit. He takes a room. He gets lonely. He sees a picture of Olga outside the Batumi and goes looking for her. He only wants to say hello."

"Some hello."

"He found out she was talking to a cop."

"He knew I was at the Batumi? He saw me?"

"It's possible. It's possible he is using me to get to you. I can't be sure."

"Jesus Christ."

"Yes. He is anxious about money. He sits on the boardwalk looking at the ocean and writes postcards to his father. One has the Statue of Liberty on it. Our boy is ironical. He wants the money to give his father. The father lost a leg in the Afghan war. In Moscow, he sells his shoes outside Belorus Railway Station. 'What do I need good shoes for?' his father says to him. He says, 'For three generations my family has grown up believing, now nothing is left, just western shit, shitty westerners that look down on everyone, and traitors like Yeltsin who pander to them.' " Tolya knocked back a drink and continued.

"I had to be careful. He keeps changing rooms. When I met him after he killed Olga he had a room in Brighton Beach. He said it annoyed him because there was a girl playing sad music."

"What kind of music?" I asked; I already knew.

"A flute."

My stomach lurched.

"It was his idea to be the first person to bring such samples into America. He read about the poison gas in Tokyo subway, you recall? Lev saw his chance. If poison gas in Tokyo, why not plutonium in New York? He has no politics except hate. He only wants the money."

"Who's the buyer?"

"The Brighton Beach mob probably. There had been feelers out from New York looking to get into this game. Lev arrives, he meets the hoods. Then suddenly his contacts dry up. Lev is stranded. They cut him loose."

"Where is he now?"

"He moves around. Yesterday, I saw him in a room out near the airport. The Palace, the hotel is called. The name made him laugh, he said. It's a hotel for old people. 'Mutants like me,' Lev tells me."

"He moved after he beat Genia up," I said.

"What?"

He had moved into my cousin's house, then beat her up; it was a message for me. "Nothing. Go on. How did he get the stuff in?"

"Lev had practice. He had been humping samples around Eastern Europe. He knew his way around the atomic gangsters' third division. He knew the ropes. He drove trucks down to Varna. He ran packages through Ukraine into Croatia. The flow of traffic there means border checks are nonexistent, guards can be bribed.

"Most sample merchants never go beyond the border towns where they hand over their stuff, he told me, but he was different. Lev wanted more. He hated the Saturdays in muddy market towns on the Croatian border, hated the peasants who stank, hated pretending to buy and sell spare tires and dusty vegetables.

"Once, Lev went even farther. Once, he did the trip down to the Mediterranean, then Sierra Leone. He hated it. It meant doing business with Lebanese who run the ports there, who, it is said, work for Hezbollah, people Lev detests as much as Jews. In Africa he handed over his samples. Someone else took them by sea to Mexico. It was Lev's biggest adventure." Tolya stopped and licked his lips. "I need a drink."

"Do you believe this?"

"Yes." Tolya waved for a waiter. None came. He went and got a bottle of red wine from the bar.

"At some point, Lev begins getting ideas. He decides he will be the first to transport samples into New York."

"He's crazy."

"Probably. He decides to travel direct. Moscow airport was easy, he says. A few dollars to the right people, his luggage went directly to the plane without inspection. A nice young lady escorts him to the VIP lounge where there are no metal detectors and offers him French Champagne. He asks for Russian."

"He asks for Russian?"

"Yes. Says Russian Champagne is better." Tolya Sverdloff grinned.

"Jesus."

"He chooses to fly through Frankfurt. You know why?"

I didn't say anything.

"He recalls the Pan Am plane that crashed over Lockerbie stopped in Frankfurt. He remembers transit passenger luggage that is interlined is rarely inspected in Frankfurt. Not that it matters to Lev. Most of what he carries cannot be detected by X-ray, and the other he carries in a bag over his shoulder. On board, he sips his wine. He muses that if the plane goes down, the explosion will be much bigger than Lockerbie."

"He's sick."

"Yes," Tolya said and I figured he knew the AIDS. "But smart. At JFK there are no metal detectors for passengers disembarking."

I was sweating. The house with the girl playing a flute. Olga. The radioactive material in a fake Samsonite suitcase.

"Lev settles in. Soon he goes shopping."

"Shopping."

"Yes. He tells me New York City is filled with knives, everywhere you can buy beautiful knives. One knife he lost. He buys another. Then he confides in me. He wants to use this knife on some Jew who is after him. He hints. He is testing me."

I said, "So you pass the hate the Jews test."

"Yes. In his room at this Palace Hotel, I notice a nice laptop computer. 'I got it off a Jew cop,' he brags. He tells me how sometimes he goes to this sweatshop opposite the Jew's building and watches him like he is at the movies. Jews are soft, he says. Idle American Jews. He wants to kill a Jew."

"How did he pick up I was involved?"

Tolya shrugged. "A man with glasses, maybe. A hood, or one of your own guys who works both sides of the street."

"You think every cop has his hand out here, like Russia?" I was angry. "So you saw this suitcase he was using for some kind of arsenal?"

"I'm getting there." Tolya ignored the sarcasm. "The small suitcase has a false bottom. Underneath, containers with pellets of enriched uranium. Plutonium scraps inserted into steel disks resembling hockey pucks. Soluble salts of cesium in a thick lead jar. In the carry-on bag, three glass vials filled with a suspension of Red Mercury. Maybe more." As he recited the list, Tolya's face was slick with sweat; this stuff worried even Anatoly Sverdloff.

"He showed me the certificates. The stuff is authentic."

"Who wants it?"

"Anyone who wants to make a bomb. For terrorists, samples are delivered as proof the seller has access to the goods. For small-time hoods, samples are good for ransom. For bribes. For small scale terror, samples are good. I showed Lev I was impressed."

"You looked at the stuff?"

"I saw enough." Tolya shrugged. He looked around the bar. It was almost empty. "What choice did I have? I wanted him to believe in me."

"What about his contacts?" I said.

"I told you, they cut him loose."

"Why?"

"I was coming to that. Zeitsev's people are not stupid. They cut him loose because Lev made one very big mistake." Tolya Sverdloff paused and slurped down the dregs of his wine.

"What mistake?"

"He killed General Ustinov."

Chapter Three

THE PIECES WERE SPREAD OUT LIKE A JIGSAW I COULDN'T PUT TOGETHER: the knife; Roy Pettus' conversation with the customs inspector who was a Polack; his hints about nukes; Maxine's coy warnings; the creep following me, maybe from the beginning, following Lily because of me; now this. I said to Tolya, "You really think he killed Ustinov?"

"Yes. But it was a sideshow," he said. "Except that it put you in the frame."

"And Lily also."

"What?"

"Nothing."

He tossed some money on the table and said, "Let's walk."

"Where is he? Where is he?" I had my hands on Tolya Sverdloff's neck, but he shook me off like a bug on a bull. "Where the hell is he?"

"Waiting for me to get the money for him. Back in Brighton Beach waiting to cash in."

"I'm going with you."

"You do that, we don't get the stuff."

We walked silently down Broadway. He was holding out on me.

"How come he trusts you?" I asked Sverdloff again. He stopped at a flea market that was still open, operating under a stand of lights.

"He wants to sell the stuff. I promised him money for his father. I made him trust me. He's a believer, this Lev. His kind never give it up. He wants to believe. He has no one else. So he believes me."

"How do you know he'll deliver?"

"He needs the money."

Wandering among the insomniacs who shopped at midnight in the flea markets on Broadway, Sverdloff picked up a painted matrioshka off a stall and held it close to his amused face. Along with imitation Rolexes and fake Vuitton bags and Jimi Hendrix T-shirts, Russian dolls had become a staple of flea markets. I glanced around at the insomniacs who stood idly, smoking. He could be here, this Lev. He could be anywhere I was.

The creep trusted Tolya Sverdloff for the same reason I was going to trust him; I had no choice. He was an operator. He bargained, cajoled, plundered stalls for what he wanted, his huge face white like a misshapen moon made of floury dough.

There were a couple of old Blue Note albums on a stall, but the discs were scratched. Tolya wrapped his leather coat around him and tried on a Nigerian cap. The stall owner chatted, smiled, offered discounts. I saw Tolya was smooth enough to have been one of Ustinov's men in the old days.

"You remember when you first read 1984?" he said idly. "For me, it's the biggest deal in my life except when first hearing Beatles, maybe, or first fuck. Penguin edition. White and orange. A guy in my class gives it to me. I'm standing in the stinking school toilet, I know this is provocation, you could go to jail for reading Orwell. This boy, he's named Patrice for Lumumba, pulls it out of his waistband. 'Wanna try it, Tol?' Bang! Like a gun. Like dirty pictures. I read it. Next day, I knew everything was fake."

"I always knew. I drew wigs on Lenin in my school book. I listened to Voice of America on shortwave."

"*Willis Conover's Jazz Hour?*" Tolya smiled nostalgically.

I said, "Yeah. Well, it's swell reminiscing with you about the bad old Moscow days, but you want to tell me why you didn't grab him, this Lev you maybe dreamed up?"

"Because he only showed me some of what he's got, and we need it all. Because we got to get that suitcase and I need the money to get it. Because I didn't dream him up. Because," he said, inspecting a secondhand Nikon, "I'm only a Russian tourist and who will believe me?" He put down the camera, paid for the hat, and headed toward the street. A chilly breeze blew.

"So what's this Red Mercury stuff?"

Tolya Sverdloff stopped under a streetlight. "The worst thing ever made. Worse than plutonium. More lethal. Heavier. A few ounces, you can make a nuclear bomb big enough to blow up a city."

"And hair grows on billiard balls."

"You think this is crazy Russian stuff? You think this is sci-fi? You think I am a dickhead dumb-ox Russki? You think if it doesn't go boom it won't kill you? You think if it's small-time creeps like Lev with a suitcase it's a joke. What? You will only believe if there is a big warhead, plenty of hardware, a cast of thousands. Okay. Boom!" He shouted so that half the people in the street turned round. "Boom!" He grabbed my sleeve. "You been away too long to believe there are people who do this stuff? You have been living with your head up your behind, Mr. American Policeman."

It was what Sonny Lippert always said.

"This is only the beginning. Let him get away with this there will be more, much more. You think it can't happen? Do you think a scientist whose kids are starving in some hellhole in the Caucasus won't sell plutonium scraps for a few bucks to feed them? Come to Moscow and I will make you a believer."

"Not on your goddamn life," I said. It was almost cold out but I was hot with panic.

"Suit yourself. But watch your back, Okay? He's following you. He's dangerous."

"Jesus! What else?"

"He is sick. Very sick. He doesn't care who he hurts. He's a loose cannon out there and he's dying."

"How much money does he want?"

"Ten thousand only. You want me to arrange it? Get me the money, I'll arrange it."

"I'm thinking," I said.

"Think fast."

"Or?"

He grabbed my arms and said, "Hunt him down and kill him."

The next morning, it was after ten when I swung my legs over the edge of the bed. I went to the window and shoved it open and a blast of cold air hit me. Across the street, in the window of the sweatshop, two Asian women sat sewing bridal veils. The young one smiled at me and waved. She could see into my window perfectly. It would be where Lev had sat at night, watching me.

He knew my address. He had my computer. He knew my name and face and friends. He had seen me with Olga, with Genia. Lily. He had watched me through my window at night from across the street; my life was his TV show.

And he was sick. He told Tolya he was sick and he had cut me and bled on me. I picked up the phone, but who could I call? I was unofficial, Sonny Lippert had cut me off, even Roy Pettus was reluctant to take my calls. At Danny Guilfoyle's no one answered. Dan was probably out on his boat. If only I could get to Danny, I thought. I put Miles Davis playing "Kind of Blue" on and thought about eating. Instead, I got a beer out of the icebox and sat on a kitchen stool.

"You can't go on like this, man," Ricky said when he arrived. I had forgotten he was coming over for breakfast. He grabbed the beer out of my hand and switched off the stereo. "That music could kill you this early."

"My little geisha," I said. Thank God for Ricky.

"Concubine."

"What?"

"Japs have geishas. We have concubines. You questioning my

sexual orientation, you androgynous piece of shit? Where are the eggs?"

The Taes were getting ready to close up for a few weeks. They were going to Hong Kong to visit the new in-laws and I wanted to say, "Don't go." I told Ricky some of what Sverdloff told me. He was skeptical. I think Ricky was a little jealous of Tolya Sverdloff.

"You're telling me this nuke food is coming into Manhattan, the Bronx, and Staten?" Ricky sniffed some olive oil and grimaced. "This is no virgin." He tossed the bottle in the garbage and opened a fresh one. "You considering doing something stupid, Artie?"

"I don't know, Rick. What am I thinking?" I reached over to the stereo and put Stan Getz on.

"Don't do it. Or let me come with you. I may be beautiful, but I'm tough." He tossed his cigarette in the sink so it hissed and went out.

He was tough. His uncles taught him martial arts stuff when he was a little kid and he could fly across the room and kick you in the kishkas so you wanted to die. I once saw him in action when some bastard came on to Dawn and he went ballistic.

"I'm taking some vacation," I lied. "Go to Hong Kong with the family, Rick. Eat good."

Ricky wrote a number on a pad. "Leave me a message there if anything goes wrong." It was a local number.

"Where's there?"

"What's the difference?" He looked out the window. "I'm not going to Hong Kong. I met someone, okay? Maybe it's better Pop doesn't know. Okay?"

"Okay."

He poured olive oil in a pan and fried the eggs and put them on a plate. "Eat," he said.

"Thanks."

"He's a swimmer. A pro." Ricky gave me a sly, pleased look.

"So," I said, aiming for cool. "He's here for some Gay Games thing."

Ricky laughed it off. "You think I plan to spend my vacation watching a bunch of fags doing sports? I only want to fuck the guy, Artie," he said and for the first time I saw him as a grown-up, his own man. Ricky out of the closet was Ricky unleashed.

"What's his name?"

Ricky changed the subject. "I talked to my cousin."

"What?"

"I told you something bothered me about Sverdloff from the beginning. I talked to my cousin Don in Shanghai."

"You have a cousin in Shanghai named Don?"

"Yeah, Don Ho II. It's his stage name. He has six nightclubs. Hawaiian themes. Listen, he remembers Sverdloff. They were chummy on the commie rock circuit years ago. Sverdloff used to broadcast out of Russia to Shanghai. Before Tiananmen Square, when rock was hot and good. He could speak Chinese, all kinds of dialects, and he could put one over on the official antbrains in both countries. He was, you should forgive the expression, an artist. Guess what Sverdloff's call sign was."

"Tell me his call sign," I said to humor Ricky while I ate the eggs and because Stan Getz cheered me up.

"Red Mercury," Rick said triumphantly. "And you didn't even have to open your fortune cookie."

"You really believe in this dreck? This Red Mercury?"

"It's real, babe. Red Mercury is the stuff the Sovs put in their nuclear weapons to make them smaller and hotter. Real rare. Lethal. Elusive."

"You know why all those Cold War thrillers worked so good? Because you can't make up crap that's weirder than what Russians believe."

"Trust me," he said. "I did physics, remember? It's real. And Artie?"

"Yeah?"

"If your Polack killed Ustinov by mistake, who was he really after?"

Things weren't bad enough. I called the doc, who said the test wasn't back. Monday, he promised. Lily Hanes had also stopped taking my calls. I went looking for her at her building on Tenth Street and the doorman, José, said she was out. But he remembered me from the other night, and that and fifty bucks persuaded him to let on as to how he figured Lily had gone to her gym that was a few blocks east; he had seen her with her gym bag.

In a room where the walls were covered with mirrors, a couple dozen white women in skin-tight gear punched the air in time to a litany of requirements; the guy giving the orders didn't have a whole lot more muscles than me and I wondered what he had. Lily saw me and broke ranks and ran across the floor.

"I didn't figure you for a health nut," I said. Her red hair was tied back with a yellow scarf and her high forehead was dripping sweat. Unlike the other women, she wore baggy shorts and no makeup. There were violet circles under her eyes and she looked her age. I liked her better this way: She seemed vulnerable.

She backed me into the corner where a plastic pitcher of green juice sat on a table.

"It was a mistake," Lily said wearily. "I'm sorry. I didn't mean to come on to you for nothing."

"It wasn't nothing," I said, getting in between her and the room, the class, the mirrors, the trainer. I cut off her view of them, then I glanced over my shoulder.

"Who's the guy?"

"That is Kickbox."

"That's his name?"

"No, his name is Jamie. He teaches kickboxing. It's all the rage," she said, but at this, at least, she grinned. "I hate exercise. Someone at the office gave me a course, a sort of gift. A booby prize for Teddy's wrath. He wants to fire me because of all the attention. It's not a good time for me. I'm trying to quit the smokes without turning into a tower of blubber."

I knew I had to tell her about the blood and the AIDS test, but I was chicken and instead I said, "Be with me."

"It was a night. Period. One night. I don't know what you are and I don't want to know. All I know about cops is Mel Gibson and Morse, and I've had it with politics. I just want to get away from the whole bloody nightmare," she said. "I asked around about the missing pages from Ustinov's book. I asked Phil."

"I'm not Mel Gibson and you don't have to pay me off, you know."

"I think the pages are in Phil's safety deposit box in the bank. I don't know what he edited out, but there was something. I'm going away for a while."

"Where to?"

"Away. Away. Okay?"

"Anyone bother you again?" I said.

"I'm not sure. Some more phone calls. A car I keep seeing outside my house. I don't know."

"I'll take you away. Come away with me."

"It's you I want to get away from." She brushed the sweat out of her eyes.

In the background, Mr. Kickbox watched himself in the mirrors.

"You don't get it, do you? You're in the middle of this. I'm no wuss, but the creep knows where I live and I don't want to wake up like that girl on Brighton Beach with my fingers in a jar." She held out her hands in a gesture of despair and sat down hard on a chair. I crouched beside her and she put her hand on my arm as if to steady herself. "I'm scared, Artie. People think there's always solutions to a puzzle, like a book. If you connect the dots, you get a picture. But things just happen. Sometimes it just goes on and on and people keep dying and there's no reason."

Lily Hanes was real smart; it was the thing I liked most about her, along with her noisy good humor, and her curiosity, the self-possession, the lack of guile. Okay, and the legs.

"You said it was a great story. I could help you get it." I was begging.

"Don't con me. Last time I got obsessed with a story, I ended up in an East Berlin jail. It wasn't great."

"Does Phillip Frye know about us?"

"Probably."

"Is this about Frye? You're going away with him?"

"Not exactly," she said and pulled herself off the chair and looked at the moving figures in front of the mirrors.

"Can I ask you something?" I said.

"Sure."

"He's married, isn't he?"

"You checked?"

"I asked around. What do you see in him?"

"He used to make me laugh. He introduced me. He knows everyone. He reads everything. Like this Australian friend of mine said once, I thought he could be my wonder bra; I thought he'd make me bigger. It didn't work out."

"There's something else."

"Yeah, he scares me a little."

"How?"

"He's a manipulator. Every time I get free, he finds a reason to need me. Look, I gotta go. I'm sorry. I really am sorry."

I could smell the sweat and the perfume. I grabbed her hand. "Lily? How come a woman as great as you isn't married?"

She laughed. "This is an old-fashioned question." Lily kissed my cheek. "I don't know, Artie. I really don't. I'll see you around."

I went home.

On the sidewalk outside my building, my cousin Genia's little girl was gazing at a doll with pink hair on a street stall. I spoke to her in Russian and she pushed a note in my hand. When I turned to buy her the doll, she ran away.

Genia's note invited me to Brighton Beach Sunday to drink tea and eat. The old man, her father, hated my guts, so I figured the invite was some kind of bait. I figured Pop had been gossiping on the boardwalk and I bet he put it around I could be bent cheap. I wondered who was interested.

Chapter Four

"MR. COHEN, I AM ELEM ZEITSEV," A VOICE SAID IN ENGLISH.

Outside my cousin's house, in Brighton Beach on Sunday, leaning against a snappy black BMW convertible, was a slim, polished, good-looking man, forty maybe. He wore a blue denim work shirt from the Gap, faded jeans, loafers, no socks. He was extremely polite and the hand he offered in greeting was beautifully manicured.

"Your cousin tells me you might be interested in working with our company," he said. He was pretty bald about it.

"You're asking me to dance?" I said and he only smiled and

held open the car door. I slid onto the buff leather seat, then he got in.

"If you like dancing," he said.

Zeitsev drove us to the end of Brighton Beach Avenue, past the Menorah Home for old people; at the Holocaust Memorial Mall, he turned onto Emmons Avenue.

Where Sheepshead Bay began, most of the signs were in Italian. Lundy's, its frescoed walls restored as lovingly as some Florentine church, announced itself as the biggest restaurant on earth. In the canal opposite, fishing boats advertised half days of fluke fishing; the fluke were running, the signs said. Behind the suburban villas that faced the canals, in the gardens, satellite dishes sprouted like ears.

Zeitsev pulled into the gravel drive of one of the houses and turned off the ignition. Three men in suits stood in the garden. "Some friends of ours," he said and stayed in the car.

"What work did you have in mind?"

"We have an organization. A legitimate one. There are always corruptions. I guess you know about Agron and the tommy guns and Ivankov and all the nonsense you read."

I nodded. "I read."

He checked himself in the mirror. He had good hair. "Some of us have always understood American democracy. It is what we want. You know, my parents used to call me Jack, because they said I looked like JFK? You think so?"

"Sure, Jack. You've got the hair," I said.

"Most of our people have never done anything for themselves. They are frightened. To get anything in Russia you had to make deals. To outsmart the police or the state was to be a good guy, a dissident. For most of these people the law is the oppressor. We try to help them. We provide services. Justice."

I kept my mouth shut. Unlike the hoods in silk suits at the Batumi and the sleaze at the Arena Café, Elem Zeitsev was not a crude man.

"There is anti-Semitism everywhere, even in America. We become successful, and because this is America, the authorities cannot persecute us for being Jews. So they say we are gangsters." He laughed. "Do you think I look like a gangster?"

"Depends who's playing the part."

Zeitsev snapped open the glove compartment. "Swiss chocolates. Teuscher," he said, putting a box on the seat beside him. He took some socks from the glove compartment and a tie from his pocket, and put them on. In the mirror, he adjusted the tie like a vain little boy on a visit to the relatives. He was pretty charming about it. "My uncle thinks nice boys wear a tie to show respect. I may be forty-six. I may have graduated from Columbia Law School. In this family, I am a boy."

"We can do some business if you want, Jack," I said.

But one of the suits had signaled Zeitsev and he was out of the car, silent, preparing himself for the encounter in some way I didn't understand. The preparation, I realized later, wasn't about respecting the uncle, but about replacing him.

"Yes, of course," he said. "But first come and meet my family."

The formal living room was dark, paneled in oak, hung with mirrors in gilded frames. On the mantelpiece were family photographs framed in heavy silver.

The old man sat in an armchair in front of the fire. Zeitsev, my Zeitsev, the younger, fussed with his tie and tripped on the oriental rugs that were piled ankle deep on the floor. The soft chatter of about a dozen people in the room ceased; they all turned to watch.

Elem Zeitsev leaned over the old man and gave the uncle a kiss smack on the mouth the way you used to see Brezhnev kiss other old commies like Ceauçescu. Smack, right on the kisser. It was enough like a scene from a movie that I had to try not to laugh.

Zeitsev stood up and held his hand out to a plain woman with dull hair who wore a doe-colored suede dress and pearls big as grapes. A canary diamond in her ring was turned in toward the palm, as if she despised the gift. Zeitsev pushed her in my direction and she pressed her thin lips together to squeeze out a smile.

"Mr. Cohen, this is my wife, Yekaterina Alexandrovna," he said. "Speak English, Katya," he added softly.

She spoke halting English; I spoke some Russian back; we made dry conversation about the weather. She was a daughter of the nomenklatura; Zeitsev had probably married her for the connections. I wondered why she'd married this mob; maybe it was love.

"My wife breeds dogs," Zeitsev said, and she smiled a little and showed me a room with half a dozen little dogs, hairy things, lying on the floor like mops, whining. "She has her own kennels. Perhaps you'd like to visit," he said.

"Sure," I said.

Zeitsev worked the crowd. The other women, his cousins, were flashy women in alligator heels and big Bulgari jewelry with colored stones. I saw the blonde with the great posture I had seen at the Batumi.

The old man, Pavel Zeitsev, was the star attraction. He gazed at a small television set on a table beside him and between his hands he held a ginger cat he seemed intent on strangling. The animal sprang out of his grasp, but the old man shuffled after it and brought it back with the weary resolve of a time-serving torturer.

Zeitsev was the brains in Brighton Beach. He had been in the Gulags as a young man, they said; he had belonged to the Black Empire of Crime and had the tattoos to show for it. He was untouchable, so far as the law was concerned; he was a pillar of the community, he was a poet. He read poems over the radio; Russians were impressed.

He delivered the usual litany: corruption in America; bent cops; the need for discipline. "We are not western," he said, taking a hockey puck off the side table and manipulating it like a rosary between his fingers. "We have tried your suits but they do not entirely fit. Another tape," he ordered the younger Zeitsev, who changed the videotape and said to me, "My uncle owns several hockey players."

"Teams, you mean," I said. There was no answer.

He was silent for about ten minutes while I sat and watched hockey with him, then I asked about his poetry. With the sly wink of a pornographer, he beckoned me to an old-fashioned glass-fronted cabinet.

Fondling his books, he showed me first editions of Robert Frost, Walt Whitman, Emily Dickinson. I had passed some kind of test.

After that, the children were brought in and there was lunch in the dining room where I got to sit between the uncle and the blonde babe. I had never seen so much caviar in my life, or such big eggs, and after that and the borscht and the dumplings, a couple of babushkas hoisted a side of beef onto the table. There was little talk. The more this crowd drank, the more silent it got. There were a few desultory toasts and the old man went back to his television. I got Elem Zeitsev to one side.

"Can we talk? Jack?"

"Of course." He led me to the porch in back of the house.

"Business, Jack," I said casually, taking a cigarette out of a pack in my pocket. He lit it for me with a plastic lighter that cost a buck. Zeitsev knew his part did not include a wiseguy's gold lighter.

"My uncle likes you," he said. "He says you are a cultured man. What kind of business shall we do?"

"I'm thinking of getting interested in radiologicals," I said. "Plutonium, uranium, Red Mercury. Industrial uses, of course." I bluffed as best I could. "Experimental medicine. To help the sick."

He laughed. "We don't touch the stuff," he said easily.

"I'm disappointed."

"We get cowboys now and then. Sample men. Scrap merchants usually. With certificates. Without. I feel for the bastards. There are first-class physicists who get fifty dollars a month. They have families to feed in Russia, but it's not for us. It's illegal. This is small stuff for small-time terrorists with popcorn money." He was an engaging fellow.

"Could it be more interesting if this was big stuff? Very big?"

He nodded very slightly.

"Any offers recently, Jack? I'd be very grateful for some help. A favor." I figured I sounded like a two-bit actor playing a hard-boiled cop in a B picture. But it seemed to go down okay; Zeitsev was smiling.

"I'll let you know. I'm glad you have become part of the community," he added, without any irony so far as I could tell.

Elem Zeitsev offered me a ride home but I said I'd take the subway and he laughed. "A man of the people?"

"Sure," I said. "I like people."

"May I be in touch?" He was amiable and impassive.

"Sure," I said. "I'm looking for something touching."

The back door of the house opened and the old man came out, one of the hairy dogs on a leash. A thin man in a suit helped him and when he turned around, I saw it was the bookkeeper with the glasses.

I walked. I needed air. The surreal afternoon had made me forget the AIDS test for a while. And anyway, what could I do except wait?

Elem Zeitsev knew about Lev, I figured. Tolya was right: Lev brought the samples to Zeitsev, things got hot, so to speak, Zeitsev cut him loose. Halfway to Brighton Beach, I called Genia; the little girl said she was getting her hair done and I found her at the Charming Lady Beauty Salon. For a while, I stood in the door. I could see Genia under a steel helmet and she was animated, in spite of her bruised face, by the company of other women gabbing in her own language. The lotions and shampoos gave off a rich, acrid smell that mixed with the excited voices.

"Americans make shit," one of them said. "Buy the Sony, I'm telling you." Her friend replied in Russian with a grunt. Genia looked up and saw me.

I sat in the chair next to her.

"I met Zeitsev," I said. "Both of them."

She hushed me. "I know. Of course, I know."

"You think I should do business with them?"

Genia withdrew into her dryer; a Russian beauty magazine lay in her lap.

"Tell me about your girl," I said.

"Mr. Zeitsev offered to pay for her music lessons."

Genia and the women looked up as the door opened, the chimes jingling "Midnight in Moscow." A uniformed cop removed his cap and tried smiling. No one smiled back. Around here all cops were bad news.

"Tell me about the man you rented a room to. A Pole?"

She shook her head.

"Please."

"I don't remember," she said.

"He beat you up."

"It's a mistake," she whispered. "I don't remember."

"You want to come out for coffee? We'll buy something for the child?" I said to Genia, but she shook her head.

Outside, the street was jammed. I stopped into the Arbat Café and drank beer, watching two men in ponytails and Calvin T-shirts eat dinner with their women; the women laughed hysterically. The talk was all about money. In the street again, I leaned against the building and breathed in the silky blue autumn air for a minute, trying to shed the sick feeling the place gave me, and the panic.

I saw him.

From the back, I recognized him, the tilt of the head, the shape of the jaw. I had seen him a dozen times on the video, I knew him from Tolya's description, from the crummy snapshot I carried everywhere. I knew him. It was Lev.

Almost casually, I had come looking for him, and he was here, maybe looking for me, meandering down Brighton Beach Avenue, caught in the drift of shoppers. For a moment he was trapped between two enormous old women who carried him along through the crowd between them, as if to his wedding.

One more time, I had no weapon; Zeitsev would not have let me in his uncle's house with one, but I started walking anyway. Then I ran.

The shoppers screamed at me. An old lady straddling a camp stool fell over when I scrambled past. I ignored them all and followed him, up to the boardwalk, onto the beach. Sucking in air that came off the ocean, I ran after him, tripping over clotted piles of seaweed and beer cans and used needles. Here was where creeps shot up when they had no place left to go.

He was breathing hard. I could hear him breathing as he slalomed between the struts that held up the boardwalk and on to Coney Island.

I knew the face. But I'd know the face anywhere. I had dreamed about him, smelled him, had his blood on me. If he had AIDS, I probably had it. A cloud shifted; the sun was in my eyes now. I squinted as I ran. I couldn't see if he had the suitcase with him. Red Mercury they called the stuff in the suitcase he couldn't let go of, had to sell; if it could kill him, it was also his redemption.

Something glinted. There was a knife in his hand and he raised it and turned toward me, and in the bright autumn sunlight, for the first time, I saw him full face: Lev Ivanov, if that was his real name, had once been a good-looking man. I couldn't tell how old he was, but his cheeks were sunken like an old man's, and the pale Slavic skin was pitted with lesions and bruises. Lank yellow hair, what was left of it, fell over his forehead, and the eyes that almost glowed in the sunshine were empty of anything human.

"I'll buy your stuff. I want the samples," I shouted at him in Russian. "I have money. I have it," I said. "Lev," I called him. "Lev Ivanov."

I thought I saw him hesitate, but maybe he didn't hear me or wouldn't trust me and he threw the knife at me in an arc and it glittered in the light that streamed through the rotting boards. I covered my face and ducked and when I looked up, Lev had disappeared into the dark recesses under the boardwalk.

I ran. But it was pointless and I was winded. Maybe I should have chased him harder, but he was gone. I got the subway up to Park Slope where Tolya told me he was staying with a friend in the record business. At one of the tidy brownstones, I rang a bell and a man with corn rows and denim overalls came out on the stoop. I said I was looking for Sverdloff. He said he was a record producer, this was his house, the information I had was correct, except for one thing: He had not seen or heard from Tolya Sverdloff since his own last trip to Moscow ten years earlier.

Chapter Five

THERE WAS NOTHING FROM TOLYA WHEN I CALLED MY MACHINE. SON-ofabitch. Nothing at all. Whose game was he playing?

"Watch it," I shouted at a kid on a skateboard who almost slammed into me as I stood on a corner using a pay phone that had chewing gum stuck in the receiver.

"Fuck you," the kid shouted. He was maybe ten years old.

Tolya had disappeared. I figured the Taes had already gone to the airport, but I tried. Ricky answered. "We're not leaving until later," he said. "Ma took a message for you downstairs," he said hesitantly.

"Spit it out."

"Your friend Maxine called. She says she got some news from a doctor friend, that mean anything? She says if you want you can meet her."

"Where?"

"That pier by the river, Twenty-third Street, they got a skating rink there. She has her kids. You want me to come, Artie?" But I had hung up. I got on the subway.

I tried feeling ironic, but I was busy making deals, like a kid does: If I'm okay, I'll be good. But all I could think of was the creep. Lev's face stayed in front of my eyes like sunspots. I couldn't blink him away. The sickly Slav face in the light filtering down through the cracks in the boardwalk, the look of a diseased man who didn't care, who would do something terrible if only to give the world the finger. The eyes, or what I had seen of them, were completely empty, like sockets in a skull.

Seeing him like that, I knew instinctively he had told Tolya the truth. He had the goods. Somewhere, he had this stuff, this red mercury, and I had to get it. But he wouldn't deal directly with me—the Jew cop. And Tolya had gone to ground. Sverdloff had lied to me. Don't trust Tolya Sverdloff, Gavin Crowe had said in the Chelsea Hotel. Don't trust him.

The subway grunted and stopped and I got out feeling wired. Like worms were under my skin. I didn't want to die. I didn't want to be sick. I got out of the station and walked over to the pier. I tried to pretend there might be a god looking after Artie Cohen and I could promise him good behavior in return for good news.

Maxine was standing at the edge of the rink watching her kids stumble around on Rollerblades. She had on shorts and a grubby blue shirt. She didn't look so great, her face was pinched and nervous and she sucked on a Snapple bottle like it was a pacifier. She didn't kiss me. She just looked at me and said, "You have to stop, Artie. You hear me? You have to stop this crap."

"I don't need this," I said quietly.

She was distracted. Something was worrying her. She walked in little circles at the edge of the rink while in the background people slid on Rollerblades, fell, laughed, shouted. Maxie looked around. Something was wrong and she wasn't going to tell me. I thought it was the AIDS test. I thought she had the results and she didn't want to tell me or touch me.

"Did you get it? Tell me." I grabbed her wrist and she wrestled free from me.

"Yes," she said. "Yes, I got it."

So that was it. I shivered and turned in the other direction so she couldn't see me. I thought I might puke.

"You don't have AIDS, Artie. The test was negative."

I could have cried with relief. I put my arms around her and tried to kiss her cheek but she didn't want any. She pulled away again.

"Hey, be happy for me. Okay?"

"Sure, Artie." She seemed distracted. I followed her glance, but Maxie was only looking at one of those he-shes that live by the West Side Highway. This guy was in bike shorts with a codpiece, his beautiful face made up like a woman, gold curls cascading down his back. He braked his skates, then, with elegant gestures, took a container of yogurt out of his bag and started eating from it.

"Wow," I said. "Look at that." I was trying to get Maxie to talk to me, to lighten up, but she was on the edge of panic.

"The kids look good," I said, watching the twins, who were a few yards away giggling helplessly as they fell on top of each other. Sometimes I wish I were seven. "You want to tell me what this is about if it's not about the test?"

"It's about your running wild all over the city and I'm getting the raw end," she said. "People know we're friends. They know I help you out."

"I lied for you a few times, Maxie. You remember? You remember that time you fucked up and I covered for you?"

"You can be a real prick when you try, Artie. I was pregnant. I was out of it. So I fucked up. Okay, I owe you. But you ask too much, Artie, you really do. You think you can do your charm bullshit and I'll tell you anything you want, you know? Look, I'm gonna tell you a couple things, okay, and then I want you to stop. I want you to leave me alone and let the pros find out who murdered Ustinov and the girl on the beach. They got a gun, you know. A match for the weapon that killed Ustinov."

"I heard." I thought of Sonny at the game at the Garden. So he was telling the truth. "What else?"

She shrugged. I didn't think she knew about Lev. How much did she know? She looked out at the rink again, at the blur of bodies, and for a minute I felt angry at all the careless people having mindless fun.

"Maxie? Hey. I'm sorry. I'm grateful you got the test results. I was scared shitless, okay? So that's it, I'll leave you alone."

"Fine," she said.

"What couple things?"

"What?"

"You said you were gonna tell me a couple things."

"You know the knife that guy cut you with, you remember?"

I touched my face. "Here. He cut me here. Hurt like fuck."

"You already got my sympathy, babe, alright?" she said. "The knife was hot."

"Hot?"

"Radioactive. Hot."

"How do you know?"

"Roy Pettus asked me to check it out. With a Geiger counter, you know? We checked it out. It registered. It was hot."

"I see."

"Does it make sense to you? Does it?" She didn't know about Lev or the suitcases.

"Maybe. Do you want me to tell you about it?"

"No. I don't want to know. I don't want to owe you. I don't want to know what I don't need to know. I'm not like you. You should get a family, Artie. Get real."

"How come you're so pissed off?" I asked because Maxine was normally a real mild-mannered girl, a friend, and suddenly she was frantic, like she was ashamed of something and wanted to cover up. One of her kids—Annie—raced over to her and asked for money for Cokes.

"Hi, Artie," the girl smiled.

118

"Mr. Cohen to you," said Maxine, and gave her daughter some change.

"What was the other thing you were going to tell me?"

She glanced behind her. "I have to go."

"You waiting for someone, Max?"

She looked over her shoulder again, but there was only a young couple, the husband on Rollerblades with a baby in a backpack. "No. The jar Roy Pettus sent me. With the girl's fingertips. It registered too," she said again. "I would never think of it, but Roy, you know, he has this obsession. It was hot. The jar was hot like the knife."

"Max, do you know anything about radiation?"

"No. Once in a while we get a call from the nuclear medicine people over at the hospital, usually when the monitor goes off by mistake. We get a call to check stuff out, but it's always laundry, rubber gloves, that kind of low-level shit. The real stuff they got specialists for. Radiologicals are not exactly a high priority in Brooklyn, you know."

"Can you test a corpse for radioactivity?" I was thinking of Olga.

"From what I know, probably. I'm not sure."

She looked at her watch, waved at her kids. They skated toward her, then draped themselves over Maxie and begged for another half hour. She told them to get their skates off.

"What's the hurry?"

"I got to get home."

"Let me get the girls some pizza or something."

She was twitching like some kind of puppet and I wanted to know who was pulling her strings or if I maybe just had bad breath, figuratively speaking.

"Art," a voice said from behind me. It was Sonny Lippert. He was not wearing blades.

"Shit, Maxine. You set me up. You told him I was coming."

Her face was hot and red. "I had to, Artie," Maxine said. "I had to. I couldn't keep lying for you. You're going to get yourself hurt." She looked miserable.

"You can go now," Sonny said dismissively to Maxine. "I'll

take over here," he said, as she touched my shoulder and hurried away to get her kids.

"Oh yeah, and thanks, sweetheart," Sonny called out, but Maxine was out of earshot.

"You don't listen, do you? I got to schlep over to this fucking pier to tell you you have got to stop this shit," Sonny said when we were at the concession stand drinking coffee.

"I don't know what you mean, Sonny."

"I hear stories, you turn up in Brighton Beach, you're hanging with the Zeitsev crowd—you working for them now, Artie? You still a Russian deep down? Did they get to you? They will, you know. Or they'll get to someone you care about, if there is anyone, know what I mean, babe? Go away. Go to the island. Go stay with Danny. Or—" He let the sentence dribble away into his coffee cup.

"Yes? Or?"

"Tell me what you know."

"Why the fuck should I?"

"I'll shut you down."

"Ask Roy Pettus."

"Sure, and maybe I should also call Saddam Hussein for information."

"Tell me what you know, I'll tell you what I've got," I said.

Sonny looked at me and gave his version of a smile. "That won't work. That won't work at all. We got plenty. We got what we need. I got good men in Brooklyn. I'll get the bastard with or without you, and I'll get whoever set him up."

What he was really scared of was I'd break the case and get the credit. That's what he couldn't stand. But Sonny shook me up; he could come down hard on me. Where was Tolya? Where was he?

"Can I go now?" I said.

"Sure," he said.

"I'm going on vacation, like you said to."

"I'll check," he said. "And Artie—"

"Yeah?"

"Be careful who you screw with. It could make you sick."

* * *

120

I got a cab home in time to see Rick drive away from the curb, his parents in the car, luggage loaded up, taking them to the airport, then going on some adventure of his own with a new friend. I stood on the pavement and waved and felt alone. I went upstairs. The building felt empty. I looked across the street at the window where the creep had watched me. For the time being I wasn't going to die from AIDS; there was that anyhow.

I took a bunch of beer and went up on the roof and thought about what Ricky said before he left. We were talking about nuke shit and this Red Mercury stuff, and he said "If I was you, I'd ask a Russian."

Chapter Six

ON THE DOOR OF THE FAKE TUDOR HOUSE IN A PRIM SUBURBAN GRID the nameplate read: andy feder. I figured maybe I made a mistake. But the taxi was already gone.

My goddamn car was in the shop again. It served me right for driving an antique. I had loved that Mustang once. Never own anything that eats while you sleep, Ricky said; the car ate my money. I wanted a big red Caddy with brand new leather seats.

I looked at the house. The rush of stuff was getting to me. There was too much, too many threads, Ustinov, Lev, Zeitsev. Now I was on Long Island. Like some bum digging in a garbage can, I was hoping for scraps. Lev was out there, but where?

"Artyom? It's you?"

The screen door flew open as if I had been expected, as if someone was watching for me.

"Is it really you, Artyom?"

"You're Feder now?"

All that was left of the skinny nerd I knew in school were the wet brown dog eyes. Andrei Melorovich Federov. He wore baggy shorts, the pockets stuffed with mysterious items. "Can't you be more like Andrei?" my father would say when my teachers told him I was smuggling rock and roll records into school. That was when Pop still expected things to work out, poor bastard.

"I am Andy Melvin Feder now. Sometimes Mel. You always had the American name of Art. Me, I have become Andy Feder. Sounds Jewish, yes? Better to sound Jewish in the community, scientifically speaking." He peered at the driveway. "You have no car?"

"In the shop. I took the train."

We pounded each other on the back a lot, like men think they have to, but what the hell, I really was glad to see him. We had met a few times when he first got to America, I didn't feel comfortable with it, he went out west. I let it drop. Which is why I didn't call ahead. I figured maybe he wouldn't see me.

I followed him into the house. Both his parents were dead, Federov said; I only remembered the father, a pint-sized Stalinist whose own father had fought the revolution and named his only son Melor. Marx Engels Lenin Organization Revolution. In my generation, people named their kids Gagarin and Fidel; I didn't know what they called them now, Tiffany probably, and I didn't care. But Ricky said ask a Russian. Here was one authentic Russian physicist on Long Island, U.S.A.

"I was sad when you did not come to my wedding or reply to my calls," he said, and I knew I would have to atone with Moscow guy talk about American cars and Russian soul things. He took me into a suburban kitchen jammed with appliances.

"Look. Electric bagel slicer!" Federov poured coffee into mugs and pulled open the refrigerator. "You would like?"

"I ate already."

"It must be fifteen years. I have not seen you since I first arrived in America," he said mournfully.

"These are all yours, Andrei?" A snapshot of five kids was on the refrigerator.

"All mine. Yeah. Big blonde one is wife, ha ha," he added.

"Russian?"

"Yes, naturally. But high class. How about cake?" He sat at the table and I sat opposite him. He reached for the refrigerator again and pulled out a coffee cake.

"Talk to me first," I said. "Tell me about nukes."

"Nukes?" Feder guffawed. "What kind nukes?"

"You tell me. Nukes. Radiation. Warheads in every former Soviet craphole from Ukraine to Kazakhstan. Fallout. Draw me a picture."

Contemplatively, he drank the coffee and ate some pastel-colored mints out of a cut-glass bowl. "Give me something to work with, otherwise this is a lecture in Physics 101, you want this?"

"No."

"So Andy guesses maybe you are interested in spill of radioactive materials—radiologicals, nuke food, what you like to call it—from former Soviet Union, right? Who are bankers? Who are sample men? Mules? Scrap merchants."

"Scrap merchants?"

"Poor slobs who collect insignificant amounts to sell. Low level. So you are perhaps interested in meaning of the sudden appearance on the world market of plutonium. Enriched uranium. Men with samples for sale?"

"How do you know?"

"Information is always available. Sometimes, the more information the less knowledge. You think because I'm Russian, I'm stupid? This is always your problem, Artyom." He had become hostile; he knew me from way back.

Feder said, "The FBI opens an office in Moscow. Where? Smack in the middle of the embassy compound. Nice assignment for suicidal guy from Indiana. Everyone knows about the trade in radiologicals. Stuff leaking out of secret Sov cities. Arzamas, Tomsk. Turns up in Europe. Sell it to terrorists. Iran, maybe. Maybe Libya. Maybe you found this stuff in Brighton Beach?" For the first time he was interested.

"Maybe."

"Please. Please!" He opened a drawer, grabbed a knife, slammed it shut. He began slicing a piece off the cake that stood on the table. "Why else would you be at my house after fifteen years, asking about radiologicals? You hated science at school. All you cared for was jazz music. Rock and roll. If you find any of this stuff in New York, this is big deal."

Andrei spoke to me in a mixture of Russian and English. His English was slipshod, as if he couldn't hang on to the present. Maybe the comic immigrant version he slipped into was only a cover. But what could he be covering for in this suburban paradise?

"Andrei, Andy, Melvin, whatever, talk to me."

The veins on his nose popped, then he calmed himself. "We've known all this for years. Years. No one listens."

"You want to show me your lab?"

"My day off," he said cautiously.

"What's your work?"

"Environmental stuff. Nuclear waste storage. Vitrification. You want to discuss fine points vitrification?" He was sarcastic.

"How long you been here now?"

"Ten years. Before that, Los Alamos Atomic Laboratories. Then Brookhaven. Now here."

"Really."

"Why not? I'm a good guy. My daddy was a dissident," he said, completely reinventing his past. "I am a U.S. citizen. I was even a U.S. soldier. Captain Feder. You are a citizen also?"

"Yup, Citizen Cohen. I'm a cop. Was a cop."

He giggled. "I guess us Sov boys like institutions, huh. What kind cop, Artyom?"

I didn't trust Federov and I wasn't going to let him in on my current shaky status with the NYPD, but I needed what was in his head. I played it for old times sake. I said, "Yeah, you got it, Andy. I'm on special assignment. Very hush-hush. High-level cop stuff. You'll keep it that way won't you, Andy?"

He nodded slowly, then looked at the last piece of cake, a shifty, covetous look. He scooped up its remains and ate; crumbs covered his chin. "Tell me," he said, with a manipulative gleam in his little eyes. "Tell me who killed Gennadi Ustinov?"

"I don't know."

"But as soon as he dies radiological stuff turns up in the city?"

"Come," he said. "Let's go out."

We drove the short distance to the lab in Andrei's Chevy Suburban. In a little park, we sat on a bench. I smoked. Down the hill, a yellow bus let workers out onto a green campus where some lab buildings stood. A boy in high-tops cut the lawn with a mower big as a tank; the grass smelled sweet.

Federov hunted his pockets and took out a few candy bars. He offered me a Baby Ruth. The Snickers he ate whole, like a snake devouring a rabbit. He was a lot more nervous than he said. Was Captain Feder still military? Obliged to report every encounter?

"Okay, you get material for weapons in various ways. From spent fuel rods in nuclear power plants. From special places that make weapons-grade plutonium just for bombs. For years we thought you needed special weapons-grade stuff to make a bomb. Wrong. The British sold us Americans low-grade stuff, and we made a nice bomb with it anyway. Also, you don't need much. Also, for terrorism, you don't have to make a bomb at all. You have only to make terror. You want I draw you pictures?"

"Draw for me."

Federov took me literally. He dragged some crumpled paper out of his pocket, took a ballpoint out of his shirt pocket and sketched for a minute while he talked.

"Okay. Plutonium bomb, you need few pounds, but precision work. Uranium, you need maybe fifty-five pounds, but a crude bomb works okay. So. I make my bomb. I put her in a rental van. I drive it to the garage at World Trade Center, then run like hell. Boom. Explosion brings down one entire tower. But this time, it kills everyone inside. Also at least one hundred thousand extra from blast and radiation. Maybe more, depending on contamination, meteorological conditions, air vents, run-off systems. Manhattan is drenched with fallout. He looked at me, then went on talking.

"This produces nausea, vomiting, diarrhea, hair loss, lesions, cataracts, anemia, that's short-term. Long-term? Cancer, leukemia, depending on length of exposure. Trauma from being irradiated can mimic the same symptoms. Massive opportunity for infection. The immune system kaput."

I shivered slightly. "Like AIDS?"

"Like AIDS," he said.

Bingo! I thought: Radiation sickness looks just like AIDS. Lev, the Atomic Mule, didn't have AIDS. He was dying from what he had in that suitcase!

"Terrible burns, so bad you have to peel off skin. Enough? You know a terrorist doesn't love even the idea of this?" Federov's voice rose with enthusiasm for his subject.

"From what? From plutonium?"

"Plutonium if you burn it and it gets in the air. Plutonium if you breathe it in. Strontium 90 replaces calcium and presto, bone cancer. There's cesium, a nice little killer if it's uncontained. Plenty of things."

"What if there's no bomb?"

"Even with samples you can make trouble. Poison air vents, water supplies."

I lit up and leaned back and closed my eyes for a second; the sun was warm. "What do you know about Red Mercury?"

"Why?" Federov's posture changed. His flabby body went taut with intensity. He got up and started down the hill. "Let's walk. Maybe I will show you my lab," he said. "So, Red Mercury? You have it?" He was walking fast. What the hell was the hurry?

I said, "Maybe. Maybe not."

He grabbed my arm. "You don't know what you have, do you? You don't know that Red Mercury as toxic powder can be irradiated to form liquid, then implanted with rare isotope to make Red Mercury 20 20. That it can help exploit the hydrodynamic flow properties of a heavy liquid to design a nuclear trigger. Possibly, it's a neutron emitter."

"In plain English, okay?"

"In English, it is very toxic, highly radioactive. In liquid form, you can use it to make bombs, to make paint that makes planes invisible—stealth technology. In English, it is very deadly. More than plutonium. Heavier. I've never heard of any on the international market. Never. It is the most closely guarded of all secrets."

Reaching into his baggy shorts, he pulled out two tennis balls and juggled them casually. "I'll show you in English. Two tennis balls of red mercury in a nuclear bomb the size of, let us say, a salad bowl and bye-bye Long Island."

He knew what he was talking about. I knew for sure that Andy Feder was still military. He had been walking steadily toward a wire fence that surrounded some of the lab buildings; security was low key, but even I could spot the muscle.

"What else?"

He grew evasive. "I don't know," he said, but he knew alright.

As a kid, Federov was a lousy chess player. His face told you everything. "You ever go home these days, Artie?" he asked.

"My home is New York," I said stiffly.

"You never change." Federov put his hand on my shoulder. "Come on, Artie. Let me show you labs. We can meet some real chipheads, real computer nerds who can maybe help you."

"I think I better get going," I said. "You've been a real help."

"Do you have Red Mercury?" Federov edge toward the labs as I backed off. He grabbed my sleeve. He was pissed off now. "You think I'm threatening you? You think I going to have big fat security guards arresting you? Don't be asshole, Artyom. Is bullshit. You got more danger traveling Long Island Railroad. But if you have got Red Mercury, I must have it. Please! With this you can make bomb that fits package of cigarettes. Please, Artyom. For years I have wanted to see this. Please."

The old paranoia swilled around me. I didn't wait to find out why he wanted me inside the lab. We Sov boys love institutions, he said. He loved them, he meant, and I wondered again who Andy Feder worked for these days.

"Be careful," he called out in Russian as I ran for the train. "It will kill you."

Chapter Seven

"HE'S BEEN FRIED. FRIED. I'D SAY HE'S SO HOT, YOU COULD PULL HIS chain and he'd glow in the dark." The medic switched off his Geiger counter, zipped up the body bag and pulled off his green rubber gloves with a snap as if he'd just finished the dishes. He looked down at the bagged body that lay on the platform in Penn Station. "I don't know what he's got, but it's plenty radioactive."

I was real edgy after the visit with Federov on Long Island, so when I got off the train and climbed the stairs into Penn Station, I half expected someone on my back. The way Penn Station is set up, the way you have to go up and down separate stairs to the various platforms, I didn't see the dead man right away, didn't see the guys from the Hazardous Materials squad in their moon-suits. My train pulled into a different platform. As soon as I climbed the stairs to the main terminal, I spotted the extra cops, the frantic security men, the FBIs with their bad suits and ashy faces. I know Penn Station pretty well; I worked a case there once.

The terminal was heaving with bodies. People pushed through the crowd, like swimmers among schools of unfriendly fish. I got a half-dozen elbows in my side. A woman in spike heels ground her shoe into my foot, and I shouted, "Watch it." She screamed back, "Lick your dick."

The terminal was in permanent chaos, renovations never fin-ished, loose electricals dangling like evil weeds. I was hyperven-tilating. I could feel the weight and heat of the bodies. The noise was relentless, that low-level insistent din that comes sometimes just before a crowd panics. Maybe it was my imagination.

At a Dunkin' Donuts, I stopped to get a Coke. There were too many cops around. Next to the donut shop, I spotted a transit cop with enough flab on him to fuel Times Square. Brenner, his name tag said.

"What's going on?" I said and Brenner yakked, trying to be pally with me, but his eyes drifted to donuts sizzling in a bucket of fat. I went and got him half a dozen. He talked. He pointed to the entrance to one of the platforms, maybe a hundred yards away.

"Something going on," he mumbled, lips covered with pink sugar.

At the entrance to the platform, I found a cop I knew slightly. "I don't know what it is. They just told us no one goes in. We had a bastard of a time clearing off that platform. Maybe they're hold-ing some perp down there."

God knows why I was interested. Maybe I didn't want to go home. Maybe I already knew. I got the cop to let me through. I went down the stairs into the semi-dark of the platform. Above me, the noise from the terminal surged like quadraphonic surf, then receded. That's when I heard the medic say "He's fried."

* * *

The platform was almost empty. I squinted in the gloom. A couple hundred yards along were a few Bomb Squad guys in dark blue jackets; others from Hazardous Materials squads were zipped into protective gear, some with gas masks. The TV pictures of the Japanese subway disaster came back to me, people in the train station dying like flies from Sarin, the nerve gas.

I wasn't completely surprised to see Roy Pettus.

"Poor sonofabitch." Roy, holding a gas mask in his hand, stared at the dead man on the ground. One of the Haz Mat guys, the chief I guessed, took Roy aside. He let me listen.

"I'm not sure and I wouldn't guess for anyone except you, Roy, because I know you got that obsession. This time you were right. This is some kind of radiation thing."

"Christ," Roy said and I thought I saw him cross himself.

"The package we found with the dead man? I got a pretty high reading. I won't know for sure until the lab calls, but if I was gonna guess, I'd say he was fried by something very hot that works very fast. Something like cesium. I want to evacuate this place. Fast. You want to keep that mask on."

"Wait for the call," said Roy.

"We can't wait."

"Where's the guy who found him?"

Pettus waved at a black kid so young there was down on his upper lip. He wore a knitted hat with a red pompom.

"You live in Level Three?" Pettus asked politely.

"Yessir," he said. "In Three."

The caves under the tracks at Penn Station were the last stop for a bewildered tribe of the homeless, nomads chased from parks, from doorways, even public toilets. A friend in Transit took me down once. It was like some Orwellian housing project; the levels even had numbers.

"You knew him?" Pettus gestured toward the man on the ground.

"He was a regular. He came to use the washing machine. We liked him. We saved the puzzle for him."

Beggarman, homelessman, I thought.

"Puzzle?"

"He liked to do that *Times* crossword puzzle. He knew a lot of stuff."

"Did he have a name?"

"I don't know. He didn't say. He liked drinking and the puzzle. Sometimes he looked around in the lockers upstairs, see if there was anything interesting, he said. Sometimes he found interesting stuff. When he stumbled in half dead, I figured it was his heart. That's why I got hold of a conductor."

"Anyone else around?"

"It was the middle of the day. Most everyone out working the streets, you know?"

Pettus nodded. "Everyone out?" he said to the Haz Mat chief.

"What about him?" The chief pointed at me.

Pettus handed me one of the masks and said, "Put this on. And tell me what you are doing here?"

"I was passing. Who's the kid?"

"He lives down in Three. He tells a conductor on the platform some old man is dead. He talks about a package. One smart cop goes along and figures there's something funny. They clear off the platform, God knows how, close it down, call Bomb Squad in. You heard the rest."

The chief was talking into a portable phone. "It's the lab, Roy. The package is hot whatever the fuck it is. Real hot, like I figured. I want this place fully decontaminated. I want it shut down. I want everything and everyone monitored. I want to know the extent of contamination. Ventilation systems. It gets airborne, we're in trouble."

"Worst case?"

"A lot of sick people. Some dead. Panic. You hear me? Roy? I want this place decontaminated."

"What place?"

"The whole goddamn station and all the trains, if I had my way. If there's one package, there's another. There's always a second package."

Roy said, "Give us half an hour to find the other package. If this gets out, the panic will be worse than the thing itself. You quarantine ten thousand people, you got global panic. I mean global."

The chief looked down the platform. A little group of men in moonsuits worked with Geiger counters and hoses.

"What choice I got?"

Lev had been in here. Of course he had been here. In my gut, I knew. Had he followed me earlier when I left for Long Island? Was I the bait for Lev, or the fish he planned to hook with the packages that leaked radiation. Was I merely a bystander who got in the way, accidental roadkill?

"I want to see," I said to Pettus.

"See what?"

"Where they found it."

"No."

I pushed Roy a few feet from the others. "I need to see. I need to know. This is about me."

He went and mumbled to the chief and came back. "Let's go," he said and a guy from Haz Mat gave us hot-suits that felt like wrinkled toilet paper when you put them on and rubber gloves. The face masks smelled of camphor, the gas masks that went over them smelled of rubber. It was hard to breathe.

The black kid said, "Let me come too. I know how the old fellow hid his things."

"No," Pettus said.

"He was my friend," the homeless kid said simply.

Pettus looked at me and someone fitted out the kid with a suit. We stood on the deserted platform huddled together for a minute. Then Roy Pettus grabbed a walkie talkie from one of the guys. "Let's go."

An officer from Haz Mat picked up a Geiger counter.

"Ten minutes," the chief said. "Not more. You understand?"

We went through a rusty iron door that led to a tunnel underneath the tracks. Pettus went in first. I could smell rust and sewage; I could hear the complicated sounds of the subterranean city and trains overhead in every direction.

"Be careful, detective." Pettus' voice echoed back at me inside the tunnel; I realized he always addressed me by a title because Roy Pettus was a shy, formal man and didn't know what else to call me.

The sound of our feet on the metal rungs banged into the musty darkness. We climbed past a series of underground storage centers, then emerged into one of the cavernous chambers. Light came from a couple of bulbs that dangled from a metal crossbeam. Steampipes hissed out warm dank air; a washing machine had been hooked up to one, and above it was a laundry line neatly hung with jeans, T-shirts, underpants, and a pair of stockings. A rat scampered across someone's cardboard bed. The homeless had set up housekeeping, and even through my mask, the smell was potent, a dank, Dickensian smell. The Geiger counter chattered softly.

"They found him here," Pettus said briefly.

We searched the cave as best we could. "Nothing," Pettus said. "Goddamn it. Nothing at all. I'll have to let them evacuate."

"Wait a minute." The kid was on the floor. He crawled under one of the makeshift beds. Cunningly inserted under the mattress was a flat box—the second package. He opened it. Inside were some scraps of paper. He gave it to Pettus who looked through the crumpled paper and gave me a single sheet. "You read this stuff?"

I nodded. "Yes, I read it." It was in Russian.

"Anything?" the chief said when we got back to the platform.

Roy handed him the piece of paper from the box the kid found. They muttered together.

"Okay, I'm gonna take your word, Roy. I'm only gonna close down these holes, this platform, but it's on your head. You tell your people to keep their mouths shut. No media. Nothing." He looked at me. The kid with the hat hung around now aimlessly; he had lost his home.

"Come with me," Roy Pettus said to him. "We're going to get you looked after now."

"Was I good?" he asked, this skinny black kid with faint down on his lip who lived in a hole in the ground.

"Yes," Roy Pettus said. "You were a hero. Thank you."

We made our way to the street through one of the tunnels. In the street, all of us squinting like bats, the chief herded us into a van that was waiting. We took off the protective gear. The chief said, "Everyone gets checked out, okay? I'll be in touch with phone numbers."

"Let me see the note again," I said to Pettus.

"Keep the gloves on," he said and handed the note back.

I had to make sure. The ransom note was written in Russian. The package in the station locker was a warning, it said. There was more. He wanted to sell. Wanted money. It was from Lev, but I had known all along.

"Ten grand," I said. "All he wants is ten grand in a locker in the station. He says he'll give you the stuff. Give him the money, Roy, for God's sake. We're never going to find him. He'll go to ground. He'll hide the samples. No one in Brighton Beach will talk. Get me the money and let me do it."

Pettus said, "We don't do that. We give it to him, it never ends. It goes on and on." There was something he was holding back.

"What really brought you into the station today, detective?" Pettus asked and I told him.

"You took the train going out to the island, too?"

"Yes."

"Who knew you were going?"

I thought of Ricky. "No one. You think someone followed me?"

"Is that a possibility?"

"Yeah, sure. Anything's possible. Why not?"

"How come you took the train?"

"My car's bust again."

"Gimme a smoke," Pettus said.

"I thought you quit," I said. I gave him one, he lit up and gulped the smoke like it was manna. "You trying to tell me something?" I said.

"Okay. The first package we found with the old man who died?"

"Yeah?" I stripped off the rubber gloves.

"It had your name on it, detective," said Pettus.

"What do you mean?"

"The package was addressed to you."

Chapter Eight

CONSIDERING THE OLD DEAD GUY GOT A PACKAGE ADDRESSED TO ME, I figured I owed him something, so I went to his funeral. I had gone home from Penn Station and stood under the shower on and off for an hour, feeling as if my body were fried. I was scared. A month ago, I never thought about nukes. Now everywhere I went, there was a connection—the dead bum, Federov. All I could do was keep moving forward. I sent all my clothes to the cleaners.

I fixed a sandwich out of some prosciutto I found in the back of the icebox, made coffee, put Gerry Mulligan doing "Round Midnight" with Monk on the CD to remind me there was life out there and grabbed the phone, working a bunch of old contacts until I got what I wanted. Which is how I found out they were probably going to plant the bum from Penn Station in the next two or three days in a public graveyard.

Prisoners from city jails work the burial detail at the public cemeteries, and I let one of them con some cigarettes off me. He leaned on his shovel, enjoying the smoke and the clean fall day. "That's the second one like that we've buried the last couple of months. The second one they wanted a hurry-up special delivery stick 'em in the ground job for. Usually with them John Does they take their time on the autopsies, so what's going on?" he said.

I didn't answer. I got in Dorothy Tae's station wagon that I had borrowed because I'd had it with trains, and I broke all the speed limits on the FDR until I got to Brooklyn and Roy Pettus' office.

"You want to tell me what's going on?" I said to Pettus after I banged into his office, bullying my way past the guard and past Pettus' secretary.

Four agents who sat in the room with him, suit coats hung neatly over the chair backs, muscles straining at their pants, looked up from their paperwork. They had crewcuts and mid-western faces. Bland as mashed potatoes, they stared at me with distaste. New York, their expressions said. Pinko liberal faggot Jew, they were thinking.

"Can I help?" said the oldest of the agents, who had a face more like a pumpkin than a potato. I ignored him.

"So?"

"Sit down," Pettus said. "Sit down."

"I don't want to sit down. Just tell me how many others there have been. I'm out watching them bury the guy from Penn Station in the public dump, someone says there have been others."

"What the hell did you go there for?"

"I thought someone should, okay. Okay? Don't stonewall me, Roy."

"It was before you were involved."

"But you didn't bother telling me."

"That's right."

"Why not?"

In the background, the pasty-faced agents shifted uneasily, pretending not to listen.

"You got to tell me something," I said. "You've got to tell me if this shit ever came into New York before."

"No, I don't. And I don't know. I'm not sure. That's what I'm trying to tell you: I don't know, detective. It's all rumors. Conjecture. A whispering gallery. Except for you, of course, running around putting your nose in stuff you can't fix. You know, Pat," he said to one of the agents, "maybe we should call Sonny Lippert. Tell him who we got in here."

When he got angry, Roy's face wrinkled up like a violent old baby who was in awful pain but couldn't cry. "You want to know? Here," he said, grabbing up a sheaf of paper and waving it in my face. He threw it at me. "You want to deal with this? Should I tell you about all the nuts in New York with nukes on their mind? The schizo copycats just waiting for something to ape? Should I tell you about how we could have public panic on a twenty-four-hour basis, if people knew there's nukes out there? You want to know why I do what I got to to suppress stuff like what happened in Penn Station?" He looked ready to crack.

"How about the nutbag I got who says he's selling plutonium in the Penta Hotel? I got black Muslim militants upstate doing errands for their pals in Chicago, who might be greasing the pipeline for stuff coming in through Mexico from Sierra Leone,"

135

he said, and I thought of what Lev told Tolya. "I got Israelis who tell me we told you so, then sell nuke technology to South Africa. Nothing ever gets proved. You think it's hard to get stuff across borders? You ever crossed the border from Juarez into El Paso? You're a white guy in a nice Hertz rental, no problem, how ya doing, amigo, welcome to the U.S.A."

I got up and paced around, waiting to see if Sonny Lippert showed.

"Sit down, detective, I'm not through," Roy said. "Any sign of nuclear terrorism, the government sends in the hotshots from the Nuclear Emergency Search Team and they are good. Sure they are, but so what? So they stop some two-bit terrorist. There's plenty more. And someday they won't even have to import it. One of these days they'll break into one of our lousy storage facilities. Did you know this country is dripping with nuclear wastes?" Roy asked.

"The government just lies like they always did. They contract companies to run the nuclear industry who hire PR people who lie. No, I apologize. Sometimes they don't even have to lie. They just buy into the whole corporate message all by themselves."

I had never heard Roy Pettus so angry. When Roy thought about this nuke stuff, he saw it like he saw the bombers in Oklahoma or the gas spill in the Tokyo subway or the explosion in the Paris Metro or Penn Station. He could see people dying like flies in a tunnel or on a bridge or a skyscraper and he saw himself, Roy Pettus, helpless to stop it.

"No one gives a pig's dick, either. Radioactive materials are unpredictable, unstable, the statistics are unreliable, you know why? I'll tell you. Because the information has been classified for too long. Because the populations subjected to it got railroaded. Got it? You know what they did to my family? Five generations served this country in wars, then the government stuck a missile in our backyard in Chugwater, Wyoming, you understand? Didn't ask, just came on in and put it there. Now how about you level with me, detective?"

"Why didn't you tell me before?"

"It wasn't your business. It wasn't anyone's business."

"How many have there been like the bum?"

"We're not sure. We're not sure what we were seeing. I can't afford any rumors." Pettus looked down at me with hard eyes.

"What was in the package the bum died from?"

"We think it's a thing named cesium."

"You make bombs from that?"

He said, "Mostly it's used for medical stuff. Cesium 137, a little goes a long way. Doctor in South America opened the wrong shutter on a teletherapy device, he was dead in a week. It doesn't matter what the stuff is, you raise the issue of radiation, unless there's an emergency the public doesn't really want to believe it. I got a country in denial, okay? That's what I'm dealing with. Now you talk."

I told Roy what I figured he needed to know when one of the agents called out to him, "Lippert's on the phone for you."

"Tell him I'm on vacation. Please," I said. "Let me get out of here without seeing Sonny, okay? I'm asking you, Roy, please. You remember last week, by the river? You mentioned Red Mercury?"

Roy nodded. I walked to the window and Roy walked with me and we stared out.

"I heard there's a guy who has some to sell," I said.

Pettus told his men to take a break and when they had gone I told him the rest of what I knew about Lev.

"What do you want from me, detective?"

"Help me find Anatoly Sverdloff. I told you about him. He's a Russian, probably on a legit visa. With a phony address in Park Slope. Pick him up, but do it quietly," I said.

Roy said, "I'll call you."

Chapter Nine

I WAS DREAMING I WAS ON A PLANE FOR MOSCOW THAT COULDN'T LAND when the phone rang. I fumbled for a light and pushed over a glass of water. It shattered on the floor. I looked at my watch; it was six in the morning.

"Artie? Hillel. I been trying you almost two weeks. What's the matter? You don't like me anymore?"

I knew Hillel Abramsky had been calling. "I'm sorry. I been up to my ass. Really."

"I got this client I figure might interest you. Okay? Come by lunchtime. We close early Friday."

"Hilly, I got a lot on." One more blind alley and I figured I'd freak.

"Come," he said.

My best source in the diamond district, Hillel Abramsky's a good guy. I could hear him singing even before I opened the door to a back room on the second floor of the shabby building on Forty-seventh Street. It was lunchtime and the workbenches were mostly empty. Only Hillel sat at his bench, face half covered by a pair of welder's glasses thick as Coke bottles, a diamond in one hand big as a walnut. He held it up to the light contemplatively. Meanwhile, he sang.

Abramsky saw me, pushed up the glasses onto his head, shook my hand, and introduced me to a man in skin shoes. It was Tomas Saroyan. From *The Teddy Flowers Show*. The missing guest.

"A beauty," Hillel said, looking at the diamond, and sang some more of his ecstatic diddle diddle diddle. Saroyan tried to restrain himself, but I could see the irritation. Saroyan did not become rich waiting around for Jews to sing folk songs and contemplate their art.

"How much longer?"

"I don't know. Could be an hour. A day. A week. This is a big-dollar item. You want I should chop it any old place, lose maybe half? It's your stone, mister."

"It's been almost two weeks."

"Look, mister, go eat. Okay? You'll feel better."

"I'll wait."

"I'll buy you lunch," I said, as the other cutters began filing back from their meal. I like Hillel a lot; his wife sends me fabulous chopped liver, he has great Klezmer records and even though he can see around the sides of people, he's always cheerful; for Hillel Abramsky, religion is better than Prozac.

"I'll bring him back in an hour," I said. "How's the family?"

"Wonderful. The baby comes next week. Maybe in time for the holidays. You'll come to the bris?"

"How do you know it's a boy?"

Hillel shrugged. "I can tell."

"Who are you?" Saroyan said warily.

"Go with him. Go," Hillel Abramsky said like a housewife trying to get rid of vermin.

Outside on the street, more men in beards jingled millions of dollars' worth of diamonds in their pants pockets along with quarters for the phone. With Hillel's help, I had discovered crooks hiding out with the Hasidim. These evangelicals figured if some Russian hood was willing to trade in his chestwig and gold chains for a black hat and long curls, well, even the outward show of faith was a beginning. You could hide out easier in Crown Heights than Miami Beach.

Of this, ethically, Hillel did not approve. Deals on Forty-seventh Street had always been done on trust, by his father, his grandfather, millions in gems traded on a handshake, a whisper. So Hillel helped me. When Tomas Saroyan arrived with a diamond big as a walnut, Hillel figured I could be interested.

"You're a cop," Saroyan said sullenly.

"That's right. And I want to talk about why Gennadi Ustinov was killed on a TV show that you happened to also be on. Maybe other things."

Saroyan's skin loafers must have cost five hundred bucks. Snake, probably.

"Nice shoes," I said. I bought hot dogs from the cart on the corner and handed him one. He held it gingerly like he was used to better.

"I'm in a big hurry. I did not come to New York City to talk about shoes. This man there has been weeks preparing to cut this diamond."

"Relax," I said. "I'm not interested in your diamonds, for the moment, anyway. I don't actually care if you are the expensively shod slimebag you appear to be. All I want is to hear what you saw on Teddy Flowers' show, the night of the shooting, and what, if anything, you know about Gennadi Ustinov. Take me through it. How did you get on the show?"

Saroyan tasted his frank. "A friend in Moscow. English guy, Gavin Crowe. He said I could meet important people. Good for business."

"What kind of business you in?"

"Import export."

"What kind?"

"I help people get things they need."

"You mean you're a personal shopper," I said and bought a cream soda. "You shop for Zeitsev?"

"Excuse me?"

"Never mind." He understood. "Go on."

"I told the police everything I know."

"Tell me everything you know. Tell me something you forgot to tell them."

Saroyan sized me up. He was a fleshy, handsome man, thirty-five, thirty-six, but he had a low forehead where greasy hair grew in curly tufts; he looked like a monkey.

"Cementing international relations is important to me." Suddenly the man oozed diplomacy. "You said you are Cohen?"

I nodded.

"Being Jew, you will understand. I am Saroyan. I am Armenian. I hate Soviet Union which destroyed my people."

"I thought that was the Turks."

"Ustinov was KGB. Someone kills him for revenge." He peered at me. "What can I do for you?"

He would figure that like every cop he met back home, in America all cops were also bent, or could be folded. I let him gamble.

"What have you got?"

He was silent.

I said, "Tell you what. Show me good faith, Armenian to Jew. Show me where you stash your goods."

He twitched like a man shooting craps for high stakes.

"You don't want your visa to run out before my pal Hillel finishes your diamond."

"You know Grand Hyatt Hotel?"

* * *

A half hour later, Tomas Saroyan scuttled out of the hotel. "I have your word?" he said. "I have your word this is between you and me, if I show you this stuff?"

"Sure you have my word. You called Zeitsev, didn't you? Didn't Zeitsev tell you I was his friend?"

Saroyan slid silently into the station wagon, inspecting it with a certain contempt.

We rode in silence. Saroyan reached into the pocket of his Versace blazer and took out a Gucci notebook and a Mont Blanc ballpoint. He started clicking the pen's mechanism. Click click click. Click click click.

"Do you mind? Huh?"

"Belt Parkway," Saroyan said.

"I know how to get to Brooklyn."

I got lost. In the tangle of roads and belts on the way to an area between Brighton Beach and the airport, I ended up in a nature preserve near Jamaica Bay. Some kind of crow or raven swooped down in front of the car and I almost crashed it. Saroyan looked smug and directed me to a garage on a busy street. A couple of guys sat out front and worked on a bucket of Kentucky Fried. One waved at Saroyan. He took me out back where there was a second shed. A half-dead mutt passed for a guard dog.

I gave the dog a piece of candy bar I found in my pocket; it looked grateful. "I hope this is good. I didn't come here to view some sorry-ass chop shop."

"Don't worry," Saroyan said. He was nervous. He was showing me his wares as a trade-off so I wouldn't think too much about his other scams, and I wanted him by the balls in case he knew about the sample trade in radiologicals. But maybe he thought I could be had for a couple Rolexes.

Saroyan unlocked the door. He flipped a light switch. I looked around: It really was Aladdin's fucking cave. Saroyan shopped to order and he bought good. He bought designer labels, gold, diamonds, Rolex, Cartier, Patek.

There were no windows; a powerful air conditioner hummed. Crates were stacked neatly against the wall and there were objects covered with quilted moving blankets. A large Chubb safe stood to one side.

"Show me," I said. Saroyan looked over his shoulder and began pulling away the quilts.

Beneath the blankets there were three Steinway pianos, gleaming ebony grands. Persian rugs were bundled in neat coils. Dozens of top-of-the-line stereos and TVs, Aiwa, Sony, Mitsubishi, stacks of Macintosh PowerBooks, IBM PCs and software, Gameboys and Nintendo. There were crates of china, glass, silver, toys, CD players and discs by the dozen. A whole container of bikes from Specialized stood near the wall. He pulled off more packing blankets and showed me racks of fur coats, neatly bagged in plastic. There were dresses, suits. Armani, Chanel, Donna Karan. And Gucci bags, and Vuitton. On a shelf were cartons of small items by the gross: Calvin T-shirts, Hanes panty hose. He opened the safe and I walked in after him and he showed me boxes of gold jewelry, antique porcelain figurines, loose stones, rubies, emeralds, diamonds.

"Cars?"

"Another place. You want to see?"

"I trust you. All to order?"

"Sure. We are Russian shopping channel, so to speak. We got a lot of these places. L.A. New Orleans. Put in order in Moscow or Petersburg, Mercedes, black, red, silver, new one, vintage, Rolls Royce, Lexus, shop in New York City, ship back via Vladivostok, Odessa, the Baltics. It arrives as good as new. It is new, fully loaded, customized if you want. Antiques also. I got one client giving his kid a 1947 MG for his birthday."

"You keep the stuff here all the time?"

"We move it fast," he said.

"The cops aren't stupid."

"No," Saroyan said. "But cops like shopping also."

"It's been informative," I said.

"You like to do little shopping?" He was an oily prick; I had a vision of Saroyan in striped pants with a carnation in his buttonhole.

"Maybe later." I looked around. "What's that?" I pointed to a small crate by the door.

"Spare parts. You want to see?" He pushed it in my direction. I said no. I had already seen the name. Sometimes you get answers in dull little boxes. Already I was wondering why Saroyan got spare parts for his fancy cars from a dump like Cosmos Auto Supply.

Saroyan was real pissed off when I dropped him at a subway stop and he walked down the steps right onto a wad of gum that stuck to the fancy shoes. Then I called Hillel Abramsky and told him about Saroyan; Hillel said it would be inconvenient for him to return Saroyan's diamond for at least a couple of weeks what with the New Year coming next week and the baby also. Then I went to Brighton Beach.

Cosmos Auto Supply was a front. It was run by Johnny Farone, a skinny, affable Italian with half glasses, a nylon shirt with short sleeves and a club tie; his door was always open was his motto, he said.

The shop was small and dusty; cobwebs in the windows broke up in the light. The weather had turned cool for good, the sun shone, the ocean was blue and silky; it was painfully lovely all day every day.

Car parts in boxes were stacked everywhere. Farone also sold air conditioners and old-fashioned fans that gathered dust on the windowsill along with order books and invoices and cardboard boxes. There were brushes, valves, cranks, pumps. A tire stood against the wall underneath a religious calendar and a plastic crucifix. I had checked Farone out with a guy I know at the Six Two and he said Farone was okay. He was one of the rare non-Russians on the Beach and he depended on the station house for his well-being and sometimes just for company.

Farone offered me espresso and we sat around shooting the breeze. I got around to asking what was new in the way of business.

He shrugged. Business was pretty good. He could export a lot of stuff these days, car parts, air-conditioning units, whatever. "Maybe this interests you?" he said, trying to please. Johnny Farone was the kind of guy who liked doing favors; it put him in the black. He reached into his desk and pulled out a file folder, and from it extracted a greasy Xerox. It was an official letter and it was in Russian. He went to the toilet and I could hear him taking a piss while I looked at it. He came back.

Farone shrugged and said, "Can you read it?" I guess he assumed everyone around here could read some Russian.

I nodded, leaning on the doorjamb while I read it. I read it again. The subway rattled overhead and the beige plastic crucifix on the wall vibrated. The paper was slick and crumpled. Farone folded his hands calmly over his desk. It was an invoice for Red Mercury.

Farone shrugged and said, "What's this stuff? Who knows? I got clients want something, I find something. I got people with stuff to sell, I find clients. You know? The guy comes in, he sick, man. Real sick. I think to myself this here one sick dude, you know? AIDS. He got the AIDS thing. Hair falling out. Teeth gone. Sores on the mouth. He can hardly sit he's running to the bathroom all the time. Sores. He wants to sell me this stuff. You wanna see the video?"

"You videoed this?"

"Sure, always. Help with burglaries. My kid sets it up, why not. I got a check-cashing service. Guy forges social security cards, a video gimme some backup."

He ran the tape: It was Lev.

I said, "You bought the stuff?"

"Yeah, sure. I agreed to buy." Farone laughed. "Sure. Sure. Sure. I did a deal with some Russkis to buy this stuff. I'm a broker, you know. I got deals with people. I'm the middle man. I don't even know what it is. I ask around. Somewhere I heard Saddam bought some, a million bucks for a couple pounds of the stuff. I ask some more. I hear there's guys in the Midwest looking at polymers and lubricants and aerospace technology who want it real bad. They want a sample. Me, I never heard of it. Guy offers me this Red Mercury stuff on spec, I ask around. I say, why not?"

"You ever see the stuff?"

"Nah. That's not my deal."

"Really, I heard you got a sample," I bluffed. "Should I get a warrant?"

"You a cop?"

I nodded.

144

"Hey, I'm a cooperative guy, everyone knows Johnny Farone is friends with the police here."

"Where's the sample?"

"There ain't no sample, honest to God," he said and crossed himself. "You wanna search, go ahead, please be my guest."

I read the piece of greasy paper over and over. Red Mercury.

"Give me that videotape," I said.

He said "Sure" and stuck it in a brown envelope and gave it to me. From the mess on his desk he extracted more paper.

"Look, man, what I want a sample for? You can see the thing right here. Here." He handed over the paper, this one tidy and in English. It was a purchase order from a company in Los Angeles.

"What I want with samples when we already done the deal same day I get the offer, for eighty pounds of the stuff," Farone said. Even low-life tell the truth once in a while and Johnny Farone was telling me at least what he knew.

A few minutes after I left, there was an explosion in an empty lot a few yards from Farone's shop; it blew his windows out into the street and burned a top-floor apartment; no one was home though. That night, at the Coney Island end of Brighton Beach, another fire took the roof off a house; a family of seven was incinerated. The cops attributed this to a faulty space heater. The only reporter who noticed the small squad of discreet decontamination experts out in the middle of the night worked for a Russian language paper, and who the hell cared about that? I never found out if it meant anything. As Lily Hanes said, sometimes things just happen. She was right. It was more than two weeks since Gennadi Ustinov died and I still didn't know why.

But I knew Red Mercury was the trigger. I knew a man with a suitcase was out there, running loose, desperate, cut-off, dying, somewhere in the city. He knew where I was, who I was, he left me packages with stuff in them that fried people, packages with my name on them. I also knew it wasn't local. Nothing's local in the city unless maybe you're talking a couple pizza guys that got shot in Queens. Everything's linked: Chinese hoods running illegals from the old country, Russians manipulating the real estate market, creeps like Lev trading in red hot stuff. This thing wasn't local, it wasn't just Brighton Beach. It started in Moscow. Lev, Ustinov, Red Mercury, the radioactive shit that could kill a million people and fit in a pack of cigarettes. It would end in Moscow. I knew it would end there. I started drinking early that weekend.

Chapter Ten

After i left farone, over the weekend, alone in my loft, I checked all my contacts, my notes, my dossiers, one at a time. The Jewish New Year was starting the beginning of the week, the city shutting down. I retraced my steps. I crossed the city, went back to Brooklyn. No Tolya. No nothing. Roy Pettus, who was in a lousy mood and didn't take my call at first, said he was coming up empty, too, but I couldn't tell how much he was sharing. I tried Maxine, but her husband said she was at her mother's with the kids and I knew he was lying. I hadn't felt this lousy since the year before we left Moscow. There was this thing in the pit of my stomach and I couldn't digest it.

I was going around in circles that ended back in Brighton Beach. I couldn't keep away. I was looking for the creep, for Tolya, for what? I didn't know what.

I hit the bars first, then the cafés and clubs. At the Batumi, I recognized a few faces in the crowd and one of the waiters greeted me by name. Someone offered me a drink; a girl asked me to dance with her. As if I now belonged, they talked to me in Russian; I had become one of them.

At the Rasputin, a fancy new joint that looked over the boardwalk, the women ate French food with their minks on. I ran into Elem Zeitsev there, or maybe he ran into me. He introduced me to a couple of lawyers from Wall Street he was entertaining, and then he took me into a private room. He didn't say he knew what I had been doing; maybe he didn't know. Sipping a Martini straight up with a twist, he asked pleasantly if we could do some business now.

"Have you got what I'm interested in? What we talked about at your uncle's house? Can I count on you now?" I said.

"Yes," he said, "I think we do," and I never knew if he was bluffing, if he could really put his hands on some plutonium, some Red Mercury. "Does that mean you're in, Artie—can I call you Artie? Does that mean you want to join us?"

"Sure," I said, and let him buy me some drinks and introduce me to his wife's cousin, Marina, the blonde. Marina was friendly. She danced with me. We drank together. She told me she liked Billy Joel and sang to me.

Later, I got smashed on the Absolut. I scared the shit out of myself. I was one of them, now. When I stumbled out the door late that night, Zeitsev called out, "Happy New Year, Artie Cohen."

If I was "in" with these hoods, how would I climb out? Who would help me? Who could I trust?

Chapter Eleven

"ME YOU CAN TRUST."

In Dan Guilfoyle's backyard in Sag Harbor, the whoosh of cars from the road was muted; the fog licked the motorboat Dan kept at the little landing dock at the edge of his property. He put his paw on my arm. "I'm sorry I was out of action, Art, darling. Fish were running good."

Dan was pushing seventy and retired, but he was in great shape. Around him and Dinah, I could let go, maybe even catch a night's sleep. After a couple nights drinking in Brighton Beach, I had to get out of town or crack up. And maybe Danny could help.

"Sonny Lippert called looking for you. I said you were shacked up with the brunette in Amagansett."

"Thanks, Danny."

He had been my first boss, he was a brilliant detective, street smart, institutional smart, incorruptible. We sat in his yard. Dan poured cold white wine from one of the North Fork vineyards he owned a piece of.

"I been thinking about you." Dan shifted his weight.

"Yeah?"

"Well, Ustinov gets bumped off, I think of you. You want to take me through it? Don't give me the political rap. Talk homicide to me, okay? From the beginning. How did you hear about Gennadi Ustinov's murder, for instance?"

For an hour or two, maybe longer, I sat in his yard in Sag Harbor and told him everything, from the night Gennadi was shot on TV, and everything that had happened since. He listened quietly and sipped the wine.

"I'm not going back to Moscow, Danny. I'm not, you know. I don't care what."

"Calm down, kiddo." Dan got up and stretched. "You say it's an accident, the logic says it was a hit, the evidence says nada. Zilch. I got to tell you, I'm not sure I buy this nuke business," he said.

"Let's work backward. If the shooter was aiming at someone else, who was it? Who? Who except Ustinov? Zalenko? I seen him on TV, I think. This fellow is crazy. I'm a crazy old guy, but this guy is crazy crazy. Could it be Zalenko? The stripper? They did her in the end, maybe they went for her on the show? But why do it in public, like that? Excuse me, Artie, I gotta go take a piss. Age," he grumbled.

Through the window of the old house I could see Dinah, Dan's wife. In her sixties, she was still stunning: coffee-colored skin, black hair just turning to steel. She had been a nightclub singer once. She came out, set a platter of barbecued shrimp on the table, and said to Dan who reappeared, "See this boy gets some rest." Then she got in her silver Mercedes and went off to visit her sister in Nineveh Beach.

"How do you know about the nuke stuff?" Dan said.

"I got to be friendly with this agent. Roy Pettus? You hear of him?"

"You got a lot of friends, Artie," he smiled, but he added, "Love 'em and leave 'em."

"You mean I'm a whore."

"Come off it."

"You taught me right, Dan. You always said in New York City it's who you know."

"Lemme talk to some pals at Immigration. The system there's shot to hell, but I still got a few lines out. Lemme turn this thing over in my head," Dan said. "You want to stretch your legs before we turn in?"

We walked into the town and down Main Street toward the marina. Dan loved this place where his father was born. Grandfather, too. When he retired, after a stint at Customs and Immigration, he came back and took possession of the place. We passed the Paradise Grill where Dan generally ate breakfast with some other guys, and I remembered once how his oldest son would hover, unsure if he had a right to join these leathery old men, most of them ex-cops.

"Sit down, lad, right there where your father sat when he was a bridegroom and his father before him," he had told his son, Danny Jr., once; it made me jealous, this belonging.

It was fall and night came on faster, but it was still mild and a fog was blowing in, running across the yellow moon that was reflected in water thick and still as wet silk. In New York, I was home. Always had been. Knew it like a village. Out here, over the bridge, in America, I was only a visitor. Dan belonged. I didn't want him to see how lonely I suddenly felt. I made dumb guy talk instead and bought an ice cream cone.

"I love when the girls are still out without coats on," I said idiotically.

Danny wasn't fooled. "You don't have to charm me, Artie."

The big boats were alight. There was a faint sound of music and muffled laughter and ice on glass from the big sleek yacht at the end of the marina. Kids eating waffle cones on the dock stopped to gape at it. On deck a blonde in a sarong gazed down and waved; her fingernails were gold in the night lights.

I wanted to board the big boat and sail away.

"Whose boat?" I said.

"I don't know," Dan said. "Let's get some sleep."

Back at his place, Dan went to bed and I sat out in the garden and read a Tony Hillerman novel. It was terrific stuff—Indians, dead men's teeth, the high desert, ritual healers—not exactly familiar territory for a fat-ass city Jew boy like me, except in the way the clans were connected. Maybe I'd go join a tribe. The Navajo might have me. They didn't like death either. Dances with Cohen, I thought. Dances with Nukes.

I ate some of the shrimp, finished the wine and watched the moon trail through the trees into view. Night birds perched in a dead tree in the next yard and tittered. Crickets screamed. The fog rolled up to the edge of my feet. I felt someone watching me from the water, or maybe I dozed off and dreamed it. I woke up an hour later, still thinking of the big boat in the marina; I couldn't get it out of my mind.

In the morning, while Dinah slept, Dan and I drove up to the beach for a swim in his baby-blue Corvette. It was Dan got me into the vintage car business.

"You're too old for this piece of garbage," I said.

"Screw you," Dan said affectionately, then pulled into the Candy Kitchen for breakfast. Dan hailed a few friends.

Farmers sat at the counter stirring half and half into their coffee, eating fried eggs. Summer was over, but there were still agents who talked deals and local studs who ate pancakes and talked conquests.

A pair of women with cruel faces and handsome bodies arrived wearing Spandex bike shorts; their kids were as silky as the women were hard, made of the stuff that good American money could pull from the gene pool in one generation. The little girls wore jodhpurs, sipping milk with the world-weary panache of Bette Davis consuming gin. Behind the counter, fresh-faced girls with big cheeks served up breakfast, wondering if they would ever make it off Long Island. Class in America, I thought. Great tits, though.

As I turned to look, I saw the old man at a table in the back. He was flipping packets of sugar off the back of his coffee spoon, trying to amuse a little boy beside him. He was tan as fine leather and he wore a black linen shirt, white shorts, loafers, no socks, and a gold watch on a worn leather strap. His head was bent toward the child; the carefully barbered hair was white.

The little boy was beautiful and alert, and he smiled as the packets flipped off the spoon onto the table like tiddly-winks. The man cut up his egg in small squares and tried to cajole the little boy, then ate it himself. I craned my neck for another glimpse. I don't know if he saw me; he was fierce in his attention to the child. "Eat, honey," he seemed to say to the boy. "See how good it is," he added, infinitely patient, putting the egg into his own mouth.

I realized why the big boat had interested me; it was his boat. His boat.

"What's the matter?" It was Dan who was still eating his eggs, but I had already taken the check and was halfway out of the booth, a twenty in my hand.

"Let's go."

As fast as I could, I got out onto the sidewalk and waited for Dan who appeared with a bag of muffins for Dinah.

"Who was he?" Dan said.

"Chaim Brodsky," I said.

Dan was interested. "You know Chaim Brodsky?"

Chapter Twelve

CHAIM BRODSKY LIVED QUIETLY IN A GROVE OF BUTTERFLY TREES NEAR Georgica Pond in East Hampton. The lawn rolled away from his house like a carpet up to the edge of the dunes.

The main house with its porches and porticoes had been built in the nineteenth century by Minard Lafaver. The pool house, where we met, was modern. On the wall was a Matisse, a huge amazing thing you could see from outside or in, the colors glittering and wild in the daytime, subdued and mysterious at night. Everywhere you could hear the ocean rustle against the beach.

Sooner or later, I would have ended up at Brodsky's. I knew I'd have to go the minute I saw him at breakfast. A note was hand delivered to Danny's. Would I come for a swim?

Had he seen me? Was it a coincidence? It didn't matter. He

would know I was around and no one refused his invitations. I don't know why I was reluctant; maybe because he was part of my past.

With me and Brodsky, there is some blood, in a way. My grandmother's younger sister, on my mother's side, had gone to America with her first husband and later married Brodsky. She died a few years after, there were no kids, and Brodsky remarried, but the rare occasions we met, he never let me forget we were family.

"Swim with me, Artyom," Brodsky said when I arrived and we had kissed and I changed. "Swim with me." He removed his robe. It had his monogram embroidered on it: CB. CB were Brodsky's initials. CBM was Brodsky's media group. It had taken me all this time to get it: CB were the initials in Ustinov's diary the day he died.

Chaim Brodsky was seventy-five but he was a rangy powerful man who swam with obsessive regularity in ice-cold water during the summer when it was hot. All afternoon he swam laps. He gestured at the pool and I climbed in after him.

He flicked a button on the blue Fabergé pool clock that measured laps, and began swimming. The numbers on the clock were made of tiny jeweled goldfish, the thing having been made for, but never used by, one of the daughters of the last Czar when swimming was all the rage in Edwardian Petersburg.

Chaim Brodsky swam silently. I swam beside him. He glanced at me, his eyes, through the goggles, as pale and cold as Ustinov's; in this way, they looked alike. After a few laps, he stopped at the shallow end, stood, and talked.

"How is your aunt?" he said. He meant Birdie.

"Birdie is fine," I said.

"And your mother?"

"In her own world."

"Yes, I heard. I'm sorry. She was a beautiful woman, your mother." Something in his voice unnerved me: he said it like a man who had seen my mother naked. Brodsky added, "I knew everyone in Moscow at one time. I knew all the foreigners, of course. I brought books. Films. Do you remember?"

I remembered. "I was only a kid."

The sun shone. There was no sound except the water and the rustle of the butterfly trees and the faintest tumble of a mild surf beyond the green silk grass and pale dunes.

"I hate to leave this, even for a day," Brodsky said mournfully.

"Leave?"

"Moscow. I have to go to Moscow next week."

He sighed and we swam again. He had been doing business with the Russians since Stalin died. His father had been one of the few successful Jews in Kazakhstan, way back, just after the revolution, and when they came to America, they traveled first class from Odessa.

Brodsky had been born and grew up a rich boy on Riverside Drive. After Harvard, he took over his father's business. He had exclusive deals all over the Soviet Union; he knew everyone who mattered on both sides: Brezhnev, Gromyko, Andropov, later Gorby. He knew Harriman, and Armand Hammer was his best friend. I remembered pictures of Brodsky at Nixon's funeral. With Nixon gone, Brodsky owned the franchise, was the man who knew Russia best, although he was modest about it, refusing most offers from presidents of corporations and presidents of countries.

Brodsky was the only man in America who understood how things worked in Russia: the relationships between the old nomenklatura and the new politicians, the Moscow mafias and ethnic clans, the atomic gangsters and capitalists, the KGB and CIA. He knew about the Swiss bank accounts, gold deposits, oil. He was intimate with the network of foreigners in Moscow that had always been secretly powerful and intellectually influential. He knew about wheat and beef and diamonds, and he kept dachas in Nikolina Gora near Moscow and on the Black Sea, or so it was said; when I was a kid, there were always rumors about Chaim Arnoldovich Brodsky.

For a while, he had an apartment on the banks of the Moskva facing Gorky Park; Birdie had taken me there once when I was a child, to shake his hand and see his Chagalls. Brodsky had been the handsomest man I had ever seen; his dark blue cashmere overcoat was tossed casually over a chair and I had nuzzled it—I was maybe nine or ten—and I had never felt anything so soft. I imagined Brodsky and Birdie had been lovers once, a million years before, but maybe it was only a boy's fantasy.

Brodsky's father made money in Russian oil; he made even more in minerals and, later, electronics and satellites. I don't know how much he was worth: billions, though. Then he sold everything and retired to East Hampton.

"Swim," Brodsky ordered gently as I lagged behind. I swam. I could hear a lawnmower in the distance, counterpoint to his soft voice. He still spoke the rich slightly patrician New York English of his boyhood; the voice was urbane but young.

Rumor was Brodsky had retired in order to expand his collections of first editions, to edit Nabokov's letters because they had been friends, and to write his memoirs. Mostly, he said to reporters, he would simply live. He believed in life, he would say, offering the Jewish toast: *"Le Chaim."* It was a marvelous act, all of it. I knew I hadn't come before because I wouldn't want to leave. The real world seemed grubby after Brodsky's.

I could barely keep up with him, slicing through the water. He turned over and did a backstroke, his head always out of the water, the sharp eyes gazing up at the sky but alert, as if he had 360-degree vision. There wasn't an ounce of fat on him. I sucked in my gut and kicked hard. Then he pulled himself up to the ledge of the pool and sat.

"I wish you came to see me more often," he said almost wistfully. "Tell me what you've been up to."

So I asked, as casually as I could, if he knew of a substance called Red Mercury. He kicked the water thoughtfully.

"Red Mercury is one of the last great Soviet secrets. Few know about it. It was a substance of heavy metals and—but the science is not the issue and I'm afraid I'm not awfully good at it. Years ago, when bomb production was down, there was terrible paranoia about the West. A few physicists felt if they invented something brilliant, they would be honored by Stalin and safe from the purges, poor fools. And they did it. They invented a substance so potent, a very small amount could do enormous damage. A few ounces could produce a nuclear explosion. It had critical properties unlike anything else. There are references as far back as 1950.

Brodsky went on. "It was only tested a few times in the Arctic Circle. The fallout was so toxic, the mutations were horrible—and covered up, of course. Stalin asked the scientists if they could, theoretically at least, make another substance just as potent, just as Ivan the Terrible had once asked his architects about St. Basil's. They said, the physicists, because they wanted to please him, yes. He had them executed as enemies of the state."

I was silent.

"If you have encountered Red Mercury, atomic smuggling is out of hand. It's something I know a little about. I worry about this. Did you know that many radioactive isotopes have barely any signature, no fingerprints? The Russians don't keep their books properly, so no one knows what's missing."

He wanted to swim and we swam and when he stopped, he talked some more, about nuclear waste, weapons, about radiological spills and the secret cities in Russia. My view I got from Brighton Beach; Brodsky's was global.

"The Russians will never give it up," Brodsky said. "When warheads are decommissioned, more plutonium becomes available, it's degraded, unstable. They don't care. They see plutonium as a national treasure. They believe we encourage rumors about atomic gangsters in order to cast the Russians as bad boys out of control. To force them to dump their whole program."

Brodsky leaned against the side of the pool and pushed his swim goggles on top of his head. "It will get worse. There will be hijackings, kidnappings, accidental explosions. The whole cast of terrorist activity will change," he said. It was what Roy Pettus had said.

"Who killed Gennadi Mikhailovich, do you think, Artyom? I mean who set it up?" he asked suddenly.

"I don't know."

"It was dreadful for you, I know. For me, too. We were good old friends. I loved him very much." This man was straight as a die, I thought; none of the corruption he had encountered had tarnished him. Maybe all that money kept him clean.

"I'm glad we have met again. I have missed you," he said and I was flattered; I had not met him more than a dozen times in my life.

"You'll come to my party tomorrow, I hope." It was a command.

Chaim Brodsky got out of the pool and onto his feet, allowing me to help him. On the blue tiles of the terrace, I saw a pair of feet like flesh-colored fish. Brodsky gestured to a servant who held out a terry-cloth robe for him, then he pointed to the body that belonged to the fishy feet and said, "Artyom, I'd like to introduce you to my guest Phillip Frye."

Lily Hanes was at the party the next night; she was there with Phillip Frye.

The sky over Brodsky's estate was rich as chocolate and the stars had been sprayed around promiscuously as they often were on island nights in the fall. I took Dinah Guilfoyle with me because I didn't want to go alone; I guess I knew Lily would be there with Frye, and Dinah could still make a spectacular entrance; she wore an old silver Fortuny gown that looked liquid.

Frye gave me a regular guy handshake. He was a tall handsome man with a vividly English face I couldn't read, ruddy, animated, secret, and it reminded me of those evangelicals like Wilberforce in my history books, always agitating against slavery or sheep grazing. Frye was to publish Brodsky's memoirs. He spoke beautifully and told good jokes. Lily laughed at his jokes and Frye kept his arm around her shoulders. I felt jealous and lonely.

Brodsky's place was lit up with lanterns and flares and citronella wands wrapped with lemon-scented yellow flame. Fireflies stacked up over the trees like planes waiting for permission to land and inside the house a famous pianist played Gershwin songs and Russian folk tunes.

There were movie people, a group of Russian dancers, writers. I wouldn't have been surprised to see Sonny Lippert, but maybe he couldn't cadge an invite. Across the lawn I saw Teddy Flowers sucking up to a Hungarian billionaire, and a famous poet sat alone eating lox. I quelled my dread with vodka.

With his handsome French wife, Paulette, Brodsky moved among his guests happily, and food and drinks were served by beautiful young people in black who smiled without effort.

I drank steadily. Dinah kissed me goodnight and said she had ordered a cab and wanted to get back to Dan. I drank some more. There was delicious stuff: great wines and flavored vodkas from a private distillery Brodsky owned. There was caviar from his own fisheries on the Caspian Sea. Ustinov should have been there, it should have been in his honor, a party for his book. But he was dead.

I wandered out onto the lawn where people drifted up toward the dunes through the old oaks and butterfly trees. Lily Hanes sat on an old wicker chair; she was alone. She had had her hair cut off, short as a boy, I'd noticed earlier, and she looked wonderful, but she was quiet. I had liked the noisy, opinionated woman I'd met; something had gone out of her.

"Hi."

"Hi," she said.

"Can I sit?"

I was surprised when she said "Sure."

"Smoke?"

"I quit," she said. "Sort of."

"Great party," I said. Pretty banal. I wanted her a lot. She stretched out her legs, a mile or two of pale gold tanned leg.

"I was surprised to run into Teddy Flowers here."

Lily said, "Don't be. Chaim Brodsky owns Teddy Flowers. And Phil. And me, I guess. In the nicest kind of way, of course. He's pretty benign compared to most of the new media grandees, you know? He reads books. He has taste, at least. They're all here."

"All?"

"His stars. The writers. The ass-lickers. Everyone who has anything to do with Russians. Even a few Russians."

"Did you ever get to see the pages from Ustinov's book?"

"I asked Phil. He wouldn't give them to me. He said there was nothing," she said, but she averted her eyes.

"Can you get them?"

"You'll have to ask Phillip."

"You're still hooked on him, aren't you?"

"Look." She turned toward me, shrugged. She had big shoulders for a girl.

"I'm looking."

"I really don't want to get involved with this story. You get involved, you get hurt."

"Is that why you won't see me?"

"We talked about it at the gym. It was a mistake. You're too good to waste, Artie. Find some nice woman. Have a life."

I ached with desire. But I knew it was over with us. I put my hand on her arm. It was warm. She got up, then leaned over me and kissed me. Like drowning in honey.

"I have to go now," she said. "Phillip will be looking for me."

Brodsky took me aside later and we sat in his study and he asked me to work for him. "Doing what?" I said.

"This and that," he said. As he had described earlier, he said. Help with his proposals. Help with the memoirs. I had the languages. I was family.

"I'm just a cop."

"You're much better than that," he said mildly. "I need your help, Artyom." Ask a man for his help if you want his collusion, my father used to say. "I'd like to know who killed Gennadi Mikhailovich, of course," Brodsky said. "He was a friend. Shall I offer a reward?"

"Will you tell me why your name was in Gennadi Ustinov's diary?"

Brodsky smiled sadly. "Yes, of course. We planned to meet in town that day. As I said, we were great friends."

"May I think about the offer?" I said.

"Of course," he said, his arm briefly around my shoulders. The gesture did not suit him.

"Be well, Artyom. And let me see more of you. I promised your grandmother once to keep an eye on you."

I held out my hand. His eyes hardened and I wondered if he thought I should kiss his hand, but instead he kissed me on the cheeks three times, the Russian way.

"Chaim Arnoldovich?" I spoke Russian. He liked that.

"Yes?"

"You keep a boat in Sag Harbor?"

"Yes."

"What is her name?"

"She is called the *Mercury*. For the god with winged feet." He smiled, the benign smile of a courtly old man. "For the Roman god with winged feet," he said. "The god of commerce and of thieves."

I stayed on. Through the windows of the pool house, I saw a group clustered around Teddy Flowers. They were watching the late news. On the screen, in Africa, people were dying in the biblical brown dust, piles of bodies tossed in pits. Famine. Cholera. Hacked to death. On the walls, the Matisse glowed.

Outside, on Georgica Pond, the other guests ate and drank and laughed. I opted for the laughter while I could, or maybe it was to prove something to Lily, and I chased a very young girl with wet black hair into the grove of butterfly trees where I caught her for a while.

Chapter Thirteen

RICKY TAE WAS DEAD.

I found him on his face on the floor of my loft, one leg twisted under him. I couldn't find a pulse. Like a broken animal he lay there, and I knew they had come for me. A few drawers were overturned, a few books tossed on the floor; whoever had murdered him had barely bothered to make it look like a burglary—the desultory gestures were almost a taunt.

I had come home from the island, leaving Dan working his phone, looking for information about Lev from his pals in Immigration. The Expressway was jammed with overheated cars stinking up the air and by the time I got out of the tunnel, I was wiped. Before I went home, I stopped across the street for some iced coffee. I sat there in the coffee shop for an hour, more maybe, drinking coffee, looking idly at my building. While I was there, drinking the miserable coffee, they killed him.

Ricky had been coy about his plans, I remembered. Some guy he was meeting—the swimmer?

He had my keys. They probably hit Ricky when he came in with my mail or to borrow some music, the way he always does. They caught him by surprise. Caught him, broke him in half, killed him. In my place. I called Hong Kong. I got Dawn in the middle of the night. I handed over the lousy job of telling her parents to Dawn.

Waiting for the ambulance, I found the plastic bag. It stank from rancid fat. Inside was a bloody leg of lamb, the blood and fat congealed in cold white lumps. In the old days the Russian butchers' union supplied a lot of the hitmen and they left a ram's leg for a calling card; this was some half-assed mockery. I knew who had done it.

The EMS people came. They carried Ricky out on a stretcher. I went in the ambulance with him to St. Vincent's. I sat in the same waiting room where I sat the night Gennadi Ustinov died.

A doctor told me he wasn't dead. "It's a miracle."

Ricky wasn't dead. He was in a profound coma—a vegetable, worse than dead—but not dead. They stuck a lot of tubes in his mouth and arms. They wired him up to equipment that let his body imitate life. Nothing could be done about his brain unless he came out of it. Unless he did, Ricky was a cabbage.

It keeps happening. People don't die. Instead, they enter some twilight zone, suspended where I can't get at them. In Israel, my mother sits forgetting herself in her Alzheimer's half life; Gennadi Ustinov went into a coma before I could tell him stuff I needed to tell him. Now Ricky.

A few years ago, Aunt Birdie started writing me how many of her friends in Moscow had had strokes. How these old people now lay, like secondhand fruit—Birdie's phrase—in nursing homes and hospitals where they once locked up dissidents. The land of the nearly dead. I understood why people could prefer Stalin's time to Brezhnev's; at least there was a crude certainty.

It always makes me laugh, those fictional cops who deliver

themselves of pithy certainties about murder and morality, life and death, then go and beat someone up and feel better. It's all horseshit. All of it. Everything is horseshit except being really alive.

Ricky couldn't talk; you couldn't bury him. Where was the creep? Where was Lev? Where was he? Where was Tolya?

I went home and waited for Dawn to call me and tell me when the Taes were coming. I looked around and wondered if the creep had tracked his radioactive garbage in with him, if my place was hot, if it would kill me. I phoned Roy Pettus at home and he told me to get out fast until he could get the place checked out, but I had to wait for Dawn's call.

"I got us on a flight tomorrow morning." Dawn's voice was hollow as she gave me the details.

I took a shower and, wrapped in a towel, I sat on the edge of the toilet and smoked a joint and thought about Ricky. I couldn't stop crying. I think maybe I was crying for myself, too.

I picked the Taes up at JFK the next night. They had gone away sleek and youthful. They came home to New York old. Two tiny shriveled figurines, like broken tin toys someone forgot to turn the key in, they shuffled toward me, lost among the sunburned holiday-makers. They crept through the terminal and into my care and stood, arms by their sides, looking lost while Dawn got the luggage. They leaned on each other helplessly because their son was in the hospital instead of me. When I saw them, I knew I would have to do the thing I was most afraid of; I would have to go to Moscow. I would have to go. I had to know why Rick was beat up, why the creeps were all over me, in my loft, the only real place I ever owned.

"I been chewing it over," Danny said when he called. "I really think it was what it seemed. A mob hit on Ustinov. Then they got lucky because this hitman, this Polack, had some other agenda and everyone took their eye off the ball."

What agenda?

Chapter Fourteen

THERE WERE MAYBE A HUNDRED PICTURES OF HER. A HUNDRED PICTURES stuffed behind the dresser, underneath a loose floorboard, rolled up and placed carefully in cardboard tubes. All of the pictures were of Lily Hanes.

Head shots. Full length pictures. The same picture in some cases, blown up so big every pore showed and Lily's face was distorted, a hideous parody. Some had been drawn inside cartoon bubbles. There were pictures of Lily in fancy underwear, in a fur coat, at the Eiffel Tower, in Red Square. Pictures of Lily as a *Playboy* centerfold, even the *Playboy* typeface. These composites had been exquisitely made, elaborately retouched, lovingly airbrushed, each of them placed in the cardboard tubes or inserted into a clear plastic sleeve. It was a professional job.

"She is a friend?" It was the first time my cousin, Genia, ever showed any interest in me and she held my hand as she pulled out the pictures she had discovered hidden in the room she rented out to transients. She had not rented it again and only when she got ready to make some repairs had she discovered the cache of pictures. Scared, she had called me.

I said, "The last one you rented to was sick?"

She nodded.

I showed her the picture of Lev. "He was the one who beat you?"

"Yes."

Lev had been aiming at Lily Hanes when he shot Ustinov. Somehow, Lev knew Lily Hanes. Had known her. He had planned to kill Lily and he had missed.

Gennadi Ustinov had died accidentally, hit by a bullet intended for someone else like those that cut down kids in New York every night, by chance. Lev had been telling Tolya the truth.

I got hold of Roy Pettus. He got his men to take the pictures away. I slept in Genia's front room that night because her father was away and she was frightened. Before dawn, someone banged on her door. It was one of Pettus' men.

The agent said, "Come with me, please." He was young and he looked terrified.

In the street, I grabbed a gun from my car, then the agent—I never got his name—climbed in a van that was waiting. I got in with him.

The sun was just coming up and the streets were empty. It was Yom Kippur and everyone was home, sleeping or praying or just taking it easy. On this Day of Atonement, in Brooklyn, it was cool, silent, and beautiful. The ocean air smelled clean, salty. The young agent pulled up in front of a neat house on a side street in Sheepshead Bay. The fishing boats were just visible and their banners fluttered.

KATYA'S KENNELS read the sign outside the house. I recognized the name: It belonged to Zeitsev's wife, the dog breeder with the unpretty face. The lawn was green and trim. Pink geraniums grew in a window box. Painted wooden cut-outs of dogs and cats decorated the front door. Roy Pettus was waiting.

There was the low babble of voices, the distant slap of the ocean, and the fishing banners in the breeze, but nothing else. A few of Pettus' men worked silently around the house. They were wearing hot suits. Silently, Roy handed me a mask. I put it on. We walked across the lawn; it was wet from the dew. I could feel the pulse in my neck. My mouth was dry.

"I want you to see. I want you to look. You can't go in," Pettus said and pointed to a ladder set up underneath a window.

"You went in."

"That's different."

"I'm going in," I said.

"Two minutes. Two minutes, detective, that's all. Give him a suit and take him in," he called to one of the men in protective gear.

Inside the little house was a scene straight from hell.

All I could think of was a newsreel I once saw about the effects of radiation on pigs. Pigs. Pink pigs.

I remembered that. I remembered the newsreel. Seven hundred pink pigs had been wrapped in silvery stuff, like tinfoil, and chained inside pens the shape of mailboxes. The pigs couldn't move inside the pens; the pigs filled up the pens, and they were chained inside and the boxes were locked and left out on the sand a few yards from ground zero somewhere in Nevada.

After the bomb went off and the mushroom cloud went up, the pigs kept squealing. They seemed to have been fried alive but they squealed; it was all you could hear: the deathlike quiet of the moment after the bomb and in it, the shrill, endless, helpless squealing of seven hundred pigs.

In the kennels was the same eerie noise of helpless animals baying for life. The dogs in the cages were dead and dying. There was fur on the steel bars where they had tried to ram themselves free. There were teeth on the floor, and bone. Here and there were the charred remains of little animals. A cat screamed somewhere, then ran into view, its skin hanging off its backbone. You could see its skeleton like X-rays.

Pettus had to drag me away. We stood on the pavement and he yanked off his hood.

"What was it?"

"We think it was a very small device. A small amount of fertilizer, some chemicals. A homemade bomb. It didn't go off."

"What killed them?"

"I don't know. Something that was inserted in the weapon leaked. Something that would have turned it into a crude nuclear device. Something toxic enough to do this even without the explosion. It could be anything, but I'd put money on cesium. Soluble salts maybe. Add water and stir."

"How come it didn't go off?"

"Accident. A screw-up. Luck. Luck," he snarled this and glanced at the building.

The first person in on the dawn shift was in the hospital now, Pettus said. When she arrived and opened the door she didn't know what she was seeing. She took a deep breath; it made her sicker. The night man was already lying in his own vomit. He was dead.

It was a message from the creep. From Lev. Up yours, it said.

Up yours to the mafia that had cut him loose and abandoned him. To the authorities. To me.

"Everyone out," I heard Pettus shout from the lawn. I stripped off the protective gear.

"Your apartment is okay, though, detective. I got one of the men to give it a thorough going-over. The Geiger counter didn't even register."

One of Pettus' men had a cellular phone and I grabbed it and called Zeitsev. He was cool. He knew nothing.

"He got in touch. We threw him out. I told him 'What do we want with samples of this shit? We are legitimate businessmen.' You've seen what he did to my wife's business? You've seen this?" There was cold rage in his voice. He hung up. I felt a hand on my shoulder.

"If the bomb went off?" I asked Roy Pettus.

He said, "It would have contaminated the whole block. Maybe more. The copycats would have a field day."

"He's here, isn't he?"

"Yeah," Pettus said. "He's close. I can smell him."

When we found him on the beach, Lev was bleeding badly, trying to drag himself under the boardwalk as if it offered protection. He tried to stumble to his feet, then fell over. He performed this act as if it were a ritual, over and over. Sand got in his mouth and he tried to wipe it out; it was full of blood.

Blood covered his jacket, the plaid shirt, his pants, his hands. Tufts of fine blond hair stuck out of the skull-like head and his cheeks were sucked in like an old man's; he had no teeth left.

"Where's the shit?" I said in Russian. "Where is it?"

"I have it," a voice said behind me, and I turned and there was Tolya Sverdloff, holding the two suitcases in his hands like a porter. There was blood on his leather coat and it blew open in the brisk wind driving in off the ocean.

Pettus said, "For Chrissake, put them down. Is this Sverdloff?" he asked me.

"Where the hell did you go?" I yelled.

Sverdloff gestured at Lev. "I had to get the suitcases."

165

"I know about your call sign. Red Mercury. What the fuck does it mean?"

"I called myself the nuclear DJ. It was my joke. A long time ago."

"A joke?"

"Yes, a joke. That was how we lived, by jokes. You forgot."

Lev stumbled blindly around, tripping on garbage piled up under the boardwalk.

This man had killed Gennadi Ustinov. Olga Gross, the stripper. The old man in Penn Station. He had come after me and Lily. Ricky was in a coma at St. Vincent's because of him. He left a trail a mile wide. He looked pathetic, though, incapable of so much violence, but what did I expect? Did I want him to shout "Top of the world" like Cagney in *White Heat*?

Instead, Lev stumbled toward me. He tried to butt me with his head. He fell flat on his face.

Roy Pettus grabbed my arm.

"Let me," I said.

"I want him. I want him to talk to me. I want to know the rest of the story. Ask him."

I asked him in Russian but he only snarled and tried to crawl away. I recognized in him boys I went to school with, Russian boys with stringy blond hair and high cheekbones who lived in communal apartments that stank; we despised them because their parents were peasants. They had grandmothers who kept icons, who silently recited the ancient liturgy: Beat the Jews. Beat the Jews. Beat the Jews.

I looked at Lev. His people were the anti-Semites and drunks; they had been the Party faithful once; now they were nationalists, they were Leonid Zalenko's fervent followers.

"What about Lily? What about Lily Hanes? How come you had her pictures in that room you rented at my cousin's house, why Lily?" I was yelling in Russian but he only grunted—like the pigs dying in the newsreel.

Lev tried to get up. Come on, I thought. Get up. Come after me. I want to kill you. Give me an excuse. The adrenaline pumped. I moved fast. I had my gun out.

I shouted, "You tried to kill Ricky, you came into my home," but Lev, the monster, shook his head. Tolya yelled, "When was Ricky attacked?" and I told him

"He's telling the truth," Tolya said, but I didn't want to hear.

Roy Pettus reached for my gun. "Don't do it, detective."

I heard the sirens scream.

With an expression of hatred like I'd never seen on any other human being, with mewling noises like the dying cats, like the pigs chained to their pens, with the noise coming out of his mouth with the blood and saliva, somehow, Lev lunged for Tolya and the cases. He tried to get them, to grab them, the cases he had carried halfway around the world, that were killing him, that he couldn't let go of, couldn't give up. He grabbed at them as if for his own death.

I don't know if I shot him because he went for Tolya, out of pity because he was pathetic and I had power, or because of what he did and who he was. I don't know if I killed him because I'd have to go back to Moscow. Dread drenched me with cold sweat and I shot him. Because of Moscow. He pulled at my jacket, dragging me down, then he fell over, and lay there while the sand turned red under him. It was over.

A special squad took the suitcases away and Tolya said quietly to me in Russian, "He was telling the truth, you know, about your friend, about your friend Ricky. It wasn't him in your loft. It wasn't Lev."

"How do you know?"

"I know because I was with him. I was with him all the time, trying to get him to give me the shit. It wasn't him."

Cops swarmed over the beach now. Was it true? Was that why Roy Pettus' men couldn't find any trace of radioactivity in my loft? If it was true, then who beat Ricky up? Who came for me? Who?

I said, "Is this also a joke?"

"Come to Moscow," Tolya said. "I'll make you remember."

Part Three

MOSCOW

Chapter One

At Sheremetyevo airport, on the other side of the barrier, Tolya was waiting, wrapped in his leather coat. He stood at the back of the crowd that was packed in solid against the barrier and he towered over it.

I had slept most of the trip. As I made my way through customs, I felt like someone had hit me over the head. Up close, in the greenish lights of the terminal, Tolya looked somehow older than when I remembered, older than when I saw him ten days earlier in Brighton Beach.

"I'm here to take you home," he said. I wanted to run away.

It felt freakishly warm that morning in the countryside. Thirty miles from Moscow, the woods crackled with the sound of Russians picking mushrooms, or maybe it was my imagination. Everything came back with those sounds, the crisp snap of leaves, the shouts of delirium over a good mushroom crop, the mournful voices of the elderly celebrating the sadness of the season. Soon there would be weeping. I didn't know whether to laugh or cry.

At the edge of a stand of slim pale birch trees, at a bend in the river, a woman in a white bathing suit stood pensively, up to her knees in the water, smoking a cigarette. She had dark hair cropped very short. The trees made a filter for the light that fell on her bare tanned skin like a lace dress. For a moment there was no other sound except the noises from the woods and music from a radio in a café on the narrow beach. It was playing "American Pie."

"Svet! Svet! It's me. Tol."

Tolya Sverdloff's voice boomed from behind me, and he rolled down the bank to the river like a kid or a dog. The girl in the river looked up, burst into a smile and ran toward him, jumped in his arms, and hugged him. She was a big, soft girl, but he carried her easily up the hill and held her toward me as if she were a gift. He took off his jacket and wrapped her in it. "You're crazy to be swimming this time of year."

"Put me down," she said in Russian, laughing.

"I'm sorry," he said and put her gently on her bare feet on a pile of leaves. She had mud on her ankles, like brown socks. I remembered how the sand on the beach in Nikolina Gora was deceptive, how it just sat on top of the mud so you got brown socks when you walked in it. I'd had sand in my shoes when I watched Lev die on Brighton Beach. When I killed him.

"I'm so glad you're here." Her eyes were shining with pleasure.

"I saw her only yesterday. She gets carried away," Tolya said to me. "This is my cousin Svetlana Orlova. We sometimes call her Kitty."

"For the character in *Anna Karenina*?" I asked inanely.

"No, for *Gunsmoke*." Her English was good; I realized she thought I was American.

"When we were children," said Tolya, holding her hand, joining her game, "we got bootleg westerns. We used to act out western movies here in the country. I was always Jesse James. Svet was always Miss Kitty."

All the time Tolya was talking I could feel my heart racing. He turned to me. "And this is my friend Artemy. His western name is Artie."

Svetlana looked straight at me. She held out her hand and I fell in love with her.

Chapter Two

"NOT MY CUP OF TEA, DARLING," BIRDIE SAID, LETTING ME IN THE DOOR, waving a paperback book at me. "Not like that Arthur Hailey," she added with a melodramatic little sigh. "Or that clever Stephen King. Such a smart boy."

Birdie Golden smoothed the pages of her book twice, then replaced it in its regular spot in the glass-fronted bookcase that she had brought with her to Moscow more than sixty years ago. Her novels were meticulously lined up, her name written in the flyleaf of each one in the flowing cursive taught by the New York public schools a long time ago.

Tolya had dropped me off and I found my aunt in the same apartment on the outskirts of Moscow where she always lived. She was sitting at her bridge table in the window, one leg under her like a teenager. The front door was open; she was expecting me, and she got up and kissed me briskly as if I had only walked out that morning instead of a quarter century ago.

"Birdie knows the value of a good book," she always said, and she was no snob, for almost no one wrote a better tale than that Arthur Hailey, Birdie said. Of course she knew it was rubbish, not literature at all, but such a good tale.

"A good yarn, am I right? You always loved that word when I was teaching you English. A good yarn, you would say, but is it woolly? Sit," she added. "On the good chair. It's not cold in here? It's cold? Am I wrong? You got big, Artyom."

She went into the kitchen and fussed with a teapot.

"Your English is good." She was brisk. "I taught you well. Am I right?"

Birdie taught me English with a New York accent from the time I was five or six. She "walked" me around the city, reading to me from Alfred Kazin's *Walker in the City* and Gorki's *Journals*. Later there was Walt Whitman, Stephen Crane, Washington Irving. We admired Thomas Paine and she made me read Fenimore Cooper and Poe, Henry James and Melville, Lincoln Steffens and O. Henry and Edith Wharton. We worked our way through Dos Passos and Hart Crane, Clifford Odets and Irwin Shaw. We visited Harlem with James Baldwin and Long Island with Fitzgerald. What the books must have cost Birdie in favors I never knew, but she made me love New York long before I got there.

"You'll have cake." It was a command. I could see she was not ready to discuss Gennadi Ustinov. There was too much pain in it for her; they had been friends for a long time. When things were bad, he helped her out.

"I'd love cake."

Through a curtain, I saw the tiny kitchen was jammed with things I'd sent and she hoarded: boxes of cookies, jars of coffee, packages of support hose, a salami, chocolate, aspirin, and cheese, all piled on a shelf in promiscuous disarray. Waiting for the kettle to boil, she held up to the light a box of fancy soap I got at the duty-free. She sniffed it, inspecting the legend on the box from a half-remembered place, trying to decode the meaning. She came back from the kitchen with a tray of cake, pickled eggplant, cookies, bread and butter, and tea.

She was unchanged, except for the shrunken bones and wrinkled skin that hung on them, loose, like an old slipcover. She was as opinionated as ever, and just as alert. I noticed she used terms of endearment more often, though, but maybe she just felt it was an old woman's only way to seduce. Birdie had never been a huggy woman, but age had mellowed her a little. She now sprinkled her talk with Yiddish phrases as if her own childhood had reclaimed her.

"Sit. There, on the good chair, sweetheart, by the window," she said again, pointing at the folding chair that belonged to her bridge set, her legacy. "We brought our furniture. We planned to stay."

Out the window, carefully patched with newspaper, the raw ground around Birdie's apartment house was visible. The buildings stuck up like rotten teeth from muddy gums. Directly below her apartment was a state store.

Birdie came and stood next to me, leaning hard on my arm.

"Every day they come. Every day they wait in line. You know what I think? They wait from habit. From habit. And for leftovers that go cheap. You know what? I went in the shop first time in two years and I saw things I never saw since I was a girl. Pork roasts. Chickens with flesh on the bone. The old ladies come to stare at things they will never eat before the worms eat them. One old lady hit the shopkeeper with her handbag. You know what happens if he should sell you for less?"

"Tell me."

"Don't humor me. He finds himself hanging on a meat hook in his icebox. Sooner or later. The mafia takes care of these things. Mafia. Some mafia, am I right?"

Birdie returned to her chair and I sat opposite her. "Can I smoke?"

She was irritated. "No," she said.

174

"The mafia! This is all anyone talks about these days. This is perfect, here in the capital of moaning and whining, finger-pointing, blame-laying. There is no discipline. No respect," she muttered. "Birdie is pretty disgusted, you know? The mafia. You don't like your lot, you should improve it, not blame it on the mob," she added.

"From mafia, of course, I knew the real thing," she said, drifting back in time to her childhood when, as a little girl in the lovely big house in Flatbush, she had met real mafia gentlemen in alpaca coats and Homburg hats. They tipped their hats to her mother and brought her gifts of barley sugar lollipops in the shapes of flowers and animals that came all the way from Italy. Birdie's father was a top lawyer who knew men around town, and in this way she encountered Lucky Luciano and Bugsy Siegel when they came to call. This was real mafia.

I listened and Birdie rambled and I wasn't sure she understood that I had been away at all. There was a noise like a cup rattling on a saucer when she talked; she had succumbed to false teeth and they fit badly. Birdie was so proud of her teeth in the old days. "You know how I earned money to come to Moscow?" she used to say. "Milk. I had marvelous teeth. In New York City, I posed for milk advertisements."

Birdie sat and drank tea and talked. It was bad times, she said, but if bad times meant you could no longer afford to get your shoes heeled, if you had any pride left you did not go on the street to sell them. You stayed home. If you were on a fixed rouble pension, you sat home and watched the new millionaires on television.

She, Birdie, always had a little something put away, she told me. After sixty years in Moscow she was still Abe Golden's daughter and she never went completely without. She picked up a photograph in a painted wood frame and held it to the murky light. In it I saw Birdie Golden, aged twenty-two, wearing a summer dress and white leather sandals, standing in Red Square. Birdie had arrived with two Vuitton steamer trunks to join the revolution. Abe Golden's daughter traveled first class.

Birdie Golden would go first class again, she said. She often thought about herself in the third person, particularly when she

175

was trying to work out her next move. In the mirror over the glass-fronted bookcase she sometimes caught a glimpse of herself and was startled, she confided to me. Younger people never understood that you didn't get to feeling old; you were just yourself, and if you were Birdie, you were always twenty-two, always ready to take on the world, ugly but sexy. The mirror held only an old woman, thin hair in an untidy bun, gray eyes thick with cataracts. "Enough with the self-pity," she said half to herself.

"Help me with this, Artie darling, please." She knelt beside the bookcase where the paperback novels were lined up in order of her preference—the Arthur Haileys, the Ross MacDonalds, the Robert B. Parkers—she was crazy about that detective Spenser with all his recipes and his lovely girlfriend—and she felt along the back until her fingers stumbled on a hidden latch. She pushed it and a panel gave way. She extracted several notebooks, set them aside, and took out a slim photograph album. Birdie put it on the cream-colored leather top of the famous bridge table and opened it.

"Can I smoke?" I said.

"You asked me already. You think that I am senile? No, you cannot. It's bad for you. For me also, am I wrong?"

Birdie opened the album. Inside, the photographs were covered in tissue paper: my mother in a gypsy costume, smiling broadly; my father as a handsome man in his thirties with other handsome men, one in a rakish beret, the other with a cigar: Che Guevara; Fidel. His friends. Idols of my childhood. A third showed him winking at the camera, laughing, his arm around a comrade who was laughing too, both boys standing on the banks of the Moscow River, the way Tolya and I had stood there this morning, these two dashing in bathing suits.

"Diplomatic Beach Number Three," she said. "I knew they met foreign girls there. I got them condoms. Your grandmother was furious."

The other boy was Gennadi Ustinov.

There were more: me in my school outfit looking dull and idiotic. Me in my car in New York, a picture I'd sent her when I first arrived. My mother on her wedding day in a stylish suit and a little hat; a cracked formal portrait of Birdie's parents taken in a studio in Minsk before they left for America at the end of the last century.

There were pictures of young Comintern workers on bicycles, on picnics, in Red Square, waving breezily, smiling merrily. Saucy girls in summer dresses laughed at the camera. Boys posed at jaunty angles with their bikes. These were Birdie's comrades.

"All dead now," Birdie said sharply.

"How is Bela Nikolayovich?" I asked, inquiring after the last of Birdie's beaux, a courtly Hungarian diplomat who had become a Maoist briefly in the sixties, then given it all up to practice Zen Buddhism in a monastery outside Moscow that stank of cats.

"Dead. Everyone's dead. His best time was the war when he felt it was virtuous to work for the intelligence service. My eyes can see one hundred eighty degrees, Nicky would say. But he's dead. So is everyone else. Or gaga. You know what I hate, Artyom? Stupid old people." Birdie shrugged.

"It was not for this we came." She gestured at the patched window, at the deputies on television spewing venom at one another. At the podium, one man swayed. "A drunk. All drunks. We were for order. For discipline. We came to stay." Birdie was still committed, a true believer.

I had heard the story but it was Birdie's great story and I settled in to listen. Birdie was unwilling to cast herself among the forlorn, although the little sideshow in which she figured was one of the saddest in the history of this sonofabitch country. Birdie was among the foreigners who, enamored of the great socialist enterprise, went to the Soviet Union in the late 1920s and early 1930s. Later on there were the spies—the Philbys and Blakes—who ended up in Moscow, but they were professionals who had run out of road. "We came to stay," she always said.

Birdie's generation went to the revolution with their bridge tables, their Singer sewing machines, and their books. "We went because we believed," she said. The equality of man, the dignity of labor, with a kind of ingenuous fervor they believed. Most were urban intellectuals who didn't know a tractor from a tank; Birdie herself attended tractor driving school in Alexandrov, although she had come via Bremen, with a pocket full of her father's dollars. For a time, she sewed workers' clothing in a commune populated by western true believers.

"The early thirties was a time of no cynics," said Birdie, launching herself into her favorite tale while I ate more cake and she nodded approval. "The only cynic was Stalin. You want me to tell you who killed whom?"

"You told me," I said, and she grunted.

Birdie worked as a typist at the Comintern. Lenin's instrument for world revolution pulled in kids like Birdie who sat in the building next to the Bolshoi Theater in their good American sandals and plotted the overthrow of capitalism. Recruits like Birdie Golden read foreign papers, listened to the BBC World Service. "We took the pulse." She removed her eyeglasses, voice brisk with the undiminished ring of New York City.

For Birdie, solidarity was sexy, the classless society rang with poetry. Free love was in the air, and folk music. It was an enticing culture. I thought of Lily Hanes and her parents who were believers.

"I knew them all," Birdie said, recalling the leaders of her youth. Whatever horrors they might have perpetrated, they had been handsome men in exciting times. Birdie used to claim she also once dated Paul Robeson, which always made us laugh. "They were all poets."

"Chairman Mao was a poet, too."

"A mouth like your mother, you've got." Birdie winked as if I had passed some test.

Birdie had given away her money to the revolution and her husband, Guram, a Georgian, a Red Army officer and a very handsome man. For Guram and their boy, and for the cause, Birdie, like the others, took Soviet citizenship. When the purges began, these hybrid creatures were doubly vulnerable to Stalin's obsessive xenophobia. To their own embassies, they were now foreigners. No one cared.

In 1937, Birdie's husband, who was my mother's uncle by a previous marriage, was arrested; he had an American wife and was, therefore, labeled an "Enemy of Nations". He spent eighteen years in the labor camps. In 1939, Birdie, the wife of an "Enemy of Nations", was also arrested. Stefan, the child, was dumped in an orphanage for the "Children of Enemies of Nations".

From fear, Stefan quit speaking English. Speaking English meant you were a spy. When he was nineteen, he drowned. My father said it was suicide. My mother told me it was murder. Guram died from it.

"He had a broken heart," Birdie said as if it were a disease, like cancer. "Everyone I knew went to ground. They stopped speaking English because it could kill you. They forgot who they were. They spoke in whispers."

Not Birdie. Birdie was Birdie. She got out of the camp. She holed up in a Moscow apartment. The war came and went. Stalin died. Joe McCarthy died. To Birdie they were the same person.

Birdie's rebellion was to teach English privately to as many kids as wanted to learn; she gave us all real passion for the language, for America, for New York. We were ripe for it. We were little kids when we saw grown-ups weep for the beautiful dead young President, John Kennedy. America was the land of the free, the home of the brave and Elvis. Everyone knew that.

Now, in the apartment where I spent so much time, I remembered it all; I could retell Birdie's tales like a liturgy. It was who I was.

Birdie took my hand. Hers was as dry as snakeskin.

"What do I believe these days, you are asking yourself, eh? You think I am like these pathetic creatures who first believe all the bullshit then nothing? This woman Doreen, you remember her, the Englishwoman with the beautiful skin? She spent the war in a room without windows or mirrors. For some years she slept. Birdie does not sleep. Birdie is not pathetic." She spoke softly. "Birdie does not weep for Stalin or Gorbachev who spoke peasant's Russian or Yeltsin, or herself. Stalin murdered the Soviet way of thinking. Ours was not to reason why. Ours was just to do or die. Now I reason. Birdie Golden will die a reasonable woman. You want more? You like my stories? Soon I will be dead, my stories over."

"Are there stories about Gennadi Mikhailovich Ustinov? You never told me stories about Uncle Gennadi."

"You mean you want to know if he betrayed your father."

Birdie showed me a photograph of my father and Ustinov in their army uniforms.

"Poor bastards having to do army time, especially back then." I thought of my own miserable days in the Israeli forces.

"They loved it, you idiot," Birdie snapped. "They could play soldiers. They wanted to be heroes. It was the late fifties, early sixties, it was patriotic. They were officer class, not conscripts. They loved it."

I made a face.

"What do you think your father was?" Birdie said.

I drank my tea.

"He was KGB. He chose it. He loved it. Both of them, you understand? It was in the blood. You're just like your mother," Birdie said. "She was noisy and unrealistic. Did you know she had been a fine journalist? But she balked at doing what you had to do, she could not decline politely while paying lip service to the possibility of cooperation. She had a mouth on her. I loved her for that. She made a lot of trouble for your father, but he loved her anyway. At least he did that."

"What?"

"What? You thought he was a saint? He was KGB. So was Gennadi. They did things," she said.

I didn't ask, but Birdie didn't let me off the hook.

"Did Gennadi betray your father? Did he report what your mother said, her jokes, her anger at the system, her efforts to get information to her foreign friends? I don't know. Gennadi was in love with her, of course."

I guess I had always known.

"He was in love with her before your father, and Gennadi had a way of talking, you remember? He could charm the birds off the trees. But your mother liked your father better."

"I see."

"Oh don't be a baby. He didn't betray your father because of that. If he did it, he did it because he believed in the system. He was a handsome man, Gennadi was. And he always came to see me on my birthday, every year." Birdie lit up.

"He loved you, Artyom. When you would not see him, he was

180

badly hurt. In the end, he knew too much about all this." Birdie waved her hand—she meant Moscow, Russia, life. "He knew almost as much as Birdie." She was drifting. "You saw him in New York?"

"I didn't see him."

"You got my fudge?"

"I ate it all."

"I want you to help me, Artyom."

In my whole life, I never heard Birdie ask for anything. It had been a legend. "If Birdie ever needs something you will have to guess what it is," my mother said once. "She will never ask. She has pride a foot thick."

"What do you need? What can I do for you?"

"You're married, Artyom darling?"

"Don't be a Jewish mother. I was married. Once."

"Once? For five minutes when you were eighteen you were married. And what happened? You fooled around and she left you. Schmuck! That Eviva was a little big in the ass, maybe, but for an Israeli, she was not bad." She fastened the rheum-clotted bird's eyes on me.

"I was bad." I grinned. "I was very, very young."

"Marry. You'll live longer."

"Tell me what do you need."

"Tell me who killed Gennadi Mikhailovich."

I told her about Lev and the hit, and the mafia, and she made a face.

"Not that crap. Who set it up? Who sent the assassin?"

"It was an accident."

"Don't be silly." Like me, she couldn't bear that his death was random, meaningless.

"I'm tired now." Birdie closed her eyes. "But you can have a smoke before you go." She paused to let the drama build. "So. So guess who I saw?"

She had grown old after all. She changed the subject without noticing. She had my hand in hers and held on tight.

"Who, darling?"

"Don't darling me. Don't give me that look. But I'll tell you who I saw," she taunted.

"Who?"

"Chaim Brodsky," she said, triumphant. "Suddenly after all these years, Chaim calls up Birdie. When was it? A few months ago. So. He wants to visit. To schmooze, he says. For old times' sake. Sure, and the Pope is Jewish. I am high-handed: 'Excuse me, Chaim Arnoldovich, you are a famous man so I owe you some respect, but I am some years older, so you will have to come to Birdie. I don't go out.' 'I'll send a car,' Chaim says. 'You'll come to the Metropole to dine with me.' A car he sends. Some car! He says it's a Mercedes Benz car. More like a hearse, and German yet."

"Can I ask you something, Aunt Birdie?"

"Did I ever say no? Did I ever lie to you? You asked me everything. I told you. What?"

"Did you ever sleep with Chaim Brodsky?"

She made a face, then burst out laughing. "Well, I taught you to ask questions, didn't I? Once. One weekend."

"You loved him?"

Birdie fussed with her photograph album and blushed.

"What did he want?"

"My notebooks."

"What notebooks?"

"Notebooks, notebooks. I keep notebooks. Birdie kept notebooks, thirty, maybe forty years. How Chaim knows? Gossip. Rumor. The usual. Everybody knows Birdie writes things down. Only Chaim is smart enough to know this is worth something. Information. Always worth something in this cockamamie country. Chaim knows better than anyone; he's all over the place, buying stuff, newspapers, TV, those satellites. Oh, he never uses his name; Mr. Chaim Brodsky is retired, a diplomat, the Mr. Knows-it-all about Russia. But I know it all." She sipped some tea.

"I knew people, I wrote things down. Some years there was nothing much to do. During the war. During purges. So Birdie stays home, keeps quiet, and writes in her notebooks. Who notices what an ugly old woman is doing, right?"

"What kind of things?"

"You want more cake? It's all right? Go on, finish the last little piece."

"Thank you." I ate the little piece of cake.

Without my noticing, it had grown dark. Stingy yellow lights flared on in the apartment buildings on the other side of the raw courtyard. I shut the homemade curtains for Birdie and switched on a lamp. In the pool of light I saw how old she was after all. I reached for my bag.

"A little schnapps?"

"Why not."

I poured some Scotch from the duty-free bottle I'd brought into the teacups.

She said, "What kind of things? All kind. Who I met. Who I saw. I wrote down what I knew. Politics. Money. Who is sleeping with whom. Andropov's socks. Did you know he wore silk socks? Paul Robeson. What a voice!"

"Did you give Brodsky the notebooks?"

"You think I'm meshugga? Of course not. I wouldn't give Chaim Brodsky a Band-Aid if he slid down a fifty-foot razor blade into a pool of iodine, so to speak. The notebooks are for you. I want a promise you will take care of them, when I go." She smiled like an old cat. "When I go. Which is soon, but not yet."

"Of course. I promise. Aunt Birdie?"

"This whiskey is very nice, darling. What?"

"Did you ever hear of something named Red Mercury?"

Birdie chuckled. "Oi from the Red Mercury. Suddenly everybody is after it. This is all I hear from foreigners, people writing books, making movies. So much talk, so much chatter. Of course I heard. It's for nuclear weapons. But these reporters, you know what I tell them?"

"What?"

"I tell them I got connections. I can get some Red Mercury. Maybe. They even offer me money." Birdie wept with laughter.

"Can you?"

From the next apartment came the sound of anger. A kid cried. A cat screamed. Birdie rubbed her forehead wearily.

"Why not sell the notebooks to Chaim? He's frigging loaded, excuse me."

"It's all right. I don't want Chaim's money. You think Chaim is a great man? Okay. But he has been friends with bad men. Men who busted unions. Who stole poor people's pensions. Men who bombed innocent babies in Cambodia. Vietnam. He was friends with Henry Kissinger, Margaret Thatcher, even with Richard Nixon. He is friends with bad men now. But I'm tired," she said, and I could see it depressed her talking about a man she once loved who had abused the ideals she lived for.

"I'm tired."

"Should I take you back to America with me, Aunt Birdie? I could fix it."

"What would I do in America?" she said sternly. "This is my place. I'm just tired."

"What else do you need?"

"I need to rest now is all. Come tomorrow."

"Can I bring someone?"

"A girl?"

"A girl."

"She's pretty?"

"Very."

"Then come with your girl, Artyom. Come Wednesday. I can have my hair done Wednesday."

When I kissed her, I felt her bones, thin and brittle as cheap chopsticks. I picked up my suitcase.

"How bad are these other friends of Brodsky's?"

She looked at me. "Bad enough to try to kill me."

Chapter Three

FROM THE TIME I HAD LEFT BIRDIE'S UNTIL I GOT TO THE HOTEL WHERE Tolya fixed me a deal, someone followed me. Maybe ghosts. Maybe spooks. I sat in a cab in a daze, smelling the fumes from the cars, from Moscow itself, watching the back of the driver's head. He had long hair.

Was Birdie right? Was Chaim Brodsky a bad man? Had I been

so flattered by him I didn't see it? He had not told me he had seen her in Moscow, but so what?

I didn't believe Birdie. She was old. She lived in the past. She was angry because a man she once loved had been friends with Richard Nixon and because her world had disappeared.

Who could blame her?

This Moscow was an alien place to me; for Birdie it would have been a living death. There were billboards and neon, ads for Coke and Mars bars, Versace, Chevrolet, *Playboy*, sex clubs. The street names had been changed. The roads were jammed with cars. I saw Alfas, BMWs, Jeeps, Buicks, Range Rovers. A Mercedes with tinted windows sped up the wrong lane, lights flashing, spewing pebbles, pollution, corruption. I picked up a copy of *Izvestia*; it had a business section. There were beggars next to the newsstand.

I remembered plenty, of course, but mostly what I remembered about Moscow was its emptiness compared to New York: so few cars and shops, no advertising. Not anymore. My head jerked around. I thought I saw some Moscow cops in a blue and white Chevy.

I told the cabbie to drive around for a while. I saw two men behind the Slavianskaya Railroad Station dump a body wrapped in sheets. Seconds later, a couple kids with flashlights came to pick over the trash, and seagulls wheeled screaming overhead. In front of the Belorus Train Station a few women, old as Birdie, stood selling their possessions, motionless, garments held out in front of them. I noticed what other tourists had noticed; I was a tourist, too.

The cab stopped for a light, a little kid, a girl maybe five years old, pushed her face through the window and begged for change, offering a copy of *Cosmopolitan* in exchange. She had a clown's face. For a few coins, she performed a little jig for me.

Poor Birdie.

I loved Birdie, but what did she know? How could she know? Before I went to the hotel, I went to Ustinov's building, looking for his daughters. His wife had died years earlier. A caretaker told me the daughters were long gone, both abroad, one to Vietnam as a venture capitalist, the other to Cuba with her husband, who was a Havana musician. The old Communist empire had its fantasy destinations, too, hot exotic countries where the women were lovely: Vietnam, Cuba, Ethiopia. "At least the Cold War is over," I said to the caretaker at Ustinov's building. She shrugged. "It's never over. It is not over until two generations of us are dead." I got to the hotel, too tired to notice much except that the theme music from *Chariots of Fire* played through a muzak channel in the ceiling like a bad dream. I took a sleeping pill.

When I woke up it was morning. Svetlana was sitting at the foot of my bed, looking at me and smiling and watching Al Roker read the weather forecast. I was pretty sure it was a dream. Al was followed by Katie and Matt standing in Rockefeller Center.

"You recognize these people?" she said.

I nodded. It was *The Today Show* from New York on the Superchannel. I was in Moscow twenty-five years after I left and I was watching *The Today Show.*

"How did you get in?" I said idiotically, groggy from the pill.

"I asked the chambermaid. I said I was your wife. I was very nice. She is called Irina, the maid."

"You are very nice," I said. Svetlana stood up and took off her jacket. She took off her sweater and her jeans without any fuss and I got up and put my arms around her and we went back to bed. There was no small talk, no jokes, no self-conscious comedy, no foreplay. She was completely straightforward. She wanted me.

Later, we got dressed and went downstairs and ate breakfast. In the dining room, a woman in a black dress played Andrew Lloyd Webber on the piano, entertainment for the businessmen. As we left the hotel, I stopped at the desk and got a key for Svetlana.

Outside was her little yellow car. The lemon, Svetlana called the acid yellow Trabant. "A friend in East Berlin sold it to me. After the Berlin Wall came down. He fixed it up for me for a joke."

The used Trabbies were big with Moscow's new money, the rockers and artists who considered Mercedes or Rolls uncool. My father would not have known if he should cry or laugh. My mother would have considered it very funny.

"My little lawnmower with engine." Svetlana patted her car. "It breaks down all the time, but I like it."

"Very chic." I was grinning like a fool. She looked wonderful.

She wanted to buy some groceries, she said, and we walked around to the back of the hotel where there was a supermarket.

At the entrance, an elderly man stumbled up the steps. He had the face, the beard, the hat of an old Jew. A couple of kids with acne sprayed on their faces taunted him. They yelled at him: "Kike," they yelled. "Get out of our country." One kid knocked him over.

Svetlana helped the old man up, then turned on the boys and let them have it. She did it instinctively, not for show, and when she was done, she went into the store and started inspecting bags of fruit.

"That was very nice," I said.

"What was nice?" She peered at some frozen fish.

I tried to figure out what was happening to me with Svetlana. I had been afraid of coming to Moscow for a quarter of a century. I arrived, I fell for this woman who was now reading labels on frozen fish dinners and laughing. I pushed the shopping cart for her and she filled it up slowly and we talked. I wanted her more than I'd ever wanted anyone, but I didn't mind waiting either. There was no effort in any of it; she was somehow placid and passionate at the same time; I felt turned on and calm. While she was inspecting ice cream flavors, I put my arms around her and kissed her.

"Let's go to your room," she said, and simply abandoned the shopping cart that was piled high with groceries.

After Svetlana left, I finally unpacked and then I went out and walked. In the Arbat, a band of men in clown suits played "Hava Nagillah." They played "Putting on the Ritz." In a shop window, six TVs were tuned into Mexican soaps and people pressed their faces to watch *The Rich Also Cry.*

I crossed the city to the old Radio Moscow Building where Tolya worked.

Kiosks had sprouted everywhere. You could buy anything; I bought newspapers. Tons of them. I read while I walked. Headlines in the tabloids claimed that Attila the Hun, Hitler, and Jeffrey Dahmer had been unloaded by evil space aliens who wanted to infect the godly Russian people. I read how Chechens had learned the real value of intercepts and ham radios from the Charles and Di story.

"Imagine," Tolya said when I found him and we were drinking coffee in the cafeteria in his building. "Imagine, I go to do a story in the Caucasus and I meet this bunch of mountain men. Real Chechen outlaws, you know? In a hut, in those coats made of hairy sheepskin. About six of them and pissed out of their skulls. They pass me the bottle and we all crouch over this ham radio. They're laughing and listening. To what? Intercepts of Prince Charles and Princess Diana talking to their lovers. Prince Charles tells his lover he wishes to be her Tampax. The Chechen chief asks me: 'What it is this Tampax?' Their eyes bug out of their heads. They think, how wonderful to intercept any conversation, any information. They're enthralled by the possibilities of ham radios. When Diana dies, these people are heartbroken, tear hair out, they build monuments to her, Diana becomes their goddess. Think of it, Artyom. In the mountains."

We went out through the main lobby. On the wall, a yellowed photograph showed a man in a cardigan and glasses reading behind a vintage microphone. It was the first broadcast from Radio Moscow, the caption noted; the man was speaking the words: "Workers of the World, Unite." The triumph on his face was potent, I thought.

I was glad to see Tolya. The truth was I needed him. I could get around, even with the street names and subway stops changed, but I was scared.

"Are you okay?" Tolya peered at me.

Yeah sure, I thought, swell. Apart from the fact that I took a big whiff out of a killer suitcase on the beach in Brooklyn ten days ago and I might be about to drop dead from radiation poisoning, or find my dick on the floor one morning. At least Lev's blood had tested negative for AIDS when they took a sample from his corpse. At least that. But it was completely surreal to be back in Moscow.

I had fallen in love with a Russian woman at first sight, but who could I tell? Ricky, poor bastard, was still in a coma, hanging on to the world by his fingernails. My Aunt Birdie, it seemed, had been keeping better records than the KGB for the last sixty years, and was either so crazy or so smart she could die of it. I still couldn't prove the connection between Ustinov's murder, the nuke spillage into New York, the dead dogs, Olga, Lev. Who hit Ricky if Lev didn't? The evidence said he didn't.

Also, I couldn't see how anyone functioned in Moscow. All I saw was that Tolya's own boss still had seven phones with rotary dials on his desk; all I saw was, in Moscow, the traffic lights were sporadic because rats had chewed through the cables.

"You're looking at this like an American," Tolya said as we started walking. "That is no logic here."

The rumor mill in Moscow turned relentlessly, rumors of god-fathers and crime bosses, rumors and half truths. Moscow was big with American kids who, playing at journalism, helped spread the rumors, Tolya said. They gathered in Trenmos for burgers or the Raddison Hotel for cappuccino or outside the Bolshoi for Ecstasy. On the side, they dealt in whatever was going, canned fruit or radiologicals. The rumors they spread for fun; the fuck-you generation.

"Tell me more about this Red Mercury call-sign bullshit." I told him about Rick and his cousin in Shanghai.

"Don is cousin to your friend, no kidding? It's a small world. Comrade Don was one helluva great guy, we had some times in the old days, on the circuit. A groovy guy. He had fabulous bootleg Beatles albums."

"Can we dispense with the good old commie rock and roll days nostalgia?"

"You like jazz, of course," Tolya said dismissively. "So. Red Mercury, sure, I made this my call sign for two reasons. Like I said, I was the nuclear DJ. The big explosion. The authorities went ballistic. People didn't know about Red Mercury, so I told them. I was lethal but elusive, man. We had fun then, you know? You had to have fun or you died. Me, I was the Jesus of Cool."

"What an asshole you were," I said admiringly. "Can we get a drink somewhere, a beer maybe?"

"You need it bad?"

"Of course not."

"Good. Because first we will make a stop. At *Izvestia*. To see a friend. My young friend Eduard is very offay with Red Mercury. People still say offay?"

"Mmm hmmm! I love that smell of napalm in the evening. I love that movie." Eduard Skolnik looked at the poster of *Apocalypse Now* on the wall of his office at *Izvestia*. Skolnik was twenty-five, a hotshot young reporter who wore a flak jacket and a baseball cap backward. He worked out of an office decorated with movie posters and beer bottles.

"Morning," I said.

"What?"

"The smell of napalm in the morning."

Eduard smiled. He reached into his desk. "Want some?" He held up a glassine bag filled with white powder and dangled it from his fingers. "Coke is extremely chic in Moscow; if Gorby was the sixties, style-wise, this is the seventies. You wanna see disco? I could take you, if you want. Only much wilder. Girls. Boys. Slave auctions. A club where American girls strip for Russian hoods. Whatever you want." He made a show of sniffing and rubbing his gums.

Eduard and Tolya gossiped a while, then Eduard said idly, "Someone is buying a lot of newspapers. TV companies. Even Tass. Tass for Chrissake. Tass reports Armenians in Siberia kidnap the son of a reputed Red Mercury dealer, someone tries to buy Tass. A Czech reporter writes he buys Red Mercury on the black market in Vladivostok, someone tries to buy the reporter. Let me show you something." Eduard's English slang was a whole generation hipper than Tolya's.

He popped a video into a VCR, hit the remote, and Jimmy Swaggert came on apparently speaking perfect Russian. It was eerie, like religious karaoke.

"Sorry," Eduard said and changed the tape. He was in the video himself, in a room with a desk where a fat man sat. There was nothing else except a ham radio and a metal box. "I got a friend to shoot this undercover. Watch."

The fat man opened the box and removed a steel rod. He took a hammer out of a desk drawer and kneeled on the floor and began hitting the rod. He banged on it, mouthing disgust in the direction of the camera.

Eduard said, "He's offering me a sample. Says it's plutonium. Maybe it is."

Dust flies. The man laughs.

" 'Don't worry,' he is saying," Eduard picked up the narration. "It's only detergent that's spilling out. They put it in to counteract the radioactivity. The guy used to be a scientist. Now he's a scrap merchant. He sells samples. Packed in detergent. Usually to what we call laundry men, guys who pass on small amounts of money for the big bankers. Packed in detergent." Eduard giggled and rubbed a little more coke into his gums.

"It's a two-way street, of course. You wanna smuggle cocaine, invent a myth about uranium. You want plutonium, make a legend about dope. I know people buying up poppy fields around Chernobyl; the flowers grow real big. The opium money is big. Hot poppies." He laughed again. "You want more?"

I nodded.

"You want beer?"

I said yes and Skolnik rummaged in his desk and produced cans of Bud.

"Look. It's out of control. And everyone knows. There's no inventory on any of it. We aim to please, however. If some US State Department retard says all the nukes from Kazakhstan are safest in America, hey, we are happy to celebrate. We like parties. I met one Russian general who had an entire warhead ready to ship to the Libyans. So what? It's the tip of the iceberg and I am talking the Titanic. You think I'm some conspiracy theorist? You bet I am. The only thing to do is get rid of all the plutonium. The Russians never will. So, bingo, mutually assured destruction. MAD. It's a mad, mad world. *Mad Max. Dr. Strangelove.* Nuclear leaks. Terrorist spills. Slow death this time. Real slow, man. A million cases of dementia. A million mutants. Let me show you something else." He put a different video into the machine.

Snowy fields. Forests of birch trees. A Soviet city, broken apart—

ment buildings, like Birdie's, crumbling, the mud frozen solid, the statuary shattered. A stretch of clean snow followed, then a gate, a factory, steampipes.

"What am I looking at?"

Eduard Skolnik swallowed beer and froze the picture.

"This is one of the operations around Tomsk 7. You see? This is a plant that makes weapons-grade nuclear fuel. The same plant heats a town of half a million people. The Soviets linked their civil and weapons economy in a way that can never be taken apart. Never. You understand? Never? You see those pipes? They travel nineteen miles through virgin forest—the only virgin in the forest." A joker, this Skolnik, a Tolya in the making. "All over the country, there are nuclear plants. The power that fuels them also fuels cities, factories, apartments, schools. You want to see footage of children born in Semipalatinsk? I got home horror movies." He grabbed a few tapes off his desk. "You want me to take you? You want the tour? I can do plutonium buys. I can do Chernobyl, half day, whole day. What do you say?"

"I want a drink," I said.

"You sure?" Tolya said.

"What, you're my mother now? Yes, I'm sure. You want to come?" I asked, but Eduard was on the phone.

"Be careful," Tolya said. "You could get killed."

Eduard waved breezily. "Not!" he called out. "That would not be cool at all, man."

"Let's go to the Metropole." Tolya buttoned his coat. "Maybe meet someone interesting. Maybe Svetlana will come."

"Don't you ever go home?"

Tolya shrugged. "My wife left me for a Jew. Rich guy. Smart. Who can blame her? She lets me see the kids when I want. We're friends."

It was the first time he ever let on he had troubles. I started to say something.

Tolya turned away. "It's okay," he said.

In the subway, we were jammed between bodies; the stink of sweat and perfume and Russia made me gag. Tolya towered over me. After a while he shouted, "You thinking of making it with my cousin?"

"This is your business?"

"It's my business."

"Fuck off."

I felt his enormous fist close around my upper arm. "Listen to me, you American running dog imperialist piece of shit. She's my cousin. I love her. You be good to her, or I'll cut your heart out while it's still ticking."

"Let's get out." I was having trouble breathing.

We squeezed out of the train. Tolya pinned me against a wall.

"I'm all she has. She likes you. I'm serious. Promise me, on your mother's grave."

"My mother isn't dead."

"Stop the crap. I want your word."

This was old-fashioned stuff, but I was thrilled because it meant Svetlana did like me.

I looked up at Tolya and in Russian I said, "I promise."

We walked to the end of Gorki Street which had been renamed Tverskaya. It is pretty fucking disorienting to discover the streets of your childhood have new names. Also, it had tourists and beggars and strip clubs that advertised nude dancers, legs spread, clits showing. At the corner was the old Intourist Hotel. I remembered sneaking in once to sample the espresso coffee. I couldn't actually remember the boy who did it, only the bitter taste of the coffee. Or maybe it had been some other hotel; things from the past blurred. Now, men in thin Italian shoes loitered on the pavement speaking into cellular phones. "Bizinessmen. The last great steal on earth," Tolya mused.

In Red Square, the soldiers had simply vanished. The goose-stepping troops outside Lenin's tomb were gone. A few tourists wandered in and out. A crew was filming an episode of *NYPD Blue.*

Red Square always frightened me, especially when we marched on May Day or pledged ourselves to the revolution at Lenin's tomb. I was always sick before; my father always made me go.

The tomb itself was terrifying. The shrunken figure of Vladimir Ilyich, the backlighting, his syphilitic orange glow, my horror that I would be trapped inside.

The year we were in the same grade, Andrei Federov noticed Lenin's ear had dropped off. He said so in the loud, proud, formal manner of the ass-licking top boy he was. The tomb was shut and we were held inside while guards, waving their AKs, grubbed around on the floor, looking for Lenin's ear.

You're a traitor, I would say to myself when my grade visited the tomb. Here is this great man who has invented a wonderful, marvelous world just for boys like you and you are thinking about his ear and whether they had to pull his guts through his nose to embalm him, like the Egyptians did to make mummies of the Pharaohs.

Tolya said, "Lenin's in the mausoleum, Lenin's out, they keep changing their minds about this place. Depends on tourist trade."

Put Lenin in, take him out.

I made Tolya walk with me. I glimpsed Planet Hollywood. This was Planet Moscow where everyone spoke English, the suits were good, Russian tourists hoisted video cameras, old men in suit jackets stiff with war medals held up pictures of Stalin.

The first forty-eight hours was like being high, like hallucinating, everything came at me at the same time. I saw people with AIDS dying on sidewalks, there was talk about a dying population, about the Chinese eyeing the borders in Siberia, about sex and shopping. People talked and talked. Get money. Kill Jews. Go West. Go East. Moscow was running on a zillion watts. Electrification means neon! Power to the People!

In the underground shopping mall in front of the National Hotel where Lenin spoke from the balcony people slammed Visa cards onto counters jammed with stuff. "Look, Artyom," my father would point to the hotel balcony. "Vladimir Illych spoke there."

There were lights, noise, talk, jokes, horns, hookers working, beggars wailing, sirens shrieking, new capitalists, old commies, Moscow was jammed; my head was swimming. How my mother would have loved it; I felt empty because she wasn't with me; how she would have celebrated, not just the politics but the life.

Tolya pulled my arm. "I got to check my brokerage account," he said. He pointed to a modern building and said, "Troika Dialog, the biggest brokerage firm in Moscow." I followed him into a trading room where young guys in button-down shirts worked the phones. Other rooms, other guys, speaking English, cuff links with dollar signs. Wanna buy some stock? Futures? Oil? Gas? Platinum? Gold? One man stood on a strip of bright green Astro-Turf and worked on his golf swing. Others ate Big Macs out of take-out bags.

Tolya did his deal and said, "Only the surface is modern, like always in this country, always I am reminded of the Air India pilot who could fly a 747 and believed also the world was carried on the back of a turtle. Traders buy and sell electronically, but speed is illusion. I think I do real estate," Tolya laughed. "Pop gave me little piece of land, I think I turn this into real estate."

We headed back to Red Square. In the crowds I suddenly saw Lev. I saw him everywhere, his pale Slav face on beggars, on forlorn travelers with shabby suitcases. I fantasized he wasn't dead. He had followed me to Moscow.

On the street, Tolya met someone he knew who whispered to him that a hundred nukes were missing that week, nukes you could fit in a suitcase, available for purchase. The wind blew harder.

Winter was coming. They could survive anything. Tolya said, "Things change and do not change. Here we got a thousand years of fear. So no one believes anything."

"Not even money?"

"Maybe money."

The Metropole glowed with money. Outside, the art nouveau exterior had been restored, so the green and gold tiles glittered. Inside, there was marble and glass and brass, potted palms and security guards whose jackets bulged visibly with weaponry. When I was a kid only foreigners went to the Metropole, or people with heavy connections, and entry was strictly monitored. Nothing much had changed, except the cast.

In the bar, along with the hangers-on looking for a story or a deal or a piece of negotiable gossip, we ran into Gavin Crowe.

Crowe was anybody's, temporarily at least, for a few whiskeys in the Metropole where he held court. Currently, he was drinking with a hood from New York in a silk jacket; the man said he was a union official, or a private eye, I can't remember which. Both, maybe. He was clearly also CIA, one of the old new boys of the Iran-Contra generation, self-aggrandizing, still believing in all the spook hocus pocus in spite of the fact the organization let a mole like Aldrich Ames run the show for years; in all that time, not a single CIA agent noticed what a rookie from NYPD intelligence would spot in five minutes. I kept looking at the door; Svetlana was late, if she was coming at all.

Crowe left his friend. "What's up, man?" Crowe said. Tolya introduced me.

"We've met," I said.

Crowe introduced a couple of American kids who hung on him like the holy grail. "Been here long?" he said in Russian.

"A few days," I said in English.

A waiter asked me what I wanted in English. I answered in English. Everyone figured I was American and I let them. When I spoke Russian, I heard myself talk with the weird inflections of someone who's been away too long; I had to pay attention to pick up slang.

Crowe bragged. "Me, I've been here donkey's years. Eight? Six? I think, Tol? I'm part of the scenery. Gone native. *Dasvedanya*. Etcetera. Whatever. Hey, did you hear the fascists are proposing official pogroms again? Bloody anti-Semites."

"But what about the English?" a low voice said. "I have heard people often discuss the arrogance of the Jews. In Shepherds Bush, not Smolensk." It was Svetlana who had come up behind us. She put one arm on her cousin Tolya's shoulders, and took my hand. I touched her arm; the flesh was round and soft.

"Darling Svetlana," Crowe cried. "Have some Champagne."

"What do you know about nukes?" Tolya asked Crowe.

"I'll have beer, please." Svetlana looked around briefly. All the men at the bar looked at her. She gave off sparks.

"I know everything about nukes, darling," Crowe said. "What do you need, or is this a little fishing expedition for our friend here from New York?"

"Who trades in radiologicals?" Tolya said.

I sat silently looking at Svetlana, listening to Crowe.

"Well, let me see." He swallowed some whiskey. "The intellectuals, so called, trade what they can, in between whining over the withdrawal of state subsidies. Naturally, they disdain all material things, but a poet has to eat. There are Jews, natch, racially different, addicted to moneymaking, so my most Russian friends tell me—therefore, they would deal anything. Maybe someone who did not get his 'profit tax?' Crowe was bitter.

"The Azeris have drugs, but also flowers, very lucrative flowers, you know. Also the film industry. I have many, many dear friends in the film industry. The Georgians run the casinos, the Dagestanis do the muggings, the military is making war on some awful place like Grozny because the local mafia failed to cut them in, who does that leave for the atomic mob?"

"Please, Gavin, really." Tolya mimicked the accent, grinning at me. "This stuff I can read on the Internet."

"The sixty-four thousand dollar answer is: everyone," said Crowe. "A million comrades worked in the nuke trade. And don't let's forget the locals who sell gossip they invent to foreign hacks, then tell them that in Russia, gossip and rumor are as important as fact.

"The nuke thing is one honeypot of a story, kiddo. So. Do you want me to take you to talk to someone? Or maybe you want to actually buy the shit?"

"I want to buy. I want to know who's got it, who sells it. I'm not interested in small-time hoods. Only players." Tolya ordered a beer.

"Okay." Crowe nodded. "What else? And by the way, how's your delicious mama? And that absolutely fabulous little dacha of hers?"

Tolya got the drift. "Gavin, find me someone who's trading Red Mercury. And Gavin?"

"Yes, my love."

"When you've got it, why don't you come out to the dacha? We'll have a party."

Crowe nodded and disappeared into the men's room.

"He's not stupid. He knows people," said Tolya.

Crowe returned. I had to get away. I said I had work. "I'll see you guys."

As I turned to go, Gavin Crowe, who had perched on a bar stool, making him almost my height, flung an arm over my shoulders. He leaned on me with greasy good fellowship. I shook free.

Svetlana had an evening class. She was learning Portuguese because she had a yen to see Rio. She said quietly, "Artie, maybe I can help." We were still in the bar and she lowered her voice. "I was a journalist once," Svetlana said. "I know some people."

I asked her to see what she could get on Ustinov, maybe Brodsky. She nodded.

"Why did you quit journalism?"

"I was very young. I couldn't stand all the lies I wrote," she said and took my hand.

Gavin Crowe watched us go. "So long, detective," he shouted at me in Russian so everyone heard.

Chapter Four

"GOOD EVENING, MR. COHEN," SAID THE TATIANA AT THE DESK OF MY hotel, plucking a sheaf of faxes from my box.

I had never stayed in a Moscow hotel before last night. In Moscow, I had barely been in a restaurant. These were for anniversaries or weddings, unless you were working class, in which case you went out only to drink yourself stupid on Saturday night.

If the Tatianas and Natashas at the desk were impostors in this glassy modern hotel, a few miles from Red Square, so was I; I felt like a fake impersonating myself. I felt fifteen and young for my age. I had never stayed in a hotel, or come into Moscow through an airport; we hadn't traveled much once my father became a non-person. I had barely been outside Moscow except to the sea a few times and once when Birdie took me on the train to Warsaw. I was shocked by how much the Poles hated us Russians.

When we left for good, we went by train to Rome. I felt ashamed. We left like poor immigrants. I'm never coming back, I swore. I told my mother. Never. My mother had smiled, but I saw how weary she was.

"Can I help you with something else, Mr. Cohen?" the girl said. I figured she had probably read my mail and retailed the information, maybe to the portly sweating little general manager who popped up from nowhere like a freaky jack-in-the-box. From his name, I guessed he was Lebanese. He hailed me with damp bonhomie and invited me to a VIP cocktail party currently underway in the bar on the mezzanine, he said. I took my key and climbed the stairs and, from the lobby, the general manager and the girl watched me.

In the bar, groups of bored businessmen licked salt off their fingers as they ate peanuts. The band wasn't bad. A fat boy with long black hair played a tiny mandolin and sang "Worried Man Blues." A girl in a fringed vest sawed brilliantly at her violin, stomping her foot, crying "hee haw."

I was operating on beer, cigarettes, and adrenaline, and testosterone. Wiped out, I sat on a turd-colored naugahyde sofa, ordered Scotch from a waitress.

A woman in a leather suit approached. "Do you mind?" she said. She sat down next to me, fiddled with a gold cross that hung around her neck and took a magazine from her bag. I glanced over. The glossy magazine was named *Domovoi*. She flipped through articles about how to treat servants ("Servants More Educated Than Yourself"), where to buy handmade pianos, Gucci's new look. The new Russia. I shoved the faxes in my pocket.

The woman crossed her legs. She put a cigarette in her mouth and scavenged in her bag for a gold lighter; it must have weighed a pound.

"Cartier. Special." She held it toward me. "I am waiting for my daughter. I do not like her to be in such places." She gestured airily around the bar. "So vulgar. My daughter is brilliant. Very cultured. We do not know if she shall go to school in England or Switzerland." Curiosity overcame vanity, she took glasses from her purse and looked at me hard.

"You seem familiar," she said and I figured it was some kind of come-on until the daughter arrived.

She was a sullen girl, about fourteen, with a petulant lower lip you could hang an umbrella on. She had the mother's face, and in it I recognized a girl I had been to school with twenty-five years earlier. The mother had been in my class. I got the hell out of the bar before she figured out who I was.

Along with the memory of snow on the gold onion domes and the smell of disinfectant and vomit, if you were ever a kid in Moscow, somewhere in the back closet of your brain lives a girl at school who would betray anyone for a good report card. Little Nazis, with pale skin, blond braids, Young Pioneer neckerchiefs always properly tied, she and her cronies whispered in teacher's ear about the rest of us. They were obedient. Their parents scraped together a life out of favors and coercion.

"These people grew up with their moral sense in their butts," Tolya said when I told him. "We called them the buttocracy. I went to school with a kid whose father was a favorite of Brezhnev. He cleaned his personal toilet in the farthest dacha."

In the elevator, a camera was pointed at my head. The place was rigged solid with security; a businessman had been shot in the Rossiya in his bath the other day, left to stink until the maid found him decomposing in the tub. By the time I got to my room, I was gasping for air. Paranoia was catching and I was like a fish out of water.

I locked the door, checked nothing had been touched, pulled out the Scotch, poured a couple of inches and stretched out on the bed.

Were Russian beds always so short? Did the blankets always have holes in the middle? I had forgotten.

I spread out the faxes. I read the faxes. Dan had news from friends at Immigration; so did Roy Pettus.

Lev Ivanov, as he called himself, had entered through New York JFK, using the pseudonym and his own photograph. Pettus also enclosed a note from a detective in Munich. The Germans had picked Lev up a few years back. He was suspected of humping plutonium samples, but they couldn't prove it and they let him go. No one so carefully enforces the civil rights of suspects as the goddamn Germans.

The Germans also sent Roy a picture and he had faxed it. The healthy handsome man with thick hair was unrecognizable as the demented sick man who died on Brighton Beach.

His full name was Ivan Borisovich Kowalski, aka Lev Ivanov and who knew what else. He was part Polish. His mother was dead, his father alive somewhere in Moscow. Our boy really was an Ivan.

From habit I switched on the TV. There were German channels, French, the BBC, NBC. On CNN, I registered the names of seven fine hotels in Malmö. Over the television was a window; my room looked over a courtyard. It was raining. On the other side, a girl in an office was working late and she saw me and waved.

I dialed Roy Pettus and heard the call bounce off a bunch of satellites. When I left, I had told him Birdie was sick in Moscow; he didn't believe me, but he wanted answers. He agreed to help. I got through and asked him to fax the old picture of Kowalski to Lily Hanes. He already had. I hung up and dialed the home number of the FBI guy in Moscow; Pettus said he was a buddy; no one answered.

On my bed, I found a sweater Svetlana had borrowed that morning and I put my face in it and it smelled of her perfume, which was rich and familiar. I had never wanted anyone this much in my whole life. It wasn't just I was bruised by Lily Hanes' brush-off. I don't know what it was: sex, maybe, but something else. Something completely reflexive. Like in the books. In operas. Like the way Stan Getz plays "Time After Time."

"Will you invite me to visit New York City one day?" Svetlana had said that morning, as if all she had to do to read my mind was lift its corner.

"Yes."

"Good," she had said. "I would like to visit where the streets are made of gold and Calvin underpants," she added, grinning like a voluptuous cat.

"Come home with me now," I had said, "for good."

"I can't do that," she said. I pretended not to hear.

* * *

201

There was a nuclear emergency at the hotel later. A meltdown. I was sweating with fear. Over an echoing loudspeaker came an announcement that shook me out of an uneasy sleep. The voice ordered all Jews into the courtyard. Hundreds of people poured out in the rain. In the middle of the yard was an immense heated swimming pool. Steam rose off the surface. People were swimming but were ordered out, again by a voice over a loudspeaker. Then, from the end of an old-fashioned crane, a horse was lowered into the pool. When it was hoisted out with the same crane and pulley, two of its legs had been amputated. I woke up, shaking.

When Svetlana arrived, she told me it was a very Russian dream. "I'm hungry," she said and we read the room service menu like kids, ordered food, a BLT for me and melon and ham for her, and ice cream and strawberries and a bottle of white wine. She ate the melon with her hands, letting the juice run down her mouth.

"You know the best thing about the new Russia?" She smiled. "Me."

"Fruit. So much fruit."

So Svetlana was on my bed eating melon with her hands when Lily Hanes called.

Roy Pettus had informed Lily about the pictures of herself that the killer left in the room in Brooklyn as soon as we found them. Roy had now passed on what information he had, including the Munich mug shot of Ivan Kowalski with the handsome healthy face. And then she had remembered.

I don't know if she had actually remembered before, but I doubt it, and it didn't matter. Her voice was tense, but cool. She told me about the Ivan she had known a long time ago.

When she knew Lev, he was still an Ivan, that was the irony. Johnny, he called himself; it was his western name, he said. It was almost ten years earlier when she knew him in Moscow.

"What else?" I said.

She met him in the bar at the old National Hotel in those early heady years of glasnost. He was a good-looking boy then. Lily said, "It was just a fuck for me."

There was static on the line, then I heard Lily again. "He started

202

talking about coming to America. About green cards. I backed off. He was never heavy about it, but I was nervous. I left Moscow a week later. I never thought about him again. I met loads of Russians and I sure as hell didn't put together some crazed killer with that pretty boy in the bar. End of story. Banal, huh?"

"It always is."

I scribbled as Lily talked.

"I didn't recognize him on the show. I didn't recognize him on the tape. He had changed completely. I only got it when I saw the old picture and I heard his real name. Jesus, I thought. A one-night stand. It's me he was after when he killed Ustinov. It was me."

"Are you okay, Lily?" I was stroking Svetlana's leg. It had a peculiar curve where the knee rose and met the thigh, a long sinewy muscle, like a bike rider's. I wanted to ask Svet if she liked riding bikes.

"I am better. I decided to take all this on instead of running away from it." Lily's voice was quiet.

"What did he do, his job I mean?"

"Who?"

"Your Ivan."

"I think he worked at a magazine. Something photographic, maybe. I met him at a reception at Novosti. Does that help?"

"Good," I said. "Great. Thanks." I could hear the hesitation.

"Artie, I'll try to get something for you. If I can, I'll get in touch. Somehow, I'll get in touch," she said, then changed the subject abruptly. "So how's the big Piroshki these days? How's Moscow?" Lily was self-conscious. I sensed she wanted to stay on the phone.

Svetlana was reading contentedly and caressing the soft pocket of flesh in the crook of my elbow.

"Interesting. The weather's warm. Hot almost."

"It's cold here in New York."

"How's the boyfriend?"

"I don't know. I haven't heard. Keep me posted, okay?"

"Sure, Lily. Yes. Take care of yourself."

"Look, about that dinner. I wasn't such a doll to you. Maybe I can make it up? When you get home, maybe?" she added. "I'm asking this time."

There was a pause. The silence filled up with embarrassment.

"Thanks," I said. We both knew it was too late.

I must be defective, I thought. Morally defective. Ten days ago, I was half in love with Lily Hanes, now I was crazy about Svetlana. Besotted. But this was different. I was planning to marry her, if she'd have me. I was ready to stay in Moscow if I had to. I could already feel its gravity tugging on me. When she looked at me, it was like she was winding her legs around me forever. Maybe I was such a lumpen guy that's what I really wanted.

"You believe in synchronicity?" I said to Svetlana when I hung up the phone.

"Probably." She smiled. "Your girlfriend was calling?"

"I don't have a girlfriend. Except you. If you want. There's no one else. No one."

Before Svetlana, I had never really kissed a Russian girl. She tasted of melon.

Chapter Five

SVETLANA KISSED ME ONE MORE TIME, OPENED THE DOOR OF HER YELLOW car, and let me out into the bruised night. Shadows moved across the courtyard of a building made of stained concrete blocks. The sky looked charred, a red glow around the edges, even in the dark.

"I'll wait for you," she said. "I'll wait there, look, there's a telephone. If there is trouble."

"Go home. There won't be trouble. Go home. I'll get a cab." I put my hand on the black hair that was like silk and kissed her on those bee-stung lips. I kissed her again.

"Marry me," I said, but she didn't hear and she was gone with a wave.

I had trouble finding the place. A crude sign indicated the upstairs floors were some kind of student hostel. I held up my lighter and squinted and, in the flickery light from the flame, the ghost of a young African went silently by. He had a serious face, lips pursed with concentration, wire-rimmed glasses. I called out, but he was gone; I wasn't sure if he was real. There were echoes, metal rang on concrete.

Eventually, I stumbled down a dank flight of stairs. The man named Dubovsky greeted me with a wrestler's handshake, took fifty bucks off me, and motioned me to a chair. *"New York Times,"* I said. He whispered to a younger man in the shadows. A few other men sat, legs crossed, smoking.

On a makeshift stage, under hot pink lights, a girl got up and, wiggling, removed her clothes and began rubbing her naked breasts very slowly for our edification. She stripped to Tina Turner, then sat down abruptly on the edge of the stage and was replaced by a second girl who took her clothes off to Edith Piaf.

We were five journalists, so called, me and a Swede, two Danes and Gavin Crowe. We had each paid fifty bucks to Dubovsky for this demonstration at what he called his school of erotic art. The girl on stage was twenty, tops.

"Glad you could come," Crowe called, patting the seat next to his. I was here because Crowe told Tolya he heard rumors Dubovsky was connected through one of the mafia clans to someone in the atomic mob. "You remember, Artyom, in Moscow rumors are more interesting than fact. There are no facts, all information is tainted, go with the rumors," Tolya had said. I remembered.

A very pretty girl climbed on the stage and began her act. She had wonderful large breasts, smooth skinned, big hard rosy nipples.

"What's her name?" Crowe asked Dubovsky.

"Tell them your name," he shouted at the girl.

"Madonna," she said.

"Tits real?" Crowe sniggered.

"My girls? Always." Dubovsky's forehead was wet.

Madonna finished her act. There were a couple more acts and then Crowe brayed, "Let's have the big tits back."

"It costs more," Dubovsky said.

"The *New York Times* will pay," Crowe answered.

The lights were dimmed. Someone switched on the boom box and there was classical music then the whistling of a train. Madonna reappeared; she wore an old-fashioned cloak and a large hat and long gloves. At the end of the act when she had removed the G-string and was naked, she came down off the stage and stood in front of Crowe and whipped him with her hair. It was Olga Gross all over again. I thought of miserable Olga in her room, the dirty pink bra, the cheap vodka, her fingerless body in a garbage bag on the beach in Brooklyn.

Crowe had one hand on his dick. With the other, he tossed a cigarette onto the floor and reached out and squeezed the girl's breast hard.

"That's enough," said Dubovsky. The girl backed off, the lights went on. Dubovsky got my elbow and escorted me out, up a flight of stairs and into a room where there were a few brocade armchairs and a table with vodka and snacks on a tray.

"Have a drink." Dubovsky had a mean face with pig's eyes. His wet mouth never closed over the ragged teeth.

"Welcome to the Eroticacademy," he said. I could smell him, as he added, "Sometimes known as School of the Erotic and Entertaining Arts. Here we make art. Striptease without art would be like gynecological checkup to music."

I lit another cigarette. Took out a pad and pencil and asked about his school.

Dubovsky got his girls by advertising in provincial newspapers. There was a contract that obliged the girls to live in the building—there were dormitory rooms down the hall. Somehow, he got them to sign up and pay for the training, but he was pretty vague and I couldn't figure where the profit was. The fee the girls paid was peanuts.

Consider Madonna, Dubovsky said. Once she led a dreary life going nowhere, stamping out metal parts in an automobile factory in Rostov. Now she was "dancing" in Moscow. "We attend to all of our girls' needs. We house them, we feed them. We do everything, including arranging even the toilet paper. In exchange, they give away all their human rights," he noted and added "ha ha." His eyes that were pinholes of contempt.

"I insist on physical beauty and an inborn artistic sense."

No girl could be more than twenty-six, at which point her date expired. Here, at the school, they did dancing lessons, posture, fashion, and what Dubovsky called "flexibility and the Oriental Arts"; I did not think he meant Kung Fu. Without his permission, no girl left the premises. Without it, not even a phone call, he said. He drank some vodka. "I understand women. You know what I was before I was businessman?"

"What?" I said.

"Gynecologist," he said.

Dubovsky spoke some English mixed with the coarse Russian. "In daytime, girls study. At night, demonstrations, for visiting journalists, also businessmen—potential employers."

"What kind of work?"

Dubovsky poured me vodka from a bottle on the table.

"Work. Traveling work. We are good to them."

Dubovsky's wife, Vera, appeared and helped herself to a drink. She was a platinum blonde in a Lurex sweater with a voice so shrill it could crack Coke bottles. It was Vera who had decided the medical profession was too corrupt for a man of his sensibility— she actually said this—and suggested the school.

"I was nurse in circus," said Vera.

"When the Soviets went, the stopper came out of the bottle," Svetlana had told me. "Plop"—she stuck her finger in her cheek and made the sound of a cork popping. "Moscow became sin city. Sex shows. Floating gay disco. Hookers of all kinds, and all dying to meet a bizinessman."

Businessmen were the new comrades, the new nomenklatura, the new Party members. It was already old news in Moscow, but not for me. I had read about it, seen it on endless breathless television reports at home. But I had left a priggish, puritanical country obsessed by the notion that capitalism was the devil's work, where sex was rarely mentioned; business was to socialism as sin to the Catholic Church. And now they were everywhere, the hookers, the businessmen, World Bank guys in tasseled loafers I ate breakfast with at the hotel. Russian venture capital hoods drove Rolls-Royces and Dubovsky had his school. The new bizinessman didn't want a night at the Bolshoi, he wanted dirty fun. Dubovsky could do the business.

But where was Dubovsky's profit? It bothered me. "An investment," said Dubovsky. "The girls agree to turn over a percentage of their pay when they begin work."

"What percentage?" I scribbled stuff earnestly like I saw reporters do. From next door Sting sang something pious on a stereo. "Where do the girls work?"

"A few in Moscow, mostly we send them in other countries. Good jobs."

The wife nodded.

"Firms who make showbiz in South America or Middle East." He warmed to the subject.

"With Arabic countries, of course, I am not eager. These men are not gentlemen. But you got to take a chance. Work is work and, of course, Dubovsky is providing a kind of service to his countrywomen," he said. "I make order out of the chaos in women's heads."

I was pretty dumb not to spot it right away: Dubovsky ran a brothel. The demonstration was the come-on; after that you took your pick.

"I want to talk to you, man to man. You understand." I showed him a roll of bills. "Get rid of the woman."

He told his wife to get lost.

"If I want to take one of the girls away, to make, like you say, showbiz?"

"No problem. If the price is right."

"You had a girl named Olga Gross?"

"Maybe, maybe not. Who remembers? She was good? I take only first-quality Russian girls. You want this Olga Gross?"

"Sure. Look it up. I can pay. You got girls already traveling with guys like me?"

"Sure, I got girls everywhere, Italy, Rumania, Croatia. Global market. Russian girls are best."

"U.S.A.?"

"Sure, Brighton Beach, Los Angeles, why not."

"I want a private demonstration."

"Which one?"

"Olga."

"Olga's away on business," he lied.

"Your best girl. Young. Clean," I said. "Big tits."

"How long?"

"A couple hours."

"For the *New York Times*," he said, "two hundred dollars."

"Give me the one named Madonna."

I gave him money. I showed him more. "And find out about Olga for me."

Gavin Crowe sauntered in, sipping Scotch from a plastic pint bottle and zipping up his fly.

"Madonna is at the end of the hall," said Dubovsky.

There was no dancing. The girl who called herself Madonna lay on a stained cotton bedspread, her legs spread, her mouth in a parody of a lascivious smile as I walked through the door. A boom box was turned on low. I reached over and turned it up; it was Billie Holiday, but I'm not sure the girl had any idea what the music was; it was just noise.

She was much younger than I'd thought, maybe seventeen. She rubbed herself. She had a fantastic body. She was tasty goods. Succulent. But she was a kid. She was also badly bruised, the purple marks like fruit stains on her pale body.

"Get dressed." I grabbed a robe from a chair. I threw it in her direction.

"Don't you like me?" She tried to fondle me. "Should I give you blow job?"

I put the robe over her and said, "You can speak Russian with me. Get dressed. I want to talk."

She pulled the robe on and dressed inside it, like a schoolgirl. In T-shirt and shorts, she looked like a child.

"Did you know a girl named Olga Gross? Anna was her stage name." I lit her cigarette and put some money on the table.

"Olga was a good friend. Is she well?"

"Have you been abroad working?" I asked, putting some dollars on the bedside table. She glanced over.

"Yes."

"Where?"

"Germany. Croatia. Ukraine. Rumania. You won't say I talked to you?"

"I won't tell."

"I need money to get help. I am sick."

"Sick from what?"

"Tell me about Olga."

"She's dead. I'm sorry."

The girl bit down on her lower lip.

I said, "Where else have you been?"

"I don't know the names, in Arabia."

"Dubai? Kuwait?"

"Maybe."

"Will you help me?" She grabbed my hand as if for her life. It was what Olga Gross said to Tolya in the Batumi in Brooklyn. I nodded. She tried to smile, but her lips were cracked and the lesions around her mouth were ugly. I should have spotted it sooner.

"You carried samples?"

She nodded.

"You knew?"

"No."

"What did you think it was?"

"We thought we were going abroad to work. We were working girls. Dancers."

"People asked you to make deliveries."

"Yes. Sometimes."

"Who to?"

"Men. Border towns. Croatia. Germany. We took what they asked. We put the packages in with our makeup."

Like Olga, like Lev, this girl had carried radioactive samples across the borders, then spilled out into the West with them, lost among the refugees and the chaos.

"Did you ever find out what you were carrying?"

"Eventually."

I whispered: "Plutonium?"

She nodded.

"Other things?"

"Yes."

"Red Mercury?"

"Yes."

"How do you know?"

"One night we—me and Olga—were in a little town in Croatia. A disgusting place, horrible food, drunken soldiers. We ran away to our room. Olga liked a dare. Let's look, Olga said. We thought there might be drugs. Olga opened a package. There was something red. It looked like nail polish. We knew it wasn't drugs. Later, someone told us."

I showed her Lev's picture.

"He worked as an escort for the girls."

The door flew open, the girl cowered against the wall, Dubovsky and the wife appeared and she started slapping the girl. Dubovsky had a 9-millimeter pistol, a Gluck. He held it at my head while the wife worked the girl over. I just watched. They made me watch. I wasn't Clint Eastwood. I wasn't Harrison Ford. I wasn't anybody, just a schlemiel who hated his life right now. I didn't help her. I couldn't fix it. I didn't save her. I felt like I'd been hanging on by a bungee cord and the elastic had given out. I just stood there with the cold metal against my head and Billie Holiday playing and the girl screaming from pain, certain that if I moved I'd be dead and so would she. I think that's what the good Germans always said.

"You want this for your girlfriend?" Dubovsky laughed. "It can be arranged," and I prayed to God he was bluffing, that Svetlana had the brains to get the hell away from this dump. Was she outside waiting? Did they know?

The wife hit Madonna again with her open hand and there was a crack. The girl fell down.

"Enough," Dubovsky shouted. "Enough!" I guess he needed his girls alive. Here was his profit, these girls, like this one huddled in a corner trying to stop blood pouring from her mouth with her hand. Dubovsky's girls were Atomic Mules.

Chapter Six

SVETLANA WAS WAITING IN HER CAR, FEET ON THE DASHBOARD, READING a paperback novel, when I stumbled out of that hellhole into the street. There was something fearless about her, like the way she drove. She took me home, made eggs, ran the tub. While I sat in the warm water, she started making phone calls, fixing to get Madonna out of Dubovsky's place. In the morning, when I left her, Svetlana was at it again, cajoling, begging, laughing, demanding, offering an exchange of favors. "Be careful," she called and kissed me as I left.

The Novosti building lobby stank. It was the overripe apple stink of disinfectant and of vomit I had smelled at St. Vincent's the night Ustinov died. The stink of Moscow mornings.

When I was a kid, Novosti had been a thriving honeycomb of a place where Birdie worked as a secretary for a while on one of the English language magazines. I used to visit so I could look at the girls in the magazines and practice English on Birdie's friends, other Moscow foreigners who all knew one another.

Dozens of magazines had been published here, disseminating Soviet propaganda, but with a sugar coating for foreign consumption. Now, part of the building housed the "Up and Down Club"; Tolya said it was the dirtiest sex club in Moscow.

I wandered corridors Kafka would have recognized for nearly an hour, knocking on doors, peering into dusty rooms where plants had died on the window sills. I stumbled on archives of photographs and magazines. It was a whole history of the public relations endeavor that was the Soviet Union. I asked about Ivan Kowalski; no one knew anything. I asked for a Lev Kowalski, thinking maybe his comrades called him that, and met blank faces.

On the walls of the corridors were black-and-white stills from *Soviet Life* in the sixties: a man driving a car with a bear in the back; Khrushchev and JFK shaking hands. I thought how the old leaders, at their best, looked like animals: Brezhnev looked vigorous, like a bear. Not quite human, but powerful, animated.

"Hello?"

In the last room at the end of a corridor, a pair of forlorn guys, both in glasses, both wearing cardigans, sat around a room fiddling with bits of paper. They jumped up when I entered, glad of company. They shook my hand with that stiff jerky European shake; they bowed slightly. I had forgotten. I said I was a reporter with the *New York Times*. Just looking around, I said.

"You have heard of this fellow, Nicolae Borescu?" the one called Rudi asked hopefully.

"Who?" I offered them smokes. They helped themselves eagerly. I hated this.

"He is Rumanian publishing magnate. They tell us he buys our magazines, to make new *Russian Life Magazine*."

"Don't bet the ranch," I said. Rudi's English was minimal; his comrade spoke none. I felt sorry for them. I reintroduced myself in Russian.

"But perhaps you know Mr. Chaim Brodsky. He is also planning to buy some publications, perhaps all of Novosti."

"You know this for sure? Is there someone who can confirm this?"

"Sure. Sure. Go, Sasha." Rudi pushed his colleague toward the door. "Go. So," he said, standing at attention. "Tell me, Artemy Maximovich, how it is in New York City." He was wistful, hankering for news, using the patronymic as if I were a visitor who required respect.

I showed him Lev's picture. He did not hesitate.

"Sure. Of course. Ivan was our friend. We called him Lev. He disappeared. We thought he was drunk. Maybe cocaine. Maybe he got sick, we thought. What happened to him?"

"I don't know," I lied. "I'm trying to contact him. Can you tell me anything?"

Rudi was voluble, thrilled by the presence of a visitor, and he swept clean a cracked leather armchair, gesturing toward it, sucking on his cigarette with anticipation. "Wait."

Disappearing into a closet, Rudi came back with a large folder. He held it against himself.

"Lev was a specialist. He was a kind of genius, you could say.

213

Lev retouched photographs. He remade them. Lev could make people disappear. Look."

Rudi opened the portfolio and I saw: pictures of the presidium gathered on Lenin's tomb for May Day. In one, Andropov had no hat. In another, his hat was on. It was brilliantly done for its day—you could alter anything on a computer now, no sign would remain—but back then it was painstaking stuff, an art. I thought of Lily. Of the pictures of her he had fixed.

"The original model," Rudi said, pulling out a book that showed a famous picture of Lenin making a speech and Trotsky mounting the platform. Rudi turned the page. "Look closely. Look, Trotsky is gone, but they forgot his elbow. They left Trotsky's elbow in. We used to tease Lev. 'Don't forget the elbow,' we would say to him. Lev never forgot." He looked at me.

"Do you know why the Soviets failed? There was always some nut like me or Sasha who kept the original pictures. Someone who could get the facts out to the West. There were always so many places to publish over there. Then comes Gorbachev and glasnost, and nobody cares if his hat is on or off. Everyone knows the truth. More or less. Lev lost his job."

"He was angry? This Lev?"

"No. He was a sweet guy. He met an American girl. He was crazy about her. He said he would marry her and live in America. He was obsessed. He became a little strange, but it was strange times, you know? He showed us her picture, but she never answered his letters. Then he disappeared. Do you want his telephone number?" Rudi opened a notebook, licked a pencil stub, and copied out a phone number on a scrap of paper.

"Shall I try it?"

I nodded.

Rudi dialed, listened, hung up. He made another call and talked some more.

"Lev's father has moved. He has no telephone. But I have found an address. I'm sure he would be pleased to see a friend of his son's from America." He inhaled his cigarette deeply, a look of intense pleasure on his face.

"Thank you."

214

Sasha returned, looking pleased. He spoke as formally as if in a classroom. "I am pleased to confirm that I was right. Mr. Chaim Brodsky is to buy Novosti Press." He smiled and we all had a cigarette.

"Nice cigarette. Tasty," Sasha said.

I felt for these guys. It could have been me.

"What's your work now?" I asked them.

"We wait around. Maybe somebody will buy us. We try to keep the archive together. Tough times. Do you think things will be okay, Artemy Maximovich?"

"I don't know." I put all the cigarettes I had in Rudi's drawer as discreetly as I could. "And my name is just Artie," I said, and went to see the father of the man I killed.

Chapter Seven

THE MAN PRIZED OPEN HIS DOOR WITH RAGGED FINGERNAILS AND A screwdriver.

"I have sold my doorknobs for bread," he said when he saw me on the other side. "I am Kowalski, Boris. You are?"

"My name is Cohen," I said stiffly, as if I'd learned Russian in school. "You are the father of Ivan Borisovich Kowalski, sometimes known as Lev?"

"Yes, we call him Lev sometimes. It was also my father's name. He sent me this." He stroked a brown cardigan he wore as if it were a fine cat, and I assumed he was half cracked, the way you do with the old or sick, in Moscow especially. Then I caught myself. His eyes focused and for a moment, there was real intelligence in them.

"I'd like to speak about your son."

"Lev is dead." It was a statement.

"Yes."

"Good."

He stood back to let me in from the fetid hallway. Kowalski had covered the windows with old copies of *Pravda* and only a weak light showed through the lies.

Like Birdie, he apparently lived alone.

He hobbled on a homemade crutch and a crude prosthesis. As he led me into his room, the man's skull showed beneath his skin and a section of his head was concave, as if it had been battered in with a mallet. The sweater he wore was cashmere, but his filthy undershirt had food stains on it.

"Good," he said again. "Then he is released."

On the chair, on the floor, on the windowsills, were stacks of paper. First Birdie, now Kowalski, old people in Moscow seemed to be imprisoned by paper. In their miserable rooms they guarded their documents as if only the paper attached them to their own memories. Above the television set, which was also piled with paper, was a cheap icon. Next to it was a picture of Lev.

"Sit down, please," Kowalski said. "I will make some tea."

This was a man too weary even for hate. Once, it had been a face made for hate: lean, a jutting jaw, faded blond hair, skin tight around the mouth, a pale Polish face with light hard eyes. But illness had eaten much of the flesh and all the ambition.

"I am glad he is dead. They made him into a monster. You knew him?"

"He tried to kill me," I said.

"Why have you come, then?"

"I thought you would want to know."

"You are a policeman?"

"Yes, in America. I need to know who your son was and what he did." I offered the old man a pack of cigarettes. He took one reluctantly and I lit it for him. He smoked with three fingers. The other two were missing. I wanted to say: I killed your son. I shot him on a beach in Brooklyn. But I kept my mouth shut.

He poured tea and put four cookies on a saucer. He sat in an armchair covered with tattered rose-printed fabric and removed his leg. He put it aside and started massaging the stump, which was covered with a brown sock. Waiting until I finished my tea and ate my share of cookies, he said formally, "I am grateful for the news. What do you want?"

"How did Lev get his samples?"

"Please," he said and pointed to a plastic curtain. "In the kitchen."

Behind the curtain was a worktable. On it stood a set of vegetable scales. A row of stainless steel disks the size of hockey pucks were neatly stacked to one side. There were metal containers and clean jam jars. On a yellow plate there was a dusty bunch of purple beets, leaves still gray with soil.

The lead soup cans were used to carry cesium or plutonium, the hockey pucks fitted with uranium pellets, he said. All samples.

"What about certificates?"

He opened a drawer and held out a sheaf of official documents verifying the scientific characteristics of the samples.

"Forged?"

"Some. Some real. Not expensive," he said. "Easy to get from research institutes."

The samples, Kowalski explained, were the point and he showed me his tools that included a bent potato peeler.

"They made my son into a mule," Kowalski said. "They made him carry this shit." He spat it out. "He did not know what he was carrying, not at first."

"Who made him?"

"Who? Mafia. KGB. Bosses. Godfathers. They said he was escorting girls. Driving trucks. Does it matter what? Or who? Whoever. It is not our fault. It begins with Americans. In Brooklyn." He showed me a postcard from his son.

"How did he get the samples he took to America? Who gave them to him?"

With no expression at all, Kowalski replied, "I did." He shifted his weight, grimacing. "I didn't do this for money, you understand. I am not a money-grubbing Jew addicted to money. Do you understand me, Mr. Cohen?"

As he talked he shuffled papers back and forth across his table. "I did this for my son. I had nothing to give him, so I gave him death."

Currently, Kowalski was employed as a caretaker at a nuclear research institute outside Moscow. He spoke stiff, educated Russian and I could follow easily. It was the formal language of my grandparents' generation. What he told me, as far as I could grasp it, was this.

Too old for the draft, he, Kowalski, had been sent to Afghanistan with the Corps of Engineers to look at the possible use of unconventional weapons. He was older and slower than the others, he tripped on a land mine, lost his leg, they shipped him home and demoted him. He was already sick because, earlier in his life, he worked at a facility that made plutonium pits, the core for nuclear weapons. He worked with his head near a steam pipe and his hands in a glove-box that sometimes leaked.

In those years, Kowalski and his wife, who had since divorced him, said nothing. They were good Party members. If the state said that there was no danger from radioactivity, then who was he, Boris Kowalski, to disrespect his betters?

Then came glasnost and he began to read. Around the same time, Lev was fired from his job. No one needed pictures fixed anymore Lev fell in with a bad crowd, foreigners, mafia.

They invited Lev to do errands. He drove a fruit truck to Varna for a while. They paid him well. He realized the money wasn't about fruit but for what? Drugs? He escorted girls to Croatia, to Germany. Dancers, they told him. He knew the girls were whores. But the money was good, the work easy, and Lev liked the girls. A few of the girls got sick and Lev told his father about it.

"I then understood it was radiological samples they were carrying," said Kowalski. "I knew they had radiation sickness."

On the road, Lev made a friend who knew how real money could be made. He asked his father for help. "We would retire and live together in a lovely dacha in the country, he said. I agreed. Everyone was doing it. After all, it was our family business, so to speak."

Minatom, the old Soviet atomic energy agency, had been a country in its own right. It still employed a million people. Everyone was broke. At the lowest level, illegal trade was active: plutonium, uranium, lithium, cesium, even garbage like "Yellow Cake" would sell somewhere. Boris Kowalski simply walked out of his institute with whatever he needed on a regular basis.

"We are all angry. Many of us have not been paid for months. For years. So we make business. I did business for Lev." He put one hand over the other and cracked the knuckles.

"How?"

"How? I put the materials, the samples, in a saucepan. In my lunch box. What difference does it make how?"

He put his hand over his face. "But once, I took the wrong material, or someone played a trick. I took cesium and it made Lev very sick. I knew because another worker took some and was exposed over his whole body. He was dead in two weeks. But I had already given the samples to my son."

We sat silently. I didn't know what to say so I ate the last cookie.

"I wanted Lev to stop. It was too late. He was addicted. To the power, the chance for money. To death. He was a sample merchant. A mule. He was an Atomic Mule, he said, and he would work until he dropped. He wanted to make one last run. He wanted to run plutonium to America. To be the first. I think he had other plans."

"What kind?"

"A girl. A girl who betrayed him."

He shuffled papers around and took out a picture of Lily Hanes, ten years younger, in furry earmuffs that were white against her red hair.

"What else?"

Kowalski shrugged. "Do you know the effects of radiation? Shall I tell you how it was for my son? The blood dies."

"I know."

Kowalski lit a stinking Indian cigarette from a pink packet. Outside it had begun to rain again, hail this time. The pellets hit the glass. A police siren wailed into the Moscow dusk. I wanted to tell Kowalski I shot his son.

"Who did he think he was selling to?"

"In Germany, in Bulgaria, these places, he was selling to middlemen. Bankers. Italians who clean the money—you say clean money?"

"Launder."

"Yes. Terrorists. Libyans, maybe, Iran, sure. Who knows? Who cares? You can buy anything here these days."

"Anything?"

"Sure."

"Plutonium?"

"Plenty."

"Red Mercury?"

"Harder. More expensive."

The rain fell like lead against the window.

"Lev was a good son." He began to weep. I thought about his son's passion for knives.

"Who wanted the stuff in America?"

"I don't know."

"Can you find out?"

"Me, I am nobody. Nothing. Maybe the big bosses at some institute can tell you."

"Your institute? Will you take me?"

"It will cost."

"How much?"

"A new leg."

When he rubbed his stump, I understood. Boris Kowalski, who had cheated the system that betrayed him and destroyed his son in the process, wanted, as compensation, a better leg.

Chapter Eight

"GIVE ME A FEW ROUBLES," KOWALSKI SAID TO ME LATE THE NEXT NIGHT when we arrived at the institute in Svetlana's car. I gave him a wad of crumpled money.

An hour out of Moscow, we were outside the gates. An old woman sat in the guardhouse snoring. Kowalski banged on the iron railing and she opened her eyes. "Hello?" She looked up. "It's you."

"It's me, mother." He gave her the money. "I left something at work. You understand." The old woman nodded, and raised the gate, and spat out into the night.

"Give her a few cigarettes," Kowalski said and I passed a pack out the window. The woman bobbed her head with a subservient grin. God, how I wanted to go home. I reached for Svetlana's hand. It was getting cold.

The place was deserted. A pale frost covered the muddy yard. A machine like an old tractor chugged lethargically, sending a stream of steam onto the cool night. "Helium." Kowalski snorted. "We sell it to make cash fast. Wait here."

Kowalski left us in the car and walked toward a dirty yellow stone building, then gestured us to follow.

"Stay in the car," I told Svetlana. She shook her head. "What if there's a radiation leak or something?"

"Are you worried I might have sick babies?" she asked.

"Yes."

"Then I'll wait," she said, and I knew she was going to marry me.

Inside the building, Kowalski led me to a room that looked like a school science lab. It was pretty rundown. There were ragged charts of transuranic elements on the walls, outdated microscopes, a gas ring in a corner with a tea kettle on it, a chalky blackboard, a few desks and piles of paper. Kowalski sat down heavily, leaning on his crutch, lighting one of his Indian cigarettes. Silently, he watched the windows.

"We'll wait."

"What for?"

My back was to the door when it opened suddenly. I turned. A middle-aged woman had arrived. She was wrapped in scarves like a dancer. Slowly, she peeled off the garments, then sat on a desk.

Kowalski introduced her as Valya Golitzine. She was a scientist, he said. Top rank.

"How much?" She spoke to Kowalski who looked at me.

Opening my wallet, I showed her cash.

"Not enough. You speak Russian?"

I nodded and showed her more money.

"Okay." She stuffed the notes in her jacket pocket, glanced around the room, picked up a shopping bag, and removed from it a large can of Nescafé, a bottle of vodka, a glass, a salami, and a small loaf of bread. She put them out on the desk in a row, surveyed her work, and smiled. "We have half an hour." Her fingers fidgeted with the booze.

Like a pupil, I sat in a chair facing her. She had a thin handsome face, a Roman nose, dark eyes, dancer's graceful arms. She pulled the lid off the Nescafé, paused to light a cigarette, took out a jar about six inches high. It was lead. She put on rubber gloves then extracted a glass vial filled with a glutinous mass. It had a pinkish color. It looked like nail polish.

"Red Mercury," she pronounced. "This is Red Mercury."

"Can you make a bomb with it?"

"Of course."

"How much do you need?" I asked.

Valya pointed to the water glass. "Half this."

"How does it work?"

"Do you know science?"

"No."

"Okay. Red Mercury does not exist in nature at all. Like plutonium, it is entirely man-made. It is used in a nuclear trigger. Put it around the plutonium heart—Americans say pit—at the center of a nuclear device, it compresses. It allows you to use less plutonium. Much less. With it, you can make a bomb much smaller than any others. You can use it in grenade launchers. Even single grenades. Personal nuclear bombs. More?"

"Yes."

"The first batch of Red Mercury was made many years ago in a remote region. It is unique. Sometimes it is bonded with strontium. It is highly radioactive. The rare radioactive elements give it a distinctive signature unlike any of the other radiologicals. It is very easy to smuggle."

"How is it transported?"

"It exists as powder. As liquid. The liquid can be implanted with certain isotopes to make Red Mercury 20 20. You need a particle accelerator. We have one. We rent it out by the hour now. Like a whore." She was drinking steadily and had begun slicing her salami.

For a few more minutes she lectured me. Red Mercury 20 20 was real killer stuff.

I had heard some of this from Andrei Federov; I had to be sure: "You use it for stealth technology?"

"As paint, yes," she said. "Or you might make tiny bombs with it. Easy to carry. Easy to hide. It was the one great Soviet secret, mercury and antimony oxide. In the West, few knew. A paper was written for Du Pont in 1968, then nothing. Even your Los Alamos labs dismissed Red Mercury," she said, and I recalled that Federov had been at Los Alamos.

"Then, twenty years later, Du Pont applies for a patent. Twenty years' secret research? Who knows?" Glancing more frequently out the window, Valya kept at the salami. "The designs needed high-powered computers. We don't have high-powered computers here." She snorted contemptuously at the crumbling lab. "We haven't got anything here."

I asked why officialdom denied its existence.

"Corruption. The moral illness of secrecy. One academician who knew perfectly well it existed said it could not exist because it was 'outside nature,' even after the KGB confirmed to Yeltsin that it did exist. We have suffered from too much secrecy." She plucked a crumpled copy of a letter from one of her pockets and threw it at me. "Read!"

It was a letter from Dubna to Yekaterinberg concerning a supply of Red Mercury. Laughing bitterly, she pulled out more paper.

"Red Mercury is wonderful because it is so easy to carry." She fumbled in her purse. Triumphantly, she showed me what looked like an ordinary lipstick. She pulled the cap off. "Like ordinary mercury, Red Mercury is very soft, very ductile, very susceptible to heat. Under the right conditions, I can make it into a lipstick. Like this." She waved it under my nose, laughing as I recoiled from it, then she took a mirror from her bag and made up her mouth with it.

"Get some scales," she ordered Kowalski.

Valya continued slicing the salami with scientific precision. Kowalski found some rusty scales. She dropped pieces of salami on it.

"Look. One hundred grams. Quarter of a pound to you. With this much Red Mercury, you can make a frightfully nice little device." She put more salami on the rusty scales, then broke off a small piece of bread and added it with a little flourish. A quarter pound of salami sliced. A quarter pounder. Jesus, I thought. She talked about the stuff like it was hamburger.

"Smuggling is nothing." She popped the pieces of salami in her mouth and washed them down with vodka. "Like plutonium, Red Mercury is easy. Undetectable. Put it in a steel can in your handbag, walk through the Green Channel at customs, you're over the border. Nothing to declare!" She began taking things out of her bag and throwing them on the table. "You can fit scraps, samples, in a tennis ball, a glass rod, a cigarette pack, a jam jar." She was enjoying her own performance. "If you can't make a bomb, you can make a time bomb. I know a woman who poisoned her husband by putting uranium pellets behind the toilet. It took some years, but she said, 'So what?' I said to her, 'Didn't you poison yourself?' She said, 'It was worth it.'" Valya pointed to a camera overhead and said, "American cameras. We can't man our own facilities, we have the Americans to do it. Two billion dollars. They provide security experts, locks, alarm systems, electronic fences. There are sites so secret they're still not on the map, sites with one rail line in and out where no Russian goes unless he is official, we are speaking of Arzamas 16, Tomsk. But Americans come and go. We are not yet really on full American security, but at the Kurchatov Institute, the security cameras send images to the American nuclear research headquarters at Los Alamos." She snorted. "Imagine. Russians fail to notice a break-in, the American scan alerts Los Alamos. Your most secret city once upon a time. Such irony. Once upon a time we stole the atomic secret from Los Alamos. Now we give you everything back. Fucking Americans."

There were Americans watching me, too, I thought.

Valya Golitzine finished her vodka. She was drunk. Kowalski sat sullenly in a corner rubbing his stump. He had been a good Party man and he disapproved of her laughter, but she was his superior and he waited for her to finish.

A night watchman rapped on the door, then opened it, putting his head in. Valya greeted him, took a few notes from her purse and gave them to him. He tipped his cap, she offered him a slug of her vodka, he accepted, then waved and left.

"With Red Mercury, finally we have the technology to make bombs the size of that salami that could destroy a whole city." Sodden, she repeated herself. I let her ramble.

"It was tested?" I asked.

"A few times. In the north. We misled the outside world. In Minatom, in the Ministry of Defense, we lived in a closed state. We knew we could earn billions by exporting our special nuclear technology. Gorbachev knew. He wanted to use it to finance reforms. The documents were destroyed during the coup. Yeltsin knew. Here." She threw more paper at me. It spilled out of her bag.

"What does it sell for?"

"Two hundred fifty thousand dollars for a kilo, maybe more. There were stories about corruption, about businessmen who stole it. Corruption is everywhere. Rumors. Nobody talks to the scientists. Nobody pays us."

I looked at the coffee can. "Who were the buyers?"

"America, Britain, France, Germany, anyone working on nuclear or stealth technology. Israel, South Africa. Iraq, Saddam paid a million for a kilo of Red Mercury."

"How does it travel?"

"Diplomatic freight. Zurich airport is a customs-free zone. Mexico has open borders with the U.S."

"Can I buy a sample? For testing?"

She shook her head. "Too dangerous."

"Why should I believe any of this?"

A few workers had begun to arrive for the early morning shift and Valya closed her coffee can full of tricks and put it in her bag. She snatched one last piece of paper from her bag and snapped it shut. It was a letter of transfer from an American company agreeing to broker Red Mercury at two hundred ninety thousand dollars per kilo. There was technical stuff about the use of the substance in aerospace, electrotechnology, its potential for polymers. Techie double-talk, I thought. Then I looked at the signature. The letter had been sent by someone at a P.O. Box in Los Angeles with reference to Cosmos Auto Supply in Brooklyn. I had seen an identical letter in Johnny Farone's hands.

"You may believe me, or not, but it is true." Valya wrapped herself in her shawls. "Please forget you have met with me." She tossed the vodka bottle in a garbage can, bowed slightly, and disappeared through the door, heels clicking on the linoleum floor, leaving me believing the nightmare, but without any proof.

Chapter Nine

THE NEXT MORNING, GAVIN CROWE TOOK ME TO BUY RED MERCURY samples from a woman named Tania in a flat above Ismailova Park. She wore a feathery pink angora bolero and little spike heels that went tippy tap on the marble floor and she held out her hand to be kissed and a box of Turkish delight. I knew it was risky getting into bed with Crowe, but he was sleazy enough to have the contacts. I took Eduard Skolnik with me. They had met. It was a small circle.

"Gavin tells me you are looking for something? Sure, I can help," she said. "Of course. No problem."

The sweet, powdery, pastel smell of the Turkish delight drenched the apartment and the particles of sugar seemed fixed in a suspension of sunlight. There was a wet bar in the middle of the apartment and a wall of ficus trees against a mural of minarets and belly dancers. Turkish music played from a stereo.

A pudgy woman with bright eyes and a mole on her nose, Tania sat with the candy in her lap and her feet on a pink silk footstool. Tania smiled and put her arms around Crowe who snuggled up next to her, like a lapdog, on a pile of silk cushions. Tania was nice. Very relaxed, very pleasant. A servant brought a tray with arak and coffee and she poured it for all of us, then handed around a bowl of pistachios. In a corner sat a small man eating radishes, his semi-automatic on the table. He did not look at us.

Crowe barely spoke to Skolnik who amused himself tossing pistachio shells into an old brass spittoon.

"So, you would like to purchase Red Mercury. It is quite popular these days," said Tania. There was no melodrama; I could have been buying toilet paper.

"Purely theoretically. Purely from a journalistic viewpoint."

"Of course. Of course. How much would you like to have?"

"What else can you get? If I wanted it. Say that I wanted something else, theoretically."

"Anything," she said.

"Plutonium?"

"Sure."

"Cesium?"

"Naturally."

"What else?"

"Beryllium, lithium, uranium, enriched uranium, 'Yellow Cake,' californium. Anything. Any compound. Whatever you like."

"It's that easy?"

"Sure. Sure."

"Hardware?"

"Not my line, but I have good friends."

"For Red Mercury, how much?"

She giggled. "For you, two fifty a kilo, or do you want a sample only?"

"A sample."

Suddenly, Eduard smiled boyishly at Tania as if he had been through all this before. "Make us a deal, Tania darling. We're the good guys."

She shrugged and ate candy. "Okay, fifty grams, ten thousand. Less is not worth it."

"You could make it travel?"

"Of course, anywhere. Same as FedEx. Perhaps we should use FedEx. Or DHL." She giggled impishly some more.

"When can I have it?"

"When you like."

"We'll call," Skolnik said.

I said, "I'll have to get the money. I assume you want cash."

"Naturally. Come Monday," she said. "After Monday I am away. How long? Who knows?"

"We'll call you," Skolnik said to her.

"Come Monday." I knew we were small potatoes and Tania didn't waste time.

"I have to go. Svetlana is waiting for me." I meant it as a taunt. For a second, Crowe's face was crippled with hate.

Tania offered her plump hand. "I like Americans."

Crowe stayed behind. He didn't like Skolnik or me and he barely looked up when we left.

"Where will you get the money to buy this Red Mercury?" Svetlana asked when I met her at Gastronome No. 1.

"It's called Yelisayev's now, like it was before the revolution," she said, waving at the shop and kissing me. Her arms were full of cheese and chocolates and coffee to take to Birdie in the evening. I followed her out of the store.

"Maybe I can fake it."

"Please, Artyom, not with these people."

"Then I'll find the money. I'll get the money. Somehow."

"Should I get it for you?"

"Of course not."

"Shall I show you where I work? You asked me about Mr. Brodsky, about Chaim Arnoldovich. Maybe I can show you something." She stashed her purchases in her car.

"Yes. Show me. I want to know."

She had on white jeans and a plain white T-shirt; a blue sweater tied around her shoulders. Her hair was slicked back behind her ears; it was like black gold, and her brown-green eyes like cat's eyes. She was lightly tanned and the freckles on her arms were gold in the sunlight. A rich scent came off her skin as she reached across me and shut the door. I sniffed like a dog in heat.

"What is it?"

"What?"

"The perfume."

"Joy. From Tolya." She handed me an object wrapped in a little pink cotton kerchief.

"A present," she said.

It was a dark red pear.

Inside the palatial old building on the outskirts of Moscow where she worked, Svetlana led me through the stacks of film cans, neatly arranged in row after row, thousands of silver rolls of film, some well known, some secret, some forgotten. It was going to crumble, Svetlana said as we wandered through the avenues of metal cans. "Film dies."

An old woman hurried toward us between the stacks, felt slippers sliding on the parquet floors. She opened her handbag and took out some veal sandwiches and handed them to Svetlana. Svetlana gave me one. We sat on the floor, our backs against the films, and ate. The sandwich tasted great because I was eating it with her.

"The old woman says she is afraid for her job. The archive is being sold."

"Has anyone ever looked at all this stuff?"

"I don't think so. I want to show you something." Leaning on my shoulder, she pulled herself up and took a large gray ledger from a shelf. "This is the log. You asked me to look for certain things and I checked the files, this log. People write down which films they have borrowed in it. Sometimes it is interesting to know who has looked at certain films."

"What did you find? You found something, didn't you?"

Svetlana crouched next to me. "Look at these entries."

During the last few months, Birdie Golden had been to the archive twice.

"What did she want? What did she see?"

"Come on. I'll show you. I made a little compilation just for you."

In a small wood-paneled room, Svetlana threaded film into an old-fashioned editing machine. She turned off the lights and we sat together on a pair of hard chairs and watched the clips. I felt groggy. The film seemed to be from a bunch of dull documentaries made for Soviet television, about industry, the media, technology. There was ass-achingly dull narration in commie-speak. There was nothing special. I yawned.

Svetlana laughed. "You're an impatient man. There. Look."

The film clips Svet had strung together had one thing that would interest Birdie: shots of Chaim Brodsky. Brodsky the visiting dignitary. Brodsky receiving flowers. Brodsky with Andropov, Gorbachev, Yeltsin. Brodsky in laboratories. Inspecting printing presses, shaking hands with workers and scientists.

I thought of Birdie sitting alone in this musty archive, in the dark, watching him on the screen. "What do you think?"

Svetlana said, "You tell me."

"She was in love with him once. I wish I thought this was an old lady's obsession. I wish. She saw him a few months ago."

"Perhaps then she wanted to bone up, you know, be respectful of his work."

I laughed. "Respectful? You don't know my Aunt Birdie."

"Let's go. Let's go to Birdie's now," I said. We were in Svetlana's tiny apartment and she was getting ready; for an hour I had sat looking at her in the bath. I felt married.

I put on my jacket, took an old .45 automatic Tolya kept from his army days, inserted the clip loaded with hollow points into the magazine, and dropped the gun into my raincoat pocket. I had been uneasy since we left the archive. Birdie's phone was constantly busy when I tried it.

Svetlana saw the gun. "So many guns. We have become like Americans," she said. "It is a suit that does not entirely fit us well," she added, smiling to take the edge off what she said.

"Am I an American?"

"Oh yes," she said.

"Let's go. You have everything?"

When we got to Birdie's building, it was almost dark. I could just make out her entrance. We went in.

Svetlana said, "I think the elevator's broken."

"We'll walk up. Okay?"

In the hall, the lights were out. I had a penlight and we followed its beam as we climbed the stairs. I took Birdie's presents from Svetlana; the bag was heavy.

Going up, I saw the walls were covered in graffiti; the stink of piss was harsh.

On Birdie's floor, there were the usual sounds of a TV, of people shouting, fighting, babies yelling, a piano lesson. A metronome went tick tock tick tock. Water dripped.

"I'm looking forward," said Svetlana, smoothing her hair. "Do I look all right?"

"Wonderful." I kissed her and knocked on Birdie's door. There was no answer. I rattled the knob. Still no sound.

"Birdie?" I called.

"Stay back," I said to Svetlana as I slid a credit card in Birdie's door and worked it back and forth; the door gave way. The doorknob came off in my hand. In the dark, someone ran down the stairs. My hands were sweating, I clutched the grips of the .45, my pulse raced in my ears.

I reached for the light switch. Nothing happened. The fuse was blown. I flicked my penlight around. The place had been destroyed in a fury, crockery pulled off the shelf and smashed to pieces, glass panes in the bookcase smashed, shards of glass scattered on the floor, the books pulled out and ripped apart methodically, paper like snow on every surface. The shelves had been torn out, broken, slashed. I knew the notebooks were missing.

Birdie was tossed on the bed. Ricky, I thought. Ricky all over again. I touched her neck; there was a pulse. The phone had been pulled out of the wall.

"Get help. Get an ambulance," I shouted to Svetlana.

In the hall I could hear Svet pounding on doors, shouting, begging for help. No one came. From every side, there were faint noises, a whispering gallery of frightened people crouched behind locked doors, like rats or mice, waiting for the trouble, whatever kind it was, to go away.

We wrapped Birdie in a blanket and carried her down the stairs, my legs aching. The Trabant was too small and I ran into the street and found a cab; the driver, head thrown back on the seat, snored peacefully.

I grabbed his shoulder and pushed two twenties under his nose. He helped us get Birdie in. "Where to?" he said.

"Do you know the Borodenko?" said Svetlana. The man nodded.

To me she said, "Go. Take Birdie. Meet me at the Borodenko. I have a friend there."

Svetlana climbed in her car. In the backseat of the cab, I held Birdie and the driver put his foot flat on the pedal. He was a decent man. If you ever believed in the perfectibility of man in this fucked-up country, this was the kind of guy you had in mind: squat, solid, decent, quiet. An OKnik, Birdie used to call them. There weren't a lot of them; that night we got lucky.

Svetlana got to the hospital first. Her yellow car was parked outside the Borodenko, a green stucco building with creamy plaster, most of it eaten by acid and time and disrepair, decayed as if the architectural cake had gone stale and cracked up. Before the revolution, it had been a hostel for aristocratic young ladies.

In the lobby, I stood helpless, holding Birdie, waiting for Svetlana. In the half-dark room the bulbs were all mostly out. A couple of rows of patients sat smoking, drinking tea if they could hold a cup steady. Stray cats and dogs ran around on the marble floor that was awash with spilled tea, blood, mud.

"Come." Svetlana reappeared with a young doctor. "This is Viktor," she said. "Come."

Viktor took Birdie from me, and holding her, ran. We followed down corridors where rusting stretchers were strewn like the aftermath of a train wreck.

Viktor disappeared. A few minutes later he was back. "I got her admitted. We'll wait in my office. We will have to wait. She has had a stroke," he said.

The office was in a large room where about a dozen doctors worked at shabby tables. There was one phone. Everywhere, drawers were dislodged and tossed on the floor, some crammed with tattered paper, some with bags of lunch. Smoking, Viktor perused an X-ray on a primitive lightbox. He had a desperate case, he said. He had to make a choice. There wasn't enough medicine for everyone. "If you were in a burning building and you had only time to save one, would you take the cat or the Gauguin?" He said it with an expression of desperate irony.

I could no longer slip back into this Russian way of talk. There was always talk. After a couple bottles of brandy, even that big oaf of an egomaniac who spoke five languages, a natural skeptic who had traveled, even bloody Tolya told me he considered writers more important than doctors.

"You're pretty cheerful about it," I said to Viktor, angry about Birdie, taking it all out on this young doctor.

"What should I be?" He grinned ruefully. "If we only thought about the problems, we'd drop our arms to our sides and cry. Let me show you our work."

He led us to a ward with a dozen beds in it. In all of them were children.

This girl had been operated on five times, Viktor said. That one, from Kazakhstan, was seven, with a tumor half the size of her head. A baby lay on her side, her young mother beside her, a pair of tiny red shoes under the crib. Viktor described their condition: one child was going blind; another had a tumor that weighed a pound. The nurse flirted with Viktor who smiled back.

"Viktor takes care of some children who were born near Chernobyl," Svetlana said.

He said, "We do what we can, but the government does nothing. Nothing. Malformations, mutations, disease. It hit the children hardest."

For years, since Chernobyl, he said, he had lobbied the government for help. "I talk, I argue, it's like gymnastics for the brain," he said. He wrote to the Ministry of Health; nothing happened. Eventually, he and his colleagues went directly to the site to make their own study—how many malformations and mutations, how much disease.

"We have no good food, no decent bathrooms, not enough dressings or syringes or catheters. Nurses sell the clean needles to drug addicts so they can feed their own kids. Once, someone used dirty needles here. Four children who came in with brain tumors left with AIDS. We never have enough. So we choose who will die, by default." Leading me down a hall, Viktor said, "This is paradise compared to Semipalatinsk. You would not want to see the babies born with two heads. I left because I couldn't take it."

As we walked the greasy corridor, a nurse waved her arms furiously at Viktor. "I have nothing. Nothing. The patient is human, not a dog."

Viktor shrugged and examined a little boy who padded up to him in the corridor. Viktor prodded the boy's head kindly and the boy was docile and kissed him.

I was impatient.

"I'll go see," he said. He came back in a few minutes, looking grim. "I'm sorry. Your aunt is pretty frail. It appears someone hit her with a blunt object. She has a blood clot. It may be she has also had a stroke. We have to wait. If we operate, she could die. She is old. She may revive, but I think she will lose her speech."

"I want to see her."

"No," Viktor said. "Come tomorrow."

He took us to the front entrance and shoved his hands in the pockets of his white coat and Svetlana kissed him. Viktor shook my hand.

"There is always a chance. Always. Perhaps your aunt will recover. God is strange. Everything is chance here," Viktor said to us in the dirty lobby. A little girl had attached herself to Svetlana's hand. Viktor took the kid from her and held her in his arms. "Through one door is a fantastic surgeon, the next a fantastic bastard. In Russia, everything drops into the same bowl: diamonds, old shoes, cabbages, shit, pearls. Sometimes it is hard to find the pearls."

Chapter Ten

At a cooperative in the north of Moscow where plastic limbs dangled from a rack like pots and pans, I tried to get a new leg for Kowalski. A pair of women—they were twins—sat at a large table painting these limbs the color of jaundiced flesh. "You will have to bring the patient for a fitting," one of them said without looking up from her work, but before the leg could be fitted, the cops found Kowalski. He was strung up from the light fixture in his miserable apartment. The ruling was suicide, but who would care?

It was like falling down stairs in a bad dream on the way to hell. Everywhere I went, people died. Now it was Birdie. I had called the hospital a dozen times; there was no news. I went to the hospital and held her hand. I talked to Birdie. Her hand was dry and cold, she couldn't speak or hear me. And I didn't know how to get the money to buy Red Mercury on Monday, but I had to get it. I was obsessed with it, to prove it, to get at it. But I knew I was running on empty.

I put in a call to Roy Pettus. It was still the middle of the night in New York, and I woke up his wife. Roy had gone to Wyoming unexpectedly; his dad was sick; he'd be back in a day or so. Did I want a number? Could she take a message?

"Come to the country for the weekend," Tolya said. "You'll feel better. You'll meet some friends." He shrugged. "Maybe some others not so friendly but useful."

I went because I didn't know what else to do.

"Come home with me. To New York," I whispered to Svetlana as we left town in her car. Ahead of us Tolya drove his dowager Zil; it had chrome bumpers and red plush seats and silk curtains in back; he claimed it had belonged to Andropov.

It was nearly dusk and I was silent, thinking about Birdie and my mother and the year we lived in a dacha in the country.

My mother never cared about material things, but she had longed for a dacha. Everyone who was anyone had some kind of country shack. The worst time, before we left, when my father had no work at all, someone, some kindly poet or musician, lent us a house in the country. So by the time my mother got her dacha, it wasn't hers; it was a place of exile.

I hated the countryside. I hated the investment in some clod of earth with Tolstoyan meaning. Put two birch trees together and you'll find a Russian nearby weeping, they used to say. My mother made it better with her games. Early mornings, we'd go to the river to watch the fat men swim. In white rubber bathing caps, they floated for hours on their backs, cigarettes sticking straight up to the sky. Squatting on the beach behind some trees, we'd make up stories about them, high Party officials most of them, powerful whales who could arrange to have men killed.

"You are remembering?" Svetlana put her hand in mine, reading my mind. It made up for everything. Nothing else mattered.

It was only a few days since I saw her standing in the river, but I felt I had known her all my life. I knew Svetlana; she read my mind. She was also incapable of secrets or smuggled message, incapable of being coy. She liked old-fashioned swing

music, Ella Fitzgerald, Louis Armstrong, and the songs from
Guys & Dolls, blini with red caviar, mushrooms in butter, novels
by Anthony Trollope and Graham Greene, English movies about
working-class characters, especially with Albert Finney, Louis
Malle, and Quentin Tarantino and her cousin Tolya. She adored
bad jokes, fresh fruit, avocados, anything cashmere, speaking
English, lying in bed all day with a book, Moscow, me. She hated
the anti-Semites, borscht, Russian intellectuals who lay around
all day whining, yogurt, duplicity, folk music, unfashionable
clothing—she was old enough to remember the deprivations. "It
wasn't so much communism we hated, you remember Artyom,
as it was how ugly everything was, how unstylish, how un-
West." She also hated getting up early, planning for the future,
and Leningrad, which she said was a city built on human suf-
fering. "They call it St. Petersburg, she sniffed, "as if Peter was
a wonderful human being. In Russia, some people think only the
furniture has changed."

A flock of geese marched across the road with stolid indiffer-
ence and she hit the brakes. The car stopped dead a mile from the
little village; it refused to start. Tolya backed up, we got in the Zil
and went for help.

"We're home!" Tolya shouted, and his mother ran down the stairs.
It turned out Tolya had a pack of younger sisters and brothers;
there were gangs of rich, stylish, smiling cousins who lived nearby. They all spoke English and they ran in and out of the house
with tennis rackets. It was chilly for tennis, but they didn't care;
they were tall and breezy and self-confident.

It turned out my generation was mostly gone. Or dead. The
High Lifeitsi who stole cars, went abroad, or drank themselves to
death in their parents' dacha. These new kids called out "Hi."
"Have a nice day," they shouted at you.

That night I went to bed early and alone. Svetlana sat up with
Tolya and the family, but I was exhausted. I didn't know what I
was looking for or at. I'd come to Moscow to find out who hurt
Ricky Tae. Birdie couldn't talk to me. There was no way I could
get the money for the Red Mercury, if Tania had it, and if I did,

what could I prove? Could I make the connections to b..
Beach? Would anyone care?

In the other rooms, the lights were still on and the phones cackled into life; the *dachniki* of Nikolina Gora were gossiping after supper.

At three in the morning, I heard animals howl in the hills. I got out of bed and wandered into the garden. It was getting cold. Were there wolves? Maybe it was only local dogs. I missed New York. I went back to bed and slept badly and I was glad when the cocks started their incessant crowing before dawn. Soon came the reassuring noise of cement mixers from the road, and the smell of coffee, and then Svetlana tiptoed into my room.

"Tomorrow, we will solve all problems," she said laughing and jumped into my bed.

Chapter Eleven

THE NEXT EVENING WE SAT ON THE PORCH, WRAPPED IN SWEATERS, IN the Russian twilight, eating sausages and caviar, bread and cheese and butter and drinking red wine, me and Tolya and Svetlana. "They say you cannot understand Russia without understanding the countryside. Everything here, all these dachas, behind the wall or the fence, are secret, like Russia," Svetlana said.

"Bullshit," said Tolya. "I'm Russian and I hate the countryside. The trouble with the countryside is there is no shopping." He and Svetlana began singing show tunes; Tolya, it turned out, was a big fan of *South Pacific*. He liked doing Bloody Mary.

"In Peredelkino you would not be allowed to sing," Tolya's father said coming out of the door, a bottle of wine clutched in each hand. "In Peredelkino," he said, laughing dismissively, "they'd be talking about Heidegger."

We sat on the old porch chairs and he poured wine for us. Lara Sverdloff stood on the steps, hands on hips, laughing, looking

...sband. Tolya's father, who was also Anatoly, was
...ctor.

...; sorrowful," he shouted, his belly hanging over his
...river picked apples in his garden today and I got
...ne shop. That is inauthentic." He grinned. "They taste
...d, to tell you the truth. Have a drink."

Sve... ...ia and Tolya sang. Lara Sverdloff laughed. Anatoly Sr. declaimed.

"This house, I built it, I put a nail in it, it is mine. You know how long I waited for a place in Nikolina Gora? You know how long? Eighteen years I waited, not like these new Russians with their kottedzh and marble fireplaces, the new aristocrats." He snorted. "They are like Westerners, like in the West, where a home means nothing, where it is easy to get and all you need is money. My house is my soul."

An expansive man, Tolya's father could, in a disarming way, discuss his soul, your house, and cold cash in the same sentence. The whole neighborhood swam in his heated pool, and all day and night he would welcome them, saying, "So how much did that wine you brought me cost?"

Cats and dogs meandered through the Sverdloffs' wild garden. Lara hurried in and out, her dark eyes glistening at the prospect of feeding so many people. The two Tolyas, father and son, built a bonfire. In every corner of the garden, we placed small stoves that gave off a warm glow.

Under the trees, a trestle table was laid with platters of food and drink: pale pink tongue with baby peas and horseradish; rice pilaf with dates, apricots and pine nuts; pickles; pickled tomatoes; smoked fish; vodka, wine, and beer. Caviar, black, red, and gold. The roast pork had a crackly skin the color of caramel.

Svetlana, who had changed into a white sweater and black slacks, wrapped a red shawl around her shoulders. She had gold hoops in her ears. I held her hand and looked at her and the sun disappeared and Lara lit more candles and more guests arrived and we ate. In the house, Tolya put music on and it drifted out. He played old jazz standards I loved: Oscar Peterson, Django Reinhardt, Stan Getz. Chet Baker played "My Funny Valentine."

A siren screamed through the woods, a light flashed; in an official car more people arrived, including a large man in a cashmere blazer.

"The presence of foreigners made him let us know how important he was," Svetlana whispered.

"Am I a foreigner?"

At dinner, across from me, wearing a Harvard sweatshirt, was a professor of ethics; he was introduced as a man who once met Wittgenstein at a train station. In Munich, I think. Maybe Vienna. Gavin Crowe showed up in a hat. His wife was an angry silent Russian woman and their friend a desiccated German with a trace of a mustache. A lawyer, she was looking for the main chance in Moscow. A couple of American kids were there, too, in thrall to a pinched blonde who had been a famous actress. I couldn't recall her name but I remembered her pictures. She and Anatoly Sr. had been a famous acting duo for a while.

The actress picked at her fruit, her little eyes hard, mean, and black as watermelon pits. Furmin, her husband, was a physicist and she watched him closely but barely spoke except to spit out *"Nyet pravda"* from time to time when she didn't agree with him.

"Gorby's science minister, a big deal guy," Gavin Crowe whispered to me. That a creep like Crowe knew ministers and bigwigs told me Russia was still a provincial society: Its privileged members all knew one another.

The desultory talk about art—eighteenth-century paintings were an obsession with this crowd—gave way to more animated conversation about money and guns. Furmin, the physicist, the ex-minister, was bitter; he was leaving the country for a better job; there was no money for research anymore, he said. Sverdloff Sr. carried out a tray of brandies. A yellow moon came up over the slim white trees. Moonlight drenched the garden, candles flickered in glass jars in the thick grass, the leaves rustled in a fall breeze and kids splashed into the steaming pool. Someone had changed the music; Paul McCartney sang "Yesterday." Svetlana looked at me and smiled.

I said, "Why are you smiling?"

"From happiness."

I loved her. But sitting in this lush country garden on a balmy fall night while Russians reminisced about their own history, I felt angry, confused, seduced. Angry because Birdie was dying and so was Ricky, both because of me. Angry because the self-regard around the table was thick as Lara Sverdloff's cherry jam. And because I wanted to claim some of my own past from this place, but it was too late and I couldn't. I was a foreigner.

Svetlana stirred jam into her tea like my mother used to. She saw me watching, then she came and sat close beside me and put her arm around my shoulders. "The scientist, Furmin, do you recognize him? From the film in the archive? Remember?"

Furmin walked with me toward the river. "You want to ask me questions? Ask me. I don't care anymore. I am leaving. Leaving." He looked at the birch trees and made himself weep.

"Leaving?"

"My country. This." He gestured at the woods and the river. "Everything has come too late. We are giving away our resources. No one listened to me. I said save the plutonium. There will be power for three generations to come, but we will give in to the Americans. Without it, we are nothing. A third-world country. There is only one good American for us." Suddenly, he sat down on a tree stump.

"Who is the good American?"

"Chaim Brodsky."

"Why?"

"He understands we have the technology to build this new generation of power plants. Cheap electricity for a century. Brodsky understands. All we need is to persuade people. Why throw our plutonium away because Americans say so?"

I believed this bitter little man. He was leaving. He was free of all of it. He had nothing to lose.

"What is Red Mercury?" I asked. Through the trees I could see Svetlana in her red shawl. She was crossing the garden with a tray in her hands and the light from candles flickered across her face. I could see she was watching the kids in the swimming pool and laughing.

Furmin shook his head. His twisted face seized up in a sneer. Crouched on his tree stump, he took off his shoes and socks. He rubbed his gnarled feet, then sniffed one of them.

"It is nothing. Red Mercury is nothing."

"Nothing?"

"Nothing. You want to know?" Furmin asked me.

"Yes."

"I'll tell you what it is. It is fear in a bottle. It is a thing some scientists invented long ago because production fell off. There was news from the West of a thermonuclear device. We were terrified. Our scientists thought if they invented something even more powerful, the West would lie down for us. So these scientists, in their labs, invented the secret substance. The Soviet marvel that blew up planes, could make radar disappear. With Red Mercury, anything was possible. It was the alchemist's stone."

"But the paperwork? The reports?"

He snorted. "All manufactured. They gave the substance a formula. They made a paper trail, reports, official letters, contracts, bills of sale, certificates of verification. It never existed. It was one of the great hoaxes. Lethal but elusive. It has become a kind of legend. The aura around it is of John F. Kennedy's assassination—one bullet, two, more, no one will ever know; all that remain are the theories. With Red Mercury, it is the same, people write theses, they make documentary films about it, novels even, even poetry. It has become metaphor. Lethal, but elusive. Poetry."

I thought of Valya Golitzine and her precise, elaborate account of the stuff. I thought of Chaim Brodsky's conviction that it was deadly. I thought of my own frantic pursuit of Red Mercury and I wanted to believe all of them, but I knew Furmin was telling the truth.

I followed Furmin to the edge of the river. "I'll sit here." He sat again and bathed his feet in the water.

"The legend was made. Red Mercury. Quite a good name, don't you think? And it became real. This is Russia." Furmin watched me. "Do you think I want to leave my country? You think I want this?"

"Why do you go?"

"My wife wants diamond earrings." He stood up and waded along the bank for a few yards.

"How do you know about Red Mercury?" I said.

"You don't believe me, do you? I suppose you have been to the institute and talked to Valya Golitzine. Stupid whore."

I was silent.

"She sells her information to anyone. She was always a whore," he snapped. "Red Mercury is nothing. Nothing. Gossip. A rumor of death. Golitzine sells it for money."

"How do you know?" I took a cigarette from a crumpled pack in my pocket.

"Give me one."

I gave him a cigarette. We smoked for a minute, then he tossed it in the river. He went back to his tree stump and found his shoes and socks and began putting them on.

"I was married to her once," he said. "I have very bad taste in women."

"Please, it's important. How do you know Red Mercury is a hoax? How do you know what these men invented is a lie? How?" I was confused. "Tell me!"

Putting his hand on my shoulder, Furmin got up wearily. He put his full weight on me and said, "I was one of them."

Chapter Twelve

LIKE A BEAR, TOLYA CRASHED THROUGH THE WOODS TO THE RIVER.

"There is a phone call for you, Artyom," he shouted. "From Lily in America. She left a number. You're to call back." He handed me a scrap of paper.

We left Furmin standing by the river and went back to the house. I kissed Svetlana. Tolya went to help his mother with a stove that had gone out.

I wrapped my arms around Svetlana and kissed her as hard as I could.

"What's the matter?"

"Get Tolya."

The three of us stood on the porch. At the table the toasts were getting longer. Furmin returned and whispered to his wife and abruptly she got up and they left the garden. The moon sailed in the white trees.

"What is it?" Tolya said.

"I don't know. I'm not sure. Something is wrong. I want you to disappear for tonight. Take Svetlana back to Moscow. Do it now. Go somewhere safe."

"Safe?" He smiled.

"As safe as you can. Your car is fixed?" I asked Svetlana.

"Yes. At the garage in the village."

I walked them quietly to the edge of the garden.

"Something's going on. I don't know what it is, but something. I want you to go to Moscow. Get your things. I can make arrangements. I want you to both come to New York."

"I can't," said Tolya.

"Why? If bad times are coming then you're a dead man. Take your kids and come. You still have a visa."

"This is my home," he said.

Svetlana was different. She believed in very little.

"Did you ever? Did you ever believe?" I had asked her.

"Not for a single day in my entire life. Not when I was a little girl and put a wig on Lenin in my schoolbook." I was startled because I always figured only I had committed this atrocity.

"I think perhaps I will send Svetlana to the West with you," Tolya said.

"What? Like a parcel?" She let out a torrent of Russian, eyes blazing, fists clenched. "You don't understand." Then she kissed us both and said to me, "But I will come. I will send myself."

"I need the phone. Somewhere private."

"Come on inside."

Tolya took me into his father's room. On a large desk were scattered film scripts, piles of newspapers and magazines, books, labels from exotic brandies, a couple of telephones, an answering machine, a fax, two tennis rackets, and a damp bathing suit.

"Here, you're at home." He grabbed my shoulder. "It will be okay. Okay?"

"Okay. Take care of Svetlana." I picked up the phone.

"She'll be okay. I promise." He tossed me the keys to the Zil. "I have to do a few things. We'll get Svet's car and meet you in Moscow. At your hotel."

Tolya lumbered down the stairs and into the garden where people were dancing. I saw Gavin Crowe put on his hat and leave.

I dialed the number on the scrap of paper. The international lines were tied up. It would take an hour. Maybe more. Through the window, I watched Svetlana kiss Lara goodnight and then Tolya picked up her little suitcase and I watched them walk away toward the bend in the river where I first saw her.

I started to run out after her. Wait, I wanted to yell, but the phone rang and I went back into the study. Wrong number. I slammed the phone down, and when I looked out of the window again, Svetlana was gone.

I tried the hospital and got Viktor. Birdie was dead.

I was glad she was dead. Birdie without her speech was a ghost. At least I had seen her. At least we had talked. I would mourn for her later. But her notebooks were gone, if there had ever been any notebooks.

I sat and smoked. People started drifting into the house to drink tea. A few minutes later, the phone rang. It was Lily Hanes.

I said, "I've been trying you. Where are you? Where is this number?"

"I'm at a friend's," she said. "I went out to call."

"How did you know I was at Tolya's?"

"The hotel told me. The hotel knew where you were," she said, but I hadn't told the hotel anything at all.

"Talk. You can talk. It doesn't matter. Nothing is secret here," I said, and Lily said, "I saw the pages."

"How?"

"Please don't ask me how, but I saw the missing pages from Ustinov's book."

"Tell me, Lily."

She told me.

"Take care of yourself, Artie," Lily whispered. "Be careful."

"Call Roy Pettus," I yelled, but there was static and I couldn't tell if she heard. Then we were cut off.

I got out of the house without anyone noticing. The Zil wouldn't start. It sputtered, then died, and I began to run.

I was running hard toward the village and the garage where Svetlana had left the yellow Trabant. I ran along the wooded path. The moon had turned sickly yellow and was sliding behind clouds. The birch trees were colorless, ghostly.

Gavin Crowe had left the party without a word to anyone. So I knew. It was Crowe. Crowe who kept turning up. Crowe had been on TV with Ustinov the night he was shot, where it all began. Crowe who was an old pal of Phillip Frye, who published Ustinov's book and set up the publicity, including the television show. Crowe knew Olga in Brighton Beach and the other girls, the Atomic Mules who worked at Dubovsky's whorehouse. He took me to see Tania who ate Turkish delight and sold Red Mercury that didn't exist. It was Gavin Crowe who said rumor was more important than facts. His father had been a petty spy, an English bastard. "Perfidious Albion" like my own father said. "Anyone's for a price."

I had been blind. Uncle Gennadi. Olga. Birdie. Lev himself. Ricky as good as dead. I wasn't a hero. I was only a cop who wanted to get married and have a life. Svetlana. Crowe loved her and couldn't have her.

I stumbled over a tree root. An animal yowled. If they got to Rick and Birdie, they could get to Svetlana.

The path to the village was empty, the road slick with gasoline someone had spilled and I slipped on it as I ran. More wolves howled in the hills, or maybe it was only Russians out at night picking apples or the last of the mushrooms. Leaves crackled and startled me, but they were the leaves under my own feet. I ran faster and faster, past the little church that had been freshly painted, the door open, an icon blazing among candles on the altar as I ran past. From a distance, I heard the explosion.

I was too late. The fireball twisted up into the dark night, red, yellow, the trees black against it.

I was too late.

I kept running and when I got there, Tolya grabbed me and

dragged me to the side of the road and pushed me on the ground so I wouldn't see the body parts hanging from the trees.

Hours later, I think it was hours, maybe around dawn, I lay on my bed in the hotel, the bottle of Scotch on my chest, my hand around its neck. I'm not sure how I got back to Moscow from the country.

"I'm coming with you," Tolya had said.

The explosion had missed him. He had taken Svetlana from the dacha to the village garage. The yellow Trabant was at the garage where she had left it, alongside a white Ford Bronco.

"I'm so thirsty," she told Tolya, and he said he would run to the shop for cigarettes and a Coke. She was thirsty. She was dying for a Coke, she said to him.

"Pick me up at the shop," he called. As he left, he saw her give the mechanic some money for fixing her car. He saw the man count out her change. Saw her smile at him.

"I'll get you a Coke," Tolya had said to Svetlana. "I said I'll get you a Coke, that's all I said to her."

I didn't want Tolya to come to Moscow with me. I told him to stay behind and look after Svetlana. To bury her.

I wanted to get Crowe myself.

Gavin Crowe had sold me out; only Crowe had the connections. He knew the name of my hotel. Only Crowe knew in advance that I would be at the Sverdloffs. He was a creep, a cripple. Maybe he had done it for money or because he loved Svetlana or for cheap thrills. He had taken me to the apartment near Ismailova Park, to Tania's apartment, to show my face to the hoods who could arrange a car bombing. I knew it as soon as Furmin told me Red Mercury was a hoax. Crowe hadn't taken me to arrange a purchase; he had taken me to show them my face.

I looked at my hand and saw I was holding the kerchief Svetlana had given me with the pear in it. She was dead because of me.

Slowly, carefully, I packed and put my suitcase next to the door. Then I lay down on the bed in my coat to think. I drank some Scotch, waiting for Crowe to answer my phone call. I knew he would call because I told his answering machine I was ready to deal with Tania, to buy Red Mercury, to cut him in. Would he be surprised I was alive? Was the bomb intended for me? For Svetlana? Both? Crowe sold me out, but who did Crowe work for?

The phone rang. I looked at my watch.

When I heard the voice on the other end, I knew what Lily Hanes had told me on the phone was true.

Chapter Thirteen

"I'M SORRY TO HAVE SURPRISED YOU, ARTYOM. YOU WERE SURPRISED? Perhaps not. But thank you for coming." I found Chaim Brodsky seated at the back of the synagogue. It was early, but a few elderly men waited under the portico, and the main doors were open. Inside, light played off the blue and gold ceiling with its painted green trees. It glinted off old wooden pews and the chandeliers. In the vestibule, an old man saluted me. "Shalom," he said.

A few men in the front pews prayed and gossiped. There were no bodyguards I could see, but Brodsky's would be discreet, one of the men at prayer, or standing in the back. In a dark blue overcoat and a gray hat, Brodsky sat, hands folded, face set in a faint smile.

"I'm afraid that, like every other old man, I have begun to think about my roots. My grandfather prayed in this place, I like to imagine. I like to come here from time to time."

"That's crap," I said quietly. "This is a travesty. Also a cliché."

But Brodsky knew I wouldn't kill him in here, although I think he chose it for the drama.

"What's the matter with you, Artyom?"

It was Saturday morning; slowly the men began arriving, filling up the benches, bowing to the altar, shaking hands. The room was restless with men.

Upstairs, a few women filed in and sat and looked down and chatted.

"I'm sorry about your friend. Is that what you want me to say?"

"You killed her. You killed Birdie."

"I was right about you, Artie, you're a clever man. And I value you for it. Birdie's time had come; she had become tiresome. It's not much fun being old."

The noise of chanting and gossip muffled our conversation.

"You're a monster."

"Oh no, not a monster. You think that I am Dr. No? Or Dr. Strangelove? No, Artie, I haven't got any poison pussycat, no piranha tank, no mob of men with tommy guns. I am sorry to disappoint you. Even the trappings, the big boat, it's for politicians and the hoods who understand power only with reference to the movies. Actually, I dislike boats."

"Where's Paulette?"

"She's resting." His voice was tender. "You are fond of her?"

"Yes."

"Me too." He said it simply; for a split second, like lightning in a storm, the steel-cold eyes lit up.

The Scotch and some pills I had taken made me numb. I found I could go for a second or two without thinking about Svetlana; I had no feeling, except an obsessive desire to kill this man. Instead, I sat and listened.

"What do you want?" I said.

"Only to keep the monsters of destruction under control. There are twenty-five thousand nuclear warheads in this country, and there is chaos. We're looking at a military junta. A country increasingly hostile to the West. I want to help. I have given up all my other business. I was tired. Tired of doing business with hoods in and out of the government. My generation is all dead. Everyone I liked is dead."

"Birdie said the same thing."

"Did she? Yes, she knew, of course."

"You killed her for the notebooks."

"Do you have them?"

I didn't answer. A man and his two sons pushed past us, looking for a seat.

"I'd like to have them, please," Brodsky said. "The notebooks."

"Is that why you called me?"

"In part."

"You own billions of dollars worth of hardware, satellites, television companies, but you can't get your hands on some notebooks that belonged to a little old lady." I laughed. "How did you know where I was?"

Brodsky smoothed the fingers of his gloves. I remembered something Roy Pettus told me the morning we had breakfast in Brooklyn, the morning after Lev cut my face. "Someone accessed your file," Pettus said that morning.

"It was your people. Wasn't it? You accessed my file. When you knew Gennadi Ustinov was coming to New York."

"I had to keep track of you. I knew he would contact you. Have you got those notebooks? Should I say I'm sorry about the girl again?" He leaned closer to me. "Tell me, why did you come when I called this morning? Surely not to kill me." He smiled gently.

"Was it meant for me, the car bomb?"

"Oh, it doesn't matter, really. A diversion. I don't know. I haven't anything to do with that side of things."

"And Ustinov?"

"That was an accident. I was very sorry."

Ustinov's shooting was an accident that opened a freaky box of tricks, and in it was Chaim Brodsky.

"Sorry Ustinov died or that it was an accident?" I asked, but Brodsky ignored the bitter question, and as the temple filled up, the background noise grew, the men praying, whispering, constantly moving.

"Everything passes. What is it, perhaps six or seven weeks since Gennadi Ustinov died? Do you think of him often? Did you before? We were very close once, but he was a fool in the end. He was a believer. He believed. His death made things difficult. It meant people began asking the wrong questions. People like your Mr. Lippert. Perhaps Miss Hanes."

"People like me?"

"All you ever had to do was come to me, Artie. We're family."

"The missing pages in Ustinov's book, you had them deleted."

Brodsky shrugged. He made a tiny gesture, like a man bidding at an auction, and, quietly, two men materialized at our side. They stood against the wall, well-dressed men, watching Brodsky and me.

"Gennadi always had a taste for melodrama. He wrote some nonsense about me and what he liked to call atomic terrorism. I thought it better omitted. That was all. His murder was a mistake. Some of what followed was planned, some random. It always is. It always is."

Lily Hanes had said to me, "Sometimes, things just happen."

"So Ustinov knew about you and the nukes. Didn't he?"

"Yes."

Gennadi Ustinov was killed for what he knew by mistake, I thought. "Birdie knew?"

"In her way."

"Was *The Teddy Flowers Show* a setup?"

"It wasn't necessary. Phillip Frye planned to promote Gennadi's book in the normal course of things. Mr. Flowers is terribly malleable. And Phil Frye understands his business."

"And you own them both. A lot of effort for a few pages in one book."

"There might be other books."

"Did Flowers let Lily Hanes sit in for him on purpose?"

"No one has to tell these people anything."

"They know the corporate message."

"It's in the bloodstream."

"And Crowe?"

Brodsky shrugged. "Crowe? A nothing. A messenger. A toady. I'll give you Gavin Crowe, if you like, Artyom. You can do what you like with him. Will that make it better? Will that help? I'd like to help."

The synagogue was packed now. Brodsky looked at the massed bodies of men attending to their God with noisy reverence.

"I've had enough of this now. Will you come with me?" He got up and buttoned his coat. Automatically, I held the door.

"Thank you," he said, pleased, and left the synagogue; I followed him. Out the door, between the white pillars, down the steps to the street.

The bodyguards followed a few steps behind. At the curb, a man in a suit and cap waited in a gray Volvo, but Brodsky waved him away. "It's a lovely day, let's walk."

We walked. The Volvo followed us, keeping pace.

"I love my country," Brodsky said. "There is no other place like America. But we are ruining ourselves. We are greedy. We don't want to pay taxes. We've destroyed the educational system. Our kids carry guns like chewing gum, they are growing up like animals. They have no moral life. We have done it to them."

He sighed almost inaudibly.

"We have a media which is completely amoral. It purveys whatever entertains the people, who conspire in their own exploitation. Before long, we will have executions in public on television with advertisers buying time. We have given the country away to the zealous little shits of the right wing and the Christian Coalition who preach law and order. In truth, they cause the chaos and killing, pro-lifers, so called, who shoot doctors. No one will stand up to them. And they do nothing at all about the waste from nuclear weapons. It is going to kill us." Brodsky grew angry.

"There is no discipline. Perhaps it's too late. Perhaps the Chinese have got it right. Happily, not in my time. No one promised us more than two hundred years of democracy, Artyom." He adjusted his hat. "Do you think a few years of democracy have made any difference here?" He gestured to the broken Moscow streets around us, busy now with shoppers, tourists, hustlers, beggars.

"Tell me, Artie, which is stronger? Fear? Love? Let me tell you about how we have turned the planet into a nuclear garbage dump. At Rocky Flats in Colorado, and Oak Ridge and Handford and Amarillo and Utah and Nevada. Us. The Russians. What shall we do with it? Fire it at the sun? Bury it in glass? No one knows, you see. No one," he said.

"Here in Russia, the whole country is a stinking atomic dump. But plutonium is a national treasure. They think we want to take it away from them. To take away their power literally and figuratively. They're right, of course." Brodsky looked at me.

"Russians love electricity. Power to the people. You remember?

In plutonium reserves, they have a century's worth of power, a means to blackmail the West. Without it, this is a third-rate country with a few violin players. But you know. You know all that."

The car kept pace with us. We skirted Red Square, and Brodsky turned to admire St. Basil's with the sun sparkling off the gold domes, then walked down toward the river.

"You can read these things in the newspapers. There are no secrets, only idiots who cannot read them."

My hands were terribly cold. I started sneezing. Brodsky gave me his handkerchief. He summoned the driver who had kept pace with us in the car. We got in.

Brodsky kept talking. His voice was low, but hard.

"I try to help. I pay their scientists through my foundation. You met Furmin?"

I nodded.

"He understands the new technology."

"You own Furmin."

He smiled. "Yes. Yes, you could say I own him."

"What's he worth?"

"To me, a great deal. You can't get rid of nuclear power, Artie. The world is a plutonium-dependent economy, the way it was once petroleum dependent. Whole economies are built on nuclear power, the British and the French with their billions in reprocessing plants. The Japanese. So desperate to feed this economy they send the material by sea. By sea! Fourteen tons on a ship that takes two months. Consider the *Exxon Valdez*. Consider what would happen if such a ship broke up carrying radioactive waste. Do you think the Japanese will give up their nuclear ambitions? They have no oil. What about the North Koreans? Or the Chinese?"

I laughed. "And you're going to fix it. That's what this is about." I saw Brodsky didn't like it when I laughed at him; it was the only thing that got to him a little.

"The only safeguard is a new generation of breeder reactors that uses up nuclear fuels in a safe, self-sustaining cycle," said Brodsky.

I laughed again. "Even I know breeder reactors went out with the Bee Gees. We tried it, in the seventies, when people thought there was a shortage of uranium. The thing doesn't work, Chaim. So what's the big fucking deal, Chaim? Huh? It doesn't work."

Brodsky replied calmly. "Not mine."

"Yours?"

He put his hand on my arm and said, "Will you listen? I know all about the breeders we tried building. We need one that uses nuclear fuel in a self-sustaining cycle, that feeds itself, that is used only for civilian power, with no waste. We tried, but we quit, the way we gave up on health care, on education. The technology was wrong."

"And only yours is right."

"Only mine, yes."

The river was the color of sludge, even in the sunshine. Brodsky believed in his project, the way the Soviets had believed in Red Mercury. He was crazy, I told myself. I would kill him, I thought, but I didn't believe it. He knew. I knew. I felt paralyzed.

"What do you suppose we will do with all this plutonium if it is not recycled?" Brodsky asked.

I was silent.

He said, "We will need a war."

The car took us toward the Arbat, to Spaso-Peskovaskaya. We came to the small square; a couple of kids chased each other. There was a pretty but tumbledown church. On the ambassador's residence an American flag blew cheerfully from a pole.

Kill him, I thought to myself. Kill him before you get inside. For what? For revenge?

"What are we doing here?"

"I am staying here. Paulette is inside resting."

The car pulled around to the other side of the elegant old building, and we went in.

"I've always loved Spaso House." Brodsky gestured around the yellow and white mansion as if we were tourists, admiring the high ceiling, the gardens in back. Glancing at some pictures, he added, "I only wish we had ambassadors with better taste in pictures. Wasn't it Matlock who had rather avant-garde things of his wife? I think it was Strauss who brought in ghastly landscapes in big gold frames. I wonder if they'd take something from me."

I followed Brodsky past the cloakroom and up the stairs, past a small reception room. A maid was on her knees polishing the lovely wood floor. On the next floor up, he led me to a small suite. Brodsky took off his overcoat. He had on slacks and a sweater. He opened a cabinet and took out a bottle and poured sherry into ornate little glasses. He held one out.

"Do take off your coat."

In the pretty sitting room, we were alone. A clock ticked. I kept my coat and sat on a hard chair. The doors were closed. I could get to him and kill him, but how would I get out?

Swimming laps in his pool all summer, Chaim Brodsky did the backstroke and dreamed of all this chaos.

He had as good as killed Birdie, Ricky, Svetlana. He didn't light the match but he had whispered in someone's ear.

Red Mercury was a red herring. He knew!

"And you run this show from a beach house in East Hampton," I said.

"You'd prefer the Starship Enterprise? God is in the detail, as you know," Brodsky said.

I thought of the tacky trade in death, the dead bum in Penn Station, Lev's father, the strippers who were Atomic Mules, Valya Golitzine with her salami, the dying dogs, skins flayed. Steel hockey pucks stuffed with radioactive pellets would be coming onto the market alongside Russian dolls.

The door opened. Paulette Brodsky appeared quietly and sat on a chair against the wall, next to a window, listening, lighted up by Chaim's presence, in his thrall. She wore a yellow silk dress that was shot through with light. A maid came with a tray with a teapot and cups and sandwiches, and Brodsky waved her away and poured the tea himself and took a cup to Paulette, kissing the top of her head. I didn't know if I could shoot him in the face with Paulette in the room.

Gently, he touched Paulette's shoulder and when she opened her eyes, I realized they were vacant.

"It's early stages of Alzheimer's," he said pitifully but I felt nothing. Nothing.

He said, "Something else bothers you?"

"You buy a publishing house in New York. You bought Teddy Flowers' TV show. Tabloids in London. Some magazines on the West Coast. Radio stations all over the place. You've been buying newspapers and television companies in Russia that are worthless. Picture archives. Film archives."

"Remember your history lessons. Information is more valuable than the weaponry. Arthur C. Clark said it. Television is more powerful than an ICBM."

"How did you persuade the Russians to give it to you?"

"When Nixon died, and thank God he died because I could not have stood one more evening in his foul-mouthed presence, I became the new Nixon, so to speak. The expert on Russia. I could do as I liked. Clinton was biddable. Clinton let Dick Nixon into the White House, after all. Clinton told Yeltsin I was a hedge against fascism. Better Brodsky than a Zalenko."

Paulette had fallen into a light doze. She stirred slightly then slept again. Somewhere a party was in progress.

Brodsky talked fluently; my eyes darted around, how to get him, how to get out.

"People don't believe the danger of radiation, their governments have lied to them so consistently everywhere for fifty years. More than fifty years, Artyom, fifty years since J. Robert Oppenheimer dropped his bomb in the New Mexican desert. Did you know I met him several times? Oppie knew.

"But who remembers? You can't hear radiation like gunfire or feel it like hunger or smell it like poison gas. The Cold War is over. Instead of cleaning up the waste, we have PR men telling us radiation is no more harmful than golf." Brodsky sipped his drink.

"Golf."

"Yes. I can only help people if they are afraid. Only fear will save us."

"But the rumors weren't enough," I said.

"Not quite."

"You needed the real thing."

"Yes."

"You arranged for the samples to reach New York City."

"Not I."

255

I said, "The mob does your bidding."

"They need new scams. Gas is old hat. The government is cracking down on Medicaid fraud. It works nicely."

"But you never ask. They internalize it, like corporate guys. No one asks. No one says."

"As we said earlier, Artie, it's in the blood."

"Then why bother with the mules? The creeps? The Levs?"

"The small fry are important. The Atomic Mules, the sample men, the scrap merchants, laundry men, and whores, the mafiosi with their little jam jars and big ideas. Do you think if a Rafsanjani, a Saddam, wants something, they go to a mule? When they can buy direct from Nobel Prize–level scientists on site in Russia or one of the old republics. There are bureaucracies as big as General Motors completely devoted to the transfer of illicit nuclear materials. German bankers, Italian judges, Iranian businessmen. Only a very few care about ideology; the business of terror is business. It's a way of life," Brodsky said, then added, "So you see this Lev was a necessity. He was, shall I say, handy. Zeitsev too, he put out a line."

"And I was on the end of it," I said bitterly, as I realized Brodsky knew everything. He knew all of it, and the pretense that he was somehow aloof from the ugly petty violence, the creeps and hoods, was part of a myth he half believed.

I thought of Lev again, and of his father.

Brodsky went on, "It's the little people we need the most. Without them, the system doesn't work."

"Cannon fodder."

"What an old-fashioned idea. The two-bit crimes also keep the story alive. Radioactive material, however insignificant, smuggled into western Europe, or better still, into New York City, scares people. A few grams in Brooklyn is more frightening than a hundred tons of plutonium in Tomsk."

"And if it goes wrong? If we end up with a nuclear explosion at the World Trade Center?"

"There are trade-offs."

"You're insane, you know."

"It's the oldest of ethical questions. Who would you save, Artie? Your girlfriend or millions of people? Which is the moral choice?"

"The end justifies the means."

"Artie! As you said, no clichés, please."

"And the Red Mercury?"

"Who knows? It was useful. It sounded marvelous, don't you think? Lethal, elusive. A fabulous joke. As they say, a red herring. It doesn't matter." He turned to look at his wife. "It doesn't matter, does it, Paulette darling?"

She was still asleep, smiling sweetly.

Red Mercury was a joke.

"Lev Kowalski said he didn't attack Ricky Tae in my apartment. Did he? Someone came after me and got Ricky by mistake."

"He told you the truth. You were getting in the way. I'm sorry it was your friend, Artie. I'll make it up to you."

I got up.

Instinctively, Brodsky put his hand on his wife's arm. She opened her eyes and reached up to touch his face. He turned to me. "Is this the part where you kill me?"

"You're not going to win, you know. It's all empty talk, this saving the world. You won't get your deals now. You won't get your franchises. You can't own nuclear power."

I could see Brodsky was angry. "Someone will." He did not move.

I said, "You can never come home now to America."

"Don't be silly." He looked around and gestured to the embassy residence and what it stood for. "I am at home."

Paulette Brodsky watched. Suddenly the door opened and the maid appeared with a marine guard. Through her fog, Paulette had felt my rage toward Brodsky and she had moved to protect him, had pressed a button and the maid answered.

"Is there a problem, sir?" the marine said politely.

"Is there, Artie?" Chaim Brodsky said.

"You don't believe you can really own all the information, do you? The gossip? The rumors? The news?" I had my hand on the door.

"Only enough," Brodsky said.

"For what? Enough for what?"

"I want to own the fear."

257

Epilogue

NEW YORK

SONNY LIPPERT WAS WAITING FOR ME WHEN THE PLANE LANDED. I GOT in line at immigration, impatient to get to Ricky. Once I had been scared of this process, now I had the pushy disregard for it of a regular American.

But the immigration guy took his sweet time and we exchanged views on the Knicks. He thumbed through a book, then punched me up on his computer.

"Business or pleasure?" he said.

"What?"

"Your trip. Business or pleasure?"

Why was it taking so long? What was going on? On the other side, where the conveyor belt was already spitting out luggage, I saw a few cops I knew from Immigration, but there were always cops here when the Moscow flight landed.

It was after I got my passport stamped and hauled my suitcase off the luggage carousel that I saw two of them come at me.

"You stupid frigging dogbrain," Sonny Lippert said when the pair of cops deposited me on the sidewalk, but I think he smiled when he said it, if you could call the thing that made his mouth twitch a smile. "I'm on your side. Tell him, Roy, will you?"

Roy Pettus was waiting in a car at the curb. "Roy, tell this dick-fist ex-cop that we are on the same side. You dig, Art? If you won't listen to me, listen to him."

"Let him talk, detective," Roy Pettus said to me. Wind whipped around the terminal building, rain spattered the passengers, a double row of yellow taxis honked.

I got in the back of the car. Sonny got in front.

"We heard about the girl and I'm sorry, I am sorry, Art, but if you're thinking about some kind of vengeance, don't be stupid." In the driver's seat, Sonny turned the ignition.

"We picked up both Zeitsevs. We think Junior is going to testify. If he does, it will be the beginning. Thanks to you, we got him. Also, we stopped the nukeshit coming into the city, for the time being, anyhow. We got Moscow finally going on the atomic mules. We'll get the others. We'll do this together. Don't be a Russian. Revenge is not cool, man," he said, revving the car.

It wasn't enough. Zeitsev wasn't enough for the damage Brodsky had caused: Birdie, Olga, Ricky, Lev. And Svetlana.

"You knew I was in Moscow."

"You didn't exactly make a secret of it, Art. I put two and two together, I get four, like you. I talk to Agent Roy Pettus. Finally, Agent Roy Pettus deigns to talk to me." Lippert took off for the expressway. He drove like an old lady.

Slouched in his seat, Roy was mute. All that was visible was his head, like something in granite snapped off of Mount Rushmore. Like a wayward child, from the backseat, I watched them, spoiling for a fight.

"You knew about Svetlana?" I could barely get her name out of my mouth. "How did you know?"

"We heard. I'm sorry."

"How did you hear?" I already knew.

"Tolya Sverdloff is our friend. He's your frigging friend. He's one of the good guys."

"He spied on me."

"He saved your ass."

"You set me up, Sonny. You set me up the day you took me off the case. You said you were throwing me a bone. You knew I'd go to Brooklyn. Didn't you?"

Sonny shrugged. "I took a chance. If you cracked it, I could still take the credit and prosecute the case. You were off the picture, officially. If you messed up, I was off the hook. I could be the hero who saved you."

"Or else I would be dead."

Rain smeared the windshield. Flicking on the wipers, Sonny kept up a stream of talk. Roy Pettus sat silently.

"What about Ricky?" I said.

"Who?"

"You know who. My friend Ricky Tae. Who beat him up? Who made him a vegetable?"

"We don't know for sure. We think Zeitsev sent men after you, your pal took the beating."

"No, he didn't. I'll tell you who did it." We were on the bridge, the city visible through the rain when I told them about Chaim Brodsky. I told them everything and I could see their disbelief; they felt sorry for me.

I went home. My place was clean and someone, maybe Lois, had put flowers on the desk. On the fire escape, the geraniums were withered, yellow, dead. I pulled the shades and went to sleep for—what? A week? I got up to eat, went to sleep again, visited Ricky, then slept, twelve, fourteen hours at a time. I dreamed about Svetlana every night; it didn't bring her back in the morning.

When I finally surfaced, it was Halloween and I turned on the TV, gaping at the news while I drank coffee and took a shower. Chaim Brodsky announced a delay in his plans for a nuclear reactor due to his wife's illness; he was taking her on a long cruise, to Israel perhaps, he said, to search for his roots. Gennadi Ustinov's book made the best-seller list. A network picked up *The Teddy Flowers Show.* The murder rate in New York was down. The market was up. In Moscow a young reporter was killed when a suitcase full of documents about the atomic mafia blew up in his face; I didn't have to wait to hear it was Eduard Skolnik, poor bastard. The weather was colder. Rupert Murdoch had bought *Pravda.* And Birdie's notebooks arrived in the mail, neatly wrapped and tied, and they told me most of what I already knew and much more.

That evening when I went to St. Vincent's, I looked down at Ricky's pale face and saw a flicker of life. The doctors came, they shone a flashlight in Ricky's eyes; there was some reaction. A miracle, said one of the nurses who was also a nun. I don't believe in goddamn miracles, but I figured I'd take it.

Outside Ricky's room at St. Vincent's, I found Hillel Abramsky and some of his pals discussing Talmudic issues with a priest.

"I always liked your friend Ricky," Hillel said. "I thought he could use a little extra help. We have good relations with St. Vincent's."

"You think your God lets you pray for guys like Ricky?"

"And why not?" Hillel said. "By the way, Saroyan is a crook."

"I know that."

"You can pick him up any time."

"Thanks, Hilly. Thank you. We just did. How did you keep him from leaving? You held him hostage? You fed him stuffed derma? What?"

Abramsky reached into his pants pocket and pulled out a baggie. Inside, wrapped in some tissue paper, was the diamond big as a walnut. "Without this, I knew he would never leave. Greedy schmuck. So I kept it in my pants. I sent him a message I was on a religious retreat. I could not be disturbed."

"You could have been a shrink, Hil."

"Thank you."

I walked away from the hospital and through the Village that Halloween night, through the cool fall streets that were jammed with witches and devils. I walked all the way to Fanelli's where I sat alongside a Princess Diana in drag and a couple of ghosts. I didn't have a costume.

Halfway through my third Corona and a small mountain of fried onion rings, someone climbed up on the stool next to me. She smelled great.

"Can I buy you one?" It was Lily Hanes.

"You've been following me," I said.

"Yeah," she said. "But I'm harmless."